Redeemed by Fire

by

C J Bahr

This is a work of fiction. Names, characters, places, and incidents are either the product of the author's imagination or are used fictitiously, and any resemblance to actual persons living or dead, business establishments, events, or locales, is entirely coincidental.

Redeemed by Fire

Contact Information: info@thewildrosepress.com

Cover Art by *Debbie Taylor*

The Wild Rose Press, Inc.
PO Box 708
Adams Basin, NY 14410-0708
Visit us at www.thewildrosepress.com

Publishing History
First Edition, 2021
Trade Paperback ISBN 978-1-5092-3840-8
Digital ISBN 978-1-5092-3841-5

Published in the United States of America

"Casi?" Luc scanned the park before meeting her gaze. "What the hell? How did—"

A loud bang cracked in the air, and Luc jerked before shoving them prone to the ground.

"Stay down!" Luc held her shoulders, pinning her as he rolled further on top of her, covering her with his body.

Another loud bang and Avery jerked again.

"Shit!" He twisted while pulling his gun and then fired.

Casi screamed and covered her ears, though too late. The loud boom made her ears ring. Who was shooting at them? She tried to see, but Luc's weight had her effectively pinned. Squealing tires along with a string of Cajun curses from Luc had Casi guessing the shooter had fled.

Luc holstered his weapon when Casi spotted the blood dripping off his arm.

"Oh my God!" She pushed at him. "Let me up. You're hurt. You're bleeding!"

Luc rolled off her and did as she asked while gripping his thigh with both hands. Her gaze left his arm, drawn to the blood oozing out between his fingers. The thigh wound appeared much more serious. She tugged her phone out and quickly dialed 911. But before it connected, Luc's bloody fingers grabbed her phone and disconnected the call.

"We can't call this in." Luc exhaled harshly and gritted his teeth as once again, he applied pressure to his leg.

"You're shot. You're bleeding from multiple places. We need an ambulance!"

He shook his head. "Can't. We need to leave. Now."

Dedication

To Survivors

"And here you are living despite it all."
~~ Rupi Kaur*

You are truly an inspiration.

A Word From The Author

With each new story, as a writer, I try to grow and stretch my wings. In *Redeemed by Fire*, this novel uncovered new territory for me. My heroine, Cassanne Thomas, didn't have an easy life, and it might affect some readers more deeply than others. I want to reach out to those of you who are survivors and the people in your lives who support you.

You are not alone. If you are a victim of sexual abuse, there are confidential and free resources available to you. The National Sexual Assault Helpline (1-800-656-4673) is available 24/7 either online, chat, or by phone. They provide support services to survivors regardless of where you are in your recovery and have helped over 2.5 million people.

Pandora's Project is a terrific resource if you are a "secondary survivor"—parent, friend, or partner of someone who was raped or sexually abused. It can be overwhelming if someone you care about has been so tragically hurt. You can get information to help your loved one and help for yourself. Please seek the assistance needed to heal, no matter how much time has passed for you or your loved one.

I would like to thank some amazing people who have helped me grow in my writer's journey. First, thank you to my brave beta readers, Marla White and Jen Jeske. You make me a better writer with your thoughtful criticisms—bring them on ladies!

Next, to fellow author, JA Stone. Your Tarot card knowledge was invaluable. You rock, dude! Also, many thanks to Karine Ruatta from the World Translation Center for her help with the Cajun French words and phrases. Any mistakes are my own.

To my lovely editor, Amanda Barnett of The Wild Rose Press. You believed in me and took a chance, which I will never forget. Thank you for your guidance and mentorship. Bless you, lovely lady! She also wanted me to take credit for writing Neutral Ground's song, *The Road Taken*—my first effort in writing a song. Here's to channeling my inner Jon Bon Jovi.

And to you, my readers! Without you, it's no fun telling my tales. Thank you for picking up this book and giving it a try. If you enjoy it, please consider leaving a review. Your comments are greatly appreciated and keep me writing!

Chapter One

New Orleans, May, Present Day

Cassanne Thomas exhaled one long drawn out breath while flipping her store's sign to CLOSED. *Another exhausting and unprofitable day.* A great big catch-22. Working in the touristy French Quarter provided more income, but she couldn't manage the high rent. Hence working outside the popular district—affordable lease but less spontaneous foot traffic. New clientele she desperately needed. Crossing the compact front room, she pushed through the curtain of jewel-toned beads separating the larger back area. The clacking noise a comforting counterpoint to her exhaustion.

Her Haitian granmè would curse her sideways if she knew Casi played at being psychic instead of embracing her internal voodoo queen and following the Loa. Oh well, good thing she hadn't seen her granmè in a decade. She hadn't recently visited any of her Haitian side of the family, including her disappointed mother. Her mom currently lived in sunny California with her third American husband. The first of those being Casi's father.

She stopped beside the gold cloth draped table with five tarot cards laid out in a star pattern. The Empress, Six of Swords, The Fool, Eight of Cups, and the Tower stared back at her. Wealth and fortune, but at a substantial cost. Her client seemed pleased until the last part. Too bad. It's not like Casi's prediction would come true anyway. She didn't have real psychic powers. Smoke and mirrors were the tricks of her newly chosen career. She memorized what the cards symbolized and then studied people's body language, making intuitive guesses. At least her double degrees in psychology and sociology were helpful for something other than their intended use because her original career was toast. She must be doing something sort of right because she had several repeat clients and mostly made enough money to keep her apartment and store. Proving to herself at least she wasn't the complete and utter failure her mother believed her to be.

With another frustrated outburst of air, she gathered her hair and tied it up in a messy knot. *Damn, it was hot*. Sweat dripped down the back of her neck and beaded across her forehead and chest. She loved New Orleans but could do without the humidity. There were times, but not many, when she missed California. Tonight, the dense air made her feel like she breathed in pure water. The ceiling fans moved the damp air around, but she'd kill for air conditioning. Not that she could afford the cost. Thank God her store didn't have a unit installed. On nights like tonight, Casi would have turned it on.

She swiped up the cards and added them back into the deck, before wrapping them in a red velvet cloth and slipping the encased Tarot into a silk pouch. Crouching next to the table, Casi lifted the long trailing ends of the tablecloth. Her battered canvas messenger bag laid hidden underneath. She grabbed it and slung the long strap over her head. Standing, she let the tote settle across her front and rest at her hip. She lifted the faded tan flap and shoved her Tarot deck into the cluttered depths.

Ambling to the beaded curtain, she flicked off both switches, killing the ceiling fan with the lights. The curtain pleasantly clicked and clacked again as Casi pushed her way through the beads and crossed to the front door. She turned off the overhead light in the small waiting room, before sliding the bolt and letting herself out. Reaching into her messenger bag, she dug around until she found her keys and relocked the bolt.

She started walking. The humid air, although damp against her skin, carried the hopeful scent of rain. Slightly past eleven o'clock, Casi glanced around the dark empty street. It was later than she'd like. Her last customer, a long-term client, had frantically called to request a late reading. And of course, the session had taken forever, well past the allotted twenty-minute slot. Casi didn't have much of a choice since she needed the money. She lengthened her stride, and her low-heeled ankle boots click-clacked on the sidewalk. With the bus stop a few blocks away, she wanted to catch the eleven-thirty so she wouldn't have to wait for the last bus at midnight.

Her stomach growled. She'd skipped dinner once again. Perfect on the wallet, but not so great on keeping her energy up. Mentally cataloging what might be in her fridge that wasn't a science experiment, she waited for the light to change before crossing the street. With no cars or people in sight, why was she waiting? Snorting, she strode across the empty intersection and continued down the sidewalk. As she passed a small alley between buildings, Casi flew backward from a harsh yank on the back strap of her bag. She stumbled into the alley, trying to keep on her feet. Someone grabbed her shoulders in a tight grip and spun her around. She gawked upward into the darkly, shrouded face concealed beneath the black hood of his sweatshirt. Clenching a fist, Casi swung at her attacker.

"*Stop*!"

Her body froze at her assailant's command. Straining with all her muscles, sweat broke out on her forehead, dripping into her eyes, but she couldn't move. Additional effort only gained her a fraction of an inch before her muscles locked again. Why couldn't she move? The single word had sounded strange, like more than one voice speaking the same word at the exact same time.

"Ah, my poppet. You're a strong one."

Casi couldn't breathe as she fought to move but didn't budge. This couldn't be happening. Her adrenaline spiked, and the blood rushed crazily inside her veins, but even the added energy made no difference.

"*There's no reason to fight me, lower your arm*," her attacker ordered in his oddly layered voice.

Against her will, Casi's arm fell, relaxing against her side.

"Much better, poppet. *You're mine now. Please, follow me quietly*."

The command wrapped around her, and she started walking, trailing her abductor like a well-trained puppy. Struggling with all her might, Casi couldn't stop moving or make a sound.

Trapped within her own body, she alone heard her mental screams as the darkness of the alley consumed them.

****

Casi struggled awake. Her eyelids were weights too heavy to lift, while her head pounded as if a hammer drove nails into her skull. Bile rose up her throat, which she forced down as the sharp stabbing pain continued slicing through her brain. She had to get up, even though Casi felt like a giant boulder pinned her down and she wanted to vomit. How did she get here? Her last memory was walking to the bus stop. How could someone snatch her off the street and she had no recollection? She had to move. She had to escape.

Her lips parted as Casi inhaled a deep breath, hoping to push her growing panic aside and remain calm. Losing her shit right now wouldn't help. Used to being on her own, she relied solely on herself. Life had shown her the error of her ways when it came to putting her faith in others. If she wanted out of this situation, she had to save herself.

Her eyelids fluttered, and she forced them open. A dim light leaked from beneath a closed door sitting atop a flight of wooden stairs. She was in a lower room. A basement? In New Orleans? She couldn't tell. There were no windows. She could be on the third floor as easily as the first floor. No way to know.

Taking a deep breath, she braced her palms flat on the metal surface her body laid on, took another deep breath, then clenched her stomach muscles as she tried to sit up, only to slam down a bare inch later. Restraints held her down. Someone had tied her up. Who? A strap held her neck motionless. Her pulse raced, and her vision tunneled to pinpricks. She had to calm down.

Casi couldn't afford to faint. Not now, when left alone, she had a chance to escape.

Peering down her body to her right hand, she raised her wrist several inches before the metal bracelet of the handcuff trapping her to the table stopped her. She smiled for the first time this hideous night. Handcuffs she could deal with. For once, her high school volleyball injury would be helpful instead of a hindrance. She braced her thumb against the round rim of the cuff and gave a sharp jerk against the unforgiving metal. Her joint gave as her thumb dislocated. Biting her lip against the pain, she worked her hand through the cuff until she slid free. Relief flooded her at the freedom of one hand. A few deep breaths later, Casi's optimism deflated as she realized she couldn't pop her thumb back into alignment until her other hand got freed. This sucked. Reaching her hand up, she plunged it inside her blouse until her uninjured fingers tangled with the thin leather strap holding her necklace charm. Thank God for her steampunk fascination. She wore an ornate cross made with clockworks, fashioned with metal gears, but more importantly, the spiked bottom of the stylized piece held the answer to her freedom. It should be both long and sturdy enough to let her pick the lock on her remaining handcuff.

Tugging on the leather, it took several tries before the knot gave. She reached inside her shirt and grasped the cross resting on her chest. With a frantic glance at the stairs, she pulled the charm out. Holding it between her undamaged fingers, she aimed the hard metal point at the lock. Without being able to move her upper body, it took four tries and a frustrated groan before her makeshift pick slid into the lock. Now here's hoping her skills hadn't rusted.

It wasn't working. Her eyes filled with tears as she forced herself to blink them back. She couldn't get the leverage she needed. *Calm.* She couldn't afford to panic. Hope still prevailed as long as she kept trying. Whoever snatched her hadn't returned yet. There was still time. She could do this. Casi would do it. Holding her breath, she jammed the improvised pick hard into the lock, lifted it, and twisted. The cuff popped open. She exhaled sharply and then lifted her freed left hand. She grabbed hold of her right thumb. Knowing it would hurt, but more pain didn't matter with the chance of escaping. With a quick jerk, she slammed her thumb back into its joint. Now for the neck strap.

The tightly woven nylon strap holding her in place was a simple bungee cord. She could have released herself even one-handed with a dislocated thumb had she thought to check. *Stupid.* She had to be smarter. Finding the rubber-covered s-hook under the lip of the metal table, she popped it free. Casi sat up, rubbing her throat before reaching out to her ankles, bound by the simple means of duct tape. She tore at it until the sticky adhesive was off. Glorious freedom!

She scrambled off the table. When her bare feet hit the clammy concrete floor, she swayed, and her vision tunneled. Looking at her feet, Casi noticed her messenger bag and boots beside her. She grabbed her shoes, slipping into them before snatching the strap of her bag. Casi straightened and flung it over her head, settling the bag across her hip. At least she still had her stuff.

Footsteps creaked on the wooden boards above. She whipped her gaze upward, staring in dread at the ceiling. *Shit*! Her heart raced. *Move*. With a jerky stumbling gait, she jogged to the bottom of the steps just as the door swung open and light flooded the stairwell. *No*! Casi dove to the side and slammed her back against the wall next to the stairs, getting out of view. Metal dug into her shoulder as she braced against the damp cement wall. Footsteps started down the stairs before Casi realized the sharp edge of metal digging into her was a fuse box. Hearing the kidnapper closing, she flung the cover with a clang and flipped the main fuse, plunging the building into darkness.

Casi realized her mistake in an instant. With all the noise she made, her abductor now knew she must be loose. Surprise wasn't an option anymore. Offense became her new strategy. With no hesitation, she barreled up the stairs. She met the kidnapper midway. Ramming her hands into her captor's stomach, Casi shoved the person aside and charged up the stairs shrouded in darkness. She gained a few more steps in the bleak gloom before a hand shackled her ankle. Her forward momentum abruptly halted, crashing her to her knees four stairs to freedom. This wasn't happening! She blindly reached out, fingers stabbing aimlessly in her kidnapper's direction. She hit something soft, and her assailant grunted and jerked away.

Casi's hand slid down smooth skin, and her fingers entangled in a chain around the neck of her abductor. She twisted the links, hoping to form a makeshift garrote in order to strangle whoever it was when the links snapped. With the loss of leverage, her kidnapper fell away, tumbling down the stairs into deeper black as Casi landed on her ass. She had to escape. Struggling to her feet, she twisted, facing the open door, and flew up the remaining three steps.

"*Halt*!"

Ignoring the order, Casi kept going, escaped the basement, and ran for her life.

Chapter Two

"Why should I?" Casi plopped onto the leather sofa. "I got away. No harm, no foul." She studied her tightly clasped hands in her lap. Her death grip hid their shaking from her near miss. She needed to conceal her fear from her friend, Mason. No need to worry him any more than she already had.

"Sweetie, I know you hate cops and all, but seriously, you were abducted and chained in a basement. I truly think you should report this."

She glanced up, meeting his concerned gaze, and sighed. After escaping her abductor, she bolted to her apartment and tried to calm down. It hadn't worked. So she left and wandered aimlessly down the always-crowded Bourbon Street even with the rain until a few hours before dawn. Not wanting to return home to her empty apartment, Casi went to Mason's. He always could coax a laugh from her, making him a perfect distraction, something she greatly needed. His *out loud and proud* personality made him a better girlfriend than any of her female friends she'd left behind in California. She counted him as one of the bright spots in her life since returning to New Orleans. He had found her staring blindly into space as she sat on a park bench on the first day of her arrival, feeling the need to intervene. He had the most open, generous heart. Proven again when he hadn't blinked an eye at her unannounced arrival on his doorstep, pulling him from his bed at an ungodly hour.

Mason dropped onto the couch and grabbed her clinched hands. Thankfully, she had gotten her tremors under control. “Cassanne.” He sighed. “You know I’m right.”

Crap. He’d used her full name. Now he’d go into serious mode. “The cops are worthless. They’re not going to do anything. In fact, I wouldn’t be surprised if they run a background check and treat me like the criminal the system wanted me to be.”

“Honey, not all cops are evil. You may have been charged, but you were never found guilty. There is *nothing* to hold against you.” He pulled her into a hug and held her tight. “I can’t believe I almost lost you.”

She gave him a squeeze and let him hold her. “Yeah, what a loss.” Casi snickered, trying to lighten the mood and distance herself from her terror. “Who would you take shopping so you could dress them?”

Mason pushed her away. “Stop. There is nothing funny about what happened.” His blue eyes were wide open as his lips pressed into a thin line. He held his stern expression until a slight upward curl on one corner of his mouth spoiled the look. “Besides, you haven’t let me buy you anything in months.”

“That’s because I’m not a charity case.”

“It’s not charity if it’s simply a friend helping another friend, and stop changing the topic.” Mason stood, pulling her up along with him, and then started tugging her toward the front door.

“No, Mason. I’m not going.”

“Yes, sweetie, you are. I’ll be with you all the way.”

Casi tried to break his hold on her hand, but damn, he was strong. His entire fitness regime keeping himself athletic and chiseled currently worked against her. He claimed looking hot got him more gigs and fantastic tips as a high-end dealer on the Riverboat Casinos. Of course, the ebony hair and baby blues didn't hurt either. She sighed and stopped fighting him.

"Fine, but if they lock me up, you better bail me out."

"I've got your back, sweetie. I always do."

It seemed Mason was the only one. Casi had a really bad feeling about this.

****

In the gray light of early dawn, Detective Lucas Avery flicked off the windshield wipers. The rain had finally stopped. He pulled into the parking lot near the Yacht Club by West End Park and found a spot near the patrol cars. Grunting as he shut off the engine, he pressed his fingers to the bridge of his nose, willing his headache away. Exhaustion beat at him, but sadly the adage *no rest for the weary* held true. Getting out of the dark blue car, he grimaced as he slammed the sedan's door shut. Another body. With the increasing number of victims, whoever tortured and mutilated these poor souls had to be stopped. They needed to catch this asshole. The sooner the better.

Luc strode toward the police tape cordoning off the crime scene, but a sharp whistle caught his attention in the parking lot. He spotted his partner, Vincent Tate, the halogen parking lights gleaming off his bald dark head as he exited a shiny new limited-edition Land Rover Defender. Shaking his head, Luc marched back across the lot to greet him.

"How the hell did you get one of these?" He gestured toward the brushed silver, high-end SUV, putting his Ford Fusion to shame.

A deep baritone chuckle answered him. "It's all about connections." Vincent reached into his new ride and pulled out a travel cup from Morning Call. Coffee. He could smell the coffee beans and chicory from here. Thank the Lord for twenty-four-hour coffee shops.

"Here." He passed the cup over. "I thought it'd take the sting out of your jealousy. Besides, it was on the way, and it looks like you could use the caffeine."

Luc grabbed the coffee and took a large swallow, not caring it burned his throat on the way down. "Thanks." Another sleepless night and then the early morning call trashed him. Head pounding, he needed the additional energy. He watched his fellow detective lock up his fancy new ride and shook his head again. Figured Tate could corral a Defender on an NOPD detective's salary. Probably got it through his Army contacts. His partner and former Delta Force soldier could magically conjure things out of thin air. Luc figured being retired Special Forces must have its perks. It could be worse. At least he wasn't the cliché former Navy Seal.

"Man, you look like shit. Did Bas keep you too long at the Loo?"

"I wish."

Luc and Vincent walked toward the latest crime scene. The Fleur-de-Lis, quaintly known to the locals as the Floor-de-Loo or the Loo for short, was a popular, in-the-know, dive bar where his younger brother's band could be found performing most nights as they worked toward their big break. Bastien, more times than he could count, continued to egg him up on stage to jam with Neutral Ground. Sometimes Luc got so lost in the music he didn't make it home until the wee hours of the morning.

"So what gives with the dark bags under your squinty bloodshot eyes? You're rockin' ugly today." Luc could hear the snicker in his partner's voice. "How do you expect to hook up with the hot new forensic probie if you look like roadkill?

"Don't start. I'm doing just fine. Besides, I doubt she's here."

An uniformed officer held up the crime scene tape so they could both duck under and cross Breakwater Drive to get to the spit of concrete on the edge of Lake Pontchartrain.

"Fine, my ass. If you weren't at the Loo or getting laid all night long, why the hell do you look like shit?"

"And this matters, why? You want to date me or something?" Luc fired back.

Vincent snorted. "If I was into male Cajun white meat, perhaps, but I love the ladies too much. And they love me back. So sorry, no way, my brother."

Luc flinched. Vincent knew how much he hated the whole *my brother* tag—a New Orleans cliché from hell. Tate did it to piss him off and get a rise out of him. His partner liked to push him ever since they teamed up last year. A game, no doubt. Delta Force men never lost their cool, and Vincent tried to prove a point that he, unlike Luc, was no mere mortal. Screw that. Luc had his Cajun charm going for him. Laidback. And when he let his accent out in full swing, no one saw his temper coming.

Pushing his irritation aside, Luc ran his fingers

through his hair, messing up the longer top layers. No matter how fun and distracting exchanging barbs with Tate satisfied him, a body on the ground trumped Luc's amusement. After all, the crime would not solve itself. He really hated serial killers, and this wasn't his first *fais-do-do*. After three bodies with the same M.O., any doubts of a serial fell to ash. And now they had a fourth victim. The press weren't here, thank God for miracles. There were no journalists coming up with their lame-ass moniker for the killer and starting a public frenzy. He guessed it didn't matter though, since the cops with their own morbid sense of humor already dubbed the killer Cyclops—from the single missing eye of each victim.

He snapped on a pair of latex gloves, as did his partner while they approached the latest victim. The Medical Examiner walked up to them.

"*Quoi ça dit*, Jake?" Luc queried as he met the M.E.'s gaze.

"Nothing good, Detective." He gestured to the body lying on the ground. "Our killer has struck again. Sorry for the ugly wake up, but death doesn't respect the clock."

"Ain't that the truth," Vincent agreed.

They walked to the body before Jake continued his debrief. "Female, in her early thirties, of mixed heritage. Ligature striations on both wrists and neck, and of course, one missing eye, this time the left." Luc grunted as Vince sharply exhaled. "I won't know until I get her on my table, but I'd estimate TOD somewhere between one and three this morning. And if I laid a bet, I'd win good money the pineal gland is missing from the brain."

"So our killer has harvested again." Luc sighed as he pushed his gloved hand through his hair. "Shit, this is bad mojo." The missing gland tied these victims together. The only clue between all bodies. The killer didn't discriminate against gender, ethnicity, or the balance of their bank account. "Why the hell is he collecting those glands, anyway?"

"Maybe Cyclops has trouble sleeping?" Jake threw out his hypothesis. "The pineal gland produces melatonin which modulates sleeping patterns."

"I think there're easier ways to find some shut-eye than kidnap and torture," Vincent added his opinion.

Luc had to agree. The removal of both the eye and gland was done while alive—so torture it was. With four bodies now and no clues besides the missing glands, they were at a standstill. The victims had nothing obvious in common. None of them had any personal connections to each other. There had to be a reason for the killer's selection of targets, but the police were blind to any. His frustration grew with each body dump. He dreaded finding a fifth…

"I don't suppose we have an ID?"

"No," Jake answered. "No purse or phone." He gestured toward the uniforms. "They're scouring the area to see if the killer got sloppy this time and let something slip. Or we might get lucky with a security camera."

"As if we'd get that lucky." Luc scanned the area, a mostly barren parking lot with some trees near the water. All the businesses were too far away to have caught anything. "The rain last night won't help either."

"We'll catch him," Tate vowed. "They all eventually make mistakes."

"*Vrai*." So true. He fist-bumped Tate. "But how many more bodies before then?" Luc paced from the edge of the crime scene to the lake and stared out. The rising sun broke through the cloud cover and glinted off the water. His partner joined him lakeside.

The buzz of Luc's cell phone broke his morose glare. He reached into his pocket, pulled out his cell, and answered the call. "Avery." Listening to the voice on the other end, he felt his lips curling up in a smile. "We'll be there." He ended the call and turned to his partner.

"Good news I take it?"

"Possibly." Luc headed back across the crime scene toward the parking lot as Tate followed. "There's a chance we just got a lucky break."

Chapter Three

"Will you please sit down?"

Casi glared at Mason. Friend or not, she wanted to smack him upside his head. Why did she let him talk her into going to the police? She continued pacing the perimeter of the square interrogation room. If she sat, she would feel trapped in a box. Why did these rooms all look the same? The one-way mirrored wall, the other three walls plain gray and unadorned, the bland tile floor holding a single table and two chairs, under flickering fluorescent lights—the universal decor of law enforcement. She never wanted to see the inside of one of these rooms ever again, but here she was once more.

After arriving at the front desk and giving a brief reason of what Casi needed to report, they handed her off to a uniform to take her statement. She had gone over it at least three times when the officer asked them to wait and disappeared for twenty minutes. When the cop returned, he asked them to follow him and led them into the interrogation room, sending chills racing down her spine as she broke out into a sweat. Panic had ridden her hard. He politely asked if they wanted water or coffee, before stating someone would be with them shortly. And then he closed the door, shutting them in.

What felt like hours later, but probably was closer to thirty minutes, had her mentally climbing the walls. She was done. "No, Mason, I won't." Shaking her head,

Casi strode toward the door. "I'm outta here."

She heard Mason scramble out of his chair behind her, but she would not let him stop her. Reaching for the door, it abruptly flung inward, slamming into her shoulder and knocking her off her feet. Flailing, she fell. Suddenly, a pair of strong arms wrapped around her waist halting her backward momentum.

Caught in a dip any ballroom dancer would envy, Casi stared into the man's face so close to hers, she could easily see the green mixed into his brown eyes. She even spotted tiny gold flecks. He slowly pulled her upward, hands sliding and lingering on her hips before dropping away. He was tall, at least five or six inches above her five-foot-seven. His dark blond hair, bordering on brown, closely cropped on the sides, gave way to longer layers on top, one of which fell artfully across his forehead. Casi had the urge to brush it aside. It looked thick and silky. She blinked and took a step back. Where the hell did that thought come from?

"Ms. Thomas? My apologies, I should have knocked."

The smooth drawling tenor laced with a slight rolling accent pointed to his rural Southern Louisiana roots. The charming smile nailed the coffin lid to his Cajun roots. She wasn't about to get suckered in. California had their bounty of handsome surfer cops with alluring smiles, only to find it hid their dark, chewy cores.

"Why? It's your interrogation room after all. I highly doubt you've ever knocked."

He shrugged and glanced at her aching shoulder. "Are you all right?"

"Fine."

They stood staring at each other. He took another step into the room and she retreated a step. The door closed. *Dammit*. She shouldn't have given ground. Too late now. He gestured to the empty seat next to Mason. "Please. I'm Detective Avery. I'm sorry to have kept you waiting, but I was out in the field."

Not knowing what else to do, Casi resigned herself to her fate and sat next to her friend. The detective frowned as his gaze swept the room. "Just a sec." He turned and opened the door, poking his head outside. "Hey, we need a couple of chairs."

With his request discharged, the door closed once more. He sauntered to the wall opposite from where they sat and leaned against it before raising a slim eyebrow at Mace.

"I'm Mason Webb," Mason stated before she could intervene. "I'm staying. Think of me as her lawyer."

"Are you?"

"No, but I'm still not leaving."

"Ms. Thomas isn't in need of a lawyer as far as I know—"

"She's in need of a friend."

The interrogation room's door opened, and a large black man entered with two folding chairs in his grasp and a file folder tucked under his arm. Taller than Avery by several inches, his build echoed a football team's fullback—muscled legs, wide shoulders, and a tight waist. The man looked like he could single-handedly break a defensive line. The complete opposite of the detective already in the room, whose lean muscular build resembled a swimmer or runner more than a football player. The new detective placed the chairs on the empty side of the table and plunked himself down while tossing the file on the table. Avery lazily pushed himself off the wall and took the last seat.

"This is my partner, Detective Tate. Tate, this is Ms. Thomas and her friend, Mr. Webb."

"Ma'am." He inclined his shaved head. "Sir."

Oh, so polite. What a front, but she could see past the niceties. No one would fool her again. She crossed her arms over her chest and leaned back in the chair.

Avery took over. "I understand you had a traumatic evening last night. Would you please take us through what happened?"

She glared into his direct gaze. "I already gave my statement. Three times. I've been here for well over two hours, more like three. I'd like to leave."

"Casi…" Mason reached a hand toward her but dropped it when she shook her head.

"I'm sure these excellent detectives know how to read." She jutted her chin at the file sitting on the table.

Detective Tate smirked while Avery smiled. "Yes, ma'am, we do in fact know how to read." Avery's accent grew thicker. Like that would help. "But if you could take us through it one more time, we'd appreciate you doing so."

"If you don't, I will." Mason frowned at her.

Casi scowled. "You can't. That's hearsay."

"She's right," the deep baritone from Detective Tate echoed in the room.

So the man could speak more than just one-word sentences. He's got two in that one. She wondered if he played *bad* cop to Avery's *good* but really couldn't care less. Casi studied both detectives' expressions and realized she'd never be allowed to leave until she went through it again.

"Fine." She unwrapped her arms and let them drop, clenching her hands together on her lap. "But this is the last time."

Chapter Four

Luc studied his potential witness. Her slight frame strung tight with tension, and shoulders hunched as she stared at her clasped hands in her lap. She took a breath and raised her head, meeting his gaze directly. The open hostility in her dark brown eyes blasted him. What was her problem? He and Vince had been nothing but polite. Luc held her gaze, waiting her out. She'd speak eventually.

Ms. Thomas was beautiful even in her anger. Her high ponytail showed off her black, slightly wavy hair. Worn loose, it would probably reach mid-back. A few twisting tendrils had escaped the tie, framing her high cheekbones. She wore no makeup and didn't need it. He wondered about her heritage. Her tawny skin, a warm, light brown, looked so soft it made him wonder what it would feel like under his hands. He had to admit his attraction to her, especially when he held her in his arms after catching her. *Shit.* He didn't need this distraction—he really must be tired.

She might be the lead to breaking his case wide open. His silent treatment usually worked, but Ms. Thomas remained silent. Most people felt awkward and would fill in the quiet, but apparently not her. He cocked an eyebrow and leaned back in his chair, hoping to get under her skin and get the ball rolling. Her full lips pursed into a thin line, showing her irritation as her brows furrowed. Score. He made an effort not to smile.

"Casi." Her friend, Webb, placed his hand on her shoulder, drawing her attention away, finally breaking their gazes. "Give them a chance."

What an odd phrase. What did he mean by it? Well, if it got her talking, he didn't care.

"Okay." She turned and faced him. "I closed my shop and was walking to the bus stop." Her eyes blinked slowly as she took another deep breath.

"About what time, ma'am?" Vince questioned, trying to establish a timeline they would need.

"Late. Eleven. Probably closer to eleven-fifteen."

Luc grabbed her file and shuffled some papers. "It says here your store is on the fringe of the Quarter close to the Marigny. You're a psychic?"

"You have a problem with that?"

"No." He raised his hands, palms outward in surrender. Wow, completely prickly. She'd give a cactus a run for its money. "No problem here."

"So you were grabbed on the way to the bus?" Tate intervened, pulling her attention off him.

"I think so. I don't really remember." He watched a shudder chase through her. "I passed an alley, and my memory just goes blank. I…I don't remember anything until I woke up."

He flipped a page. "The alley between Le Lys Violet Boutique and Copy Quick?"

"Yes."

Luc made a mental note to get a forensic team there, ASAP. He held little hope, especially with the rain, but he would grasp at any straws. Plus, he'd add uniforms so they could canvass the area. Maybe they would get lucky with a security camera or a witness.

"So when you woke up…"

She glanced at her clenched hands, and his gaze followed. He noticed her white-knuckled grip. When she looked up, her hostility had fled, and fear spilled from her wide brown eyes. Opening her mouth to speak, she closed it and then chewed on her lower lip.

"Sweetie?" Her friend twisted in his chair. Leaning forward, he placed one hand on top of hers, and his other rubbed her shoulder. As she turned toward Webb, Luc noticed her blinking rapidly. *Crap.* Please don't cry. "Do you need some time?"

She shook her head and straightened. "No. No, I'm all right, Mace. It just sort of all came back suddenly." With another deep breath, she faced him and Vince once more.

"I was on a metal table. You know, like the ones you see on TV, in the morgue in medical shows. I…I…restraints held me down. My ankles were duct-taped together, there…there was a bungee cord across my neck, and my wrists were cuffed separately to the sides of the table."

Luc exchanged glances with Vince. It fit the victims' body bruising to the letter, complete with the adhesive residue around the victims' ankles. She couldn't have known the information because none of it had been released to the public. His pulse kicked up. Finally, they got a break.

"How did you get off the table, Ms. Thomas?" Had she seen the killer? Did he release her, and she fought him off? Please, let her be able to identify him.

She raised her right hand and wiggled her thumb. "I dislocated my thumb and slipped out of the cuff."

His eyebrows rose. That took some guts.

"I then used my necklace to pick the other lock."

"You can pick a handcuff lock?" Tate's head tilted in question.

"One of my kids taught me." She gifted them with a fleeting smile.

Kids? He checked her left hand for a ring and then glanced into her file, confirming her single status, never having been married, in fact. Wait. Found it. She used to be a social worker. Why play psychic in New Orleans when Thomas had skills which could earn her more money? He looked up and met her gaze, wondering about her story when her eyes widened. She slapped a hand to her chest.

"My necklace!" She whipped around to Webb. "Mason, my necklace." She appeared absolutely frantic, so Luc wasn't surprised when her friend dropped to his knees beside her and enveloped her in a tight hug.

"It's okay, sweetie. It's just a necklace. We'll find you another one. Hush."

A tear escaped from her eye and slid down her cheek. She visibly trembled. No doubt a delayed reaction to last night. Luc cleared his throat. "Why don't we take a brief break?" He met Tate's gaze and nodded toward the door. His partner agreed because he stood quickly, and his chair scraped against the floor. Luc rose to his feet and headed toward the door when her voice reached him.

"No, please." Her words were muffled as she spoke into Webb's chest.

Both he and Tate stopped and turned. She pulled away from her friend and quickly swiped a hand across her eyes, brushing away more tears. "Don't leave. I want this done. I just want to go home."

"All right, if you feel up to finishing." When she nodded, Luc returned and took his seat, followed by Vince.

"So you got yourself released." Vincent grinned at her. "Impressive job, by the way, ma'am. What happened next?"

"I was in a basement, as crazy as that sounds. There were no windows, and the only light came from the door at the top of the stairs. It opened when I tried to flee."

"Did you see who was there? Can you describe him?" Luc's pulse kicked up again and quickly crashed when she shook her head.

"The moment the door opened, I got out of sight. I landed next to the fuse box, so I flipped the mains and then charged the stairs. I…I hoped to run by him, but he grabbed me. I tried to poke him in the eyes but missed, and my hand slipped to his neck. He-he," she stammered. "He had on a chain, and I grabbed hold and twisted, but suddenly the links broke. He tumbled down the stairs, and I bolted."

"Can you tell us anything about him? Anything at all, no matter how small or stupid?" Tate asked.

She shook her head. "I couldn't see in the pitch black."

"Think. Was he tall? Fat or thin?" Luc hoped he could jar her memory. Granted, probably high on adrenaline and absolutely panicked, her mind might be blank, but if he could get her to remember something, at this point anything would help.

"I think he stood about my height, maybe a few inches taller? I'm not sure, we were on different steps. He wasn't like you," she pointed to Tate. "I mean, not height but muscles. He was thin."

"This is great, ma'am," Vince praised. "What about his face? Hair? Could you tell length—long or short? Bald?" He ran a hand over his smooth head.

She shook her head. "He wore a hoodie, with the hood drawn up. Oh!" She sat up straight. "He didn't have a beard. My hand brushed down his smooth face."

"Anything else? Anything at all?" Luc mentally crossed his fingers. At least they had the beginnings of a description if her impressions were correct.

"No. The dark…I just ran. I'm sorry."

"No apologies, ma'am. You were awesome." Vince smiled at her. "Few people could have escaped the way you did. I'm former Special Forces. Take the compliment."

Luc shuffled through the papers and found a gaping hole—the listing for the location she escaped from. He shot his gaze to hers. "Ms. Thomas, what about the location you ran from? Do you know where it is?"

He saw Vince tense out of the corner of his eye as Luc's own excitement built.

"I don't know."

And his hope crashed, smacking the ground and shattering into a million pieces. Could they ever get a bigger break?

"But I can take you there."

Chapter Five

Casi stared through the front windshield as she sat in the backseat of the detective's unmarked sedan and tried to slow her heartbeat. She didn't want to return to the house she escaped from, even in the company of two detectives. Mason left her with the two cops after a hug and an apology. He had to get ready for work. She understood. She did. But Casi would have given anything for his unconditional support seated beside her right now.

"Make the next right." Sweat beaded on her forehead, regardless of the blasting cool breeze from the car's air conditioning. Glancing behind her, she peered out the rear window and marked the procession of four patrol cars following them. She swallowed hard, her throat and mouth dry. What if they found nothing? Would they still believe her? Why all the manpower?

Detective Avery made the right. Her entire body shook, and she broke out in a full-body cold sweat. They were close. "Slow down. Slow…" She met Avery's eyes in the rearview mirror, before looking out the side window, searching the townhouses lining the street. *Shit, shit, shit.* There it was. When she had run out the front door, she'd glanced over her shoulder, hoping not to see her abductor chasing her, and had noticed both the color of the door and the embellished mailbox slot, even in the rain and darkness. "Stop." Her voice cracked. "It's the yellow door with the ornate gold mailbox." She wet her lips and took a hard swallow.

Avery pulled the car to the curb. He swiveled in his seat and faced her. "You sure?"

She could only nod since her throat had closed tightly, and she had trouble breathing. Casi felt lightheaded.

"Take a deep breath, Ms. Thomas. You're safe." Detective Avery gave her a slight smile. "We won't let anything happen to you. Come on, just one breath." His light Cajun accent curled around her.

Her mouth opened on a gasp. He nodded when she took another breath. Once reassured she would not pass out or hyperventilate, he turned to his partner. "Call it in."

"Already on it." Detective Tate replied with a smartphone in hand as he tapped on a name she couldn't make out. It didn't take long for someone on the other end to pick up.

"It's Tate. We need information on an address. Text me all pertinent info." The detective gave the location and ended the call when a heavy silence filled the car as they waited. Though the car's vents continued blasting air, Casi felt both hot and claustrophobic and yet chilled to the bone. The need to open the door and bolt crashed through her. Escape screamed inside her head. She gripped the leather seat beside her knees, trying to hold herself in place. With her hands aching and sweat dripping, Casi kept still, but only by the skin of her teeth.

Tate's phone dinged. He unlocked the screen, and his gaze focused as he read the message. He looked up, and his walnut brown eyes met hers before swinging to his partner's. He flipped his phone and showed Detective Avery the screen. As soon as Avery read it, he let out a soft hiss of air. Some unspoken communication passed between the detectives, leading Tate to nod and then dial a new number as Avery turned and addressed her.

"Ms. Thomas. Thank you so much for your cooperation. We will have some patrolmen take you to your apartment. The clothes you wore when abducted are there?"

"Yes."

Casi listened as Tate requested a search warrant for the upscale townhouse when she realized Avery had kept speaking.

"I'm sorry. What did you just say?"

Avery smiled, all sympathy and charm, which raised her hackles. "I was saying that after we have your clothing for evidence, you'll need to pack a bag because we're taking you to a safe location."

"Wait, what?"

"You can't stay at your place, ma'am."

She shook her head and grabbed the car door's handle when Detective Tate reached over the seat and stopped her with his hand on her arm.

"It's for your safety."

Her safety? Bullshit. She wanted to go home and forget everything that happened. Going somewhere unknown with cops? Impossible. Absolutely not.

"Ms. Thomas. Cassanne. Please." Her eyes were drawn to Avery's. "The man who took you is still at large. What if he knows where you live? Please, it's just for a short while. A precaution. Let us keep you safe."

She didn't feel in danger. Taken from the alley and not her home, the guy couldn't know where she lived, could he? Shaking her head, Casi didn't believe them. They were giving her a line of bullshit. They had to be. The kidnapper wouldn't know the personal info of a random victim. "No. I want to go home and stay there."

"Miss Thomas," Tate addressed her. "Just a night, two at the most. Just to be sure. Think of it as a free vacation." He smiled, showing white teeth, which glowed against his dark skin.

Avery exited the car and rounded the front, approaching her rear passenger door. He opened it for her. Casi noticed the patrol cop standing next to him as the detective offered his hand to help her out of the car. She looked between the detective and the uniform. Her stomach clenched tight, as nausea threatened to bring bile up her throat. It appeared she had no choice. One night. Two at the most, and then she would leave. Refusing Avery's outstretched hand, she got herself out of the car.

She let the officer lead her to the patrol car. Casi had hoped never to ride in the back of a cop car ever again. Granted, she wasn't cuffed and being hauled off as a suspect this time, but that didn't change the nastiness of the rear seat of a police car. Before she entered the backseat with a caged wall separating the front from the rear, she peered at Avery, who stood frowning at her. What was his deal? Did he know about California and didn't believe her? Whatever.

Casi ducked into the car and tried to tamp down her swirling emotions. She'd follow their lead for now, but the second she could, she'd be out of there.

****

She paused at the entrance to her bathroom and stared at the clothes crumpled in a heap on the floor. Shuddering, Casi forced herself to take the few steps forward, reaching the pile.

"Excuse me, ma'am."

She jolted at the cop's voice so close behind her. Looking over her shoulder, she saw the young cop, who couldn't be more than twenty, maybe less, standing in the bathroom's doorway. Oh yeah, some protection he'd provide.

"You shouldn't touch those." He motioned her out of the way as he entered with plastic evidence bags. "We need all the uncontaminated DNA we can get."

Uncontaminated? Her DNA was littered all over the fabric. With gloved hands, he squatted and confiscated her outfit. Bagging her jeans, blouse, boots, and even her underwear into separate bags. At least her bra and panties were nice and not the plain old cotton ones she'd normally wore. Behind in her washing, she had only *date* underwear left. The lacey matching navy set, a definite contrast to her ripped jeans and a plain T-shirt. Looks like her wash would still have to wait, at least for another day or two. She sighed.

The baby cop stood. "If you pack a bag, we can be out of here." He looked around. "Anything else you had with you? Something that might lead us to who grabbed you?"

Casi's gaze landed on her messenger bag propped next to the bed. She hesitated. Her kidnapper had to have touched it when he removed it and strapped her to the table. Maybe even dug through its contents. She chewed on her lower lip. If she told the cop, he'd seize it as well. It held everything. Her phone, wallet, her

Tarot cards, odds and ends of her life, everything but her keys, which were the only thing she grabbed when she left her apartment in a rush before ending up at Mason's. Casi couldn't let them have it.

"No." She shook her head. "You have it all." Besides, the lie comforted her since the kidnapper's prints or DNA had to be on her boots since the guy had removed them as well.

"All right, ma'am. Officer Rylie"—he gestured toward the other uniform standing inside the threshold of her bedroom door—"and I will wait for you in the front room." He gave her a sympathetic smile before exiting the bathroom and flicking a thumb at his partner to follow him. Finally, some breathing space. Though not much. Her crazy small apartment had just two cramped rooms. One with a kitchen stuck in the corner of the front room and a minuscule bedroom barely big enough for a double bed with a tiny bathroom hidden behind a pocket door.

Casi exhaled as she watched them leave. As soon as they left, she turned and grasped the edge of the white porcelain sink in a tight hold before lifting her gaze to the mirror. She had to admit she looked awful. Her bloodshot eyes highlighted the dark circles below. She shook her head. This day had to end. Exhaustion ripped through her, and she locked her knees to keep herself upright. *Dammit.* Why couldn't life ever be easy? It had been once. She'd had a career she'd loved, helping kids and making a difference. Her happiness and good fortune changed in a blink.

Disgusted with herself, she stared into the mirror and yanked off her hair tie. Slipping it onto her wrist, she gathered her hair and twisted it until a tight bun formed against her head before pulling the tie back over her hand to secure the knot.

Fate could go screw herself. She'd take care of herself. Opening a cabinet next to the sink, she grabbed her toiletry bag and began shoving inside items she'd need for the next few nights. Casi strode out of the bathroom and tossed the bag on her bed and headed for her closet. Yanking the door open, she reached up and pulled a small duffle bag from the shelf. It didn't take long to toss what clothes she needed, since there wasn't much to choose from. Between being perpetually broke and all her dirty laundry, packing became simple.

She grabbed her messenger bag and slung it over her shoulder and then snatched up her small duffle before marching to the front room.

"All set?" Officer Belmont, the boy wonder, asked.

She nodded. He opened the door and exited. So much for manners and ladies first. Casi left her apartment with Officer Rylie following close behind after shutting her door, completing their three-person parade.

Was this really for her safety? Or in her naïveté, was she about to be royally screwed again? They should at least buy her dinner and drinks first.

Chapter Six

Selene Walsh strode down the sidewalk, heading for the police tape cordoning off the townhouse. Her Louboutin heels tapped along in rhythm with the swing of her short asymmetrical bob swaying to her footsteps. She needed information.

"I'm sorry, ma'am. You can't go any farther."

Not shocked when the uniform stopped her, after all, he had his job to do. And when his gaze strolled leisurely down then up her body, that hadn't surprised her either. Dressed in her custom-fitted Chanel skirt and blouse, exposing her long-toned legs, retro pinup girl curves, and ample cleavage, she knew she had his attention.

"Of course, Officer." Selene smiled. "I live nearby." She inhaled and kept her smirk hidden when his gaze dropped to her breasts. "What happened?"

Selene granted him bonus points when the cop lifted his gaze and looked her in the eyes, made easy since with her heels she matched his six-foot height. "I'm not at liberty to say, ma'am."

Making sure her painted red lips pouted, she took another breath, drawing the officer's eyes downward once again. Who needed magical powers when you had a nice rack? "But you can tell me something, right?" She touched his upper arm, drawing his interest upward again. "I live alone. Do I need to be worried?"

The cop studied her for a moment before surveying his surroundings. “You should probably make sure your doors and windows are locked at all times.”

“But what happened?” She gripped his bicep tighter and stepped closer. “Just between you and me.” She made her voice breathless. “I’ll never tell a soul.” Selene saw his pulse quicken with her proximity. “Please?”

The cop’s brow furrowed before he leaned closer and whispered. “A woman was held captive inside.”

“Oh my gosh! Is she all right?”

“Yes, ma’am. She escaped.”

“Thank goodness.” She squeezed his arm one last time before stepping back. “Do they have a suspect?”

“Hopefully soon, but the investigation is still ongoing.”

“I’ll be sure to keep myself locked up tight at night. Thank you for the reassurance.”

Selene barely saw his nod as she turned and headed toward her car. Rounding the corner, she kept walking until reaching the shiny black BMW parked halfway up the block. With a chirp from her key fob, the car unlocked, and the engine started as she stepped off the curb and opened the driver’s door.

The news wasn’t startling. The glaring lack of news vans swarming the scene considering who owned the townhouse came as a surprise. Selene smiled. The cops would find nothing that pointed to the true culprit. Everything was as it should be.

****

“Fuck, man. This place is cleaner than an operating room.” Vincent complained.

Luc grunted in return. Not a speck of dust in sight.

He scanned the living room. Empty, devoid of all furniture, like the rest of the house. With their second pass through the entire building, all four floors, they still found squat. With the townhouse scheduled for renovation, all the furniture and belongings were cleared out. Searching wasn't difficult, just frustrating.

"My gut is telling me something isn't right." Luc shoved his hair off his forehead.

"Yeah, I'm feeling it too."

"*Ouais*. Let's check the basement one more time."

Luc and Vince cut through the kitchen to the open door revealing the wooden stairs, the exact ones Cassanne Thomas had described. First, he had to agree with her. Who in their right mind would have a basement in New Orleans? The area was below the water table. The amount of money making it waterproof had to be astounding. But then again, considering who owned the high-end townhouse, it wasn't surprising.

Chadwick Winston III. The legacy billionaire whose hands were deeply entrenched in Louisiana's politics. The man behind the power. It had sent chills scurrying over his skin when he had read the name on Tate's phone. Placing Ms. Thomas into protective custody became imperative once Luc knew who they were up against. The guy had tons of power and reach. Approval for the search warrant shocked him—he figured it would have been blocked. In the hours they combed through the empty townhouse, they had found nothing, except Winston and his wife were currently vacationing in Milan. Must be nice.

Minutes ago, Vince got another text, this one confirming the billionaire's son remained in town. They wanted to issue a BOLO on Brock Winston, but their captain refused unless they found something proof positive. The captain declined to put his and the department's neck on the line with only *the word of a tarnished social worker who played psychic*.

Luc jogged down the creaky stairs and hit the concrete. Still nothing. No gurney, no cuffs, no ties. The empty floor taunted him. He believed her story, and Vince backed him up. Why couldn't they get a break?

"There has to be something here," he muttered, stepping farther into the room.

"I hear ya, but we've been at this for a while, and there's nothing. The only prints found were on the fuse box, and I'll bet my military pension they'll match Thomas."

"I won't argue. I still wish the captain would issue the BOLO." Luc started quartering the room, willing himself to be sharp. They had to find something. The search of the alley where she was grabbed had turned up nothing. Last night's rain made sure of it, or their killer was that good at hiding his tracks. The frustrating news held no surprises. Still, he had uniforms canvassing the neighborhood. They might get lucky with surveillance footage or an eyewitness.

Vincent joined him, mirroring his movements from the opposite side of the room. "There's no way he will risk his career. You know it as well as I do. The man's a coward."

Luc had no answer. It would take time for the prints to come back. They needed to find something tangible now. He pulled his pocket LED flashlight, hoping more light would help.

Something sparked off to his right, catching his

attention. He strode to the fuse box and squatted before shining the beam toward the seam where the wall and floor met.

"What have you got?" Vince arrived by his side before he could say anything.

"Not sure. You have a pen or something?"

Tate snorted. When Luc glanced up, he saw the pocketknife held in his partner's hand. Yeah, that would do. He grabbed it with his gloved hand and flipped open the utility knife. He hesitated. They'd need to document it before he could unearth his possible treasure. Vince read his mind.

"Yo, Joyce, get down here. We need some photos." His bellow reached deep into the townhouse.

"Coming!" The distant female voice shouted from above. In short order, they heard her footsteps on the stairs, and she reached their sides. "The basement, again?" She crouched next to him. "What have you found?"

Luc motioned to the tiny pointed piece of bronze metal barely protruding from the base of the wall.

"Huh. Good eye." Joyce reached in her bag and pulled out a yellow plastic v-card with the number three emblazoned on both sides. Sad. This might be their only other potential piece of evidence. The fuse box being number one, and the scuff marks mid-basement stairs were two. Plopping the evidence marker down, she picked up her camera and focused, before snapping off several shots. She stood and took a wide shot for room placement.

"There you go, Detective Avery, have at it."

"Thanks, Joyce." Luc slid the small knife into the crevice as more of the concrete cracked and crumbled away, revealing a deeper hole.

"This place will flood with the next big storm," Vince predicted.

Luc agreed. One shouldn't have basements in the Parish. The rot set in below ground. With a flick of his wrist, the small knife dislodged the metal object wedged inside the interior of the wall. The clicks of the camera announced Joyce still documenting. They needed all the help they could get.

"Well, look at what we have here." Luc lifted the bronze medal with the small knife, revealing a cross made of clockworks. "I do believe we found Ms. Thomas's charm."

Vince handed him an evidence bag, which Luc dropped the cross into before sealing it shut. His gut twisted. Was finding the charm, especially after Ms. Thomas pointedly drew attention to it in the interrogation room, too much of a coincidence? Chad Winston thrown in the mix complicated everything. Was she trying to blackmail him or his son by framing one of them? Was it a con game? Her finances weren't great, and her professional reputation remained in ruins.

Luc mentally shook himself. Cassanne Thomas had given details not known to the public. The light bruising on her neck and wrists matched the victims. Plus, terror exploded across her features when she had spotted the townhouse. She could be an Academy Award-worthy actress or the genuine thing. His lips thinned, and his gaze narrowed as he studied the cross in the clear evidence bag. He shoved his cynicism aside. Innocent until proven guilty. For now, he'd trust his gut, and his intuition told him to believe her.

"Get me that BOLO, Vince."

"On it."

Luc smiled as he stood with his bagged prize in hand. Finally. His hunt now had a scent.

Chapter Seven

Gabriel gave the aged wood of the bar one last wipe, before flipping the towel to land across his shoulder. The Fleur-de-lis pub remained quiet this lazy late afternoon, but things would pick up when evening arrived along with the live music.

"Taps all full?"

He glanced up and then nodded at the bar's owner, Chris Jeske, when the man stopped on the opposite side of the countertop.

"I'm going to take off for the next few hours, try not to let the place burn down."

"You got it." Gabriel waved him off. The bar couldn't be safer with him. Little did Chris know whom he had actually left in charge. Gabriel wasn't human. In fact, he was an angel. An angel of renown. The Archangel Gabriel. He could handle the bar with his eyes closed, unlike his other situation where he craved resolution. No more wasting time. Finally, his possible resolution had arrived.

A movement caught his eye, and Gabriel glanced at the pub's entrance. He kept his groan internal when in walked his eldest brother and younger sister. Of course they'd decided to visit. They must have figured out his horn had come into play. But didn't they have better things to do? He knew his brother certainly did.

Michael and Sari made themselves comfortable on

a couple of barstools as they both gave him matching grins in greeting.

"Can I get you two something to drink?"

"Sure, surprise me with something on tap." Michael slapped the bar with his hand.

"Make mine a Cosmo." Sari's smile turned sweet.

Gabriel nodded and grabbed a shaker and added ice. Next, he mixed in the vodka and Cointreau shots before he added the lime and cranberry. He gave it a good shake before pouring the drink into a martini glass and garnishing it with a twist of lemon. Pushing it gently to Sari, he returned her smile.

"Here you go, baby sis."

"Thanks, Gabe."

"Do I need to guess why the visit?" Gabriel pulled the tap for a glass of Turbodog from the local Abita Brewing Company for his brother. A dark beer but wouldn't weigh him down like a stout. The brown ale held a more complex taste than most. Michael should like it.

With a flick of his wrist, he sent the full pint glass gliding across the half-length of the bar to land in his brother's hand without a drop spilled. He wandered back to stand in front of his siblings.

"Is there a reason we can't be here other than we'd like to see you, Gabriel?"

"Oh please, Mikey. You can try to fly that past me, but you know, and I know, you have way too many things to deal with for no ulterior motive."

Michael took a sip and savored his swallow. Gabriel was rewarded by the look of pleasure filling his brother's face. They may argue and tease each other, but Michael had the hardest job amongst all the siblings. It pleased Gabriel he could ease his brother's burden in such a simple manner.

Sari elbowed Michael in the ribs, and he caught the twinkle in Michael's gaze. Okay, this might be just a social call after all, one to relax his too serious brother. He had a feeling Sari was behind the trip, trying to get their eldest brother out of the house and away from work more.

"Is it true? Has something precious and personal of yours gone missing?" Michael's grin lit up his face.

"The feathered grapevine is never wrong, Gabe." Sari teased him.

He'd go along with the game. "Missing? Nothing of mine is missing."

"Really?" Michael drawled. "So you've recovered your horn?"

"Well—"

"Ha! I knew it." Sari clapped as she bounced on the barstool in her enthusiasm. His extraordinarily clever sister always enjoyed a good scheme. Two steps ahead of everyone in the family, she must have figured out Gabriel's plan.

"It's not lost." He tried keeping his face stern.

"So if I went to St. Brendan's church, I'd find it safely stored?" Michael raised an eyebrow, his eyes still laughing at him.

"Ah…no."

"Your horn is a powerful artifact, Gabriel. Need I remind you, it isn't something that should be out and about?"

"No, you need not point that out, Michael. Besides, I've told you, it's not missing."

"Oh, you *are* up to something." Sari grinned.

"Perhaps."

"Gabriel. Father has rules."

"Yes, yes, Michael, I know." He waved off his brother's concern. "I'm taking a page from Uri and Remi's playbook." With his aforementioned brothers and their successes, Gabriel felt the time to remove the thorn pricking in his side had arrived. He only hoped his luck would be as good as theirs.

His big brother's sigh had him grinning. Poor Michael. Always having to set the example and hold to the higher standard of the eldest child. Sucks to be the first. He decided to cut his brother some slack.

"I let it be stolen."

"Seriously? You know how dangerous the horn can be."

"Yes, Michael, I know. It is mine, after all. However, if I wanted to draw my prey out, it became necessary."

He shook his head and glanced at Sari, who remained grinning.

"Come on, Michael. Gabe's right. It's about time we took this demon out."

Gabriel studied his brother's serious demeanor, but he saw past Michael's façade. The eyes don't lie, and amusement glittered in his brother's navy blue depths.

"I hope you know what you're doing. It's been over two hundred years." Michael finished his beer.

"And has anything happened? Plus, two hundred years passed for the humans and this creature, but not for us."

"Yeah," Sari agreed with him. "You know we're like the Doctor except, like, we don't need the actual blue box TARDIS to do the whole time and space thing."

Michael's eyes narrowed, probably at Sari's comment on a popular mortal entertainment, before glaring back to Gabriel. "I suppose. Your plan better be good."

"Of course it is. Gabe's the best." Sari rubbed a finger around the rim of her empty martini glass.

"Thanks, baby girl. I appreciate the vote of confidence." He high-fived with his sister's palm as Michael stood.

Sari hopped down from her stool and gave Michael a hug. "He's got this. Come on, we should go bowling."

"Bowling?"

"Yeah, you need some fun, especially now you're loosened up with a beer."

Gabriel jerked his chin toward the exit after exchanging glances with his brother. "Go on, get out of here, you old bird. Sari will kick your ass, and I can't wait to hear every embarrassing detail." He winked at her.

They shared a laugh before his family left. Gabriel grabbed their empty glasses and put them in the dirty bin. Things were looking up for the Floor-de-Loo. The place would have to lose its nickname and go by the Fleur-de-lis permanently. It wasn't every day the place got classed up with a visit from the Archangels Michael and Sariel.

Chapter Eight

Casi jolted awake, breathing hard while the remnants of her dream dissolved. She dragged herself upright, taking in her surroundings. The uncomfortable lumpy mattress in the safe house sealed the deal on her unhappy fate. Forget protective custody, she felt like a prisoner.

After dropping off her bagged and tagged clothes to the precinct, her detail handed her off to another pair of uniforms—with no introductions—who drove her to this house about an hour outside New Orleans. The small, nondescript house on a nondescript street in a typical suburban track held little charm. When she walked past the front door, which needed another two or three coats of paint to mask its wear, the exhaustion she had kept at bay slammed into her full force.

She literally swayed after crossing the threshold. With burning eyes and not a word to her babysitters, Casi forced herself farther into the house until she entered the first bedroom she could find. She closed and locked the door behind her, dumped her duffle and messenger bag to the floor, and then collapsed on the twin-sized bed fully clothed—never even bothering to kick off her shoes. She remembered nothing after that.

The filmy grime covering the window beside the bed encased everything outside in a greasy fog. Regardless of the visibility, she could tell night had fallen. Exactly what time, she had no idea, but that could be easily remedied.

She stood, stretched her stiff muscles from sleeping in one position for too long, and went to her bags still lying on the floor. Grabbing her messenger bag, she flipped the flap and started digging through its depths for her cell phone.

"Ouch!"

Pain sliced across her finger causing her to almost drop her bag. Casi pulled out her hand and studied the angry red scratch across her index finger. What the hell? There wasn't anything sharp in the bag. Her keys wouldn't have scratched her.

She shuffled to the bed and upended the bag, spilling the contents across the cream blanket covering the off-white sheets. Tarot cards encased in their satin bag fell first, followed by her phone, wallet, keys, makeup bag, and some papers. Nothing sharp stood out. Giving the canvas satchel another shake, she almost missed the insignificant item falling out, but it hit her cell phone with a ping before bouncing away, landing in the center of the bed.

A charm, shaped like a horn, laid spotlighted by the grungy light from the bare bulb overhead. It was an odd color—a greenish, brownish, gray mottled combination. The horn didn't look like any metal she'd ever seen. Casi picked it up. No, not metal, more like a weird type of ivory or something. Maybe a polished stone? She ran her finger over the horn's wider opening and felt no rough patches on its edge. The charm appeared maybe three inches at the most and slightly curved. Where had it come from?

Centered in the curve of the bugle was an eyehook

ring where a chain or string could be threaded through. The ring didn't quite meet at the top. She found the sharp edge, which had injured her. Who knew how long it had been in her bag? So small it could have been overlooked since she bought the satchel secondhand. Maybe it belonged to the previous owner?

She ran her finger over the smooth body of the horn, before dropping it into her palm, studying it. Her curiosity peaked. The horn heated, suddenly becoming scalding hot. A shooting sting lanced into her hand, followed by a blinding pain behind her eyes. Agony crushed her skull as her legs gave out, and Casi crashed to the ground, dropping the bugle. She clasped her hands to her head and squeezed, trying to relieve the exploding pain in her skull. In seconds, the blinding agony retreated. She blinked away tears. What the hell had happened?

Sitting on the floor, she stared at the horn, afraid to touch it in case it burned her again. Casi nudged it with her foot, but nothing weird occurred. It laid there innocently. With a shaking hand, she reached out with the bare tip of her finger and touched the charm.

Nothing. Cool and smooth, the horn devolved into just a piece of jewelry again. Had the charm burned her and given her a crushing migraine sending her to the floor? Well, she hadn't landed on her ass for no reason. She needed air. She needed to walk off the lightheadedness she felt after the blinding headache.

Casi snatched the charm, stood, and stuffed it into her pocket, before grabbing her phone. Unlocking her bedroom door, she eased it open, wondering where her babysitters lurked. She padded to the front room, finding the front door closed and the living room empty. Maybe she could take a walk around the block? She stifled her snort. No way the cops would let her wander around on her own, but they might leave her be if she stayed in the backyard.

Decision made, Casi walked deeper into the house. Right before entering the kitchen, she halted when male voices reached her. She pressed her back against the wall, out of sight, and eavesdropped.

"Is she still asleep?"

"Yeah, last time I checked. I used the skeleton key to open the door this time, just to make sure."

"You read her file?"

"Of course. I like to know who I'm guarding. That was some fucked up shit in California. I'm not sure why she's still walking free."

"Because they found her innocent."

"Well, they got it wrong. Even a blind man could see her culpability. Two kids dead and she's free to live her life? Did you see their ages? Seven and five. She fucking deserves to be behind bars. That would be the ideal *protective* custody for her."

Casi squeezed her eyes shut and forced the bile back down her throat into her cramping stomach. Would she always carry the guilt of Trevor and his sister, Aimee, for the rest of her life? She'd give everything and anything to trade her life for theirs. She blinked back tears and silently inhaled a few deep breaths, trying to steady herself.

"The Cyclops should have killed her. At least this time his victim would have deserved it."

"Seriously, Dan? They found the lady not guilty, and nobody, and I mean nobody, needs to be a victim of a serial killer, or any murderer."

"I'm just saying."

"Enough. She might help catch him. Save lives. I don't care what you personally think of her, all you need to do is your job."

Eyes wide and breath caught in her throat, Casi froze, stunned. Serial killer? What the freaking nightmare? Panic set her pulse racing and her heart pounding. Wouldn't she have heard if a serial killer indeed stalked the city? It'd be all over the news, and there hadn't been a peep. That couldn't be right. Some maniac in the alley kidnapped her, not a freaking serial killer.

She had to get out of here. They were nuts, and they knew what happened in California. Even if the whole killer thing were true, would they even protect her? It didn't sound that way.

Casi's pulse kicked into overdrive, making her even more lightheaded. She couldn't curl into a little ball and hyperventilate. She had to get moving before she fainted. And there was no way she'd let herself be found unconscious by these assholes.

Silently retreating from the kitchen while the cops continued their discussion, she returned to the small bedroom. She shoved everything on the bed back into her messenger bag and slung it over her head. Jogging to the door, Casi grabbed her duffle without missing a beat.

She hesitated for the first time since fleeing the kitchen and the horrible conversation. A long head start would be awesome before they started tracking her. They had a key, but maybe if they found the door locked, they might assume she was still inside. The slight chance was worth it. He had said *this* time, so maybe they would only check the handle the next time. She locked the knob and silently closed the door. Hopefully, it would buy her the time she needed.

Sneaking out the front door, she paused on the porch. Though most of the houses had lights shining inside, the street remained quiet. Maybe the families who lived here were all eating dinner and no one would notice her. Her feet bounced down the porch steps, and she quickly crossed the lawn. When she reached the sidewalk, Casi turned left and broke into a jog.

She had paid little attention while on the way to the safe house, her bad, but she remembered passing through a small town. A town would have buses. Public transportation would get her the hell out of wherever she was. Casi didn't dare use her rideshare app. The cops could probably trace her through the program. *Shit*! Her phone!

Glancing over her shoulder and finding herself out of view of the safe house, she stopped. She yanked her phone out, pulled up the location settings, and turned off her GPS before powering it down. Hopefully, they couldn't track her. Casi shoved her cell into her rear pocket and picked up her pace once again.

She'd go to her apartment and pick up the essentials she needed, then disappear. Protecting herself became her number one priority. No one else would. It was time she got the hell out of New Orleans.

Chapter Nine

Luc studied the new bartender as he pulled a pint from the taps. The large guy echoed Vincent's height and build, showing he must at least work out regularly. The drink slinger could easily give the Loo's bouncer back up. His light brown hair, cut short and messy, made him appear young. The guy could be a model with his chiseled facial features, but not the metrosexual kind, more like the bad boy style.

"You new to the Loo? I don't remember seeing you around?" Luc picked up the fresh pint set in front of him and took a swallow as he stared the bartender in the eyes. There was something not right about him. He didn't think the guy was a criminal or anything, but his cop's instincts kept pinging every time Luc looked at him.

"Yup. I'm Gabriel. A recent hire, been mostly working days while Jeske took my measure."

"Huh. Guess you passed. Welcome to the Loo. I'm Luc."

Gabriel gave a nod before going back to work. The busy night kept the two bartenders hustling as they pushed drinks nonstop.

The live music stopped, and canned upbeat jazz took its place. Luc swiveled on his high stool, placing his back to the bar, and watched the members of Neutral Ground putting their instruments down and hopping off the stage for a break. Bastien, his younger brother and front man of the band, threaded through the crowded floor and plopped himself onto the barstool next to him. He wiped his hand across his forehead, mopping up the sweat coating his skin. Four years younger, his brother checked in an inch or two taller than Luc, with a slender but muscular build—like Bastien had a ten-pack instead of the lowly six-pack abs. Good thing too since Bas took his shirt off while on stage more often than not. He claimed the ladies loved looking at him, and it was hot under the stage lights. Well, he had impressive stomach muscles to show off, so why not? He also had their Dad's coloring—jet-black hair, worn rock star length, and cat green eyes. Luc appeared more of a blend of their parents with his dark blond hair and hazel eyes.

"Nice jam." Luc offered his fist, which his brother bumped obligingly with his own.

"Thanks." Bas gave him the once over. "Why you look like crap?" His accent drawled full out from singing the last forty-five minutes. Most people lost accents when they sang, not Bastien, his only grew stronger. "You could give the Loo's floor a run for ugly."

Luc sighed. Vince had called him on the same thing earlier this morning. He hadn't been out partying or screwing. Sadly, he just hadn't been sleeping. This past week of no rest had finally caught up to him.

"It's been a shit-tastic day."

"Do you have any other kind?" His brother's scrutinizing attention pulled away when the bartender dropped a huge sweating glass of ice water next to him. Bas gave a chin nod to Gabriel, before taking the glass and chugging half of it down. Swiveling on the stool, he turned with a frown, giving Luc his full regard.

Luc mentally sighed. It might be a different melody, but the song remained the same. Bas had been nagging him to change careers for a couple of years. He might be right. "This case is kicking my ass."

His brother raised a dark eyebrow. "It's a bad one?"

Luc nodded, before raising his hand and stalling Bastien's next words. "Yes, I know. They always seem awful, but I am a detective in the CID."

"How come they keep giving you all the nasty homicides in the Criminal Investigation Division? Last I heard there are crimes other than murder."

"What can I say? I've got the highest closing rate. I'm good at what I do." Luc sipped his beer. "Vince and I might have gotten a break today, though."

"That true?" Bastien's eyes narrowed. "Let me guess, a witness."

Luc shrugged.

"And now, you've been wondering all day if it's too good to be true." Bastien chugged down some more water. "So you're losing sleep over a killer you haven't somehow magically caught, and now your skepticism has you bound in knots." He shook his head. "Lucas, you've changed. You used to have faith in humanity." His frown deepened. "You need to leave the justice biz, big bro. It's killing your soul."

Luc broke his gaze from Bastien's, staring into his almost empty pint. Exhaustion ate at him. He'd definitely grown cynical, but it came with the territory. He saw the worst of humanity. Sometimes the belief that anything good left in the world became a bridge too far to walk. He drained the last of his beer and placed his glass on the bar before facing his brother.

"Yeah, maybe you're right."

Bastien's wide eyes and raised eyebrows revealed his shock. "It's about freaking time. I love you, bro. I hate what your job has done to you, watching it wear you down, tear you down."

Luc tried a smile, but it was the barest of movement. "I know. But what I do matters. I save lives by catching the bad guys, Bas. It's hard to walk away."

"I get it. I do. But maybe it's time to let someone else step in. You've done more than your fair share and put in the time. You need a break at least." Bastien's face lit up with a charming grin. The same one both Luc and his brother had inherited from their father—pure Cajun sly. Luckily, Luc seemed to have earned himself a reprieve from Bastien's routine lecture. He guessed his answer of at least considering walking away from his career made a splendid way to get Bas to change the subject. His brother's next words confirmed it.

"What you need is some music therapy, my man." Bastien stood up, downed the rest of his water, before slapping Luc on his shoulder. "Come on, Lucky, break's over." Luc smiled at his family's nickname. "Let's get your groove on." Bas grabbed his arm, tugging him off his barstool. "You don't even have to sing. I'll let you lose your ass in the brass section."

Luc followed his brother to the stage and jumped up after him like the old hand he proved to be.

"Here."

Luc took the trumpet from Bas with a nod and a deep breath. Putting his lips to the mouthpiece, he confidently and agilely ran through some scales, warming up while keeping an ear out for his tuning. Keith, the principal trombonist, smiled at him as he picked up his instrument and stepped next to Luc.

Neutral Ground had anywhere from five to eleven members at any given time. The core group contained Bastien on vocals and sometimes guitar—electric or acoustic, Greg on lead guitar, Drew on bass guitar, Alonz on keyboards, and of course, Phil on drums. Yes, Phil did get a rash of shit. There was no end to the amount of Phil Collins jokes he had to endure by being a drummer named Phil.

When the gang's all here, there were two trombones, two trumpets (which Luc wasn't one of normally), an upright bass, and woodwind aficionado, Bruce, who played anything, but mostly stuck with sax, clarinet, flute, and harmonica. The stage could get a bit crowded. Tonight, however, with Luc on trumpet, Keith with his bone, and Lionel on upright bass as the added additions to the core, the stage still held room for more.

At least Luc didn't have to sing tonight. Not that he was bashful or couldn't carry a tune. Singing with his brother was fun, but Luc had a gritty, rough rock and roll quality to his voice, while his brother's tone was pure sex. At least according to several of his female colleagues from the precinct kept telling him, so he'd take their word for it. Luc let Bastien do his thing, happy not to be in the spotlight.

"All right, ya'll." Bas gripped the microphone. "The Avery brothers are in the house, so let's get this party started."

Phil clicked out a beat, and then Bastien let his voice rip while the guitars growled. A beat later, the brass section kicked in. Luc kept up. The song, one of his favorites, he could play in his sleep. Bastien had taken pity on him.

Through the blinding stage lights, he saw the audience on their feet, clapping and dancing. Luc gave himself to the music. He disappeared into the hard-driving rhythm, letting all his problems and exhaustion disappear as the music took him over.

Chapter Ten

Casi made mental notes on what she needed to retrieve as she ran up the stairs to her second-story apartment. *Her passport and phone charger*. Luckily, she went digital with her banking and bills, so she didn't have to deal with having her mail forwarded. *The rest of her clothes*. She grimaced. The thought of throwing her dirty laundry into her duffle with the remaining of her clean made Casi cringe, but it didn't matter in the scheme of things. At least she wouldn't have to worry about packing nicely, which would speed things up. The bus ride and subsequent transfers had taken longer than she had hoped. Her time had to have run out. The cops must be searching for her by now.

Her hand grabbed her keys from the bottom of her bag. Good thing it would only take her a moment to gather her stuff, because the first place the police would look if they even bothered, would be her apartment. Casi hoped to be long gone before they arrived.

She frowned when she found her door unlocked. Running through her memories from when she left, Casi couldn't remember if she'd locked it or not. The cop had shut the door behind him as he left. Idiot cop. The asshole must have never secured her apartment.

Crossing the threshold, she carefully closed the door behind her, before turning on the light. She didn't want to advertise her presence if she didn't have to.

Casi froze and stood in complete confusion as she took in her tiny apartment. The room before her, even the attached afterthought of a kitchen, was completely trashed. What little furniture she had was overturned, her couch cushions and pillows were shredded, and stuffing leaked out everywhere. All the cabinets and drawers in the narrow galley kitchen stood open, their contents either shattered on the floor or broken where they stood. Her heart raced. Did the police do this? They ransacked her home. They hadn't had permission, let alone a search warrant. Taking a few tentative steps, her feet planted once more when she stood by her small kitchen table lying on its side along with two chairs. She swallowed hard against her suddenly dry throat.

Detective Avery's voice floated through her mind. *He might know where you live.* Her head swam, and she wrapped her arms around herself, hugging her center. How? Her wallet inside her bag. It would have been a simple matter for her abductor to read her driver's license. Oh God. A serial killer might truly be after her.

Casi locked her knees to keep herself from running. What could she do? Shudders racked her body while her breaths came in short rapid bursts. She wasn't safe. Casi had to disappear and fast.

Decision made, she entered her bedroom and halted, taking in the destruction. Her bedroom matched the front room. Stripped bare and ripped to shreds, her mattress laid in tatters along with her pillows and sheets. The closet doors were off their hinges, the contents pulled off hangers and shelves. All her clothes were torn. Everything ruined. Her hand flew to her mouth, covering the whimper that escaped. *So much for packing.*

Casi searched the room and saw her charger plugged into the wall. She picked her way across the disorder through the mess and crouched by the outlet. Pulling her charger from the socket, she glanced into the bathroom and noted the demolished theme of her apartment applied there as well, though there were fewer things to damage in the tiny room.

She tried to stand, but her legs gave out, and she landed on her ass. A body-trembling cold swept through her from head to toes. This couldn't be the police. This was personal. Casi had degrees in psychology and sociology. The signs of frustration and rage were clear as day. She closed her eyes and wrapped her arms around her legs, holding tight. Everything Casi owned was ruined, except for the few things she had taken with her. She needed help.

Forcing her eyes open, she unwrapped her arms and took in the carnage. Trying to decide her next step, Casi pulled her nightstand drawer lying on the floor closer, snatching her passport. She shook her head and stood. There was only one person she trusted—Mason. Digging out her phone, she powered it up and checked the time. Well after midnight. He should be home from the Riverboat Casino since he had the early shift. She powered down her phone and jammed it into her rear pocket while weaving her way past debris to the front door. Casi seized her duffle and left, not bothering to turn off the lights or close the door. After all, nothing remained here for her.

****

Luc took the last sip of beer before putting the empty pint glass on the bar. He yawned. Though fatigue slapped him, he had at least reached his Zen zone after jamming with his brother's band. He might even get some sleep tonight. Though there wasn't much of tonight left, especially if he got another early morning call about a Cyclops body drop.

He pulled out his wallet and counted out bills before paying his tab. With only two beers and mostly water, even with a tip, it was a cheap night. He slapped the money down with a nod to the new bartender and stood.

Luc turned and abruptly halted so he didn't collide with his partner. Before he could say anything, Vincent held up his cell phone.

"Dude, what the hell? Do you ever check your phone? We're on a case."

Merde! He jerked his phone from his pocket and saw all the missed calls and texts. He pushed his fingers through his hair. "Sorry, man." He nodded toward the stage. "I performed with the band."

"Figures. Doesn't matter right now." Tate grabbed his arm and hauled him out of the bar to the sidewalk. "She's gone."

"What?" Luc followed Vince to his SUV and got in.

"Cassanne Thomas is missing."

"For how long? Fled? Snatched? What about the uni's, are they hurt?"

Tate snorted as he started the engine. "They're fine. And the last time any of them laid eyes on her was around nine." He hit the flashers but no siren as he peeled out from the curb. "They didn't discover she'd flown the coop until eleven."

"Idiots. They were supposed to be watching and protecting her."

"Yeah." Tate took a turn fast enough, Luc braced himself by grabbing the dash. "More importantly, when the station sent a car to her apartment, they found the door wide open, lights on, and the place trashed. It looked like a bomb exploded."

"Shit."

"It's worse. All her clothes and bedding were slashed, torn to pieces."

Luc shoved his hair off his forehead. A cold chill sped through him. That type of personal destruction pointed to an inflamed emotion and not the good kind. "Any blood or evidence pointing to the Cyclops might have taken Casi again?"

"No. But we both know that doesn't mean a lot." Tate drove through a yellow light and kept a heavy foot on the accelerator. The flashing lights in the SUV functioned as a warning to other motorists who either came to a screeching halt or pulled off to the side of the street. All good, less chance of an accident. "We're waiting on the warrant so we can ping her phone."

"Please tell me you're driving like a demon escaping hell because we're heading to Mason Webb's."

Vincent's mouth narrowed in a tight-lipped smile. "Got it in one." He tore around another corner.

"How about Chad Winston's son? Has anyone found him yet?"

"No. Still hanging in the wind."

Dammit. He sent out a silent prayer. *Keep her safe from Brock Winston, please*. Hopefully, they would find her snug in Webb's apartment. Then he'd give her a piece of his mind. What was racing through her mind? Luc recognized her anger and hostility around police, but he hadn't thought she'd run when they were trying to protect her. Why would she put herself in danger? Why run? Nothing says guilty like running. He shoved that thought aside. Second-guessing didn't help.

All he knew was he hoped she was alive and safe. He was tired of all the dead bodies.

Chapter Eleven

Casi's foot tapped impatiently as the elevator rose. She should have called Mason first so he could've let security know she'd be arriving, but afraid the cops would somehow trace her phone even with the GPS off, she hadn't risked the chance. Her luck held, however, when the security guard on shift at the Hibernia Tower recognized her from yesterday morning's unannounced visit and let her in. He must have worked a swing shift.

With a ding, the elevator reached the tenth floor. She didn't wait for the doors to fully open before she squeezed through, hugging her duffle tight to her body so she'd fit. Stride long and quick, Casi jogged down the hall before stopping in front of Mason's door. When she reached for the buzzer, her duffle thudded into the door, causing it to swing silently inward. She paused. Did security call ahead, and Mason had left the door open?

"Mason?"

She stepped into his apartment and shut the door behind her. "Mace?"

Was he asleep? But what about his open door? She took another step and stilled. His OCD, neat-as-a-pin place, was not as tidy as it should be. A couch pillow laid on the floor, an end table askew, and some books scattered on the floor. Small things, but the items glared at her. She shivered. Something wasn't right.

Casi exhaled a sharp breath in relief when she spotted Mason in the hallway leading to his bedroom. He wore only a pair of black briefs and walked toward her.

"Mason, what happened?" She dropped her duffle and stepped forward to meet him.

"Casi." He held up a hand, stopping her. "You're in danger, get out of here."

"I know, that's why I'm here, I need your help."

"Now. You need to leave now." He pointed to his car's key fob on the kitchen counter. "Take my car. Run, Casi."

Frowning, she moved closer. A creepy-crawly feeling struck her again. "Mason, what—"

"Go, go now. Run!" She jumped as he shouted. Mason never yelled at her.

"Okay, okay." Heart racing, she snatched the key up. "I'll call you. Thanks, Mace."

She ran for the door, grabbed her duffle yet hesitated, giving one last glance over her shoulder. Mason stood in the hallway motioning for her to leave. Reluctantly, she opened the door and left. She'd get to the bottom of his odd behavior after she was safe. Jogging back down the hallway, she arrived at the elevator and hit the call button. The doors opened immediately. She entered and pressed number four. The fourth floor held the first bridge connecting to the parking garage, making it the fastest approach to Mason's car.

When the elevator arrived on the correct floor, she exited, running for the bridge. She hit the push bar for the door and blasted through, not waiting for the security door to shut behind her. Inside the garage, she searched for the stairs. Mason's parking spot was usually on the second level.

Taking the stairs two at a time, she arrived on the second floor. Casi hesitated, not seeing Mason's Mini Cooper. She turned the fob in her hand and pressed the unlock button. A gratifying chirp and a flash of lights revealed his car in the far corner near the exit ramp. She ran for the car. Pressing another button on the fob, the trunk popped open and she threw her duffle inside and then slammed it shut.

"There you are, poppet."

Casi startled at the voice weaving out from the dark near the front of the car. A figure stepped from the shadows. Wider and slightly taller than her, dressed in boxy black pants and a shapeless shirt, the unzipped black jacket with its hood up hid his face.

Shit. How many hooded figures could be out hunting for her? This had to be her kidnapper, the one who wanted to kill her—the supposed Cyclops. Casi stepped back.

"Oh no you don't. *Stay right there*." The last words echoed weirdly in the garage, sounding neither male nor female—an oddly layered voice, like more than one person speaking at the same time.

Adrenaline rushed through her, along with a piercing pain inside her skull. *Oh hell no*. Casi would not stay alone in an empty garage with the creepy, sonorous hooded figure. Heart pounding, she bolted to the left and ran for the ramp.

"*Stop*!" The eerie voice commanded.

She didn't. How had the killer found her? Somehow, he tracked her to Mason's. Casi flew down the ramp, running for her life. She sprinted past the parked cars on the ground level and fled toward the garage's opening. Dodging past the lowered security gate arm, she dashed out of the garage. Looking over her shoulder to see if the killer chased her, she blindly turned left and slammed into a wall of muscle. Two firm hands grabbed her arms. Casi screamed.

How had he gotten ahead of her? She struggled, trying to get out of his grasp.

"Ms. Thomas. Cassanne. It's okay. You're okay."

She froze and stared into Detective Avery's concerned gaze and then over to his partner standing beside him on the sidewalk. He released his hold on her and she immediately pointed into the garage.

"He's here," Casi gasped out. "Second floor."

The cops exchanged looks.

"I've got the stairs." Detective Tate turned, yanked open the door beside him, and ran for the stairs.

"You need to stay with me."

Avery's statement drew her attention. She shook her head. No way. But the detective had other ideas and grabbed her wrist, tugging her along as he headed into the garage through the car entrance.

"You're safer with me. If he gets past us, you might be taken."

He had a point. And a gun, which he drew from his shoulder holster. The holster obvious since he had lost his suit from this afternoon and replaced it with jeans and a T-shirt. Avery released her wrist. "Stay behind me."

She followed him as he picked up a jog and headed for the ramp. At the top, he slowed and stalked forward.

"Here. Stop," Casi whispered when they drew even with Mason's car. "He was standing in front of the car against the wall where the light's out." Staring at the pool of darkness, no sinister figure lurked there now.

Detective Tate approached from the opposite direction and joined them. "I called it in." With his statement, distant sirens filled the night.

****

Casi sighed as she trudged behind Detective Avery. In short order, the police had cordoned off the area and started searching. The detectives kept her glued to one of their sides at all times and had constantly bombarded her with questions about the killer, or given her the silent treatment as they waited. The cops rapidly cleared the garage structure in her opinion, considering all the places an assailant could hide. Which led to her following Detective Avery as he escorted her to Mason's Mini. She wondered how the killer had escaped. They had the two-vehicle exits blocked and the stairwell. The keypad entries secured the connecting bridges to the Tower since a passcode was needed to gain access. As spookily as her assailant had popped up, he appeared equally capable of vanishing. A shudder chased through her.

When they arrived at the Mini Cooper, she unlatched the trunk. Detective Avery reached in and pulled out her duffle before she could say a word or grab it up. With his free hand, he shut the trunk and turned, facing her.

"Come on, there's a patrol car waiting for you."

He strode away, but she didn't follow. She wasn't going back to the safe house. Especially if it were the same two cops as babysitters. With the key fob in hand, Casi glanced at the Mini Cooper. Maybe she could make a run for it? She sighed, doubting the detective would let her get too far.

Avery must have sensed she hadn't trailed behind him, because he stopped in his tracks and glanced over his shoulder. "Ms. Thomas?"

She crossed her arms over her stomach and shook her head. With a loud, much aggrieved, heavy sigh, Avery made his way back to her and stopped uncomfortably close before dropping her bag at their feet. He raised an eyebrow. "I thought," he drawled, "after the scare you received tonight, you'd be a bit more cooperative. We're trying to protect you, Ms. Thomas."

Casi studied the detective. He looked beat with his bloodshot eyes and dark circles under them, and his five-o'clock shadow bordered more on eight. His accent thick, like he wasn't making any effort to mask the dialect. She wasn't going back, but how to convince him when he appeared to be on his last thread of patience? For all she knew, he'd be on the side of the asshole cop.

"Can't I stay with Mason?"

He shook his head, then pushed his fingers through his hair, tousling the longer layers into effortless disarray. "That's not a good idea. Do you want to put Webb in danger?"

She chewed her lower lip. Would he be? The Hibernia Tower had security. Wouldn't they be able to stop an intruder?

Apparently, not liking her silence, he spoke again, but in a gentler tone. "Ms. Thomas, may I call you Cassanne?"

She frowned. "I prefer Casi."

"Casi." He nodded. "Why won't you let us protect

you?"

"Honestly?"

"That would be nice."

"I don't trust cops."

A sharp huff escaped him. "I figured that one out way early. Look, we want to help you. Keep you safe."

"Not all of you." Perhaps not even him, no matter how charming and concerned Avery appeared.

"What?" His perplexed expression added an adorable quality to the weary detective.

Screw it. She'd roll the dice and tell him the truth. Fifty-fifty odds of him backing her or the uniforms. Casi was running out of options and her returning to a safe house wasn't one of them.

"The cop, the one called Dan, at the safe house. I don't know his last name, or even the other cop's name, they never…" She waved her hand. "It doesn't matter. What mattered was good ol' Danny saying the Cyclops would have done society a favor if he would have killed me."

"*C'est le bordel*?" His eyes popped wide as he swore. Casi knew enough French to get the gist, especially with the naughty words—French being close enough to Cajun. "He did not. Please tell me you're exaggerating."

"I'm not."

Avery's fingers tore through his poor hair again. His Cajun swearing came too fast and varied for her to catch any of the words to translate them. Eventually, he ran out of curses and stood there frowning while shaking his head, before meeting her gaze directly.

"My sincere apologies, that should never have happened." He looked disgusted. "They even spoke about privileged information. Idiots. I'll have the detail changed and put Officer Lincoln on report."

She shook her head. "Don't bother. On either account. How can I trust the next set? Instead of just one of my babysitters, maybe both will feel the same way. No. I won't go back to a safe house."

"Casi, please."

She pursed her lips and shook her head again. Frustration swam across the detective's face. Casi almost felt sorry for him, but that still wouldn't change her mind. He finally broke eye contact and stared blindly past her shoulder. She studied him. He truly looked exhausted and at the end of his rope. Avery blinked a few times before returning his attention to her. His fatigued hazel eyes trapped her gaze.

"How about this? Our captain is having my partner and me stand down for the next twenty-four since we've been logging in extra hours. Why don't you come home with me?"

Surprised, her eyes widened. He held up a hand, stopping her reply.

"I know it's unusual, but I give you my word, you'll be safe." He smiled. "I have no wish to see you harmed or killed, the exact opposite in fact. Just for today, until we can figure something out. I know you have issues with the whole justice system, but I pledge to you, you *can* trust me."

She scrutinized his direct gaze. He was right about one thing. After finding her ruined apartment and the killer popping up in the garage, her freak-out scale ricocheted off the charts. Also, she would never consciously put Mason in danger. Casi took pity on the stressed-out detective.

“Okay. Fine.”

“Thank you.” He lifted her duffle and took a few steps back, giving her a bit of breathing room.

Detective Tate walked up. He nodded to her before focusing on his partner. “Ready to go?”

“There’s been a slight change in plans. Ms. Thomas will go home with me. Mind giving us a lift? My car is back at the Loo.”

Tate’s brow furrowed, causing Avery to grimace.

“She won’t go to the safe house, and I can’t say I blame her. Lincoln, the fu…The asshole, said the Cyclops should have murdered Ms. Thomas. It would have been the best outcome all around. A direct quote I believe.”

Tate’s eyebrows flew upward, and he frowned. He turned, giving her his full attention. “Did he say that to your face?”

“No. I overheard his conversation with his partner.”

“And I suppose that was the motivation for leaving?”

She gave Tate a tight smile. “Partly.”

His frown deepened before facing his partner.

Avery shrugged. “Look, it’s not ideal, but she’ll be safe.”

Tate nodded. “And that’s what matters most. Well then, come on, you two, looks like I’ll be playing chauffeur.”

“Oh, wait.” Casi looked at the fob in her hand. “I should probably return Mason’s key since I’m not taking his Mini. Do you mind? Besides, I want to let him know I’m safe. Somehow, he knew I was in danger and, to tell the truth, he acted a little odd. I’d like to reassure him."

The detectives exchanged another unspoken communicative glance before Avery swept out the hand not holding her duffle. "Please lead the way. The sooner done, the sooner we can all get some sleep."

Casi nodded and headed for the stairs.

Chapter Twelve

Lucas suppressed a growl as the security guard fumbled while unlocking Webb's door. His gut screamed at him, jolting him from his exhaustion with a much-needed shot of adrenaline. They had gotten to Webb's door and buzzed several times, then pounded on the door, but the guy never answered. They'd been waiting for security to unlock his door, and now this *coo-yôn* couldn't even handle a key?

The door clicked open. He pushed past the guard and entered the apartment, closely followed by his partner.

"Webb? Mason Webb?" Luc barked into the silent apartment. The hairs on the back of his neck rose, and all his senses went on high alert. He stalked farther into the room, noticing several items that seemed out of place. He halted in the middle of the open-style great room and glanced over his shoulder, seeing both Tate and Casi close on his heels while the guard stayed beside the open door.

"You." He pointed to Casi. "Go stand by the door."

"What? No." She scowled at him.

"Yes. For once, do as your told." He hesitated. "Please."

"He's my friend." Her chin jutted out stubbornly.

God, please save him from obstinate, opinionated women. He shot a pleading glare to his partner. Vince needed to step into the fight of corralling Casi, and by his partner's expression, Luc wasn't the only one whose intuition screeched.

"Ma'am, let us check the apartment." Vincent held up a hand, stalling her next words. "The killer stood next to your friend's car and disappeared. We can't discount him getting into the Tower and this apartment. We need you to stay by the door."

By her frown, it looked like an argument was brewing, but then she surprised him. "Fine." With her sharp retort, she spun on her sneakers and marched back to the door, stopping beside the guard. She shot eye daggers at them from across the room.

Whatever. He could deal with her resentment if it kept her alive. Luc put her out of his mind and pulled his gun. Vince had done the same. They stepped forward in unison. As they approached the granite countertop separating the living/dining room from the kitchen, Vincent peeled away, giving Luc space.

Leading with his gun, he turned and peered behind the counter. "Clear."

His partner took over point position and started down the hall, pausing before turning into an open door. He flicked on a light and stepped into the room. Luc covered his back. "Bathroom, clear." Tate's baritone echoed off the tiles.

Luc nodded and took over the lead. A coppery scent drifted from the room at the end of the hall, filling him with a certain dread. He passed a narrow door, leaving Tate to check what probably held linens as he continued forward to the open door at the end of the hallway. He carefully approached the darkened room, edging into the black space as a familiar aroma assaulted his nose. He lowered his gun as he took a hand from his dual grip, feeling for a light switch. Finding the paddle, he pressed, and the room flooded with light.

"*Fils de putain.*" Son. Of. A. Bitch. Luc stared at the grisly scene before him as Tate stepped beside him. Mason Webb lay quite dead on the floor, dressed only in briefs and a slit throat. No apparent sign of a struggle. A pool of blood congealed next to a butcher knife lying by his right hand, most likely from his own kitchen. The blood splatter streaked across his bed and splashed against the wall.

"Well, fuck," Tate stated as he took in the grisly scene. "I'll check the closet and the master bath."

His partner put action to words, while Luc slipped his gun into his shoulder holster. Monitoring Vincent, he pulled out his phone.

"All clear."

Luc nodded and hit his one-dial precinct contact. "It's Detective Avery, we've got a body and need the works. Hibernia Tower, apartment 1012." He waited for the response before ending the call and slipping his cell back into his pocket. He grimaced. Would this day ever end?

A scream next to his ear jolted Luc. Spinning, Luc caught Casi with an arm around her waist, stopping her from running into and ruining the crime scene.

"No! Let me go! Mason!"

It was like wrestling a gator, all strength and thrashing. Luc leaped in front of her, blocking Webb's body from her sight, and then used his own body to push into her personal space, forcing her to step backward, even as she continued to struggle within his hold.

"Ms. Thomas. Casi. Stop."

"Mason! Mason!"

He backed her farther into the hallway, putting a physical distance between her and Webb's body—while trying not to harm her as he subdued her. He gave her a slight shake. "Stop."

She finally quit fighting and stilled. Casi stared at him. Her beautiful brown eyes wide in horror and shock glistened with unshed tears. Her body trembled beneath his hands.

"He-he's dead?" Her whispered stammer cut straight through his heart.

He nodded and watched as a single tear escaped, sliding down her cheek. "I'm so sorry, Casi."

His quiet condolence broke her as an inconsolable sob wrenched from her. Her knees gave way, and he caught her before she hit the ground. Sweeping her up into his arms, he cradled her close to his chest as she cried into his shoulder. Carefully, he walked to the couch and gently set her down as he sat next to her. She turned and clung to him in her misery and grief, and he hugged her back.

Someone cleared their throat, and Luc glanced up to find his partner standing over them. Vincent appeared both uncomfortable and concerned. Was it Casi's tears or the fact he held her? *Too bad.* His momma and sisters would blister his hide if he turned away from her distress. What was Luc supposed to do? Let this poor woman who had been through her own nightmares collapse into tears after seeing her friend's corpse? Not on his watch.

"What?" He asked softly but with some steel,

trying not to disturb the grieving woman held in his arms.

Vincent answered as quietly and with equal force behind his words. “She was probably the last person to see him alive, Lucas.”

“So?” He frowned. “It’s not like she killed him. She’d be covered in blood.”

Tate’s brows furrowed. “She could have changed clothes and washed up.”

He snorted. “This isn’t the reaction of a killer.”

“We need to question her.”

“Later. Tomorrow. She’s been through enough.” He glared at his partner. Seriously? Couldn’t he see and hear how distraught she was?

Vince sighed with a brief shake of his head. “Fine. The team’s here and on their way up. Captain said to hand over the scene and get some rest.”

“Sounds good.”

His partner frowned again at him and Casi, not that she would know, so lost in her grief. Her face burrowed into his shoulder with her head tucked under his chin, as she leaned into him from the side in an awkward hug.

His partner finally spoke up. “I’ll handle the swap and then take you to your car.”

“Thanks, Vince.”

Tate nodded and walked to the door, greeting the team, which had just arrived. Luc pulled his attention away and back to the woman he held. He tightened his arms around her, hoping he provided a bit of comfort in her darkest of nights.

Chapter Thirteen

Once again Casi trudged behind Detective Avery, but this time he led her across a cut stone pathway leading to his small single-story house. She blinked against the grittiness in her eyes, but her swollen lids only made it worse. Not surprising considering how hard she had cried. She'd finally pulled herself together as cops flooded into Mason's apartment. Thankfully, with all the police busy with the murder, no one saw her blush as she extracted herself from the detective's embrace.

How odd, yet soothing, to be hugged by Avery. She would chalk it up to the horror and shock of Mason's death. Her breath hitched. No. No more. Casi stuffed her emotions down her throat, despite the bile making her nauseous. No more tears. She wouldn't be vulnerable in front of law enforcement again. It never ended well. They always took advantage.

She stared at Avery's muscled back as he unlocked his door. The casual look worked for him, except the shoulder holster with a gun made her nervous. Strange how the detective had offered only comfort and sincere support, never taking the opening to cut her down or cast blame.

Shocking, because she was profoundly and soul-wrenchingly guilty. Mason's death was all her fault. Somehow, she'd led the Cyclops to him, and now she would never see Mace again. Never have his unconditional support and deep friendship. She sucked in another deep breath, loud enough the detective turned before opening the door.

"Are you all right?"

Casi didn't trust herself to speak, so she nodded. He studied her intently before giving her a single nod back. Opening the door, he stepped aside, gesturing her through first.

"It's not much, but it's home."

He flicked on the lights as he followed. After shutting and locking the door behind them, he dropped her duffle down at his feet. The foyer opened directly into a living room, complete with a large comfortable-looking leather sofa, a few chairs, and a huge flat-screen television mounted above a fireplace. Rich, gleaming, dark cherry hardwood flooring reflected the overhead track lighting. The room was overtly male except for the quirky, colorful rag rugs under various pieces of furniture.

"*MEOW*."

Casi jumped at the loud feline bellow and braced herself when she saw a fuzzy brown striped mountain lion charging them. She stepped sharply to the side to avoid the rampaging cat, who made a beeline for the detective. He laughed, open and happy, as he crouched to greet the running monster.

"Hey there, sugar." Avery opened his arms wide, and from a few feet away, the beast pounced, launching into the air and landing in the detective's embrace, knocking him on his ass. He didn't appear to mind. The cat had to be at least twenty pounds, possibly thirty. It was huge. Casi stood staring, amused, and enchanted.

A rumbling, loud purr filled the quiet as Avery lavished attention on the feline currently head-butting the detective's chin as he hugged and petted the creature. "Yeah, yeah, sweet thing." His Cajun accent, out in full swing, swirled around her. Casi shivered. Damn, his voice could melt butter. "I've missed you too. Now off with you, we have company."

He placed the cat on the floor and stood, completely nonplussed by either his display of affection or the giant cat twining through his legs. Casi wondered how he kept his balance without being knocked on his butt again. With his grin still in place, he turned and faced her. She stopped breathing. The open happiness on his face, mixed with his tousled hair, slight scruffy beard, and striking looks, took her unaware. Detective Avery was gorgeous. His smile stripped years away. The world-weary, exhausted cop disappeared, now replaced by a mischievous man, who could disintegrate a woman's panties with a single glance—quite the superpower.

"Sorry about that. Cat is feeling a bit neglected." He gave a quick affectionate glance at the furry feline, still trying her best to knock her human off his feet. "I've been working long hours."

She mentally shook herself, breaking away from the spell he had cast over her. Casi raised one brow. "You named your monster cat, Cat?"

His laugh echoed through the room. "It's short for Catastrophe. And she's not a monster. She's just large for her breed."

"Which would be what? I've never seen a house cat this large."

He gestured for her to follow him as he led them

into his kitchen—a small space but had a warm open feel. “My vet said she’s part Maine Coon.”

“What’s the other half? Tiger?”

He laughed again, open and inviting. “Maybe, *cher*.” He glanced at her before opening a pantry and pulling out a bag of cat food. Catastrophe sat politely waiting, regal with her big bushy tail wrapped around her feet. He picked up her bowl, added a mound of kibble before placing it back on the floor, and then got her water dish. Crossing to the sink, he turned on the tap, dumped out the old water, and then filled the bowl with fresh. “I didn’t understand what I was getting into.” A contemplative smile curled up his mouth. “I found her abandoned in an alley during a storm, all alone. No littermates or momma. Believe it or not, she fit in the palm of my hand. My sister, Marielle, told me I was now the kitten’s human since I rescued her.”

He shrugged, slightly chagrined, as if, *what’s a guy to do*? How adorable that he let his sister bully him. It must be nice to be in a family. She had two younger half brothers from different fathers, but they weren’t close and rarely spoke.

Avery placed the water bowl next to the cat food. “Little did I know how big she’d get. I should have known by the size of her paws, but I grew up with dogs and wasn’t sure it’d be the same.” He gave Cat a quick pat before she dug into her dinner.

He filled the kettle and put it on the stove to heat and then peered into his fridge. “Hmm, not much here ‘cept pie.” Avery glanced at her. “You like pecan? It’s my momma’s. Best in the world if I do say so.”

She could only nod again. He certainly needed to tone down his sultry accent. It was killing her. Who was this man? He transformed completely from when she first met him. To be fair, he'd been polite and professional, but something seemed to have changed since Casi had broken with Mason's death. First, he wasn't trying to tone down or hide his accent. It's like he dropped his practiced skeptical demeanor and became an authentic version of himself.

He plated two slices of pie, got some forks, and gestured to the front room. "If you take these, I'll grab the tea." Suddenly, he frowned. "Do you drink tea? I've got beer or whiskey if you'd like something stronger. Water?"

"Tea's fine as long as it's decaf." It was late, or way early depending on one's perspective. It had to be close to four in the morning. She reached for the plates.

"Yeah, it's herbal. My other sister, Jolie—I've got just the two of 'em—made it. It's a blend of a bunch of stuff, but mostly some lavender buds, chamomile flowers, dried orange peel, and rose petals." He shrugged. "I'm not really into tea, I prefer coffee, but as she pointed out, tea can be better at times. She worries about me." Detective Avery blinked, perhaps realizing he might have overshared. "Uh, do you want cream or sugar?"

"Straight up is fine."

"A woman after my heart." He gestured to the front room. "Go on. I'll be right behind you."

A bit stunned with the surreal nature of her current situation dealing with the open, carefree, charming detective, she walked away, needing to distance herself and take a bit of a breather. She placed the pie on the coffee table and plunked herself onto the couch. Comfortable as it looked. Closing her eyes, she leaned her head against the back of the couch and concentrated on breathing. What a horrible forty-eight hours. She was beat.

"Falling asleep, *cher*?"

Casi pried her eyes open, finding Avery frowning down at her. She shook her head and watched as he placed a steaming teapot down and unlaced the two mugs' handles from the fingers of his other hand.

"I can show you to your room if you'd rather."

"No. No, I couldn't sleep if I tried. My mind is racing, I'd just toss and turn."

His frown disappeared. "That's what the tea's for. Jolie owns her own shop and hand blends her teas." He gestured to the steaming dark blue teapot. "She knows I have trouble sleeping when I'm on a tough case. It's supposed to calm me down enough to rest."

She hid her smile at his obvious discomfort in his sister's thoughtfulness. "Does it work?"

"Sometimes. Can't hurt. Besides, I figured we both could use a bit of comfort." He sat and unfastened his shoulder holster, placing his gun on the side table next to him. Pouring tea into both mugs, he handed her one. "It, ah, smells pretty good and doesn't taste bad."

Again, the poor detective looked like his man-card would be revoked for admitting he liked his sister's tea. She buried her face in the steaming aroma to hide her slight smile and inhaled. It did smell wonderful. Muscles loosened she hadn't known were tense. Casi looked up and found herself staring into Avery's hazel eyes, now green with almost no hint of brown. "Thank you…for-for earlier. Well, for everything. I know I've been…difficult, and you've been nothing but kind and professional. I'm sorry, Detective."

He gave her a charming grin. “Nothing to apologize for, and you’re welcome. Call me Luc. I figure if I can let you soak the corner of my T-shirt, we should at least be on a first-name basis.”

“Okay.” She took a small sip from her mug and felt herself relaxing. Maybe she could trust him?

“You should try the pie. Pie makes everything better.”

“Does it?”

“Pie is God’s miracle. Especially any made by my momma.” He shoved a chunk of pecan pie in his mouth and started chewing. Luc closed his eyes as if in bliss. Thank God he hadn’t moaned. Casi appreciated he left that out. Bad enough to find herself attracted to him, but she didn’t need to hear any sexy groans from him. It would only make her think of him naked, having sex, and what his O-face would look like. She probably shouldn’t have just thought that because a Technicolor picture just flashed across her brain. Damn, she must be exhausted if she was having these thoughts and visions.

Covering up her sudden discomfort, Casi put down her mug and picked up her plate. Her stomach growled. She couldn’t remember the last time she had eaten anything. Breaking off a small piece, she loaded up her fork and took a bite. Her eyes flew wide open when the buttery, sugary, nuttiness melted on her tongue. *Holy shit*! This was amazing pie. The best pie she’d ever eaten.

Luc’s low chuckle drew her attention. He grinned at her, eyes dancing and a bit smug. “See. I was right, *cher*. You should trust me more often.”

“Maybe,” she muttered before digging in. Casi noticed his slice had disappeared, eaten in like three bites. Men. Didn't they know they needed to savor the wonderful things? You never knew when life would pull a fast one and take all your goodness away.

She glanced at Luc, finding him studying her. Was he back in detective mode about to pounce or just curious? Finishing the last bite of pie, she placed her empty plate and fork on the coffee table and grabbed her mug.

"So before we go to sleep, I'd like us to exchange phone numbers." Luc took a sip of tea.

"Um…"

"I want you to be able to contact me directly. I'll eventually get called away, and I'll have to leave you alone." His direct gaze was serious. "I want you to feel safe."

Luc placed his mug down and pulled his cell from his pocket and unlocked the screen. Tapping a few times, he looked up. "Fire away."

It's not like he couldn't get her number if she chose not to give it to him, so she rattled it off. He typed it in, along with her name before he hit the message button. All of a sudden, Casi remembered she had turned her phone off. She yanked out her cell and powered it up. Almost instantly it dinged with an incoming text message.

"Go on. Program it in. It's L U C, which is short for Lucas."

As she added him into her contacts, Casi felt more of her tension release. He was right. After the killer found her in the parking lot, it would be nice to have instant access to help. Avery appeared both competent and caring. She guessed time would tell if she could truly trust him. Maybe she should turn her GPS back on. Conflicted, she chewed on her lower lip, trying to decide if it would be a good thing or bad.

"Hey, *cher, qu'est-ce qu'il y a*?"

She looked up. "Huh?"

Luc scrubbed a hand over his face. "Sorry, I asked what's the matter. I'm pretty beat and sometimes get sloppy. My parents had us speaking Cajun first. It's what I revert to if I'm not thinking."

Casi stopped her frown before it showed. If she thought his accent out loud and proud caused panty-melting, but when he spoke Cajun, it did strange things inside her. She didn't need this right now. "I was thinking about my GPS. I turned it off." She glanced at her phone. "Could you have traced me with no GPS and the phone off?"

"Yeah, it wouldn't have been easy, and it would have taken time, but yes, we could." His fingers pushed through his hair. "You should turn the location tracking back on. Leave your cellphone powered up at all times, and keep it with you. I'd feel better if you did. You have a charger?"

She nodded. "How do you think the killer knew about Mason?"

"Probably from your apartment. I'm sure he went there to find you or a clue to your whereabouts."

"But—" She chewed on her lower lip. "—it wasn't the police who wrecked my place?"

"Casi," Avery shook his head. "You know it wasn't us."

"Yeah, but I guess I hoped it had been the cops…"

"It's late. Come on, we could both use the rest." He stood and held out a hand. Casi hesitated before clasping it and allowing him to help her stand. "I'm gonna show you to your room and then go grab your duffle so you can settle in."

"Okay." Her stomach fluttered. He stood too close to her once again. Was he even aware? Deliberate? Still, she would not take a step back. Show no sign of weakness. She didn't want him to have an upper hand with her.

"Please follow me."

Casi tagged along behind the detective and hoped, somehow, she'd be able to forget these last few days and get some sleep.

Chapter Fourteen

Casi bolted upright in bed, heart racing as she blinked defensibly against the sunlight streaming through the window. It took her a moment to realize where she slept, her mind scrambled from fatigue. Not home in her bed, but in Detective Avery's bedroom and his bed. Jolting awake was growing old. But at least this time she knew why. Chills chased through her as the aftermath of the weird graphic nightmare clung to her. Not surprising that she had dreamt of Mason, but the last part turned downright creepy. She didn't understand where the vision had come from.

As her pulse slowed, Casi swallowed past her dry cottonmouth, but a lump caught in her throat. She needed something to drink. Wondering the time, she grabbed her charging phone. Nine in the morning. Great. She barely had a couple of hours of sleep. No wonder she still felt exhausted. Well, she wouldn't be getting back to sleep anytime soon.

She flung back the bedcovers and stood, wearing only a worn-out T-shirt from a California surf shop and her tight, stretchy yoga shorts—her go-to pajamas. Hoping there might be some leftover tea in last night's pot, she made her way out of the bedroom and padded down the hallway's hardwood floor in search of the kitchen.

The corridor dumped Casi out into the living room,

where she pulled up short at the sight greeting her—Detective Avery sprawled on the couch, fast asleep. His dark blond hair lay tousled with a thick lock falling over his forehead and almost hanging into his closed eyes. His lips were parted slightly and emitted a gentle snore once in every few breaths. The blanket he must have used to cover himself now rested on the floor, exposing him to her gaze. He'd also changed from the dark clothing he wore last night. Clad in only a pair of sweatpants, pulled low on his slim hips, Avery's bare chest was exposed for her perusal. A sight definitely worth taking a moment or three to study. The detective kept himself in shape. Her gaze drifted downward. His well-toned chest, covered in a light dusting of hair slightly darker in shade than the hair on his head, led the way to an almost six-pack. His abs weren't super defined like some gym ape, but they were there.

His sweats, which were tugged low in apparent restless sleep, exposed the lovely V on men with low body fat. One bent knee leaned against the back of the couch, and in the hollow created below slept Cat. Or she had been asleep until Casi met her amber gaze.

She held up a finger to her lips, hoping the feline read sign language and wouldn't wake Avery. The detective had looked more in need of sleep than Casi had—which said something. Turning quietly, she left the handsome cop to his slumber and light snores and snuck into the kitchen.

The teapot from earlier remained on the counter, so she made a beeline toward it. She picked it up and gave it a slight shake, thrilled to hear the slosh of liquid. It would be cold, but the taste should be fine.

Casi searched the cabinets until she found the mugs

and grabbed one. She quickly filled her cup with the last of the tea and drank. The tasty herbal blend soothed her dry mouth and throat. With a contented sigh, she walked to the sink and filled her mug from the tap and chugged it down. A yawn caught her unaware. Maybe she'd be able to fall back to sleep after all? It appeared the tea might actually hold magical powers.

After putting her empty mug in the sink, she padded across the kitchen floor. Lost in thought, confused by her rollercoaster emotions. One moment torn in pieces with grief, then terrified the killer would find her. And she couldn't discount the frustration of her growing attraction to Avery.

Casi exited the short corridor and entered the living room. She screamed as a figure jumped in front of her from the side. The barrel of a gun not a foot from her face made her scramble backward, her feet tangled, and she fell, landing on her ass.

"Shit. Shit. Sorry." Lucas crouched beside her. "Are you okay? I thought you were still asleep, and we had an intruder."

She nodded, her heart pounding as her blood raced in her veins. Totally wide-awake now, she stared as he put the safety on to his gun before offering his hand, which she gladly took as he helped her to stand. With her shaky legs, Casi didn't mind him still holding her hand once she was on her feet.

"Are you sure you're all right?" He gave their clasped palms a squeeze. "You look pale."

"No, I'm fine. Just startled. I wasn't expecting a gun in my face."

"Yeah." He frowned and let go of her hand. "My bad. I'm so sorry."

"Don't worry about it. You were only doing your job."

"It seems like I'm constantly knocking you off your feet." He shook his head. "Plus, the last thing you needed was another scare."

Avery placed his free hand on the small of her back and guided her into the kitchen. He pulled out a stool for her.

"Sit."

He stayed by her side until she was stabilized on the high seat. He walked around the central counter and placed his gun beside the sink. He twisted and grabbed the kettle, filled the pot, and put it on the stove to heat.

Avery didn't seem to realize he was shirtless and barefoot in the kitchen, or at least if he did, he appeared confident in his near-naked state as he leaned his hip against the counter and stared at her.

"What are you doing awake, anyway? I thought you'd be out at least until noon."

"Bad dreams." Casi glanced away from the all-too-knowing detective and focused her attention on her hands clasped in her lap.

The kettle whistled, taking his astute attention away from her. She watched him rinse out the teapot, measure and add the loose leaf herbs into an infuser and dangle it into the pot before pouring in the boiling water to steep. He passed her mug from the sink to her and he grabbed himself a cup from the cabinet.

"Hmmm." He studied her once again, with a hawk's sharp focus. "Come on, spit it out. My momma taught us if we spoke about our night terrors, it would leech the poison out and defang the nightmare. You might be able to go back to sleep. Was it Webb?"

She sighed. Somehow, she knew the detective wouldn't let it go, like a dog with a bone. Casi met his gaze and saw his determination. What was it about Avery wanting to protect and help her? She could probably get him to shift the topic. It might be time to psychoanalyze him off the present discussion. Her eyes dropped to his bare chest. She chewed on her lower lip before meeting his gaze again.

"Ah, maybe you should put a shirt on…"

He smirked. There wasn't another way to classify that particular smile. She shook her head. And great, now she categorized his smiles. First, the sexy panty-dropping one, the happy open one, and now the knowing smirk. She was doomed.

"I'm fine, *cher*. And you're avoiding, though I believe you're familiar with the professional term—deflecting. Now, out with it." He poured the tea into their mugs.

"Okay." She blew air into the steaming liquid, cooling the hot tea in her mug. Casi hoped Avery's mom might be right because she didn't particularly want to relive her dream, but if talking about it made it go away, well, she'd give it a shot. She placed her mug down on the counter and kept both her hands wrapped around the glass, needing the heat since she suddenly felt cold. "It started with Mason…"

"I'm sorry. He seemed like a good friend."

Casi met his forthright, sympathetic gaze. He honestly looked like he cared. She hated the fact her barriers kept lowering around him, but she couldn't seem to help herself.

"The best." She blinked rapidly, forcing her tears away. Taking a sip of tea, she felt her heart breaking all over again. How could Mason no longer be in this world? She sighed and put her mug down.

"I saw his dead body and screamed. You and your partner weren't there. A hooded figure stepped from the darkness beside his body and started toward me. I turned and ran, but all of a sudden everything went black." She swallowed hard and felt her pulse kicking up again. "Everything was dark, I floated until I realized arms were holding me, cradling me."

"Maybe me, from when you collapsed in the hall?"

She shook her head. "It didn't feel like you. Anyway, suddenly the motion stopped, and I fell until I hit a hard and unforgiving surface. I still couldn't see a thing." Casi took a deep breath. "Slowly something came into focus. A graffiti tag on the wall. The design was made up of ornate, intricate letters of red and gold in the form of a Chinese dragon. I couldn't make out what it said. It might have just been a series of initials or an acronym, but the letters definitely made a dragon. It was painted on a side of a building or maybe a warehouse."

"Huh, doesn't seem so scary." He offered her a smile, which she returned.

"That wasn't the scary part." Casi shivered, thinking about what came next.

"Well, what woke you up?"

She took another quick sip of tea. "I started having the floaty feeling again, like rising out of my body. When I looked down…" Casi grimaced. "It wasn't me. It…It was a teenager, a white kid. He had a spiderweb tattoo on his neck, and he-he was missing an eye. Blood leaked out of the empty socket. The other, um, intact eye—a pretty sky blue—gazed upward blankly."

She saw Avery tense. “Anything else, Casi?”

“He slowly turned his head to stare right at me, and-and then he-he whispered, ‘help me.’ ”

Chapter Fifteen

Selene Walsh pulled her BMW into the vacant parking spot on the street near the precinct. She turned off the engine and then leaned her head against the headrest. Closing her eyes, she willed away the persistent itching. She wanted to rub her back against the leather seat but held herself still. The raw prickling between her shoulder blades drove her crazy.

Her anger rose. What had gone wrong last night? All had been within her grasp—the angel's horn and her prey. How had the bitch escaped? Everyone fell sway to her power, no one had immunity. Her magic had worked on the girl the night Selene had snatched her from the alley. So why hadn't it worked last night, or in fact, on the townhouse stairs when the girl had first escaped? The power was simply in her voice if she willed it to be.

She was a siren. A creature of legend. Sadly, a creature now relegated to fiction, graphic novels, and cheesy television shows. Selene sighed. Amazing how through the annals of time, the myth of the sirens had morphed and twisted to the ridiculous versions seen today, nothing like her true origin and traits. Mythology had gotten so many facts wrong. Selene could lure and mesmerize both male and female, and she didn't need to sing to make it happen, nor be on or in the water.

The other historical mistake, and one she remained,

in fact, grateful for—wings. Sirens had wings, not fins or gills. She wasn't a bloody mermaid. Wings she had deployed and used to make her escape from the parking garage when the police had surrounded the building with her still inside. And now, since she had flown, her back itched from having her wings concealed. So now the timetable for her next harvest needed to be accelerated.

Selene would have to hunt, but not before a small errand. If she could extract the information she required from Detective Avery, she'd have both her wayward prey and the treasure she sought, without having to stalk a new human imbued with magic. *Two birds with one stone*. It would be so much more convenient to track down the girl who escaped her twice and who had stolen Gabriel's horn. The one artifact, throughout Heaven, Earth, and the Underworld, which could bestow upon her true death.

She needed the horn. It had taken her forever to find its hidden location—a small church in remote northern Scotland. Stealing the relic over two hundred years ago was simple. But the search had taken an eternity. Selene would not let a mere human outmaneuver her. She would take back the horn, kill the human psychic, and get on with her long life. This century held so much fun and adventure. No human would deprive her of her enjoyments, the stupid cows.

Mesmerizing the detective would allow her to retrieve all the information she needed. Exiting the car, she locked it and strode on her stilettos to the precinct. She wondered if Avery would remember her? Selene, as most would have mistakenly believed, had been the arm candy to the assistant district attorney—whom she controlled—not the curvy airhead she had pretended to be. On Lance St. Croix's arm, Selene had crossed paths with the detective on multiple occasions at various functions and police charities. She liked the trappings of wealth. Though she had plenty of money and all the supernatural power in her grasp, she found she had developed a taste for political influence. Avery and she had a passing acquaintance. Well, they did until Lance DUI'd himself in a car crash.

She entered the building and nodded a greeting to the uniform attending the front desk. He recognized her and waved her through. Entering the elevator, she tapped her Ferragamo clad foot as she pressed the fourth-floor button while waiting for the doors to close. Soon she whisked upward. In a matter of moments, the doors opened, revealing the busy floor of a police department, with multiple desks, phones ringing, computer keyboards clacking, and the hum of various conversations even at this early hour of the morning.

She stepped off the elevator and strode forward in search of Avery. Selene hadn't made it far when she was intercepted.

"Ms. Walsh? What a pleasant surprise."

Selene smiled at the commander of Criminal Investigations, who took his time checking her out. Men. They were all the same.

"Hello, Commander. I'm surprised to find you here. You're not normally in this division."

Finally meeting her eyes and not staring at her chest, the commander smiled. "We're stretched a bit thin lately, so I needed to check in." He gestured her toward his little-used office. "So what do we owe the pleasure of this visit? It's been a while."

She took a seat as he closed the door and then sat across the desk from her.

"I'm looking for Detective Lucas Avery."

"Avery? He's not in today."

Selene pursed her lips in her pretty pout. "Oh dear. I was hoping to ask for his help. But perhaps…" She let her words hang in the air, counting on him to pick up the bait. He didn't disappoint.

"Well, now, Selene. I may call you Selene?"

"Of course." She morphed her pout into a warm smile.

"Selene, maybe I can be of service?"

He most certainly could be of use. The commander as the head of the CID and the boss of the boss of Avery would be privy to the information she hunted from the detective. Time to get to work.

Selene took a deep breath and pushed her magic into her voice. "*What information do you have on the serial killer known as Cyclops*?" It amused her the police had named her kills after the wrong mythical creature. Her voice echoed eerily throughout the closed room. She witnessed the moment her unique magic swirled around the commander and enveloped him, making him hers.

He replied in a monotone. "There was another murder last night, possibly attributed to him, but we're not sure. We have four confirmed maimed bodies and no leads. It's only a matter of time before the next corpse hits the ground."

Too true. She stretched her shoulders, trying to ease the latent ache of her hidden wings. "*What of Cassanne Thomas? Where is she*?"

"Still in protective custody."

She'd assumed as much since Selene had gone by Cassanne's apartment again and found it empty and still trashed from her search for the horn.

"*Where are you holding her*?"

The commander blinked slowly. An odd reaction when the answer to her question should have been spilling out of his mouth the instant her query had ended. She pushed more will into her words.

"*Where is she*?"

"I don't know."

Her brow furrowed. Not good enough. "*Well, find out. Now.*"

He tapped his keyboard, waking his computer. Several keystrokes later, he stared blankly at the screen.

"*Well*?" She demanded, pushing yet more magic at him.

The commander swayed in his chair and sweat beaded on his forehead from the stress of not being able to fulfill her request. He finally responded in a flat voice. "Her current location hasn't been logged into the system."

He spoke the truth, lying was beyond him when enthralled. "*I need you to find her*."

Nodding, he picked up his cell phone, unlocked it, and scrolled through his contacts. After pressing on a name, he held his phone to his ear and waited for an answer. "This is Eckert. Where is our Cyclops' witness? She's not in the system." He listened as some officer babbled at him. "I don't want excuses. I want a location. Find her and call me immediately."

He hung up and stared, fixated on her. Selene frowned. Frustrated, she needed answers now, but she pulled on her self-control, calming down when she realized it didn't matter. Eventually, she'd get the information.

"*Commander, I want you to find her, and then I want you to text me the address.*" She reached for a paper on his desk and grabbed a pen. In short order, she wrote her number and passed it to him. "*You will remember nothing of this conversation. You will, after you text me the location, delete all records, even incidental ones, off of your phone. And of course, destroy this piece of paper with my number. Do you understand?*"

"Yes."

"Good." Selene stood, smiling. "*If anyone asks about my visit, you will tell them I discussed your involvement in the upcoming Jubilee charity function. Understood?*"

"Yes."

"Excellent, Commander Eckert. *Get me the information I require and quickly.*"

"Yes."

Selene left the room without looking back, assured her commands would be obeyed and her secrecy kept. She hadn't survived over two thousand years by being careless. She knew how to protect and hide, especially from other supernaturals who'd been gunning for her like Gabriel, the feathered bastard.

In short order, she rode the elevator down and exited the precinct. The humidity and heat slammed into her as she left the air-conditioned building and stepped onto the streets of the French Quarter. Not a single breeze stirred the stagnant air. If she wanted to feel like she was swimming, she'd go into the bloody river.

Selene froze in her tracks as a tingling sensation flooded her body. Like a lover's caress over her naked skin. Slowly a smile curved up her mouth as she scanned the sidewalk and street. She knew this feeling and welcomed it. The shivering touch meant a human with magic arrived near her. Her eyes landed and focused on a teenager. *How convenient.* She approached the teen and stopped in front of him.

"*Well, hello, my darling,*" her power whispered out, capturing the boy. She lifted her hand and, with a finger, lightly caressed his cheek, letting her finger trail down to his neck, landing on his spiderweb tattoo. "I'm so pleased to meet you, poppet."

The teenage boy's bright blue eyes gazed blankly at her, completely mesmerized and within her control. Another easy one.

"Beautiful ink, my boy, but I believe you're now caught in my web. *Follow me, please.*"

He obediently walked beside her as she led him to her parked car.

What a stroke of luck. She helped the lad into her passenger seat and shut the door before striding to the driver's side. Now she didn't have to wait on the commander's schedule. She hadn't even needed to hunt for her next third-eye gland.

The pineal gland, also known as the third-eye chakra, held magic. Held power. This boy had magic, and though only latent and untapped, it still held the potent energy she needed. Powerful energy to keep herself hidden so she could walk amongst humans and exploit them for her pleasure. The gland was the source of magic in humans. Hunting and killing became one of the joys she'd lived so long for. In fact, she didn't need to harvest while her prey lay awake and aware, but the torture added the spice of adrenaline, flavoring it, making the gland more potent. Besides, she liked to hear them scream.

Finding her victims turned out to be surprisingly easy since many humans who were psychics, witches, or held other supernatural abilities—whether they knew it or not—were more abundant than humans knew. Technology became her only problem during the ages, making it more difficult to hide her harvesting. People reported screams to the authorities so blazingly quick today.

Selene started her car and carefully backed out of the parking spot. She glanced at the youth sitting docilely beside her as she drove away from the precinct. The commander was correct, another corpse was about to drop.

Chapter Sixteen

Luc stared at Casi across the countertop. How the hell did she know about the missing eyes? She kept dropping information the public wasn't privy to. She had to know more than she was letting on. He forced himself to look away and eyed the refrigerator instead.

"Are you hungry? I am. I'm going to make us some breakfast." He took two strides, arrived at the fridge, and pulled the door open. "Omelet, okay?" He rummaged for ingredients, hoping to find food that wasn't moldy. He hadn't been home much lately. There had to be something besides pie and eggs that he could throw into the omelet.

"Um, sure. I mean, you don't have to. I don't want to cause any more inconvenience than I already have."

"No trouble." He threw a quick smile at her as he dumped a few fixings on the counter, before returning to the fridge to grab more. Maybe if he gained her trust, she'd open up to him some more or, at least, drop more knowledge she'd been hiding. "It's actually nice to cook for someone besides myself."

"If you're sure, but uh, why don't you put on a shirt? I mean, you might get burned or something…"

Luc placed the rest of his scavenged ingredients, which weren't much—a small soft onion, wilted spinach, a handful of mushrooms, and one lone wrinkled bell pepper—on the counter and studied Casi.

Most women wouldn't have minded the view. Sure, his muscles weren't as sharply cut as his younger brother's, but he wasn't a slouch either. He kept himself fit. Luc hoped the distraction would work in his favor. But he realized by the slight blush pinking her light brown skin, she was more embarrassed or uncomfortable. Either of which probably wouldn't aid his fact-finding mission. So a shirt became a priority.

He gave her his father's smile, all charm mixed with a bit of wicked boy. "Safety first, right?" She ducked her head, breaking eye contact, and his smile turned into a grin. "I'll be right back. Want to make some coffee? I need something more than decaf tea since neither of us looks to be going back to sleep anytime soon. The beans are in the pantry, and the grinder's next to the coffeepot."

She nodded, so he grabbed his gun and made a quick exit. He jogged down the hallway and into his bedroom, which he had loaned to Casi. Catastrophe was curled into a large ball on his unmade bed, blinking lazily at him. A quick reconnaissance of the room showed nothing out of order. All of Casi's belongings were neatly tucked away in her duffle, and her phone sat charging on his nightstand. He opened a drawer and yanked out a faded blue T-shirt. Pulling it over his head, he smoothed the cotton down before donning his shoulder holster. Next, he strode to the nightstand, unplugged her phone, and took it with him as he made his way to the kitchen.

Casi was seated where he left her, but the aroma of brewing coffee attested she hadn't remained there. Luc put her phone on the countertop in front of her.

"What about my request to always have this on

you?"

She frowned at him. "I only came into the kitchen for a quick drink. I was actually on my way back to bed when you put your gun in my face."

"And what happens if it hadn't been me?"

"I would have screamed."

"You did. And it wasn't helpful, was it?" He pushed his fingers through his hair. "If I had been the killer, you could have bolted and had a way to call for help." He shook his head. "Keep it with you. At all times."

"Fine." Casi dragged her phone closer.

Time to lay off the bad-cop vibe, but he wanted her safe, needed her safe. "Thanks for making the coffee. You want a mug?"

"Yes. Thanks. Milk, no sugar."

He fixed up two mugs and handed hers as Cat came trotting into the kitchen. She sat patiently on the floor with her bushy tail wrapped around her feet, staring up at him. Her intent easily read in her orangey eyes as clear as if she had spoken.

"Nope. Not going to work, Cat."

Luc set about cleaning then chopping mushrooms, ignoring her.

"She's staring at me now," Casi commented.

He looked down. Sure enough, Casi had drawn *the stare*.

"I swear, it's like she's talking to me, but I don't speak feline."

"That's because she *is* speaking to you. Well, commanding. She wants you to feed her. There is perfectly good kibble in her bowl. Apparently, last night's, well, earlier this morning's, isn't good enough." This time Luc met his cat's gaze directly. "It's only a few hours old. Eat what you have and lay off the newbie."

Cat replied with a huge yawn and then a full-body stretch before she turned her back on them and padded silently out of the kitchen.

"I've never had a cat. Is this normal?"

"Pretty much. Cats are way different from dogs. We humans, are here merely to be at their beck and call. Glorified servants. Sometimes I miss having a dog, but with my job, it's good she's independent and in control of the universe."

Casi chuckled. "It's good to be the queen."

"Exactly." Luc pointed a knife at her before returning to chop the pepper. Once done, he added it to the bowl which held a meager amount of mushrooms and the questionable onion and spinach. He stepped to his spice rack. Choosing a few, he seasoned the vegetables, gave them a quick stir before dumping them into a heated cast iron skillet. He grabbed another bowl and started cracking eggs. Leaving Casi to sit in silence, he hoped she'd break the quiet, so he kept to himself as he whipped up the eggs. Giving the vegetables a quick stir and assessing they were almost done, he poured the eggs into the pan.

Luc glanced up and caught her staring, so he raised an eyebrow at her. After all, it had worked in the interrogation room. It had gotten her talking.

"So um, you like to cook?"

"I do, but don't get to often enough to suit me. Hence the sad condition of my fridge."

Casi gave him a slight smile. "I can do the basics, like grilled cheese or scrambled eggs, but nothing fancy. I always wanted to learn." Her smile grew. "You already out cook me with your omelet. What's your skill level?"

He returned her smile with one of his own. "Fancy advanced, I guess."

"Really? Did your mom teach you?"

"Nah, *cher*. My poppa. He's a chef."

"Wow, how cool."

Luc folded the eggs in half and then, wanting to give Casi a bit of show, flipped the eggs over using only the heavy frying pan. Skills he had learned as a teenager working in his father's restaurant hadn't let him down.

"Nice!" she replied, but her smile disappeared. In fact, she now looked a little sad. Before he could ask what was wrong, she spoke up. "It sounds like you're close to your family."

"Yes, we're pretty tight." He tilted his head. "I'm guessing yours isn't."

A small chuckle escaped her. "Yeah, not so much. My mom is on her third husband, the first being my dad. I have two younger half brothers, but we don't talk. Everyone is in California. Plus, my mom is more interested in her social standing, so she and I aren't speaking anymore. It's kind of just me."

"That's a shame. You seem entirely worth knowing. Especially when you're not scowling and belligerent."

"I apologized." She frowned.

He held up his hands in protest. "Teasing."

Casi shook her head. "So your mother bakes amazing pies, your dad is a chef, so what's up with your sisters? You've got two of them, right?"

He plated, then cut the omelet in half and passed her one along with a fork. “Jolie and Marielle. I also have a brother, Bastien.”

“Wow, a matched set—two girls and two boys. I bet you’re the eldest.” She took a bite of eggs and nodded as she chewed. “This is fantastic, thanks for cooking.”

“You’re welcome. And you’d lose. Jolie is the eldest.”

“The tea shop owner?”

“Correct. Excellent memory.” He went back to eating.

“Well, you’re not the youngest.”

“I come next. I’m a year younger than Jolie. Then there’s Bastien, the rising rock star, who’s four years younger than me. And last but not least is Marielle, who’s in college at the moment.”

“And you’re all close?”

Luc couldn’t help but smile. “Yes. We and our extended family, we’re all tight.”

“Must be nice.”

“It is.”

His cell phone dinged, letting him know he had a text. He picked up his phone and unlocked the screen. The brief details of the coroner’s report on Mason Webb appeared. Time of death confirmation, severed arteries in the neck as cause of death, and the surprising information the wound appeared to be self-inflicted.

He highly doubted Webb would have killed himself. Everything about this case emerged screwy. His brain jumped a gear, something else didn’t add up besides Mason Webb committing suicide. He put his phone down, lost in thought as he went through the details of last night.

"Something wrong?"

Luc looked up and met Casi's concerned gaze. "Not really, just something bugging me." He took the last bite of his eggs, stalling. Vince wanted Luc to question her, and his perfect opening appeared. He might as well jump on in. "What time did you last see Mason Webb?"

"You already know the answer. When he gave me the key to his car." Her forehead furrowed. "If you don't like me grumpy, quit repeating questions."

Luc shook his head. "I realize that. What I'm asking is the actual time you last saw him."

"Oh—" She chewed her lower lip. "—I don't remember precisely, but I think after one in the morning? Maybe one-thirty?"

He sighed. "Casi, please don't lie to me. It's not going to help."

"I'm not lying!"

"You are." He gestured to his phone. "The text came from the coroner. Time of death is between nine and eleven o'clock. So quit with the pretenses and tell me what happened."

"I can't be in two places at once! I was still in your so-called *safe house* at nine." She stood abruptly, the stool skidded and teetered. "I left around ten, went to my destroyed apartment, and then made my way to Mason's. All by public transport. It took a while." Her entire body broadcasted tension and anger as she held herself tightly upright, glaring at him. "They're wrong. He was alive when I saw him after midnight. Why can't you believe me?" She turned her back on him. Her next words whispered and probably not meant for his ears.

"Why do they never believe me?"

Luc rounded the counter and placed a hand on her shoulder. "Casi, it's a science-based exp—"

She whirled. "They're wrong! I *know* they're wrong. Check the security cameras. They'll prove what time I got to his apartment."

He frowned. She's right. It would be easy to prove. Maybe she hadn't seen Webb, but just broke into his place, or had his apartment key and took his car fob? His thoughts must have been written across his face.

"Why do you think I'm lying? Why is that your go-to? I saw Mason. He came out of his bedroom wearing only his underwear. He was worried and concerned for me. He even yelled at me, which he never does. Why can't you believe me?"

"Casi." Luc reached for her, but she took several steps backward. "If I take you for your word, then what? You saw and spoke to his ghost?"

Chapter Seventeen

"I don't know! Mace spoke to me! I…" She turned, giving him her back as she fought through her frustration and the tears threatening to spill over. Mason died. The fault lay with her. Just like last time. And once again, the people who should be on her side weren't. She shoved all her emotions down tight. Enough. No more.

"Casi."

Shaking her head, she spun and pushed past him, bolting for the bedroom. She needed her stuff. She needed out of here.

Casi made it to the bedroom doorway when the detective grabbed her arm, jerking her to a halt.

"Stop! Stop running."

She turned, hand curled in a fist as she threw a punch, but he easily blocked and grabbed her wrist.

"No! Dammit. Let me go." She struggled, blindly thrashing. "I won't let you arrest me!" She couldn't go to jail again. The nightmares still haunted her. Panic set in. Her pulse throbbed in her ears as her heart pounded. She couldn't breathe. He had control of both her arms, so she blasted her knee upward, but he twisted and took the blow on his thigh.

"Shit! Casi, please. It's okay."

Before she figured out his actions, Avery rotated her and then pulled her back tight against his front. He wrapped his arms around her, pinning her arms to her side, and then he widened his stance, using his legs to subdue her own. She tried to move and found she couldn't. Casi threw her head backward, but he must have been expecting it because she never connected. She let out a frustrated scream.

She had to break away. No jail. Never again. Her vision tunneled as her heart rate spiked. Thrashing in his hold, lost in her mind, she blindly tried to break free. It wasn't until her panic maxed out and her body's adrenaline plummeted, did she realize Avery was speaking. When she collapsed in his grip, his words finally made sense.

"Easy, *cher*, easy. I will not arrest you. It's okay. Calm down."

He repeated himself over and over, his accent winding around her, reaching deep inside her. His hold was strong but somehow gentle. Though there was no give, it felt more like an embrace than a combative hold.

"Come now. You're all right. Hush. *Prend-lé aisé*. Take it easy."

Breathing hard in sharp bursts as if she'd run a four-minute mile, she felt something give deep within her. Her whole body shuddered as her throat closed. She choked. On her half gasp to inhale air, a sob burst forth, followed by another. If she hadn't been in his arms, she'd have folded in half from the strength of her cries.

"Ah, darlin'. It'll be okay. I promise."

He gently turned her in his arms, and with a hand against the back of her head, he guided her to his shoulder. His other hand landed at the small of her back, pressing her close as she cried. He murmured to her, soft and quiet and not even in English.

She lost track of time. After her tears ran their course, she blinked, opened her eyes, and found herself on his bed. She sat curled in his lap with his arms around her. Trying to lift her head, she couldn't since her body felt too heavy and drained to move. Casi could barely keep her eyes open.

Luc's hand rubbed in a gentle rhythm up and down her back. Her eyes fluttered closed, and she leaned into his solid chest. She shouldn't be doing this. He thought she was a liar. He didn't trust her, yet here she was, on his lap with his arms around her as he comforted her once again. She had to stop breaking down in front of him. Too tired to care as confusion swept her up, she'd give herself another second or two, then make herself move.

"You better, *cher*?" Luc's hand kept rubbing her back.

She nodded and, with a sigh, forced herself to sit up. Meeting his concerned gaze briefly, she extricated herself from his lap. She stood but swayed, her legs too weak to hold her. Avery's hands shot out and gripped her hips.

"Easy there."

He guided her and helped her to sit next to him on the bed. As soon as she was stable, he withdrew his warm hands. She shivered. Soon she found she couldn't stop and wrapped her arms around herself as she trembled, frozen to the core. Casi knew what had happened, what was happening, as she felt herself slipping into shock.

Avery stood and went to his closet. He opened it

and pulled a quilt from the upper shelf. Making his way back to her, he unfolded the hand-stitched blanket. The moment he reached her side, he wrapped the quilt around her.

Casi gripped the edges and pulled it tighter. She wanted nothing more than to bury her face in the cotton and shut out the world. Sadly, the detective had another idea as he squatted in front of her. With a gentle finger under her chin, he tilted her face so he could gaze into her eyes.

His hazel eyes, a muddy mix of colors this time, were so open and honest with concern she didn't doubt his worry. She just had a major inexplicable freak-out—physically attacking him and then breaking down. He probably thought her crazy, and sadly, she couldn't blame him.

"I think we need to talk, Casi." His voice gentle, using the tone one would on a spooked horse. "I'd like to know what I did to trigger you. And with your degrees, I know you know what I mean."

She closed her eyes, not able to hold his gaze anymore. Casi knew exactly what he meant. Triggers were for abused and broken people, which she most assuredly could claim. She only pretended to be strong and capable which most of the time wasn't hard to do. Triggers were words, actions, or physical touches, sometimes visual cues, sending someone back into their private personal darkness. She thought she was past all this—leaving California far behind and stuffing her trauma away—but maybe not. Did she owe Avery an explanation? Probably not but having no one to trust in her life made her both weary and sad. She chewed her lower lip. Mason was a rare man—hell, person—she'd let her barriers down so he could enter her heart. God, she missed him and still couldn't believe he was truly gone.

She heard Mason's voice in her mind.

Open your heart, sweetie. There are so many wonderful people out there waiting for you to let them in. Like you did for me.

I didn't let you in, Mace. You bulldozed yourself into my life.

True. But what would have happened if I hadn't? You wouldn't have me in your life. And that, my girl, would have been tragic.

It almost felt like his arms wrapped around her like they had been the day of their conversation. His last words from their talk flittered through her head.

For healing to happen, for good to enter your life, be open for it, sweetie.

Avery was a cop. Cops were a major trigger as if he hadn't figured that out already. But hadn't he proved himself at least a little? She couldn't blame him for thinking she'd lied since the forensic evidence all but screamed it out loud. Plus, didn't actions speak louder than words? He'd been mostly patient and caring. Hell, he gave up his bed for her when he could have given her the couch.

Casi opened her eyes and found Avery still staring intently at her. She nodded once at him before finding her voice. "Okay." It rasped from all the screaming and sobbing.

He stood and offered his hand. "Come on. Let's move this to the front room." Luc helped her to her feet as she clutched the quilt with one hand, not ready to relinquish its warmth. She still felt cold to the bone, and her eyes were gritty. He led her out of the bedroom with a hand to her spine and guided her to the couch. She curled up in a corner of one side.

"I'm going to get us something to drink, it'll give you a moment or two in private." He padded barefoot out of the room to the kitchen.

Everything inside her bubbled up, closing her throat and making her shake again. Trying to gain control, Casi willed her emotions and dark nightmares away, trying to put them back in the locked box of her mind, but they wouldn't go. She hadn't had a panic attack like this in over a year. Had she been her own psych patient, she would have pointed out that swallowing her emotions and ignoring her traumas were an extreme definition of unhealthy. Eventually, the pressure would explode, especially in high-stress situations. Like being held hostage, then stalked by a serial killer, and seeing her best friend's dead body. It was surprising she hadn't triggered sooner.

Getting herself back under somewhat tenuous control, Casi wished it wasn't late morning because she sure as hell could use a drink.

Avery appeared in front of her and held out a steaming mug. She grabbed it and wrapped her chilled fingers around the hot ceramic, pulling it close to her center for added warmth.

"It's coffee, Irish style. I didn't think you'd mind."

Bless him, he had read her thoughts. Luc took a seat on the opposite end of the couch, giving her the much-needed distance but not too far as she took a sip. Whiskey-laced coffee trailed down her throat and into her stomach, chasing away the chill deep inside her soul. She kept sipping as the silence grew between them. He enjoyed using quiet to get her to talk, but little did Avery know, Casi liked to live in the silence.

She stopped drinking and held the mug tight, knowing she would not get away without explaining herself. Reliving the past she so desperately wanted to forget kept her lips sealed and the words trapped in her throat.

"Casi, I'm truly sorry. Obviously, I did something, said something to…upset you. I never intended to trigger a panic attack. I never want to be responsible for your pain again."

Dragging her stare from her mug's contents, she forced herself to meet Luc's gaze. With a slight shrug, she dropped her eyes again after a moment's contact. "It's not your fault."

"Talk to me." He sighed. "Please. I'm just trying to understand what's going on."

"It all started with Trevor and Aimee." Casi couldn't meet his eyes, choosing instead to stare into her coffee. Was she really going to do this? Maybe open up to someone else? Mason had helped so much when she'd confessed to him. But Avery? A cop? A shiver chased through her.

"Those were the kids in your care, the ones who died."

Casi flinched, even though his words were soft and held no judgment. She nodded, not quite able to speak yet. Of course Avery wasn't going to leave it at that. He made a living getting people to spill their guts, so his leading question didn't surprise her.

"I didn't read your complete case file. The only facts I know were the kids were killed, and somehow you were charged with felony child abuse. How can that even happen when their own father killed them?"

Guilt flooded her. She hadn't done her job and protected her kids. She should have tried harder, but at the time, Casi thought she had done everything by the book and was almost destroyed because of her actions. Her life had imploded.

She swallowed hard. "California has been cracking down on social workers. They just successfully filed against two caseworkers and their superiors. I became their next shining star in their prosecution of new legislation." Casi looked up and stared Avery down. "They believed I had an improper regard for human life and a lack of vigilance."

"I find that hard to believe."

"You don't know me, Detective."

"I'd like to." He put his empty mug on the side table next to him. "What happened earlier…I don't think it had to do with your trial and subsequent acquittal?"

"Everything and nothing." She put her mug down on the coffee table, not finding any comfort in its warmth. Tugging the quilt tighter around her, she tried to figure out where to start. "They brought me in for questioning. Obviously, I was upset. I felt I let my kids down. Hell, I *did* let them down, and they died because of it."

"It's not your fault, Casi."

"I…" She shook her head. "I followed the rules. I gave my reports, both verbal and written to my supervisor. I wanted them out from under their father's household. I was waiting on approval to get them into the foster system. I thought I did everything correctly, but I shouldn't have ignored my gut. I should have pulled Trevor and Aimee out of that house and not waited, damn the consequences."

"Hindsight is great, but it sounds like you did everything you thought you legally could. No one knows the future. You're not psychic."

Ironic he should say that considering how she was hiding out in New Orleans doing just that. Too bad she wasn't. If she had the actual magical power of foresight, maybe her kids would have been alive today.

"Anyway." She took a deep breath. "The DA didn't believe me. All my reports had disappeared from the system. My supervisor didn't back me up on my verbal reports to him. So since I looked like an incompetent idiot, I was charged and arrested. I couldn't pass *go*, I went directly to prison to await my arraignment, then trial."

"Wait a sec, there wasn't bail? You have a clean record and not a typical flight risk."

"Nice to know you have faith in me, but I was being used as an example. Besides, there was bail, I just couldn't make it. It was ridiculously high." She pointed to herself. "Example, remember?"

"What about your family? Your momma, or stepfather, hell, what about your own father?"

A sharp bark of laughter escaped her. "Yeah, no. Both father figures wanted nothing to do with me. And my mom? She ran so far and so fast away from me and the ugliness of the scandal, she should have permanent whiplash." Casi frowned. "When I asked for her help, she told me everything was my fault and wasn't surprised. She never approved of my career. It wasn't flashy enough, or high earning enough. Anyway, that was the last time I'd spoken with her. She washed her hands of me. God forbid I *tainted* her, and she got kicked out of her country club."

"Oh, *cher*, that's just not right."

"Not everyone can have a family like yours, Detective."

"It's Luc, and I'm beginning to see why you have major trust issues."

Understatement of the decade. She sighed again. "Obtaining proof of my reports while in custody was beyond difficult. My laptop, which was a department issue, didn't have them, even though I *knew* I had the originals and copies on there. I always kept copies."

Luc frowned. "Someone tampered with your computer?"

"Yup, it eventually all came out. My lawyer hired a private investigator. He found my backup to my backups—a thumb drive containing all my case records, proving I wasn't negligent. Once those became public, it cracked wide open. My supervisor feared he'd be charged like in the other case, so he tried to get the entire thing blamed on me." She broke her gaze and stared at her hands clutching the quilt.

"My charges were dropped, and they released me from jail with my record cleaned. Not that it mattered. No one in my department believed me, and they even thought I had set my boss up. My workplace became a nightmare, so I quit. No one else would hire me. My reputation completely blackened through no fault of my own. So I said screw it. I decided to go back to my roots and return to New Orleans."

Silence stretched between them until she couldn't take it anymore and glanced up, meeting the all-too-perceptive gaze from Avery.

“There’s more.” He leaned forward, his jaw set. “Something happened. Nothing you’ve told me so far caused you to break down like you did. You were terrified, panicked.” His brow furrowed. “You thought I would arrest you when I grabbed you. You kept repeating you wouldn’t go to jail.”

He moved closer with a careful motion, near but not quite touching. “Tell me.”

How did he know? Her chest felt tight, and she became light-headed. Her vision tunneled, as she lost herself. Casi felt a pressure on her knee, Luc’s warm hand, even through the thickness of the quilt. It grounded her, dragging her back to herself. She looked up and found his caring face inches from hers as he leaned in closer.

“Hey there, darlin’. Breathe. Stay with me. You’re safe.”

Tears flooded her eyes. How could there be any moisture left? She blinked hard against them. “They jumped me.” The barely audible words escaped her on an exhale, but sitting close enough to hear her, he gently squeezed her knee. His compassionate support tore more fractures deep inside her, and like the waters breaching the levees during Hurricane Katrina, she couldn’t stop the flow of words from spilling out. “There was a corrections officer…he-he wouldn’t leave me alone. Everyone knew he…wanted me. So in return for favors and privileges, three women caught me alone in the showers.” She swallowed hard. “They attacked, I tried to fight, but they overwhelmed me. Among…other things, I hit my head hard and was barely conscious.”

Casi started shaking again. The slight warmth inside the quilt disappeared and cold flooded her core as her mind plunged back to her assault. She pulled the blanket tighter around her, burrowing deep in its soft cotton depths even as Luc's free hand helped her wrap up. When she continued to speak, her voice sounded small and lost. "They dragged me to the laundry room and gave-gave me to him. I-I couldn't think, or fight, he-he…"

Luc swore. She met his angry gaze but didn't feel threatened. "Tell me that bastard's serving time."

She nodded. "I think one of the inmates knew what was going down and felt guilty or found a spark of humanity. I don't really remember too much, except someone pulling him off me." She shrugged. "I'm sorry I freaked out on you. It, um, hasn't happened in a while."

"No apologies, Casi. You're under immense stress and me treating you like a suspect certainly didn't help." He squeezed her knee before removing his hand. "Thank you for opening up." He ducked his head so he could catch her gaze. "Thank you for trusting me."

Chapter Eighteen

Damn, fucking Eckert. Luc slammed his car door shut. He hadn't wanted to leave Casi alone, particularly in her present emotional state. She appeared vulnerable and lost. When he'd gotten the call from his commander, the sight of her bundled up in his grandmama's quilt looking so sad and hurt nearly killed him. Luc had no choice but to go to the crime scene. After a quick shower and shave, he dressed in clean clothes. Right before he had closed the front door, he'd seen Cat jump onto the couch. Hopefully, his oversized feline would give Casi some comfort.

He walked over to Vince, who leaned against his SUV.

"You look pissed, partner." Vincent straightened as Luc closed.

"I am." He glared past Tate, locking on to Commander Eckert, who stood just inside the police tape at the latest crime scene.

"Really wanted that day off, huh?" The bit-too-knowing smirk in Tate's smile caused Luc's hackles to rise even more.

"Piss off, Vince." Luc transferred his glare to his partner.

Tate held up his hands in surrender. "Hey now, only teasing. Man, you still look like shit. You were supposed to get some sleep."

"I did. A few hours, which is more than I've been getting lately, but unlike you, since I never mastered the art of combat naps, it feels like I haven't slept in weeks." Luc sighed. "Ms. Thomas woke up and went into the kitchen. I thought we had an intruder."

"Oh man. Everything good?"

"Yeah." Luc pushed his fingers through his hair. "Look, there's stuff I need to update you on."

"Avery! Tate! Quit gossiping and get your asses over here," Eckert bellowed.

Vince shook his head and slapped Luc on the shoulder. "I hate that asshole."

Luc trailed in his partner's footsteps toward the crime scene. They ducked under the yellow tape and stopped side by side in front of Eckert.

"It took you both long enough." The commander sneered at them. Luc gritted his teeth and kept his face neutral. But the intimidation rolled off of Vince because his large partner towered over Eckert. The guy had to look way up to meet Vincent's impassive Special Forces stare.

Luc wanted to laugh, but he knew it wouldn't be a great idea. His commander hated his guts. Why? He hadn't a clue. As his top detective, Eckert should be singing Luc's praises. When Vince partnered up with Luc about a year ago, proximity contaminated poor Tate. Luckily his partner hadn't minded because the hate-fest was all-around mutual. Usually, it didn't matter, since they rarely interacted with their boss's boss, but apparently, their luck had run out.

"We've got another Cyclops body. You two don't get a day off when there's a corpse on the ground."

Luc held in his automatic retort. It hadn't been his

idea to have the day off. Instead, he gave a sharp nod and sidestepped to get around Eckert so he could begin investigating. Anything, even another victim, was better than talking to Commander A-hole.

Eckert's grip on his upper arm abruptly halted Luc.

"I'm not done with you, Avery. You go when you're dismissed."

He glanced at the hand wrapped around his bicep and tensed. Vince must have read Luc's body language, because he stepped closer in order to, as Vince would say, *guard his six*.

Eckert, being slightly frightened of Tate, dropped his hand and took a step back. "Where's the witness, the Thomas girl? I want her location. Now."

The hairs on Luc's nape rose. Instincts leaped to the fore. Commander Eckert never went to crime scenes. Him asking about Casi was odd too. His sixth sense screamed. Something Luc never ignored. Even Vincent learned to trust Luc's weird insights. His partner shared the story of one of his Delta teammates who seemed to have a second-sight ability. So learning to roll with Luc's gut calls, or bayou intuitions, was no biggie to Vince. Luc exchanged a quick glance with his partner, hoping Vince would follow his lead. Eckert didn't need to know where Casi stayed.

"At a safe house, sir."

"Which one?"

Luc shrugged. "I'm sure it's in the system."

"It's not, which is why I'm asking. Where is she?" Eckert stepped closer, his entire body radiating tension. Sweat beaded on the commander's brow and upper lip. His total focus on Luc, ignoring Vincent completely, even his fear of the large man gone. "I've wanted to force you out for a long time. Tell me where your witness is, or I'll fire your ass right here and now."

Eckert smirked. He wanted Luc gone and losing a witness would be his commander's perfect excuse. Luc wondered if Eckert hoped for Luc not to answer. Either way, it appeared it would be a win-win for Eckert. He guessed the time came to lie like the *filthy* Cajun his commander thought him to be. Or at least share a version of the truth.

"I handed her off to some uniforms, sir. Truthfully, I was exhausted."

"Who were the patrolmen?"

"Can't say. I can't even remember their faces." A hundred percent true since there were no cops, so they wouldn't have faces. "They should have logged her location." He shrugged.

Eckert turned and glared at Vincent. "What about you? Or are you as dumb as Avery?"

"I wasn't there when she was handed off, sir."

Luc hid his smile. Tate also spoke the truth. Vince had arrived late in Luc's conversation with Casi, and after Luke decided to take her to his house. Tate had his back, especially against Eckert.

"You're both useless, and I should take your badges. Especially if you lost a witness." The commander walked away. "Get to work." He fired over his shoulder as he left.

Vince ran a hand over his smooth skull. "Huh. I guess we've been dismissed." He started for the body. "You want to tell me what just went down, partner?"

"I don't really know."

"You get one of your bad vibes?"

"*Ouais*." Luc glanced over his shoulder, picking

out Eckert in the parking lot with his cell phone pressed to his ear in deep conversation. "The creepy-crawling kind."

They lapsed into silence as they approached the body. Their latest victim had been dumped in the warehouse district, on a block of abandoned storehouses set for demolition. Their bad luck continued to hold. No working security cameras, no pedestrian traffic, just a lot of nothing.

"Hey, Jake. We meet again." Luc gave a nod to the M.E.

Jake stood when they reached the body. "Good afternoon, Detectives. Nothing new with this one, he's exactly like all the others in MO. "However"—he gestured to the corpse—"the kid is the freshest so far."The kid is the freshest so far. I estimate TOD for late this morning. Maybe I'll find something new for you when I get him on my table."

Luc glanced down at the body and froze. *What the hell*? The victim, a teenage boy around sixteen, had a single bright blue eye staring back at him. The hairs on the back of his neck rose along with his arm hairs this time. His gaze drifted down to the kid's neck tattoo of a spiderweb. *Holy shit*. He glanced to the side of the building, and there it was—the Chinese alphabet dragon.

How was this possible? Casi's nightmare had come true, except for the moving head and the creepy voice from the grave. How did she know this, even down to the finer details? Casi had been with him all morning and into the afternoon. First seeing and speaking to Mason after he was supposedly dead, and now this. He couldn't wrap his head around it. Luc grew up superstitious, deep within his heritage, but Casi seemed so normal and didn't tweak his sixth sense. He shook his head.

"What's the matter?" Luc turned and noticed Vince studying him. "Something wrong with the scene?"

He met Tate's concerned gaze. "No. Not really. We need to talk." Luc thrust his chin toward the parking lot. "Let's take a walk to your car."

"All righty." Tate's words were singsongy in his capitulation. "You and your mystery. Off we go." Without a further word, Tate spun on his heels and marched away from the crime scene.

Luc followed at a slower pace, scanning for Eckert. Another ambush from their commander was the last thing he wanted. Thankfully, he was nowhere to be found.

Vincent leaned against his SUV once again, but Luc couldn't stand still. He paced in front of his partner, his heart racing and his gut churning. He thrust his fingers through his hair.

"Come on, partner. What's got you so riled?" Vince's voice was pitched low so as not to carry. "Use your words and talk to me."

"Shit. I don't know." Luc spun in place and stopped in front of Tate. "She saw this." His words were quiet, keeping their conversation private as he waved toward the crime scene. "I don't know how, but she saw this." He met his partner's gaze. "Casi described that kid in detail, even the graffiti on the building."

"She what?"

"I know." Luc shook his head. "And before you think it, her alibi is tight. She was with me during the

TOD."

Vincent frowned. "I don't really believe in mumbo jumbo crap. There's usually an explanation. Like your weird gut insights or my Delta teammate's foresight is probably hyper-awareness of your surroundings and the subconscious piecing shit together. It just appears to be woo-woo crap." He wiggled his fingers. "So what the hell do you mean by *seen*?"

"She had a nightmare. It's what woke her up and sent her to the kitchen. After I calmed her down from having my gun in her face, I got her to open up. In her dream, she saw this location and described the body. When the dead kid's head turned to her and said, quote, unquote, 'help me,' it spooked the hell out of her."

Vince's eyes went wide as he stared at him, speechless.

"I have a bad feeling."

His partner snorted. "You got a disturbance in the force? No kidding. What the f-ing hell?"

"Between Eckert and now this, my skin is crawling."

"So what's the plan?" Vince asked.

Luc nodded. That's what he liked about Vincent Tate. Adaptable and nothing seemed to faze him. Tate had been his best partner to date. Luc may have hated the whole Delta Force superiority vibe at first, but the man knew how to roll with punches, improvise, and have his teammate's back. Luc learned to appreciate the military training and skills Vince brought to the table.

"We both can't leave, at least not right away. You mind covering? Everything inside me is screaming to get back to Casi."

"Can do."

No arguments. Nor questions. Vince had a quiet acceptance and even an excited expectation.

"Thanks, Vince." Luc shoved his hands into his jeans pockets. "Get clear as soon as you can. I've got a feeling I'll need backup."

"Don't do anything stupid, Avery. You wait if you have to. I want a Sit Rep when you arrive. Running in on your own is a brilliant way to get your ass shot."

Luc grinned. They knew each other well. If Luc could count on Vince's quiet support, his partner knew Luc threw caution to the wind with his impatience. Plus, after a year of partnering, Luc's military slang was up to par. "I'll get you a situation report ASAP. Promise."

"Yeah, right. Go on. Get your skinny ass out of here. I'll be right behind you."

Luc tossed off a sloppy salute, which earned him a grunt from Vince. He took off running for his car, whipped out his cell phone, and dialed.

"Come on, come on, pick up." The ringing abruptly stopped, and he was dumped into voicemail. He tried not to panic as he wrenched open his car door. There could be lots of reasons Casi wasn't answering. She might be in the bathroom or asleep or something. His heart pounded as he started the engine and slammed the car into drive. He told her to always have the phone charged and with her. She should have answered. His gut twisting in knots, Luc hoped to deliver only a lecture and not a call for an ambulance.

Chapter Nineteen

Selene entered Detective Avery's house and gently closed the door behind her.

"*Find her*." Her power-laced order further ensnared the plainclothes cop, who drew his weapon and on silent feet padded deeper into Avery's home.

Selene's hands fisted, remembering Eckert's call stating he still hadn't found the Thomas woman. How hard could it be to find a woman in police protective custody? The detectives should have known where their key witness had been stored. She struggled to believe they'd lost her. Eckert should have forced them to answer. Then, Selene had put two and two together. They hadn't lost her. One of the detectives personally hid Thomas, and she laid all her money on Avery. He was always such a bleeding heart and lady's man.

Compelling a cop to aid her and get Avery's address had her putting forth minimal effort. The plainclothes cop had the additional bonus of lock-picking skills. Plus, his extra muscle for backup wouldn't hurt. Not that she needed the muscle, but the way Cassanne Thomas escaped her first in the townhouse and then in the garage concerned Selene. No one, in all the centuries of her long life, had been immune to her voice. So in case it wasn't a fluke, she brought along a little help. And some subterfuge, since she wasn't dressed in her normal disguise as a hooded androgynous killer. She parked down the street in case Avery returned early. No reason to alert him with a strange car in his driveway or parked in the front of his house, especially with her own BMW. Selene doubted he'd recognize it, but why take a chance?

The cop returned. "There's no one here, except for a huge cat."

Damn. She'd been so sure. Avery wouldn't take Thomas with him to a crime scene. Same with Tate. Where was she?

There wasn't much to Avery's small bachelor pad. She looked the house up online. Just a small one-bedroom, one-bath home, though it contained a large front room. "*Show me the bedroom,*" she compelled her puppet.

The cop turned obediently and entered a hallway. Selene followed silently behind him. He stopped in front of an open door and gestured.

As Selene entered the bedroom, a large brown tabby sprang to its feet on the center of the bed, back arched, hair standing on end, and its fluffy tail spread out wide. It spat a hiss at her, then settled into a low rumbling growl as it showed its teeth.

Brave cat. It didn't back down as she approached the bed. Selene glanced over her shoulder to the cop. "*If it tries to attack me,*" — she turned back, staring into the feline's eyes—"*hoot it.*"

She smiled and took her attention off the cat. Felines were smart and had a sense of self-preservation. Plus, they could spot supernaturals better than any animal on the planet and obviously by its continuous low growl, knew a fellow predator when it saw one. She had no doubt the cat perfectly understood the situation. With the cat dismissed, Selene searched the room. Neat and orderly. The only item out of place was an oversized duffle near the door. She walked around the bed and spied a battered canvas messenger bag leaning against the nightstand. She recognized the bag.

Selene snatched the tote and dumped the contents onto the hardwood floor. Tossing the bag aside, she squatted and dug through the strewn debris until she found the wallet. She grabbed it, and she stood while opening the case. Staring at the driver's license, Selene found it belonged to Cassanne Thomas. At least her instincts were correct. She let the wallet drop. Where the hell was she? Where was Gabriel's horn? Selene couldn't sense it nearby. *Dammit.*

The still growling cat drew her attention. Too bad the feline couldn't speak. The woman had definitely been here. She left the bedroom with the cop following on her heels like a well-trained dog. Selene always appreciated dogs much more than the judgey felines.

Just as they were about to enter the main room, the front door opened, and Detective Avery entered, leading with his gun. He hadn't seen them yet.

Well, wasn't this convenient? She smiled. Now she'd have all the help she could have dreamed.

"*Hello there, handsome.*" Magic swirled around her before she directed and threw it at the detective. Avery spun at the sound of her voice, aiming his gun, but the moment her power hit him, he froze, all his muscles tightened. She walked and stopped only inches from him. Her heels made her taller, but not by much. Lifting her hand, she trailed a finger lightly down his arm, then across his weapon. "*You can put that away. You won't be using it. I need your help.*"

Sweat beaded on Avery's forehead, and he swayed while standing in place. My, my, he's a strong one. It didn't matter. He belonged to her. Avery could fight all he wanted, but the effort was wasted on his part. She pushed more of her magic at him, and satisfaction filled her when his beautiful hazel eyes glazed over, and he slipped his gun into his shoulder holster.

"*Where is Ms. Thomas?*"

The detective swallowed hard before his lips parted. "She should be here."

"*Give me your phone.*"

Avery's hand fisted before reaching into his pocket. He pulled out his cell phone and conveniently unlocked it without her ordering him. Good. Her hold on him had settled, sinking deep. He handed her the phone.

It started vibrating the moment she held it. The caller ID revealed his partner, Vincent Tate. She pressed ignore. That wouldn't do. She went to the call log, and sure enough, her prey's number was listed.

Selene trapped the detective's gaze. Pushing more magic at him, she gave him orders. "*Call Ms. Thomas, find her for me, handsome. When you reach her, don't mention my helpful cop or me. In fact, you won't remember us at all. Do it now, please.*"

She handed the phone back to Avery, who dutifully dialed her wayward quarry. When he raised the phone to his ear, she placed a stilling hand on his arm. "*On speaker, if you would.*"

He tapped the screen, and the ringing filled the entryway. It rang several more times before switching to voicemail.

"*Again.*"

Avery redialed and the phone rang again. It also went to voicemail.

"*Trace her phone*."

He blinked a few times. "I need a warrant."

"Damn it. Why is everyone so useless? *Give me your phone*." She held out her hand, and the detective placed it in her palm. She'd call Eckert, who she still controlled. The commander of CID should be able to trace a phone without a warrant or at least expedite it.

The phone vibrated in her hand once again. Probably Tate calling Avery again, but much to her surprise, the caller ID held the name Casi Thomas. Excellent.

"*Get her to tell you where she is*." Selene answered the call, putting it on speaker.

"Avery."

"Luc! I'm so sorry. I know I missed your calls—"

"Where are you?"

Selene smiled at his sharp interruption and nodded encouragingly at him.

"You were supposed to stay here."

"I know, I know. I'm sorry—"

"Where the hell are you?"

"I had to leave. Mason…I'm scared—"

"Where. Are. You?"

"I'm down the street. There's a park—"

"I know it. Stay put. Don't leave."

Selene touched the screen ending the call and then returned the phone. "Excellent." She smiled and ran her finger down his chest. "*Let's retrieve her, shall we*?"

Avery turned, opened the front door, and sprinted off before she could compel him to stay at her side. "*After him, don't let the detective out of your sight*,"

Selene ordered her pet cop, who obligingly took off running. She wouldn't be able to keep up in heels, but she could follow them in her car. Selene strode out, pulling the front door closed behind her.

Chapter Twenty

Casi stared at the silent phone in her hand. He'd hung up on her. She wanted to call him again and keep him on the line but figured he probably wouldn't answer. He must be royally pissed at her.

She sank to the ground behind the wide trunk of a live oak covered with Spanish moss and resurrection ferns. The tree hid her from the street. Casi took a deep breath and wrapped her arms around her bent legs and rested her chin on her knees, closing her eyes. Luc was on his way. He'd reach her soon. She tried to slow her pounding pulse.

Her life had turned completely upside down. Though angry with her, Luc had proven again and again he would trust her. But would he still have her back since she ran? Again. Had she broken his trust? And good Lord, what would he think when she told him how and why she fled?

Opening her eyes, Casi gazed straight ahead and studied the translucent figure standing only a few feet in front of her. Mason Webb. She rubbed her eyes again, and once more nothing changed. Mace's ghost still stood before her. She saw dead people. Hell, she had spoken to dead people.

Mason had appeared when she'd been curled up on Avery's couch nestled in his grandmother's quilt while cuddling with his cat. She thought she might be dreaming or finally had lost her mind if not for Catastrophe. The feline had sat up and stared directly at Mason's apparition.

He told her to run. Danger had followed her again. Casi sat there frozen, thinking she must be crazy. Then Cat reached out a paw and swiped at Mason. Her paw had passed straight through him. Casi screamed. Mace begged her to believe him. The serial killer knew where she hid, and Casi needed to run.

Panicked, she did exactly that. She leaped off the couch, the cozy quilt falling to the ground in a heap as she bolted through the kitchen and out the back door. Blocks had flown by when Casi ran out of air and looked for a place to hide. The park she jogged into had plenty of places to conceal her, which led her to hide behind this old-growth tree with its massive trunk.

Mason hadn't said a word since the house. No matter how many questions she'd thrown at him. He looked eerily normal except for the whole see-through thing, unlike the substantial solid appearance in his apartment. She wished he'd speak with her again.

"Casi!"

She peered around the tree. That sounded like Luc, but he wasn't in view yet. She faced forward, wanting to stay hidden until he closed the gap. Casi gasped. Mason had disappeared. Maybe a good sign, like she was out of danger?

"Casi, where the hell are you?"

He sounded closer. She stood, then peeked around the tree. Sure enough, Avery ran across the road and reached the sidewalk in front of the park.

"Here! I'm here!" Casi stepped from behind the tree and jogged toward Luc. She met him halfway and threw herself at him, shamelessly wrapping her arms around him in a tight hug. “Oh my God. I’m sorry. I’m so sorry. I know I should have called.”

He tensed under her stranglehold. *Dang*. Avery must still be angry with her. She pulled slightly away so she could see his face. “Luc?”

He shook his head and blinked rapidly. He looked confused.

“Casi?” Luc scanned the park before meeting her gaze. “What the hell? How did—”

A loud bang cracked in the air, and Luc jerked before shoving them prone to the ground.

“Stay down!” Luc held her shoulders, pinning her as he rolled further on top of her, covering her with his body.

Another loud bang and Avery jerked again.

“Shit!” He twisted while pulling his gun and then fired.

Casi screamed and covered her ears, though too late. The loud boom made her ears ring. Who was shooting at them? She tried to see, but Luc’s weight had her effectively pinned. Squealing tires along with a string of Cajun curses from Luc had Casi guessing the shooter had fled.

Luc holstered his weapon when Casi spotted the blood dripping off his arm.

“Oh my God!” She pushed at him. “Let me up. You’re hurt. You’re bleeding!”

Luc rolled off her and did as she asked while gripping his thigh with both hands. Her gaze left his arm, drawn to the blood oozing out between his fingers. The thigh wound appeared much more serious. She tugged her phone out and quickly dialed 911. But before it connected, Luc's bloody fingers grabbed her phone and disconnected the call.

"We can't call this in." Luc exhaled harshly and gritted his teeth as once again, he applied pressure to his leg.

"You're shot. You're bleeding from multiple places. We need an ambulance!"

He shook his head. "Can't. We need to leave. Now."

"How? Can you even walk?"

"Yes. Help me up."

Luc leveraged himself up with his good leg as Casi tucked herself under his shoulder. Standing, he swore again when he put weight on his injured limb but kept his feet underneath him. Luc stood there breathing hard, obviously in pain.

"Get my phone. Front pocket."

Casi saw the outline of his cell and reached in. Pulling it out, she saw the locked screen.

"Hold it up to my face to unlock." Which she did on the heels of his next command. "Look in the call log for Vincent Tate."

She scrolled searching for the number when another squeal of tires caught her attention.

"Never mind. He found us." Luc sagged a little more in her hold, forcing her to brace her legs so they wouldn't crash to the ground.

Detective Tate ran to them, weapon out, as his eyes scanned the area. "What the F, man? I guess the report of shots fired wasn't wrong."

"Later. Get us out of here." Luc stepped forward and swore as his leg buckled. He must have forgotten his injury in his haste.

Luckily Tate jumped in and helped her, or they both would have fallen.

"I've got him. Get the back door open."

Casi took off running for the idling SUV propped half onto the sidewalk at an angle. Getting to the car, she yanked open the door and stepped aside just in time.

With sheer brute strength, Tate hefted Luc in. "This is what you get for not following my advice. You get your ass shot, and now you are bleeding all over my new ride."

Luc's laugh was more of an abrupt exhale. "It wasn't my ass."

"Enough!" Casi shouted. Why were they bantering? "He needs a hospital. Get in the car and drive already."

Luc shook his head, and Casi noted once again the weird silent communication between him and his partner. She hated when they communed wordlessly in her presence.

"You still have the first aid kit I gave you for Christmas?"

Luc nodded, and Vince slammed the door shut, before turning to her. "Get in."

She climbed into the front passenger seat as Tate jumped in the driver's side. He put the car into reverse and bumped off the sidewalk, as Luc grunted from the backseat at the jostle. Tate got the SUV in gear and then headed down the road back to Luc's home.

"I don't understand. Where are we going? He needs a doctor."

Luc answered. "Gunshot wounds are reported if we go to a hospital."

She twisted in her seat, facing him. He laid slumped across the bench, still trying to staunch the blood oozing out of his thigh, completely ignoring his injured arm. "So? You're a cop. It's not like you're some criminal afraid to get caught."

With a screech of tires, Tate stopped the big SUV in the driveway next to Luc's car. This time he turned off the engine before climbing out and crossing to Casi's side of the car. He opened the back door and studied his partner.

"You owe me a detail job."

Luc flipped him the middle finger, making Tate laugh.

By then, Casi had jumped out of the car. "Stop it. Both of you."

Tate helped Luc exit. "Sorry, ma'am. Morbid sense of humor. Can you get the door?"

Casi led the way over the stone pathway. "He needs more than a first aid kit. He needs a doctor. Stitches. Antibiotics. God, maybe surgery."

She opened the unlocked door and watched as Luc growled once again, putting too much weight on his wounded leg. Neither man deigned to answer her. She held the door open as Tate half dragged, half carried Luc inside. Casi quickly shut and locked the front door and then followed them into the kitchen.

Luc collapsed into a chair, head bowed and breathing hard. It took a few moments before he could lift his head. "The kit is in the bathroom under the sink."

Tate gave two thumbs up before jogging off. Luc's gaze moved to hers. "I know this is all strange, but I'll explain. Promise. Vince has medic training from the military, but he will need towels. There are some in the drawer next to the stove. Get 'em for me, please?"

His Cajun accent was out in full force. No longer masking it, which made her think he was in a great deal of pain. Casi kept her mouth shut as she did as he asked. She'd keep her questions to herself until Avery's wounds were tended and hopefully he was out of pain. Luckily, she could keep her ghostly encounter secret a bit longer. Knowing the reprieve would be short because Luc would wheedle the full story out of her eventually.

Detective Tate entered with a huge metal box and set it on the kitchen table next to Luc.

"Wow." Casi stared wide-eyed at the medical container. "Um, are you prepping for the zombie apocalypse or something?" She had been expecting one of those small plastic white boxes with a Red Cross symbol on it. This kit resembled a heavyweight toolbox.

"Everyone should have one." Tate looked pointedly down at his partner. "Lucas hasn't appreciated my gift."

Luc's disgruntled expression made Casi hide a smile. Obviously, this was a sore point between the men. But seriously? Who would ever need this massive first aid kit? She supposed idiot detectives who refused to take gunshot victims to the hospital. At least Tate had medical experience, which he appeared to put to expert use as he examined Avery.

He frowned at his partner before gripping Luc's right wrist and lifting his arm. "Just a graze, and we don't even need to worry about any cloth in the wound since you're hit below your sleeve. Just gonna need to clean it up and slap a bandage on." He dropped Luc's arm, none too gently by Avery's apparent teeth gritting. Tate crouched, studying Luc's left thigh through the tear in his jeans, and sighed. "I hope you're not going commando under your jeans." He met his partner's gaze before glancing at her.

"Ms. Thomas—"

"Casi, please. I think the shedding of blood makes things informal."

Bright white teeth flashed as he grinned. "Casi. Would you be so kind and help Detective Avery out of his jeans while I wash up?"

Her eyes widened, and Tate grinned before opening the first-aid container and grabbing a pair of latex gloves and a bottle of iodine scrub. He stepped away and headed for the sink. Casi's attention dropped to Luc in the chair.

"Why not just cut them off?"

Tate chuckled. "They will have to come off eventually, so might as well get the process started."

With a sharp exhale, Avery unbuckled his belt, unsnapped his button, and pulled down the zipper. He caught her gaze and gave her what she thought of as his charming grin.

"Now, *cher*, this isn't how I imagined you getting into my pants."

"Seriously?"

His smile fled. "Sorry." He looked chagrinned. "I was just trying to lighten the atmosphere. I didn't mean…never appropriate for unwelcomed sexual innuendo. Sorry."

"It's okay," she reassured him. "I wasn't offended. I just don't get how the both of you can joke at a time like this."

Tate piped up by the sink. "When you deal with a lot of awful shit, it's better to laugh than go crazy."

"I suppose." Casi shook her head.

"I'll need a hand to stand so I can push my pants down." Luc braced his left hand, planted his unwounded right leg, and leveraged himself up as if he had spun a new game position making him twist his various limbs. Casi got to his side, helping him to balance.

"I, um, think you should probably do the honors. I'm afraid I might fall."

Casi stifled a laugh and raised an eyebrow. "You sure there's no ulterior motive, Detective?"

"Hey, look, Vince. She's learning." He smiled again before meeting her gaze. "Promise."

"Well okay then, hang on and don't fall."

She tugged his jeans, pushing them past his hips and bright cherry red boxers—definitely not commando. Red? White, black, or maybe even gray, but she never expected fire-engine red underwear. Avery lost his balance and landed back in the chair with his pants around his knees. Her eyes were pulled from the bright distraction down to his bleeding wound.

"Oh my God! You need a real doctor."

"It's worse than it looks. I'm in excellent hands. Vince has great training from his days in Delta Force. This is nothing for him."

She frowned and studied Tate as he arrived at the kitchen table and started digging through the medical kit. He pulled out gauze, suture thread, forceps, and scissors.

Supplies situated, Vince crouched by Avery and

started blotting the blood away so he could see the wound on Luc's thigh. "Bigger than a graze, but at least not a hole with a bullet still in. I'll call it a baby furrow, and you will need stitches."

Luc let a Cajun curse fly, eliciting a laugh from his partner.

"Sorry. You get no sympathy from me. I told you to call me and wait." Tate cleaned and disinfected the wound, all the while Luc tried to bite back more curses. When Vince became satisfied no bits of cloth or debris remained, the injury bled freely once more. He grabbed two clean towels. One he placed underneath Luc's thigh to catch the dripping blood, and the second he placed on top of the wound. "Casi put your hands here and apply pressure."

She leaned over Avery from the opposite side and pressed hard on the towel covering the furrow, putting all her weight behind it. At least the bleeding must be slowing since it hadn't soaked through the top layer. She twisted and glanced at Luc, noticing the sweat beading on his forehead before watching Tate thread a long needle.

"Come on, man, I know you have lidocaine in there. Numb my leg."

"Pussy." His partner smirked before grabbing the pre-filled syringe already lying out. He lifted a side of the towel, and without pause, he stabbed the needle into Luc's thigh.

Why Luc hadn't yelled, she had no clue. Casi shook her head. "Can I do more to help?"

Tate glanced up at her. "Yeah, put on a pair of gloves and come over to my side. Grab a bunch of gauze, I have a feeling I'll need to see what I'm doing, and the wound will still bleed once we stop applying pressure."

Casi nodded and let Vincent take over applying force. She gloved up, which in hindsight she probably should have done before. However, since she already had his blood all over her, it would have been too late, anyway. She watched as, with another ungentle prod, Tate poked Luc's thigh.

"Numb enough yet?"

Luc nodded once and then looked away, staring blankly into the kitchen.

"So," Tate stabbed the treaded needle into Luc's skin, gaining a grunt. "Will someone explain to me what the hell happened?"

Chapter Twenty-One

"Here's the problem," Luc replied through gritted teeth. The numbing painkiller had taken the edge off, but nothing could actually stop the feel of a sharp object passing through his skin and the weird tug of the suture thread. Not watching helped. "I don't really know."

"How's that possible? Start from the beginning when you arrived. Talking will help take your mind off this."

Vince tugged on the thread, and Luc felt it. Ugh. He hated getting stitches.

"Why the hell didn't you wait? Or in fact, answer my call?"

"I planned to. I..." Luc shook his head. He closed his eyes and tried to focus, but Tate's stitching wasn't helping. With his eyes shut, it only brought the sutures to the forefront, making the pain less imaginary and more real. How many stitches was it going to take? He wanted a break, but he would not ask Vince to stop now. Hell no. Luc wanted this done and over with, especially without any more ribbing from his partner. Vince had probably held his own intestines in while self-suturing his gutshot in the middle of a firefight. Stupid Special Forces.

He exhaled hard. "I remember pulling into the driveway and going to the front door. I recall being concerned I found it unlocked. So I drew my weapon and entered, but that's where my mind goes blank."

His eyes snapped open when Vince stopped sewing and stared into his partner's disbelieving gaze.

"You can't remember?"

"I know I entered my house, but then everything went blank until I held Casi in the park."

Vincent raised a single eyebrow, before returning his attention to his needlework.

Luc stared out the kitchen window, forcing himself to recall and not fixate on what his partner was currently doing. "It's weird. Like waking suddenly from a deep sleep. Startled awake. And there I was, in Casi's arms at the park, with no idea how I got there."

"Are you in shock? I mean, you were shot twice. Maybe you hit your head?"

His attention left the window to center on Casi crouched next to Tate. Her worry, a clear presence in her eyes and from the tone in her voice. He shook his head. "No. I'm not in shock. Plus, this jolting awake happened before the shooting. Before I took us to the ground. I don't understand…"

Luc stared into her brown eyes, a lighter brown than his partner's dark gaze. She had really pretty eyes, almost a rich golden whiskey brown, even when they were filled with concern. *Damn.* The more time he spent with her, the more his attraction grew. Probably not the best thing considering her history and the fact she was his only witness.

"*Merde.*" Luc frowned.

"Quit being a baby, partner. I'm almost done."

He shook his head. "The shooting. Casi had to be the target."

"What? Me?"

"Sorry, Casi. The killer might be afraid you can identify him." He met her fearful gaze and cursed inwardly by not handling that better. He knew he wasn't thinking properly since he should have probably softened the blow. He glanced away to find Vince tying off. Finally.

"Or the shooter was getting you out of the way so he could snatch her again." Tate looked thoughtful as he bandaged Luc's thigh.

"That's not any more comforting than someone trying to shoot me. Both of your bedside manners suck." Casi stood and put the leftover gauze into the first aid kit.

Tate chuckled. "*Mea culpa.*" He shrugged. "In order to keep you safe, we have to be aware of all the possibilities."

"Well, neither scenario will help me sleep tonight. And before either of you ask, I didn't see the shooter. Luc had me pinned to the ground." Instead of meeting either of their gazes, she rummaged in the metal box. "You have an antibiotic in here, right? He will need it if you're both too stubborn to let him go to the hospital."

"I do, ma'am." Vince nudged Casi aside. His partner deftly snatched up a vial and filled another syringe. "Casi, you may want to turn around unless you want to see my partner's skinny white ass." He motioned the syringe toward Luc.

Casi smiled and turned her back.

"Seriously? You couldn't get the IV kind? Or at least the one for the arm?"

"Quit complaining and drop trou."

Luc put most of his weight on his right hip, tipping slightly to the side, so he could lower his briefs to expose his left butt cheek. Vince must have been ready because with one hand, he quickly used a cold, wet sterilizing swab before none too gently stabbing him with the needle.

"Ow!"

Tate laughed as he depressed the plunger. The antibiotic stung and burned. Crap, that hurt. Over-cooked and done, Luc's exhaustion hit him. Getting shot sucked. He had just enough energy to pull his underwear back up. His jeans still clung around his knees, and he couldn't care less as he collapsed onto the chair.

"Now that I saved your sorry ass from going to the hospital, I guess you can't diss my first aid kit."

"Yeah, I guess not." Luc's eyes felt gritty, but by sheer will, he kept them open. "You can turn around Casi."

She smiled as she faced him. "Can I get you something? Coffee maybe?"

"Hell no."

"My partner is correct. Times like these require something stronger." Tate closed up the metal box. "Grab three glasses, and I'll get the whiskey."

"I'm not sure that's such a good idea." Casi frowned.

"I think it's a brilliant idea." Luc smiled as Vince walked to the cabinet holding his liquor and grabbed the bottle of Red Spot Irish. The single pot fifteen-year-old whiskey came out for special occasions only. Now we're talking. Surviving being shot and Casi not being abducted were causes for celebration. Casi reluctantly crossed into the kitchen and opened cabinets and removed two glasses. "Oh no, *cher*. You're joining us."

He heard her sigh, but she took a third glass, which Casi then juggled with the others before coming back to the kitchen table. Tate poured a generous round and handed out the glasses.

Luc raised his glass. "*Santé*."

"To health is right." Vince clinked glasses with him. "Can you ID the shooter?"

"No, not really. I got a shot off as he ran. Definitely male. White. Plus Cyclops isn't working alone. He had a driver. A black sedan, I think it might have been a Beemer."

"No lucky breaks, but at least we know more than before." Tate's lips thinned. "So who's going to state the obvious?"

"That Luc should have gone to the hospital?"

He savored a sip before smiling. "*Non*. It's time for the explanations you've patiently waited for. Thank you for stepping up and helping."

"It's the least I could do, especially if you were shot because of me."

He gave a quick shake of his head. "It's my job to protect you, even if it means taking a bullet or two."

Casi stared at him. He wasn't able to read her expression, possibly a split between disbelief and guilt. Luc couldn't blame the doubt. After everything he had learned this morning, he wasn't surprised at her distrust.

Tate interrupted their staring contest. "What I referred to was how did the killer find you?"

Casi frowned. "Do I have some tracking device on me? He keeps showing up. It's twice now."

"Well, the first is explainable." Luc tapped a finger against his glass, trying to focus and stay awake. "Your place was ransacked, right? Could be he found some mail or message linking you to Webb and put two and two together thinking you might be with your friend."

"I guess." Casi didn't look like she believed it. "But what about today?"

"That's what has us concerned." Tate slugged back the rest of his whiskey before pouring another round for Luc and himself.

Casi had barely touched hers. "I don't understand."

Luc met her worried gaze. "You weren't in the system. Something confirmed by our commander. Only myself, Vince, and our captain knew where you were."

"So what? Are you telling me your captain is in league with the killer? That's crazy."

He watched as Casi finally took another sip of her drink. At least her hand wasn't shaking. Good for her, since a serial killer kept stalking her, and she had been shot at.

Luc started tapping his glass again. "He might be, but I doubt it. Making a guess, I'd say he told someone, and it got out."

"Well, why don't you ask him?"

Tate put his glass down. "Since we can't rule him out at the moment, he's still a suspect." He turned and stared at Luc. "We've got a mole."

"Yeah, you're probably right." Luc tried to push his hand through his hair until it got stuck. He pulled his hand away and stared at the dried blood on his fingers and palms. That's right, he was covered in his own blood. Great. A walking crime scene. He really must be exhausted if he'd ignored his disgusting state. "I need a fucking shower."

"Yeah, you do." Tate smiled. "Is your grandparents' anniversary shindig still happening this weekend?"

Luc had been with his partner long enough to figure out the nonsequitur. He nodded. "I wasn't going because of the case."

Tate's lips thinned. "A change of plans is in order. You and Casi need to get out of town."

He sighed. "A good idea, I guess."

"I'll talk to the captain, make up some excuse like you're laid out with the flu or something." Tate finished the last of his drink. "I think it's best if I stay and hunt down our mole."

"Ya sure? I don't like leaving your back unguarded."

Tate smiled. "Aww, you really care. Besides, you can say hi to Jolie for me."

Not on his life. Vince had an eye on his older sister, and no way would the two of them ever be allowed to hook up on his watch. Luc shook his head. "I can arrange for you to have your own stitches if you'd like."

"In your dreams, boy." Tate stood and walked into the kitchen to crouch in front of the sink and rummage through the cabinet. He stood holding a roll of plastic wrap. "Let's get you cleaned up."

Tate walked back and then squatted. He yanked off Luc's shoes and pulled his dangling jeans off, leaving him in his bloody T-shirt and red boxers. Vince leveraged Luc to his feet. "I'll get you in the shower, then start packing a bag for you. You look like shit."

"I feel like shit."

"Is there anything I can help with?" Casi stood and joined them.

Luc gave her a crooked grin. "If you don't mind

cleaning up in here first, I'll take a quick shower, and afterward you can take your turn." He pointed at her bloodstained clothes.

"Yeah." She pulled her sticky shirt away from her body. "I definitely could decontaminate some."

"Thanks."

Tate led him to the bathroom but stopped them at the hallway entrance. "Casi, leave the first aid kit. I still need to bandage his arm."

He had time to see her nod before Tate hauled him down the hallway. His partner was right about getting Casi out of town, but he couldn't help the gut twinge thinking he might bring danger with him to his family. But since only he and Tate would know her location this time, he probably worried for nothing. Time would tell.

Chapter Twenty-Two

Casi stepped into Luc's bedroom, freshly showered and in clean clothes. Her wet hair hung in loose waves down her back, dampening her shirt, but right now it felt refreshing. All bets were off once she stepped outside in the growing humidity. Another storm must be brewing.

She dropped her soiled clothes next to her duffle by the door but held on to her jeans. The dried blood made them stiff. Could she salvage them? Besides the pair of jeans she currently wore, the blood-caked pants were her only other pair. She had packed for only a couple of days of confinement. Casi sighed.

"I think those are toast."

She tore her gaze away from her ruined clothes and met Tate's scrutiny across the room. He stood next to the closet with a shirt in his hands.

"That's what I'm afraid of. I'm kind of limited in both my wardrobe and budget. What you see is what you get." Casi waved a hand down and then up her body. Couldn't the freaking Cyclops have spared her clothes?

She gave her bloody jeans a hard shake as her frustration mounted. A clank on the wood flooring captured her attention. Crouching, she spotted the mysterious horn charm lying on the floor. She had forgotten it had been in her pocket and moved to grab it but hesitated. Would it suddenly burn her hand and give her a migraine? Only one way to find out.

Tentatively, with the barest touch of one finger, she brushed the weird colored stone. Cool to the touch. No burning heat. She picked it up and held it in her palm. Was it larger? She could have sworn it had been maybe two or three inches wide, but now it bordered on four. Weird. Must have been mistaken. Standing, she slipped it into the front pocket of her last pair of pants.

"How's Luc doing?" Casi grabbed the plastic bag she swiped from the kitchen and shoved her soiled shirt, jeans, and underwear into it.

Rolling clothes into small tight bundles and then shoving them into a soft-sided suitcase, Tate looked up. "Passed out on the couch, but he'll be fine."

"Really? It looked like he lost a lot of blood."

"He still has a lot more in him." Vince put more clothes in the bag. "Honestly, if I thought he was in any kind of genuine danger, I would have dragged him to the hospital. I've seen much worse. He'll live."

"If you say so."

Tate zipped Luc's suitcase and gestured toward her. "You almost done?"

"I never unpacked." Her duffle laid zipped at her feet. "The only thing I need is my messenger bag."

Casi crossed the room toward the far side of the bed, heading for the nightstand. She froze at Tate's side, and her hand flew up covering her mouth.

"What's wrong?" Tate spun and followed her gaze.

The contents of her bag were heaped on the floor. She had absolutely not left it that way. Did the Cyclops go through her stuff again? Stomach churning, Casi felt the blood leach from her face as she stared at Tate.

"I didn't do that." She pointed to her stuff strewn on the floor. "I think the Cyclops did."

Tate marched over to her personal items. He squatted and pulled a pair of latex gloves from his back pocket. Slipping them on, he picked up the wallet which rested on top of the mess.

Slowly, Casi approached, standing beside him. "What are you doing?"

"This shouldn't be on top. It's one of the heaviest items from your bag. It should be buried under lighter objects." Tate opened the wallet and started pulling everything out and dropping the items to the floor next to the pile of her stuff.

"Um." She chewed her lower lip.

He glanced up. "Sorry. Should have asked first. If you don't mind, I'd like to take your wallet and see if we find fingerprints. It's a shot in the dark, but you never know." Tate gestured with the now empty wallet to her stuff on the ground. "I figured you'd like to keep the contents, no reason to haul your license, credit cards, and cash to the station as well when just the wallet will do."

"Thanks. And of course, please take the wallet. Anything to end this nightmare."

He nodded and stood. "Gather the rest of your stuff and meet me in the front room."

Without another word, he grabbed Luc's suitcase with his free hand and left the room with her wallet in his other. She stared after him for a moment before crouching next to her empty bag. In short order, Casi stuffed her belongings back into the canvas satchel and stood. Taking a deep breath, she slung the strap over her head and walked to her duffle. She hoisted it up, strode out of the room and down the hallway.

Halting abruptly in the living room, her jaw dropped seeing Avery on his feet. "What do you think you're doing? You shouldn't put any weight on your leg."

"I'm fine." He gave her a small smile. "However, I think it would be better if you drove. If that's okay with you? I'm still kind of exhausted."

The detectives headed for the front door, and Casi followed with a headshake as she watched Avery limping. She froze at the door.

"Wait! What about Catastrophe? Who's going to take care of her?"

Luc stopped and turned toward her while running his fingers through his damp hair. "I'm more tired than I thought. Thanks for the reminder. She'd never had forgiven me." He gave a sharp whistle and waited.

Cat came trotting around the corner from the kitchen, tail held high and a bounce to her steps.

"There you are, sugar. Come now. Road trip."

Without breaking stride, Cat eased into a lope and ran out the door. Luc gestured for Casi to follow. Exiting the house, she found Cat patiently sitting next to Avery's car. Luc limped up beside Casi and chuckled, no doubt at her astonished expression.

"Never had a cat before. I think I trained some dog into her." He put his hand on the small of her back and guided her forward. "She loves visiting the bayou."

Tate passed them after locking up the house and popped the trunk open. "Before I head back, I'll go to the park and see if I can find any slugs or casings."

"Sounds good." Avery nodded.

He tossed Luc's bag inside, then grabbed her

duffle, placing it alongside Luc's suitcase before closing the trunk. He tossed her the key fob.

"Take good care of my partner." He faced Luc. "Try and get some rest. I've got things covered here."

Avery opened the back door so Cat could jump in. "*Prends soin de toi*."

"Yeah, yeah. I'll take care of myself, crazy Cajun. You need to do the same. Keep in touch. I mean it this time." Tate walked to his SUV. "And you know I hate that Cajun Frenchy stuff. I can't understand the shit you say."

Luc chuckled. "I'll point out you translated what I said just fine. You're learning, *coo-yôn*."

"Then I guess you better stop calling me an idiot." He shot Luc the one-finger salute before getting into his car and driving away.

Avery smiled as he eased himself into the front passenger seat. Casi quickly followed into the driver's seat and shut her door.

"Start her up, *cher*, so I can program the GPS for you."

She looked over her shoulder, finding Cat nestled against the rear window on the speaker ledge.

"Don't worry about her. She's a seasoned traveler."

Casi drew her attention to the front, fastened her seatbelt, and then started the car.

Luc reached for the middle console screen and started tapping. He pulled up the GPS and then, under favorites, punched the button labeled *bayou*.

As the navigation calculated, he faced her. "We're headed for Bayou Lafourche. My family's home is just outside, a little over fifty miles from here."

She backed out of the driveway and then followed

the directions to the I-10 roadway. Lafourche was southwest of the city, so they'd probably end up on the I-310 before hitting the US-90. Between the navigation system and her own mental map, she doubted she would end up lost if Luc fell asleep.

Accelerating up the interstate ramp, she glanced quickly at Luc and found him studying her. Focusing back on the road, she swallowed sharply as she merged safely and settled into a lane. She should thank him. The bullets that struck him were probably meant for her, and all she'd given him in return? Breaking her word and most likely his trust. With a sigh, Casi loosened her white-knuckled grip on the steering wheel and decided to confront her fears head on.

"I guess I should thank you, and I know I owe you an apology." She glanced at him and noticed his quirked eyebrow. "You saved me from getting shot or killed, maybe abducted again. I never actually shared my appreciation."

"None needed. It's my job to keep you safe, if anything I owe you an apology. I haven't been great at keeping you out of danger."

With a slight shake of her head, she kept her gaze on the road. "I haven't made your job easy, and I am sorry."

"Knowing what I know, I can't say I blame you. Let's call it even." His thick accent, a sexy drawl, filled the car and wrapped around her.

Hiding her smile, she had to admit she preferred when he didn't conceal his accent. He shared his true self with her. He must tone it down for work. She had to admit she liked the real Lucas Avery. If she wasn't careful, Casi could see herself falling for him.

Gorgeous, with his arsenal of smiles and his caring personality, he appeared the total package, even if he was a cop.

With a mental headshake, she got her brain back on track. “So on to the apology I owe you.” Casi hesitated. How in the world could she explain Mason’s ghost?

A fat raindrop splattered on the windshield, quickly followed by more. The threatening storm broke as it started pouring. She flipped on the wipers, happy for the delay, even a brief reprieve.

“Apology?”

She swallowed hard. “I ran without calling you.”

“That you did. But at least you kept your phone with you, even if you didn’t answer my calls.”

“Yeah, I’m sorry about that too.”

Silence enveloped the car except for the rapid thunking of the wipers and the pounding rain.

“Why did you run?” Of course he would get straight to the point, even if Luc’s question slurred slightly with his tiredness and blood loss. Apparently, even with his fatigue, his deductive reasoning still functioned. She wondered if he’d fall asleep again. If he passed out, she wouldn’t have to confess so soon.

“Um, I don’t think you’ll believe me.”

“Why don’t you try me, *cher*?”

She sneaked a glance and caught his drowsy smile—another to add to her collection. Why were all his smiles sexy? “All right. But you can’t laugh or get all defensive like this morning.” Her breakdown was only this morning? It felt a lifetime ago.

“Scout’s honor.”

She caught his salute out of the corner of her eye and smiled. “You were a scout?”

"I wasn't. Stop stalling and trust me."

"Your opinion of me might change and for the worse."

"Doubt it, and you're still stalling. *Dis-moi la vérité. Ça vaut la peine*."

She shot him a quick glance, wondering what he said. "In English, Cajun boy."

"Sorry." He pushed his hair off his forehead. "Tell me the truth, it's worth the trouble."

Keeping her gaze fixed on the road so she wouldn't have to witness his disbelief, she crushed the steering wheel, knuckles turning white. "So, um, I think I'm being haunted."

Waiting, with the sound of rain and the wipers as her only companion, Casi felt okay with the pause. Better than confessing her unbelievable situation.

"Haunted? By what? Is your PTSD ailing you, Casi?"

She laughed. "I wish." Shaking her head, she could only hope bad memories haunted her, instead of her best friend—except she loved Mason. Having him in her life, even as a ghost, must be better than never seeing him again. Selfish? Sure. He certainly deserved to move on instead of playing her guardian angel. She might as well get this conversation over with because Avery wasn't going to let this slide, and he deserved the truth. He could have died today.

"I, um, mean a literal haunting."

"Like a ghost?"

"Yeah, like a ghost." She swallowed hard. "Remember when you confronted me about the last time I saw Mason and you told me I couldn't have? Well, you were right. I think I interacted with his spirit."

She couldn't make herself continue—it appeared Casi liked having Avery's good opinion. Who would have thought? She wasn't surprised he figured out what she hadn't said.

"And you know this because you saw him again?"

Ding, ding, ding. Luc, too clever by far. It was probably what made him such a talented detective.

She squeezed the steering wheel before loosening her grip since her fingers were numb, unlike her inner turmoil. Taking her eyes off the road, she stared at him as he lounged sideways with his head resting against the seat, his sultry eyes half-mast, but the sleepy look didn't fool her. She tore her gaze away and studied the rain-slicked road instead.

"*Viens immédiatement, cher, Vide ton sac. Tu te sentiras mieux.*"

His deep tenor made her shiver. Damn the man. "You're doing that on purpose. Stop it. I'm taking Vincent's side. It's annoying not knowing what you're saying."

He chuckled. "It's annoying you aren't trusting me." Luc reached with his hand and tugged on a loose curl of her hair. "Come on and spit it out, you'll feel better."

Wow. She couldn't decide if it sounded better in Cajun or English with an accent. He had a point. Too late not to trust him now.

"Fine. I was on the couch having a cuddle with Cat when suddenly Mason appeared, standing right in front of me. I thought I imagined him, but Cat reacted and tried to poke him with her paw, except it went right through him."

She glanced in the rearview at the sleeping feline. Too bad she couldn't speak and be her witness to the paranormal. Since no laughter or anger erupted from the passenger seat, Casi decided Avery stayed silent, waiting for the rest. At least he might be taking her seriously. She had to give him credit because if the situation was reversed, she doubted she would take it so easily.

"He, um, warned me I was in danger, just like last time. Mason told me to flee, immediately. Completely spooked—"

Luc snickered but raised his hand in apology. "Sorry. I couldn't help but laugh at the pun."

Pun? Oh… She smiled. "I forgive you." Her smile fell. "Anyway, I thought if he came to me with a warning, I suppose I should listen. I ran out the back door and kept going until I hid in the park. He came with me, well sort of, but Mason wouldn't say anything else no matter how I questioned him. He disappeared when you found me."

"Have you seen him since?"

Casi shook her head and kept her eyes locked on the highway because she really didn't want to see if he was making fun of her. His silence killed her.

"You're taking this amazingly well. No sarcastic comment or come back? Most likely rude?" She braved a glance and found him facing forward with his eyes closed. Had he fallen asleep?

"*Non, cher*. I learned my lesson and will try not to judge you again."

Nope. Not asleep after all, even though his expressive eyes were hidden behind closed lids with ridiculously long eyelashes.

"Besides, I have firsthand knowledge of how closely connected you are to the supernatural. I'm not surprised you see ghosts, well, a ghost."

Casi swallowed hard. What the hell did he mean by that? "Do I want to know?"

He chuckled. "Probably not, but I'll share, anyway." Avery tilted his head toward her and opened his eyes. "Your nightmare? Not so much a dark dream as a premonition."

"What?" She took her gaze off the road and stared at him, eyes wide.

"You're drifting, darlin'. Eyes on the road."

Crap! She corrected back into her lane, with another tight grip on the wheel.

Avery must have taken pity on her because he continued with no additional prompting from her. "The crime scene they called me to earlier today was your dream. The victim was found in the warehouse district, tagged with the graffiti you described." Luc paused and yawned. "Damn, I'm tired." He yawned again. "And the victim, Casi. You described him perfectly down to the last detail. The only mistake? The body never spoke, thank God."

Goosebumps rose all over her body, and she shivered. "How…How is that possible? Why am I seeing Mason and having premonitions? I'm not psychic. It's all bullshit."

"I don't have answers for you, darlin'." His words slurred again within a thick accent. "Something's changed in you. Maybe your near-miss with the serial killer triggered something."

How can this be happening? It was a joke. It had to be. She didn't have any special powers, only her boring normal self. Yet…she saw and spoke with Mason's spirit. Couldn't argue with that. And how in the hell did she dream of a crime scene?

She didn't want any of this—being psychic, crazy, and stalked by a serial killer. Casi had enough. "I'm scared." Her whisper ended in a crack. Taking a sweaty palm from the steering wheel, she wiped it on her thigh. Why wasn't Avery saying anything? She wanted his calm support and assurance. "Luc?"

She glanced at Avery, finding him slumped in his seat, eyes closed, fast asleep. A quiet snore escaped. Maybe it was for the best. Hopefully, he hadn't heard her admission. Casi didn't want to rely on the charming detective, and she shouldn't. Sure, she trusted him, but…every lesson she'd learned taught her to depend solely on herself. She had to make sure Lucas Avery didn't sink any deeper into her skin, or she just might lose herself.

Chapter Twenty-Three

Selene held tightly to her umbrella. The wind and rain lashed her while approaching the unmarked sedan parked in a vacant lot. Loose ends needed tidying. She couldn't chance Avery or the girl identifying the plainclothes cop under her sway. Plus, the bastard could have killed the girl when he shot Avery. The idiot deserved his fate.

Opening the front passenger door, Selene quickly ducked in and closed her umbrella before slamming the door shut. The fact the cop waited for her here made her extremely happy. It proved her magic was working correctly. With losing sway over the Thomas girl and now Lucas Avery, worry had lingered in the back of her mind. At least for now her strongest skill appeared flaw-free. Gathering her will, she faced him and smiled.

"*Hello, my good boy.*"

He returned her smile as her magic pushed into him, strengthening her hold.

"It's time for us to say goodbye." She gently stroked his cheek with her gloved finger. "*When I leave, you will pull your weapon. When I'm safely away, please put your gun in your mouth and pull the trigger. Do you understand?*"

With glazed eyes, he nodded. "Yes."

She patted his leg. "Excellent." Selene gathered her energy for a final time and sent it out once again. "*Be sure to tilt it upward as you swallow the gun, dear.*"

Opening the door, she sprung her umbrella and stepped out of the car. She shut the door and strode confidently away in the rain. Finding Gabriel's horn became her number one priority. The high threat it posed to her doubled if her abilities were questionable. It left her vulnerable. Cassanne Thomas must have the horn in her possession. The chain holding the horn had broken with their struggle on the stairs. She had searched the townhouse, but the horn had disappeared exactly like her prey. She didn't believe in coincidences.

When Selene reached the outer perimeter of the parking lot, the sharp report of a gunshot cut through the storm. Smiling, she walked further into the stormy night.

****

Luc jerked awake when twenty-five pounds of excited feline landed in his lap, just missing his family jewels. Cat's hind end perched on his knees, narrowly missing his wound, and her front paws were braced on the dashboard as she caterwauled her excitement. Her vocabulary increased as Casi slowly drove up the lengthy gravel drive lined by old-growth weeping willows to his parents' house. At least the rain had stopped.

"Is this normal?"

He diverted his attention away from the view through the windshield to the lovely driver beside him, noting she didn't look any the worse from the haul through the storm. Smiling, he ran a hand down Catastrophe's silky back and nodded.

"Usually the passenger seat is empty though. I

think she needs to diet."

Casi gifted him with a brief smile.

"Sorry I drifted off. I meant to be a better copilot and keep you company."

"It's all right. You needed the rest. I tried to keep Cat in the backseat, but once I made the turn onto the drive, she jumped over the seat."

He chuckled. His cat loved the bayou. There were many times he tried to leave her here where he thought she'd be happiest. But apparently, Cat loved him more, at least according to his parents. After a few days of being away, his quirky feline would get depressed and spend her hours staring down the gravel drive waiting for his return. He indeed had turned his cat into a dog. Poor Catastrophe, she deserved better.

"No worries. I needed to wake up. There will be trouble enough with you driving me, but if anyone saw me passed out, there'd be no end to interrogations." His family would be a major pain in his ass once they saw his wounds. No matter his injuries weren't serious.

As Casi stopped the car in front of the house, Luc gripped her shoulder. "If you could downplay this whole thing, I'd be indebted, *cher*. I don't want them worrying more than they already will."

"Sure, Luc, maybe your arm, but I saw your thigh. It's not nothing."

"It's no big deal."

"It is. But if you want to keep this between us, fine. I'm just going to make sure you take care of yourself. Detective Tate gave me an order."

"It wasn't an order, only a friendly request." Ugh. He'd have to deal with Casi's pampering along with his family's, now. He hated all the fussing. Thank God it was early in the week. There would be plenty of time before the huge weekend bash to get everyone calmed down.

The screened porch door slammed, drawing his attention to the house as he watched his momma step onto the wrap-around porch and walk toward them. Catastrophe practically bounced on his lap. Chuckling, he opened his car door, letting his cat leap out. She made a beeline for her next favorite human on earth.

His momma scooped up the charging feline as if she weighed nothing and gave her a kiss while still closing on the car.

"*Mon chéri*, get you from there." Her narrowed eyes and furrowed brow belied the warm greeting of her words.

Luc sighed. Like that, was it? He only got a *sweet boy* when his mother knew something was fishy. Having never brought a woman home, let alone handed the driving over to one, his momma's sixth sense fired on all cylinders. He shouldn't be upset since inheriting her intuition made him the top detective in his precinct. At times like this, though, he fervently wished the skill had skipped her generation. Her internal radar always had been uncanny. Luc read her curiosity, his momma wondering who Casi was and what she might mean to her son. Might as well get this over with.

"Casi, please don't get out just yet."

"Um, sure?"

Luc opened the glove box and withdrew his personal Sig Sauer and quickly slipped the gun under his shirt, tucking it inside his waistband at the small of his back. His eagle-eyed momma would notice, but he wasn't going to go unarmed with the Cyclops in the wind. The killer had the uncanny habit of showing up in unwanted locations.

He shot Casi a quick smile. “I’ll be just a moment.” He stood as gracefully from the car as his leg would allow and carefully walked around the rear of the vehicle, hoping it would shield him from his prying momma’s eyes. Luc reached Casi’s door and opened it, offering her his hand.

Her quirked eyebrow and the barely-there smile attested to her amusement, but at least it looked like she would play along with his small subterfuges. Raised with old-fashioned manners, if he hadn’t gotten her door, regardless of the fact that Casi was the one driving, it would have added one more question to the piles gleaming in his momma’s sharp gaze.

Casi allowed him to assist her, giving his hand a reassuring squeeze when she stood. He shut the car door and then placed his hand to the small of her back, guiding her to his mother’s side.

His momma gave him a smile before tilting her face up to him. Obediently, he bent and kissed her cheek, careful not to squash Cat, who still curled in her arms.

“Momma, this is Cassanne Thomas. Casi, this is my mother, Adelaide Avery.”

“Mrs. Avery, it’s a pleasure to meet you. Thank you for having me in your lovely home.”

“*Non*. It is Momma Avery or Adel for you.” His mother took it all in stride considering he hadn’t called and told her Casi and he would be arriving on her doorstep tonight. Between falling asleep on the couch and speaking with Casi in the car, then falling asleep again, he never had managed to phone her.

Casi gave a nervous smile before giving a quick nod. His mother's attention zeroed in on Luc. Besides narrowed eyes, her lips now joined in a thin pinched line. Here it comes…

"Lucas François Avery, whatever have you done to yourself?"

"It's nothing, Momma—"

"You have a bandage on your arm, and don't think for a minute I missed your limp. *Que vais-je faire de toi*, boy? You are hurt, injured. It is something. You should change jobs."

She and Bastien were always on his case. Maybe if he told her he was thinking about leaving the force, she'd stop nagging like Bas had done.

"You don't need to do anything to me," Luc replied, answering her question. "I'm fine, but I could use some food. We missed dinner." He gave her his charming smile. It had always worked for his poppa.

She shook her head but didn't quite hide her own smile. Placing Cat on the ground, she straightened and reached for Casi. Entwining her arm around Casi's upper arm, his momma led Casi to the porch steps. They left Luc to follow. Dismissed for now, but he knew the interrogation would commence after they ate. Thank God for Southern manners giving him the delay.

Feeling the weight of his gun at his back while he walked up the steps, his amusement fled. He hoped bringing Casi home would keep her safe and not further endanger her or his family. The need to protect her triggered his possessive inner caveman. If the Cyclops made an appearance, the killer wouldn't see justice. There'd be only another body for the gators. No one would hurt Casi again.

Chapter Twenty-Four

Food magically appeared as soon as she and Luc sat at the large, well-worn, kitchen table. It disappeared just as fast. Casi hadn't realized how hungry she'd been until the étouffée placed before her held the aroma of heaven. The seafood stew over rice was the best she'd ever tasted. With a chef in the family, not so surprising. She'd have to wait until morning to meet Jules Avery. Working at his restaurant tonight, he wouldn't return until late.

Casi dropped her napkin on the table while resisting the urge to groan at her too-full stomach. "Amazing food, Mrs. Avery. Thank you so much."

"Now, *chéri*, I told you to call me Adel. With my *belle-mere* here, there are too many Mrs. Avery's, it'll be confusing."

Across the table, Casi smiled at Faith Avery, Lucas's grandmother and Adelaide's mother-in-law. The two women had fussed over Casi as much as Luc. For the first time in a long while, she felt relaxed and welcomed. She should be jealous of Luc's family, but all she actually wanted was to be adopted. Since it was only Tuesday, and the anniversary party for his grandparents would be celebrated on Saturday, the extended family and friends weren't expected until near the end of the week. Luc's sisters and brother would arrive earlier. They could turn up at any time. Excited to meet his siblings, Casi wondered how different or the same they would be to the detective.

Clearing his throat, Luc stood slowly, no doubt favoring his wounded leg as he pushed his chair away from the table. He gave a tender smile to his mom and grandma. "Thank you, beautiful ladies, for feeding us. It's getting late. I'm sure Casi is tired, I know I am. I'll show her to the guest room and then call it a night myself."

He held out his hand, offering to help her stand, but before she could take it, his arm fell listlessly back to his side as he swore under his breath. Casi switched her attention from his hand to his face and caught him staring at his mother. Adelaide had locked gazes with her son, her face blank, but her brown eyes held a fierce glow. Luc sighed and sat back down, less gracefully than he had stood. Casi guessed he realized the time to pay the piper had arrived and gave up his game of *oh, it's nothing*.

"That's right, son. Did you think I'd turn a blind eye? I fed you, gave you time to get your head on straight." Adel pursed her lips. "This is the first time since you moved out on your own you've brought a woman with you. Not only did she drive your car, but you arrived injured and carrying a weapon."

Luc shook his head.

"Don't deny it."

"Momma, can't this wait until morning?" Luc pushed his fingers through his hair. His unconscious gesture of frustration and impatience, Casi had figured out.

His mother smirked. She probably knew Luc's tell as well. "Why of course, Lucas. You go on now." She made a shooing motion, dismissing her son, and faced Casi. "Would you like some more tea, *chéri*? We can talk while my stubborn son finds his way to dreamland."

Yikes! Casi didn't think she could say no, especially after both Adelaide and Faith had been so nice and gracious, but holy cow, Luc's mom scared her a bit. She began to understand where Luc got his talent for his job.

"Momma, really? Casi is a guest."

Adel pursed her lips as she laid down the law. "Lucas François Avery, I will have my answers one way or the other."

Mother and son glared at each other, waiting to see who would flinch first. They both obviously shared a stubborn streak a mile long. Casi wasn't surprised when Luc broke the staring contest first, by bowing his head to focus on his lap. Everything she had discerned about the detective pointed to him being an honorable man raised to respect others, particularly family. His mother's wishes would always come first. Luc probably had held only a slight hope of a temporary reprieve. His wish of skating away free had been a delusion. Until Casi met Luc's father, she would stick to her assumption Luc's personality derived solely from his mother. Now that he gave in, the only question would be how much of the truth he would tell her. With his strong protective streak, Casi would bet money it wouldn't be the whole truth.

She would have lost. Luc explained about the serial killer who was dropping bodies in New Orleans. Even explaining the killer stalked her. He told his mother how she needed a safe place to stay. He justified his injury on protecting her and that Vince and he thought it best to get Casi out of town.

"So here we are." He spread his arms wide. "The danger is minimum. There's no way the killer can know where we are or how to find us." Luc sighed. "You know I'd never deliberately place our family in harm's way. And if the long shot happens, there are way too many of us for the murderer to take on."

Silence filled the kitchen. Both Faith and Adelaide's faces were etched with concern and possibly fear with their furrowed brows and thinned lips. Casi had a hard time reading them, but she knew what happened next. It always did. Especially when she felt content and safe. Casi waited for the inevitable horrible outcome. Luc may have downplayed the danger, but she knew he couldn't be a hundred percent certain the Cyclops wouldn't find her. After all, the killer proved eerily accurate at tracking her. Would he even bother with her so far out of the city and his hunting grounds?

If she were the Avery family, she'd protest Casi being there, especially during what was supposed to be a joyous occasion. She clenched her hands under the table in a white-knuckle grip, waiting for the warm welcome to disappear and be told to vacate immediately—to have the welcome mat torn from beneath her feet and the ugly looks and hatred swing her way. The meal she enjoyed morphed into a nauseous lump inside her, threatening to make a reappearance. She swallowed the bile down, wishing she'd never let Avery and Tate make decisions for her, to place her trust in them. Casi knew better. Everyone always let her down.

Adelaide stood and walked to her. She braced

herself for the hatred and banishment. It would feel doubly worse after being so warmly greeted and made to feel at home. Maybe they would at least let her spend the night because she wasn't sure how much longer she'd be able to stay awake. It had been another hellish day—her only kind lately. But she wouldn't be surprised if there were no reprieve—it's just how her life rolled.

"My poor, dear girl." Adel clasped Casi's shoulder in a gentle grip, surprising her. "I don't know how you're not a cowering wreck. I'd be a lump of senseless goo. You are so courageous and strong." Luc's mom stared straight into her eyes. "Never you fear. *Tue es en sécurité*." Seeing Casi's wide-eyed confusion, Adel translated while patting her shoulder. "You are safe, *chéri*. No harm will come to you while you're with our family."

Shock shot straight through her body. Casi felt dizzy. Speechless. She wasn't going to be tossed out? Abandoned? They wanted her here? A warm hand landed on her thigh and gave a gentle squeeze, drawing her attention.

"Breathe, Casi. Please. You're okay." She inhaled sharply, not realizing she had been holding her breath, and closed her eyes as Luc continued to encourage her. "That's right, *cher*. You're among friends. You're not alone anymore."

She shot her gaze to him, reading his concern in his eyes. Turning away, Casi saw the same expression on both his mother and grandmother.

Adelaide patted her shoulder before removing her hand. "That's right, sweetheart. Lucas speaks the truth. We're happy to have you stay as long as you need." She gave her a kind smile. “Even after things settle down, you’re welcome. You have a place here as long as you like. Whatever you need to get back on your feet.”

For the first time, Faith entered the conversation, her liquid Cajun accent filling the room, stronger than her daughter-in-law’s or Luc’s. “Most definitely. Besides, you can’t leave, I will need help with the beignets tomorrow. The rest of my grandchildren will arrive, and they will demand my beignets. They are a devouring horde.”

Luc snickered. “That we are, Grandmamma.”

“See? You must help me.” Faith gifted her with a grin.

Casi blinked away the tears filling her eyes. She wouldn’t cry. “I…I don’t know how to-to make beignets. Actually, I don’t know how to cook at all, really.”

“Don’t you worry, Casi. I will teach you.”

She quickly wiped away the single escaping tear, hoping no one noticed, but by everyone’s sympathetic expressions, it hadn’t been missed. Casi didn’t know what to do or how to feel. Nothing went the way it should have. How can they open their arms to a stranger? Make her feel welcomed? Ignore the danger she represented? Her heart galloped. Panicked, Casi leaped to her feet, sending the chair in a shrieking scrape behind her. Needing to escape, she tried to bolt, but instead of running, the blood rushed from her head, and she swayed on her feet as her vision tunneled. Before she could collapse, Luc appeared by her side, a strong arm wrapped around her waist, keeping her upright.

“Whoa there, darlin’. Everything is all right. Easy,

cher. You're exhausted. You shouldn't be rushing around."

Casi closed her eyes. Shutting everything out. Overwhelmed by her emotions, she felt like hiding, but knew she couldn't.

Once again, the Avery family came to her rescue. Adelaide closed in, even as her son still had his arm wrapped around her. Luc's mother pressed her palm against Casi's cheek.

"It will be all right. You're tired. I'll show you to your room and get you settled in. Everything you need is inside. And before you protest, we have more than enough room for you even with the celebration." Adel removed her hand, and Casi felt its absence to her bones. It had taken all her willpower not to lean into the compassionate gesture. "You just take care of yourself tonight. Everything will be so much better in the morning. Sleep in as long as you like."

Adelaide clasped Casi's hand, tugging her away from her son, but Luc didn't let go of his hold, keeping them in place. His mother frowned. "You're injured. Let me help Casi, and then I'll get on to you."

Casi witnessed another staring match between mother and son. It surprised her when Adelaide backed off first, dropping Casi's hand and stepped aside with a tiny smile.

Luc shifted her in his grip, still side by side, but facing away from the kitchen. "I've got you, *cher*. Come now, let's get you to bed."

Casi followed as he guided her along, even leaning more of her weight on him. Numb, possibly in shock, since she felt like a disembodied spirit floating along. Luc led her up a wide staircase. At the top, he turned left and went down a long hallway before stopping in front of an open door at the end of the hall.

"Here we are." Luc walked her into the room. "See, your duffle is even here. It was meant to be."

He turned, facing her, and gripped her hips with both his warm hands keeping the chill racing inside her at bay.

"You're going to be okay, darlin'. I promise." He stared deep into her eyes. "The bathroom is through the door on the right and should have everything you need, so you can climb into bed and get some much-needed rest." He studied her intently. "Do you need my help? Or do you think you're steady enough to manage on your own?"

Casi blinked. "I'm fine. I can manage."

She needed to be alone. She had to regroup and repair the walls that Luc breeched, allowing even his family to sneak in.

He nodded and slowly released her. "Okay. If you need anything, or you have another nightmare and want to be reassured you're safe, I'm right across the hall. Don't hesitate. Come right in. No matter what time, day or night, if you feel you need me, you come and find me. All right?"

She took a deep breath and nodded.

"*Fais de beaux rêves, cher.*" He leaned forward and pressed a gentle kiss to her forehead. "No more unpleasant dreams."

Luc took a step back, then walked past her. She glanced over her shoulder and watched him enter his room. Their gazes locked, and then he gave her a new smile for her collection—pure, sweet, and caring—before quietly closing his door.

With a tired frown, she closed her own door and pressed her forehead against the wood. What game was he playing? She highly doubted the detective held potential witnesses in his arms or gave them innocent kisses, or a catalog of smiles. Confusion swept through her. Too involved. Needing to step away and distance herself not only from Luc but also his family, Casi straightened and stiffened her spine. She'd learned the hard lessons on where to place her trust—only in herself. She couldn't afford to let anyone in. They either proved themselves false or died, like Mason. Either way, alone was good. Better to build her walls and stay secluded than risk the crushing blows bound to come.

As she paced deeper into the room, a small, tiny idea niggling in the back of her mind refused to be extinguished. What if she could trust him? What if she could actually have more?

Chapter Twenty-Five

Luc jerked awake. Taking half a second to appraise his surroundings, he sat up in bed, wondering what had abruptly yanked him from sleep. A muffled shout filtered through his closed door had him tossing aside the sheet. He jumped to his feet and wobbled when his full weight landed on his injured leg. Pain shot through his thigh. Right, he had to remember to move more carefully.

Glad he wasn't naked but clad in a pair of old sweat shorts and a faded T-shirt since he was staying at his parents' house, Luc grabbed his gun off the nightstand. He strode toward the door while ignoring the stinging ache from his thigh. His adrenaline pumped through his veins, sweeping away the last dregs of sleep.

Luc wrenched open his bedroom door and paused with his gun pointed down at his side as he listened. A shout followed by a groan from behind Casi's door drew him across the hall in two steps. Not an intruder attacking, but another damn nightmare. He lightly tapped on her door.

"Casi? You al' right?"

No answer except another deep moan. Screw this. He wasn't about to leave her trapped inside her mind. Luc eased open the door, stepped through, and shut it quietly behind him. Since everyone slept on the opposite side of the house at the moment, he doubted his family would wake for anything louder than a piercing scream.

As his eyes adjusted to the moonlight filtering through the sheer curtains, he spotted Casi tossing and turning on the bed. The bedcovers were flung to the floor, leaving only a single sheet twisted low around her ankles, revealing her long legs, tight stretchy cotton shorts, and her faded Jack's Surf Shop T-shirt.

"Nooooo." Her drawn-out protest more of a whimper than a word.

Enough already. He placed his gun on the tall dresser next to the door before padding on bare feet across the wooden floor. Luc wondered how he'd wake her without scaring her more. He didn't want to add to her troubles.

Was she having another premonition? Or trapped in her past? Unacceptable choices either way. He stopped beside the bed.

"Casi. Wake up. You're having a nightmare."

She ignored his order, continuing with her restlessness and mumbled vocalizations. Luc sat on the edge of the bed, causing the mattress to dip with his added weight. Gently, he placed a hand on her knee.

"Casi. Come on, darlin', wake up." He gave a light squeeze.

She bolted upright, flinging her arms forward in a shoving motion he barely avoided. Somehow, he managed to keep his seat on the bed.

"Casi?"

Blinking a few times, her breathing still rapid but at least the faraway look in her eyes disappeared as she focused on the here and now.

"Luc?"

"Yeah, *cher*, I'm here. Are you al' right? You were having a nightmare."

He thought he'd get her standard *I'm fine* answer, but when she shook her head and wrapped her arms tightly around her middle as if to hold herself together, surprise shook him. Even in the darkness, he could see her trembling. *Damn.* He couldn't leave her like this.

"Ah, darlin'. Is it okay if I hold you?"

He scooted closer when she nodded. She chewed her lower lip and kept her eyes tightly clenched shut, obviously trying hard not to fall apart. Whatever dream he'd broken her out of, it still weighed on her. He slipped in behind her, leaning against the headboard as he gathered her into his arms. With one hand, he gently pressed her head to his chest, tucking her beneath his chin before dropping the same hand to her shoulder in a light hold. His other hand landed on her hip where he softly stroked, hoping the repetitive motion would be soothing.

Casi leaned into him, giving over all her weight. Though inappropriate, he recognized she felt good in his arms, like she belonged there. The ginger and honey scent from her hair teased his nose as he inhaled and relaxed. Her trembling faded away, and she gave a quiet sigh.

"Feeling better?" Casi nodded again. "Want to talk about it? Lessen its hold on you?"

"Not really," her mumbled words barely reached his ears. "Sometimes I think I'll never be normal again."

With the arm draped across her, he gave a gentle squeezing hug. "Normal can be overrated. Were you dreaming of your assault?"

"Yes." Her voice cracked, and she tensed. She inhaled deeply, held the breath, then deliberately exhaled and relaxed back into his embrace.

"I thought I told you no more nightmares," he teased, hoping to draw out a smile or at least distract her. She was at her best when riled and arguing with him.

"Your orders didn't take. Shocking, I know," she whispered back at him.

"Well, there you go. Always refusing to take my suggestions."

"You mean commands."

"Can't help I'm a natural-born leader."

A tiny snort escaped her before she replied. "Leader? I saw you collapse like a cheap lawn chair with one look from your mom. I don't think so, Detective."

He smiled. There she was. The strong woman he had gotten to know and admire. Amazing how fast Casi could bounce back.

"Feeling better, now? Think you can get some more sleep?" He loosened his hold reluctantly, knowing he should get back to his room so she could rest.

Before he could release his embrace Casi gripped the arm lying across her chest with both hands, freezing him in place.

"Don't go," she whispered.

"Casi—"

"Please? I feel safer with you here." He felt her swallow hard. "I'm tired of being afraid."

He shouldn't stay. It wasn't right. In his mind's eye, he could visualize Vince's disapproving stare. She was a witness. He should keep it professional. But how could he ignore her soft plea? *Shit*. Luc already crossed a line, all too aware of his own growing attraction for her. He liked her. Maybe more than liked her? He really should go.

"Please, Luc."

She sensed his faltering. Screw nobility. How could he deny her when she'd been through so much? He would stay until she fell asleep and then go back to his room. No harm, no foul, and he'd get to keep her in his arms for a tiny bit longer.

"Okay, *cher*. Rest your head back down and close your eyes." He pressed his hand into her soft silky hair to tuck her under his chin once more. "I'm here, and nothing will get to you. Not even your night terrors. I've got you."

"Thank you."

"You're welcome." He pressed a kiss to her hair before he realized he burnt another bridge in his professionalism. He had to stop kissing her, he'd done it twice now.

Luc relaxed as Casi went boneless against him. As predicted, it didn't take long for her breathing to even out as she fell into an exhausted sleep. He yawned, promising himself he'd stay only a short while longer, making sure she stayed asleep. What he hadn't counted on was his own fatigue. Eyelids heavy, he closed them, letting them rest for a moment.

****

Casi stirred in his arms as the knock on the door dragged them both from their sleep. Luc blinked and watched the bedroom door crack open. He cringed, knowing there wasn't anything he could do to stop what was about to happen. Regardless of which family member entered, news would spread faster than beads in Mardi Gras, as to whose bed they had found him in. He'd never live it down. The matchmaking would be instantaneous as well as the incessant teasing.

He stifled a sigh when his eldest sister, Jolie, poked her head around the door.

"Casi, you awake?" Her eyes widened when she registered him in bed with Casi. "Oh, hey there." Grinning, she pushed the door wide open and stepped all the way into the room. Of course she did. Privacy between siblings didn't exist.

He sat up straighter and dropped his arms from around Casi as she, too, sat up and scooted away from him to the center of the bed. Still sitting so close, he easily read her discomfort.

"Don't you know it's ill-mannered to enter without permission, Jolly?" Luc used Jolie's nickname as he glared at her, which he knew wouldn't be enough to distract his sister, but he had to try for Casi's sake.

Jolie's grin morphed into a smirk. "I was concerned. It's almost noon. Besides, I come bearing gifts. Momma mentioned the dire need of clothes for Casi." She held up the bundle of garments as she walked to the bed. Placing them down on the corner, Jolie focused on Casi. "Hi. I'm Jolie."

"Um, hi?" Casi cleared her throat. "The tea shop owner, right?"

Jolie quirked an eyebrow as she switched her gaze back to him. "I see my brother has been sharing."

"Jolly," he growled. "Knock it off."

Luc tossed the sheet aside and scooted out of bed. His full weight landed on his left foot, sending a jagged pain rocketing through his thigh. He grimaced, realizing too late he had once again led with his injured leg. By the harsh inhale from his sister, his injuries were finally noticed.

"Lucas!" Jolie instantly appeared at his side. She grabbed his right arm still wearing a bandage while staring down at his left thigh where the bottom end of that dressing showed from beneath the edge of his shorts. "*C'est si mauvais? A quel point*?"

"It's not bad—"

"You should sit." Jolie pushed him back on the bed.

He stopped her by gripping her shoulders. "I'm fine. It's nothing." Her concerned gaze met his as he stared down at her. "Honest, Jolly. I'm okay."

Luc pulled her in for a hug, which she returned in kind, perhaps squeezing tighter and holding on longer than necessary. She finally released him, allowing him to take a step back. Time to make a graceful escape. He glanced at Casi, who slouched, practically hiding in the bed. Definitely time to give her some space to recoup.

"Don't let my sister harass you." Jolie grunted at his side, which he ignored. "I'm going…" He gestured out the open door across the hall to his room. "Yeah, well, um, see you downstairs." He couldn't meet his sister's gaze, let alone Casi's, as he grabbed his gun and left the room.

"I'll be just a moment. If you need something, Casi, just holler."

Crap. Jolie was following him. Quickly stepping into his room, he turned, shutting the door, but Jolie's foot shoved across the threshold stopped him. *Dammit*.

"Oh no you don't. We're having a little chat."

For a second, he contemplated muscling the door shut, since with his greater height and weight he'd succeed. He so didn't want this confrontation with his sister. They eyed each other across the entry.

Jolie quirked an eyebrow. "You taught me how to pick locks. One way or another, I'll be inside your room."

"Fine." He opened the door all the way and let his sister in before closing it behind him.

"Go sit down." Jolie ordered him just like an older sister.

He answered by crossing his arms against his chest and leaning on the door.

She glared at him. "Stubborn fool." Jolie started pacing. "Momma told me what's going on, and I have to agree with her. After you settle this case of yours, you need to quit the force."

Ugh. Was everyone jumping on Bastien's bandwagon? He could count on one hand the number of times he was wounded on the job. He loved his family, but they were overreacting.

"I'm fine, Jolie. How many times do I need to say it?"

"Fine isn't good enough." She waved her hand at him. "You were shot twice!"

Enough. He unclenched his arms and then tore off his arm bandage. Crumpling the cloth, he tossed it into the trash can next to his dresser. "A scratch. It wasn't even worthy of a Band-Aid, let alone that." He gestured to the scrunched-up field dressing in the trash. "Vince, the paranoid bastard, went overboard."

"Oh my God! Tell me you went to the hospital."

"There was no need—"

"You were shot. Of course there was a need, you ass!" Her voice rose to a loud whisper, as she tried not to shout, keeping their argument at least inside the room. "And what about your leg? No scratch there. I saw you. You grimaced. You're hurting."

He closed his eyes and counted to ten, hoping for patience. Luc didn't want to argue with her and especially didn't want to say something he couldn't take back. How in the world would he get through the rest of this week? His other two siblings were arriving today, and with his father and grandpapa already here but occupied last night, they would all need to weigh in on the matter. He would not have this conversation repeatedly.

"Lucky?" Luc blinked his eyes open at the nickname and studied her concerned expression.

"I'm sorry, okay?" Jolie sighed, walked to his side, and gave him a quick hug.

He exhaled loudly and nodded.

"We all worry. I know you're careful. Unlike certain members of our family, I get it. You live to serve and protect. You've locked away a lot of terrible people, making the world safer."

"Thanks, Jolly."

"Sometimes the family freaks out at the thought of losing you. You can't fault us for that. I love you."

"*Moi aussi je t'aime.*" He gathered his sister into his arms and held her. Scaring his family, making them worry, sucked. Luckily, it didn't happen often. He usually lived up to his nickname. "Truth be told," he murmured into her light brown hair so much like his own, "I'm leaning more to the protecting side instead of serving."

Jolie pulled back, stepping from his embrace. Surprise etched in her brown gaze. “You are?”

“Yeah, I am. Maybe it’s time to get out.”

“But what would you do?”

“Join my little brother’s rock band? Rock star has a certain ring to it, don’t you think?”

She snorted. “So not you. You’d perish if you couldn’t help others.”

“Probably right. I don’t know.” He pushed a hand through his hair. “Maybe I’ll go private. Recruit Vince and open my own security company.”

“Doesn’t sound any safer.” Jolie gave him a crooked smile.

He shrugged. At least he wouldn’t be working for assholes anymore, and he could choose what cases he took. He wouldn’t have to ask permission to do the right thing.

Jolie must have decided to let the current topic drop, knowing no simple solution existed. She looped her arm around his and dragged him to the bed where she had them both sitting in a flash. He cringed, knowing the prior conversation about his career was a cakewalk compared to the next.

“So Lucky, tell me about you and Casi…”

Yup. Who knew the discussion of quitting his job would be easier? At least she hadn’t asked about Vince…

Chapter Twenty-Six

Casi blew a fallen strand of hair from her messy bun off her face since both her hands were occupied kneading dough. She was sweating regardless of the ceiling fan spinning directly overhead. But she would not wimp out just because of the heat.

"So um, Faith, I've got a question."

Grandma Faith looked up from her own dough and smiled. "Yes, child?"

"I did a little Internet diving to prepare for this. All the recipes I read used evaporated milk. How come you use whole?" Curious, but she also needed—kneaded—a distraction from her sore muscles. Oh wow, now she thought in terrible puns.

"Because the Avery's bake in the proper way. You had the beignets from Du Monde?"

"Of course. You can't be in New Orleans without stopping at the Café."

"I'm sure you've had beignets from other shops, but they just don't taste the same or as good, *non*?"

"Yeah, now that you mention it, they don't."

Faith nodded. "When the French came to the territory in the eighteenth century, evaporated milk didn't exist. Whole milk from cows at room temperature was what they used. Therefore, we Avery's use whole milk."

"Okay, that's really cool. It's like a secret recipe."

"You're a sweet girl, *chéri*."

Casi warmed under the compliment and acceptance. She'd been nothing but welcome since stepping onto the Avery property. Though thoroughly embarrassed at being caught in bed with the detective by his older sister, she had waited for trouble to brew, expecting Jolie to be protective of Luc or even pissed. Neither happened. When Casi emerged from the bathroom after showering, she had discovered Jolie sitting on the bed. Jolie kept her company as Casi finished getting ready. Casi realized she liked Jolie and even loved the borrowed sundress she wore. It made her smile. The bright yellow cotton rested soft against her skin, and the chain of white daisies along the knee-length hem had a cool retro feel. A tiny bit large on her, but it made it even more comfortable.

"Now, Casi, we're done kneading."

She almost groaned in relief, rolling her tight shoulders as her hands left the dough.

"Look here." Faith gently shaped the dough into a ball, placed it in an oiled bowl which she then covered with plastic wrap. "Your turn."

Casi quickly and efficiently copied her, feeling a sense of pride when she sealed the wrap around the bowl.

"Now what?"

Adelaide entered the kitchen. "It's time for dinner!"

"Wait. What?" Confusion reigned inside her. Weren't they in the middle of making beignets? Besides, dinner needed food. She'd been in the kitchen with Grandma Faith and no one else had come in to prep supper.

"The dough needs to rise. It'll be another couple of hours before the next step." Faith assured her.

Casi placed her bowl of dough next to Faith's on an unused counter. Stepping to the side, she tried to stay out of the way. Jolie entered the kitchen next, followed by the youngest Avery, Marielle.

"All right, ladies, it's time to set the table." Adel clapped her hands to get the women moving.

"Momma," Marielle frowned. "Where are the boys? This isn't the 50s where the womenfolk stay barefoot in the kitchen and the men are in another room watching television."

Dinner dishes clattered as Adelaide handed a stack to Jolie. "Your brothers are helping your poppa. Since he knew your grandmamma was baking and the kitchen would be busy, he's bringing dinner home from the restaurant."

Jolie snorted. "It's not the fifties, it's the Stone Age! The men are out hunting and gathering."

Casi smiled at the easy teasing camaraderie amongst the women. If truthful to herself, her jealously started rising. She missed having close female friends. Most of her girlfriends abandoned Casi after her arrest and the others? She dismissed when she left California, being too hurt and mistrustful to put in the work to keep them.

"Why the frown, Casi?"

She glanced up at Adelaide's question, not realizing her dark thoughts had reached her face. "Sorry. Just lost in my thoughts, I guess."

"Well, none of that now. Come, we can use the help. The food should arrive shortly."

Casi nodded and joined the ladies in setting the

large table in the dining room. With nine people, the kitchen table suddenly was a little too small for the crowd. Excited to finally meet Luc's father and younger brother, she hoped to get more insight into the detective. Physically, she assumed Lucas took more after his mother in appearance. With her bright blonde hair and brown eyes, he appeared close with his dark blond hair and hazel eyes. Except for Jolie's hair in a shade matching Luc's, Jolie appeared a carbon copy of her mother's looks. Casi couldn't help or stop her interest in him—her mind kept going there.

Marielle, who looked nothing like her mother or older sister and brother, with her black hair and green eyes, sidled up to Casi with curiosity written all over her pretty face. "So is it true you're a psychic?"

"Um, what?"

"Luc mentioned you have a shop. Do you do Tarot? What about palms? Or since you're part Haitian, do you do the whole voodoo thing?"

The barrage of questions had Casi's mind whirling. Luc had spoken to his youngest sister about her? A slight smile curled up her lips.

"Did you bring your cards? Will you do a reading for me?"

"Now, Monkey," Adelaide admonished. "If you want an answer, you need to give her some air and not bombard her with questions. She's our guest, so quit bothering her."

"It's all right. I don't mind." Casi gazed at the charming girl at her side. "I have my cards, and I'd be happy to."

When Marielle gave a tiny squeal and clap of her hands in excitement, happiness flooded Casi, glad she said yes. In a small way, it would be payment for the Avery's hospitality. Though she had only her own insight and no real psychic powers, she still could be accurate. She might actually be able to help the youngest Avery solve a problem, boost up her self-esteem, or bring some joy into her life. It was the least she could do.

Casi had placed the last fork down when Adelaide looped her arm through hers and led her out of the dining room and into what she'd earlier learned was the sitting room. Though no plantation, Luc's family home wasn't a cottage either. More like a small manor, having lots of extra rooms that weren't bedrooms. The Avery's had made their money in petroleum, and the house became an heirloom handed down through the generations. She had discovered a music room, a library, a sunroom, and this room. Comfortably decorated with cozy chairs and couches, the room was appropriately named. After stopping in front of a loveseat, Adelaide sat, pulling Casi down alongside her.

"Sit, *chéri*. Let's visit before the food arrives."

Jolie and Marielle took separate chairs and settled in with expectant looks. Casi's stomach dropped. The time had finally arrived. The proverbial shoe would hit the floor. She sucked in a deep breath and held it, fighting off the disappointment. No. Wait. Often too quick to judge last night, she wouldn't make the same mistake now. Adelaide deserved the benefit of a doubt. She fought back her automatic negative reaction and tried to relax.

Adel placed a hand on Casi's knee and gave a gentle squeeze, causing her gaze to rise and meet Adelaide's. Filled with both warmth and concern, Luc's mom smiled. "Why so nervous? You were smiling only a moment ago."

She shook her head, not knowing what to say.

"I only want to get to know you better. Especially since my son has taken an interest in you."

Heat bloomed on her cheeks, and once again she was thankful for her darker complexion, which hid her blushes. Hopefully, no one would notice her embarrassment. "Um, no. Really, he hasn't. He's just doing his job."

Jolie snorted from her chair. "Is that what they call it? Wow, who knew the NOPD had such perks as sleeping with—"

"He didn't!" Casi jolted upright from her dejected slouch. "We didn't… I mean we haven't…"

Now Jolie laughed outright. "Lucky wasn't so lucky? He's losing his touch."

"Quit your teasing, Jolie," her mother admonished. "This poor *fille* has been through enough. She doesn't need more heaped upon her."

Oh. Dear. God. Did the entire household know Luc slept in her bed? It'd surprised Casi to wake up and find him still there. She had entirely expected him to have left after she had fallen asleep, but apparently, she hadn't counted on how exhausted the detective had actually been. Did the family think they were in *that* kind of relationship? No wonder she was about to get the third degree from his mother.

A couple pats on her knee drew Casi's attention back to Adelaide. "Sweetheart, I know you have nightmares, and Luc was only comforting you. I raised an honorable man."

Did Luc tell his mother *everything*? *All* the time?

Sometimes it was best not to overshare. She shot a glance at Jolie. Maybe he told his sister, and she then spread the news. Maybe having such a close-knit family wasn't such a great thing. At least the family knew they weren't having sex.

"Have you lived in New Orleans your whole life?"

So he hadn't spilled her entire life story to his family. What a relief. She still held some secrets.

"I was born there, but we moved to California when I was still in high school when my mother remarried."

"Your mother, she's Haitian, correct? It must be why you have such lovely skin."

"Um, thanks." Casi had a much lighter skin tone than her mother, since her father was white. In fact, when her mother had taken her to Haiti to visit her side of the family, her cousins had teased her. Only her maternal grandmother had made her feel truly welcomed and loved.

"I've always wanted to go to California." Marielle sighed. "I looked at universities there, but it's so far away. I'd miss my family too much. Do you miss living there?"

She didn't miss the scandal everyone seemed to know about, but the weather made her wistful. The perfect sunny day with ocean breezes felt like magic next to the sweltering humid air of New Orleans. "I do miss the Southern California weather. I can't say being able to wear the air in New Orleans is a selling point. However, it does feel more like home here."

"So," Adelaide drew Casi's attention away from her daughter. "What feelings do you have for my son? I can see his heart getting involved, and it is a mother's prerogative to be protective. If you're appealing to his romantic side to have his protection and don't care for him, know he'll always safeguard you. You don't have to play him. I won't have him hurt."

Casi's eyes widened, and she locked her jaw to keep her mouth from dropping open. Had she really asked her intentions regarding Luc? Oh. My. God! What was up with this family? Would she ever be able to figure them out? What the hell was she supposed to say?

"Um," Casi chewed on her lower lip. "I think you've got this all wrong. No offense, but Detective Avery isn't...um...isn't into me like that. As I said, he's just doing his job."

Adelaide gently smiled and shook her head. "I know my son, Casi. I've seen him with other women. You're the first he's brought home to stay—"

"But I'm not—"

"Hush now."

Casi sealed her lips at the soft admonishment, swallowing her protest. "Yes, you needed a place to stay and yes, he put you in the room across the hall from his and yes, I'm sure it was in order to be near you for your protection, but there's more. I have a mother's intuition. I've seen him with his dates, and there is definitely a deeper layer to his feelings. I can see it with my own eyes."

"Me as well," Jolie added her two cents. "It's a wonderful thing, Casi."

"I...I don't know what to say..." She glanced between mother and daughter. Were they right? Could Luc be as attracted to her as she was to him? Or was this weird physical tension between them only an illusion caused by the stress they were under? Why didn't she know the answer? She should, Casi had the degrees to ferret this stuff out.

And using him? She didn't think so. Her opinion meter held law enforcement in the gutter, so she didn't think she had manipulated Luc for protection. She actually ran from him. No. She wasn't bartering his affection. Somehow, he'd sneaked in behind her defenses, and she genuinely cared for him. Intelligent, charming, and naturally protective, the combination held tantalizingly attraction. Casi might agree with his mother's concern, except she'd also seen Luc's cynical, world-weary side and knew she held no power over him.

"You know, Momma," Marielle injected. "This isn't Victorian England where people have to express their *intentions*. Besides, have you seen how Casi looks at Luc when she thinks no one is watching? I think it's mutual."

Adelaide smiled and nodded, seeming quite pleased.

"Food's here!"

The shout from the front of the house saved her. Thank God. She dodged the bullet this time at least, but studying the expression on Adelaide's face as she rose from the couch, Casi wondered if Luc's mom thought to intervene with her matchmaking skills.

Chapter Twenty-Seven

Selene stepped over the threshold and to the side, studying the room. She'd arrived definitely overdressed for the dive bar she'd entered. Her black pencil skirt was too long, and her decorative blouse screamed businesswoman, but at least her four-inch heels fit right in. The Fleur-de-lis didn't live up to its exotic name.

"You a model or something?" A man holding a beer and leaning on the wall next to Selene eyed her in a slow perusal. She knew what he leered at as he scanned her from the points of her thousand-dollar heels, up her long legs over her generous curves, to her heart-shaped face framed by deep red hair cut in a harsh asymmetrical bob. "Kind of high class for the Loo, but what the hell. Can I buy you a drink?"

The Loo. How appropriate. A perfect name for this bar. Selene perused the man—somewhat handsome but held no innate magic or psychic ability. Pity, simply a normal lowly human.

"No, thank you. However, you could answer a question for me." She allowed a sultry smile to show on her lips. A smile that trapped both men and women alike. No need to ensnare him with her magic, when her physical attributes were more than adequate to get her answers.

"Shame about the drink, but sure, fire away, hot stuff."

"Is Neutral Ground performing tonight?"

He took a sip of beer. "Nope."

Damn. She'd hoped to find the detective through his brother. Word around the precinct said Avery hung out here all the time to support his brother's band. Irritation flooded her veins along with a bite of anger. "Pity. Do you know when they'll play next?"

"No idea, but you might ask at the bar." He gestured to the large rectangular bar with seating on all four sides situated in the middle of the room. "They probably know the schedule."

"I will." She sauntered away and smiled as she felt the man's gaze on her ass. Yes, he can look, but he'd never be allowed to touch. Finding an open spot at the sizeable bar, Selene sidled up to the well-worn wood, and a rush of pure power struck her. She gasped and searched the room. The energy exploding was so strong, she wanted to feast on its power. Its strength when consumed would last her for years

A bartender approached, and her eyes widened as her heart sped up. Oh yes, she'd found the source of all the delicious energy. Two thoughts crossed her mind. First, the power emanated from the Archangel Gabriel, who wore a human disguise, and second, thank the stars she didn't have his horn on her person. He halted directly in front of her with only the bar top separating them.

He crossed his arms against his wide chest and glared.

"Fancy meeting you here," she greeted. "Slumming, are you?"

"I could say the same to you. Why are you here? I won't allow you to hunt inside this abode."

If anyone could stop her, he could or a member of his family. Too bad he had rules in which he had to abide. Even if she killed a person directly in front of him, his hands were tied. His Father's rule about free will sucked for him. She hadn't spoken with Gabriel in centuries. Perhaps it was time to have some fun and cross swords with him. Well, verbal ones at least.

"I heard your precious horn went missing." She smiled.

His eyes narrowed. "You would know, Selene."

"Who, me?" She tried for innocent but knew she didn't achieve it when her smile morphed into a grin.

"The horn will be your downfall."

"Kind of hard when you don't have it now, isn't it?"

"Perhaps that's why I let you steal it." He smirked.

"You didn't—" Selene stopped herself. No way had he set her up. She searched for centuries to find and take the powerful artifact. The horn had been hidden in a small church in a remote section of the Scottish Highlands. She'd finally discovered the relic in the late 1700s and stolen it away. Gabriel had nothing to do with her theft. He wanted to get a rise out of her or make her doubt. It would not work. Besides, if he knew she had stolen his horn, why hadn't he done anything about it? He had plenty of time since her theft to the twenty-first century. What kind of game was he playing? She threw her shoulders back and tilted her chin up.

Analyzing him, Selene finally realized no one paid any attention to them, and the loud noise of the crowded bar had disappeared. They were enclosed in a private bubble. No doubt in fear of what she might say.

However he accomplished it, the magic must be something subtle to distract the humans because she sensed nothing, but then again, he radiated so much power would she even notice? After all, it had taken her a bit to notice their privacy.

"Answer me this." He drew her attention out of her thoughts. "Why do you hunt?"

"Why do you care?"

"You're killing innocent humans, Selene."

She shrugged. "A girl has to live. Besides, humans are far from innocent. Have you seen what they've done to the planet?" Let him chew on that.

Humans were a plague. She was doing the world a favor by culling the herd. Besides, the ones she harvested from were worse than ordinary humans. They had a potential to rise above their status, elevate themselves from the rest of the sheep, to be more with their magic and psychic abilities. Losers, the lot of them. They could be so much more, do so much more, yet most who were awakened hid or denied their abilities. And don't get her started on the ones who had the potential and couldn't unlock it. Useless. They were worse than sheep. People killed and ate sheep, so why couldn't she help herself to some glands? Seriously, Selene couldn't see the problem and didn't understand why the Archangel made such a fuss.

"You don't have to hunt," Gabriel replied, completely ignoring the whole not innocent thing.

"Of course I do. I can't walk around with wings. You may be able to hide yours, but mine take more effort."

"Go to a witch and pay for a charm."

Witches. They always thought themselves so high

and mighty when they were only tricked up humans. Though at least they embraced their power. Besides, she'd rather hunt humans for their glands rather than give witches money. "Why? When I can DIY and have the satisfaction of accomplishment."

He shook his head and glared at her. "Mark me, demon. Your time is coming." Gabriel smiled again. "Your expiration date is fast approaching. Now get out of my bar."

The magic privacy bubble popped, and noise crashed over her. Damn the feathered nuisance. He was taunting her, trying to make her doubt herself. She glared as he dropped his arms, turned his back to her, and returned to filling drink orders.

Selene spun on her heels and marched out of the bar. With Gabriel working inside, she wouldn't be able to approach Neutral Ground and ensnare the detective's brother, forcing him to take her to Avery. She needed the horn safely back in her control. Her anger rose. The angel would not best her. His false judgment rankled. He didn't like her hunting? Screw him.

When safely out of sight, Selene let her wings unfurl, punching from her skin, tearing the back of her blouse, and launched herself silently into the night. Rising quickly, the sharp-edged black feathers were hidden in the darkness as she flew to the river. She reached the banks of the Mississippi and coasted high above, drifting on air currents as she searched. The homeless abounded here, and one of them would have the touch of magic she needed.

Not that she hated her wings. She loved them. They were deadly, wicked, and beautiful. But to blend with the sheep, she had to disguise herself as the human prey she hunted. In fact, she would relish the moment she could expose her true self. Selene had a magnificent true form. Smiling, she would do so tonight and then go back to hiding herself, constrained, a bit disappointed, but gloating in the fact even the mighty Archangel Gabriel himself had to appear normal by wearing a human facsimile. She did what she needed to survive.

The familiar tingles swept across her skin. Finally. The perfect location. Isolated, remote, and no witnesses. Like a hawk, she folded her wings and plunged downward. At the last second, to break her descent, she snapped out her wings. Floating the last few feet, she landed in front of her newest victim.

Stunned, the weathered Hispanic man froze, eyes wide. Before he could gather his wits and run, Selene unleashed her magic. "*Stay. No screaming out loud but be happy to do so internally.*"

She caressed a finger down his chest. Usually she tortured her captive prey to flavor the gland. Fear with a dash of adrenaline—her favorite spices. Opening her mouth, she released her fangs, revealing them in all their wicked glory, as her fingers sharpened into claws. Smiling pleasantly, the smell of fear wafted from him.

"I can't lie. This will hurt."

Selene struck. Her razored finger punctured through his right eyeball, rupturing it. His mouth opened in a silent scream. She dug her way through his eye socket and clawed into his brain. He collapsed. Catching and holding him in her free arm, she held him upright as she tunneled through the brain and reached the pineal gland. With her sharp nail, she severed the gland free and plucked it out.

She dropped the dead body before popping the

gland into her mouth. Chewing, she moaned in pleasure and swallowed her tasty morsel. Power flooded her, energizing and invigorating. She snapped open her wings and launched into the sky, grinning. Gabriel may have his threats and his plans, but Selene would win their war.

****

Luc grimaced. “Jolly, please stop.”

His sister lived up to her nickname and laughed at him. “Oh no I won’t.” From across the table, Jolie focused back on a smiling Casi. “So he dove off the pier and started swimming.”

“How old was he?” Casi’s eyes were actually sparkling. A whole new side of her. No matter how much his family embarrassed him, Luc enjoyed seeing her happy.

“Ten.” His momma tossed in.

“And the girl?”

“I think Marla was around sixteen, maybe seventeen,” Jolie continued. “So where was I…Lucky had an adorable crush on her, and when he saw her sailboat flip over, he ran to the rescue, well, swam to the rescue.”

Luc felt his cheeks heating. Yes, his mortification continued inevitably, like a boulder rolling downhill. His family had to tell one of the most humiliating stories of his life.

“He reached her and tried to help her swim back to the shore. Only, Marla just stared at him like he’s a loon, especially after he said he was afraid she might drown.” Jolie sipped her coffee. “She told him she’s a lifeguard and was drown proof. Taking the hit in stride, Lucky offered to help right the sailboat.”

Luc bowed his head, suddenly intensely interested in his own coffee because the reveal of the punch line had arrived.

"Instead of helping, he gets tangled in the lines, trapped underwater, and the girl ends up saving *him* and swimming his half-drowned body back to shore."

"Oh no! Really?" Casi's concerned yet curious exclamation drew his gaze.

"Oh yes." Jolie laughed along with the rest of his traitorous family.

"Lucas," his poppa called from the kitchen counter where he dusted powdered sugar over the fresh-out-of-the-deep-fryer beignets. "Come get this plate."

He stood and grabbed the plate of beignets, bringing them to the table. With all his siblings, his mother, grandparents, and Casi crammed around the kitchen table, there wasn't any spare room, but no one seemed to mind. They had moved from the dining room after dinner so they could be as close as possible to the fresh, piping hot beignets. Devouring horde, indeed. Every Avery knew a plate of the tasty treats would never make it out of the kitchen, because whoever fetched the plate would stop and eat. So they all came to the source.

"Mr. Avery, these are amazing," Casi complimented.

"It's Jules," his poppa corrected while dropping more dough into the hot oil. "We don't stand on ceremony in this family. And I do believe you can also thank yourself. I heard some of this dough is yours." He winked at her.

A shy smile lit her face. "So I have to ask," Casi glanced around the table. "What's with the nicknames?"

His grandpapa took the question. "I don't remember how it all started, but somehow they all got one."

"So Jolie is Jolly." Casi turned her smile on him after acknowledging his sister. "And Luc is Lucky, but what are the rest?"

Bastien piped up. "I'm Batty, and this one here"—he pointed to Marielle—"is Monkey."

"Okay, I get Jolly and Lucky, but Batty? Monkey?"

Luc jumped in, hoping to stop the embarrassing childhood tales and deflect it to his brother. "Mare has always been our little monkey since birth." He tugged Marielle's hair. "And Bas earned his from the crazy stuff he got into while growing up. All his schemes led to trouble, including his latest." He grinned at his brother.

Casi gave Bastien a raised eyebrow in question, earning her a devilish grin from his younger brother.

"Rock star." He pointed to himself.

"That's right, you're in a band."

"I am the band." Bas smirked.

"Ego much, little brother? I'll be sure to tell the rest of the band what you said."

"You wouldn't. Besides, everyone knows the front man is the draw. Plus, it's my turn to share another Lucky tale."

Luc glared at him and tried to figure out what to threaten him with to keep his silence when his momma interrupted.

"Bastien, be nice." Adelaide poked his brother in the arm. "I'm sure you can find a less embarrassing tale than the drowning vacation mishap."

"Momma, you take all the fun away." Bastien tapped a finger to his nose in thought. "Okay, I got it. Luc and a bunch of other boys made the Varsity football team in high school."

Luc stifled his groan. Of course his brother would share the pepper story, but at least it put him in a better light than the idiot boat debacle.

"There used to be a hazing ritual for new members, I don't think they do it anymore, but they did back then. Anyway, each of the guys were assigned/challenged to eat something disgusting."

"Yours?" Casi asked him directly.

"Dead grasshoppers."

"Ewww, gross."

"Cooked right, they can be tasty," his poppa replied from his beignet post.

Spoken like a true chef, Luc thought. "It definitely was one of the easier challenges."

"So did you? What did they taste like?"

"Oh, but he didn't, did you, Lucky?" Bas continued to smirk. "You see, one of the guys had to eat a Ghost Pepper. You know what a Ghost Pepper is, darlin'?"

Casi shook her head.

"At the time," his brother continued, "It was the hottest chili pepper in the world. Seriously hot, like eat your guts out hot."

"Oh no…"

"Oh yes." Bas rubbed his hands together in delight. "Poor, clueless kid. Luc took pity and swapped. He ate the pepper and then ran for the nearest water fountain." Bastien shot him a gleeful look. "Just when he arrived at the fountain, the door next to the bubbler opened, blocking his way, but by then it was too late. He hurls, full on projectile vomit right on the person who stepped through the door."

"Oh God, who was it?" Casi leaned forward, on the edge of her seat.

"The cute cheerleader he wanted to ask to prom."

Casi's hand flew up, covering her mouth, but it did nothing to hide her laughter. Luc shrugged. It had been horrible at the time, but in hindsight, pretty funny. He didn't regret taking the Ghost Pepper hit for Todd Greenberg. There were definitely other stories Bas could have told but didn't. Thank God his momma had stepped up for him.

His poppa placed the last plate of hot beignets on the table, causing Casi to groan.

"I'm so full. I can't possibly eat another," she complained.

"Yay! More for me!" Marielle grabbed the plate, pulling it closer to her, only to get in a tug-of-war with Bastien.

"It's a lovely night," his poppa stated, as he stood next to Luc. "Why don't you take Casi for a walk?"

He appreciated the suggestion. More alone time with Casi would get him away from his meddling family, which he would be so happy to do. All day he couldn't escape his family's worry over his leg. They fussed over him, wanting him to sit and not move, keep it elevated, ice it. He needed some privacy, but if Casi was interested in joining him, he wouldn't complain.

"Perfect," his momma chimed in. "There's nothing like a pleasant walk after eating. Go on now."

Luc held in his smile. Irony, much? Their concern for his leg had now completely disappeared. They actually *wanted* him walking around. Could his parents be any more obvious in their matchmaking? Without another thought, he stood and held out his hand for Casi.

"Come, *cher*. Let me show you the bayou at night."

Everyone smiled around the table when Casi took his offered hand and stood. He turned his back on his family and guided her to the kitchen door. He wondered what Casi thought of his family, what she thought of him? It appeared she was enjoying herself. He hadn't seen her smile and laugh this much since he'd met her, for obvious reasons. It looked good on her. Better than good. He grew tired of fighting his feelings for her. Add in the magic of a moonlit bayou, and he might lose his battle.

Chapter Twenty-Eight

Casi hid her smile. Luc, probably excited to ditch his family so no more stories could be told about him, quickened his pace—injured leg or not. He guided her down the steps of the wrap-around porch and into the backyard before the screen door even banged shut behind them. He set their path across a sprawling lawn, which would be the site of his grandparents' fiftieth wedding anniversary party. A small platform off to the side for a makeshift stage and several huge unassembled pop-ups in case of rain or needed shade were already laid out.

"Sorry about that. My family means well. If you don't want to go for a walk, all you have to do is say so."

Casi pulled her attention away from the yard and focused on the man walking beside her. "I don't mind. It's fine. But shouldn't you be resting?" She glanced at his thigh.

A growl escaped him. "I have rested. All day. I'm sick of resting."

She laughed. "They did hover all over you this afternoon. Your family is amazing, and it's obvious how much they love you." A wistful sigh escaped. Envy filled her, even though she'd been here less than forty-eight hours. Did he realize how fortunate he was? How her life would have been so different if anyone in her family gave just a quarter of what Luc's family gave to him in love. His family emphasized everything missing in her life, everything she'd never have.

Luc's chuckle broke the loop racing through her mind. "*Famille. Que peut-on faire*?"

"I'm guessing you just said something about your family? Hopefully nothing disparaging. You do know how lucky you are, right?"

His smile lit up the night. "*Sans doute*."

Her nose crinkled, and she pursed her lips at not understanding what he'd said. Casi definitely sided with Tate on the annoying factor.

He took pity on her and translated. "Without a doubt, I know how lucky I am. After all, it's my nickname." Dropping his hand from the small of her back, he stopped walking and faced her. "I said, 'family, what can you do?' I love them, but they can be intrusive and apparently obvious in their matchmaking. I'm sorry. I hope they didn't embarrass you."

"Not really. But I did have to endure the *what are your intentions with my son* conversation before you returned with dinner."

"Please tell me you're teasing, and my momma didn't interrogate you." Luc huffed out, his annoyance threaded through his words.

"Not just your mother, but your sisters were there as well."

"*Merde*. I can't believe they ganged up on you. I'm so sorry. I'll speak to them."

"Don't bother. Marielle actually defended me, and Jolie was supportive. It's fine. It's best to let it go."

Luc glanced at her frowning. "If you say so."

"So are you sure you should be out here walking? I

don't want to get on Detective Tate's bad side if I failed to take care of you." She studied him. He hadn't been limping when he led her outside, but still it's been such a short time since his injury. Luc needed to heal, but by his stubborn expression, he wasn't going into the house, even if she tried luring him back inside by going there herself.

"I'm good." He took a deep breath and exhaled. "Come see."

His hand went to her lower back again and continued to guide her until he stopped her at the far edge of the lawn carved from the encroaching bayou. Far enough from the house, the intermittent beams of moonlight, escaping from the fast-moving clouds above, lit their way. Directly in front of them, a small stagnant stream about ten feet wide sluggishly flowed. The green water with algae and lumps of duckweed floating on the surface gave way to clumps of cattails before finding solid ground. Cypress trees abounded with moss-covered trunks interspersed with swamp rose mallow. The night air, thick and damp with a barely-there breeze, surrounded her with conflicting scents of green growing things and dank decay. A mist hovered low to the ground as an occasional frog croaked, and small water splashes broke the silence.

"It's beautiful," Casi whispered, afraid to break the atmosphere. "In its own creepy horror way. I keep expecting a giant alligator to attack or swamp gas to form into a ghost and haul us to the underworld."

"Ah, you're not too far off."

"What?" Her heart rate accelerated. "Joking! I don't need any more ghosts in my life other than Mason. And I certainly don't need to be eaten by a gator."

"I'm offended, Casi. Don't you think I'd protect you?"

"Ha. Ha. Maybe from serial killers, but from the supernatural? How can anyone safeguard themselves from that?"

"I'm Cajun, *cher*. Magic is in our veins."

"Hmmpf."

He chuckled again and then quieted as they stood side by side in companionable silence, staring into the swamp.

"There!" Luc whispered and pointed.

"What…"

"The light." He leaned into her as he wrapped an arm around her shoulders, cozying her into his side. He lifted his other so she could sight down his arm.

She gasped. A light. A vivid globe, bright and glowing against the night's darkness, wove through the trees. It floated, blinking in and out as it ducked behind the cypress trunks and plants low to the ground.

"*Fifolet*," Luc intimately whispered into her ear, making her shiver despite the warmth of the night.

"Fee fo lay?" Casi whispered back.

Still wrapped in his arm, he stood so close his breath heated her ear as the liquid cadence of his accent enveloped her.

"A swamp fairy. In Cajun folklore, the *fifolet* are magic beings appearing as a bright light." He leaned in closer. "They misdirect and disorient any who try to follow."

The mesmerizing light continued to dance in the distance. She could well understand being led astray when lost in the dark bayou. The light would be a means to salvation.

"Like a wil-o'-wisp?"

"*Non, cher,*" his voice dropped lower and softer. "Those are European. Our bayou faeries are much more dangerous. Evil."

"*Yoooowl.*"

The loud screech beside her made Casi leap at Luc. She wrapped herself around him as his arms embraced her, holding her tight. The horrible sound didn't repeat, but something brushed against her bare legs. Yelping, she grabbed his shoulders, jumped up, and wrapped her legs around Luc's hips, locking her ankles to keep from falling to the ground.

Her heart raced. Luc should be running. Or shouting. She leaned back, wildly looking around, seeing nothing, not even the swamp fairy. Suddenly, she realized Luc was laughing as he held her with one arm braced under her bottom and the other wrapped around her shoulders.

"Are you laughing at me?"

He choked back a snicker. "More of a city girl, *cher*?"

"You *are* laughing at me."

"Maybe a little." His charming smile came out to play. He broke his gaze, looking past her. "Catastrophe, go on now. You're cruel, taking advantage of our city, *fille*."

Her eyes widen, and she looked over her shoulder and down. Sure enough, Cat sat beside them, regally upright, her bushy tail curled around her. And if a feline could smirk, Casi swore Cat did.

"Shoo, you troublemaker," Luc ordered. "You know you're not allowed outside. You'll get yourself eaten."

Cat yawned and stretched. She gave one last aloof feline stare before she trotted away, crossing the lawn toward the house.

"Sorry I laughed. But you should have seen your expression."

She tore her gaze away from the retreating feline menace and locked gazes with Luc. "You had me all spooked out with your evil fairy and creepy swamp. What did you expect? Plus, there's nothing wrong with being a city girl."

Casi huffed, then stilled. They were so close—their noses were almost touching since she had jumped and wrapped herself around Luc. Her borrowed sundress had hiked up, baring a considerable length of thigh. Embarrassed, she sucked in her lower lip.

"Nothing wrong at all, *cher*. Not at all."

She had a feeling he wasn't talking about being a city girl. Frozen in their embrace, she swallowed hard as her heart rate sped up again.

"I suppose," Luc murmured, "Since the danger has passed, I should put you down."

He appeared reluctant. The hand on her shoulder leisurely skimmed her back, landing at her waist after a long moment. With a slow inhale then exhale, the arm supporting her from beneath unhurriedly moved so his hand gently grasped the other side of her waist.

She unhooked her ankles and let her legs drop, but his hands tightened and held her up, their bodies pressed close, gazes locked. With a slight huff, Luc gradually lowered her, sliding her down his hard body. When her feet touched the ground, it took him another long moment before he drew a single step back and lowered his hands from her body. He was still too close. They weren't actually touching, but it felt like they were.

Casi couldn't look away, couldn't move. Didn't want to. A half smile quirked up Luc's mouth, and he raised his hand. Slowly, as if afraid he might spook her, he carefully tucked a loose strand of hair behind her ear before brushing the skin on the side of her face. He lifted his finger, and she spotted the light dusting of powdered sugar. A leftover from eating beignets.

Entranced, she couldn't look away as he brought his finger to his mouth. His tongue darted out and licked. The sugar disappeared, and his hand dropped to his side, all the while he stared deeply into her gaze. Oh. My. God. Heat flashed through her, and all her muscles tingled. Her gaze dropped to his mouth as her own tongue darted out to lick her suddenly dry lips. Her eyes widen as she tore her gaze from his mouth and stared into his eyes with surprise. She accidently gave him the universal sign of *go ahead.* Would he kiss her? Apparently so. She swallowed hard as Luc leisurely leaned in and pressed his lips to hers. Soft and warm, his kiss gentle and not demanding. Casi shivered.

She stepped closer, pressing her body into his. The weight of his kiss deepened when his hand in a tender grip to the back of her neck, held her to his mouth. A teasing tip of his tongue traced her mouth and then the seam of her lips. With a sigh, she opened for him, and seemingly on their own accord, her arms twined around his neck. She let her fingers caress the soft buzzed hair before stretching to tangle in the longer length above.

Luc didn't go wild or try to force his tongue down her throat. Instead, he played. Light strokes darting in and out, coaxing her to follow and taste. She leaned into him, wanting more, which he gladly gave. He gently sucked on her tongue before releasing so she could explore. He tasted of powdered sugar and bourbon.

With a last swirl of his tongue, he broke the kiss, gradually pulling back before resting his forehead against hers. They stood quietly, his hand still on the back of her neck while her fingers played with his hair. The sounds of the swamp intruded inside their cocoon. Luc sighed, his hand dropped to her waist, and he took a slight step back.

"I should apologize." His voice, husky and low, caressed her. "I'd be lying if I did."

She stared at him. So many emotions churned through her. Luc had kissed her, and she had let him. Enjoyed it, in fact, and had kissed him back. Her prejudice of law enforcement didn't seem to apply to him. Should she allow him so close? Dropping her curled arms from around his neck, she took one step back, but found she couldn't widen the distance between them even if her instincts were telling her to.

"Say something, please? Are you okay?"

Was she? He looked worried with his slight frown and crinkled brow. She needed to give him something, instead of standing there silent in shock. She wasn't in shock, quite the opposite as warm liquid pleasure still coursed through her from his kiss. It had been so long…

"Casi?"

"Sorry." She swallowed hard. "I'm just…I…"

"Hey," Luc took her hand, entwining their fingers together. "I was out of bounds."

She shook her head. "No, don't apologize. You did

nothing wrong." Casi gave him a tentative smile. "It's not like I didn't kiss you back."

"Not very professional of me."

"I think you shortchanged yourself. The kiss was pretty amazing. Nothing amateur about it."

His smile returned, and he gave their clasped hands a squeeze. "Thank you, darlin'." He paused. A thoughtful look crossed his face. "I'm going to blame my behavior on the moonlit bayou and having a lovely lady in my arms." Luc swiped his free hand through his hair. "We okay?"

"Yes." She dropped her gaze, studying their clasped hands, trying to hide her awkwardness. With the darkness, she doubted he could see her discomfort, but he had an uncanny way of being able to read her.

His finger appeared under her chin, gently tilting her head so she'd have to meet his gaze. "You sure?"

"Yes."

His hand dropped away. "That's good, sugar. I might want to kiss you again…soon, but not tonight."

"Not tonight."

Luc's charming smile curled up his mouth. "But maybe tomorrow." It wasn't a question.

"Maybe." Casi couldn't help but smile back.

"Let's get you back inside before the bugs eat you alive. Come on now."

He tugged on their joined hands and led her across the lawn. Would he try to kiss her again? Her body tingled. She could still taste him, feel the warmth of their embrace, and remembered the slow burn in her veins hotter than the evening air. How far would she let this growing relationship go? Casi supposed that was the real question.

Chapter Twenty-Nine

Casi plopped herself down at the table in the music room. She dug through her canvas bag and hauled out the silk bag containing her Tarot deck. Marielle agreed to meet her at two for the reading, but Casi arrived early before the youngest Avery would appear. Out of practice, she wanted a turn at the cards to knock the rust off.

She shuffled the cards while looking around. Besides this table, the room held a baby grand piano, couches, and a few comfy-looking chairs. She guessed the piano made this the music room. Cutting the cards, her fingers tingled as she manipulated the deck and shivered. Weird. Shaking off her sudden discomfort, Casi mentally asked her question and flipped over three cards.

The Ten of Swords. The Fool. The Ace of Swords.

Holy sucktastic read! The first card meant backstabbing, betrayal, enemies, attack, and violence. The Fool represented not knowing what to expect and coupled with the minor arcane Ace of Swords signifying force of vision—the reading wasn't good. All these cards said trouble headed her way if she believed in their power. The simple look into her future appeared grim. Thank God the cards couldn't really predict the future.

Casi swept them back into the deck and reshuffled.

She dealt three new cards and froze.

The Six of Swords. The Hierophant. The Tower.

What. The. Hell? The new cards predicted the same as her first draw but were even worse. The Six of Swords indicated power, change, and conflict. The Hierophant ratcheted the whole severity level up. And the Tower? The Tower was the worst card in the entire Tarot deck. It represented chaos, destruction, sudden upheaval, trauma, disaster, and tragedy. This had never happened to her before—two horrible matching answers to the same question.

Her pulse started pounding behind her temples as she shoved the cards back into the deck. Shuffling, Casi gritted her teeth while preparing to pull three new cards, but Marielle entered the room on a bouncy step.

"Hey, Casi." Marielle grabbed the chair across from her and sat. She smiled, oblivious to Casi's turmoil. "Before we get started, there's something I want to give you."

She opened her closed palm and out dropped a necklace. Holding the one end of a delicate silver chain pinched between two of Marielle's fingers, it dangled. The weird horn Casi had been carrying around in her pocket now hung from the necklace.

"Since I was doing laundry, I thought I could help you. So I grabbed your dirty clothes. I always check pockets, that's when I found your way cool charm. What the heck is it made of, anyway?"

Casi took the offered necklace and caressed the horn. "I'm not sure. It feels like stone." She studied the horn and then admired the chain. "You shouldn't have done this."

"Oh no, no, no. I'm not taking it back. Besides, I

wanted to do something nice for you. You've been through so much."

"Laundry wasn't enough?"

"Nope." Marielle smiled. "I had to do my own, and it's not like you had a ton to do. I can't believe you've been wearing the same outfit for a week."

A chuckle escaped Casi. She shook her head. "It's only been a couple of days, though I have to admit it feels like months."

"Well, being targeted by a serial killer would age anyone." Marielle nodded. "Put it on. I'm hoping the length is right."

Casi undid the clasp and slipped the chain around her neck and refastened it. Taking her hand away, the fragile chain dropped to her chest, placing the horn just above her breasts.

Marielle clapped. "Perfect."

"Thank you, Marielle, you really didn't need to." Casi fingered the horn. The charm seemed warmer since she picked it up. She carefully let it drop, remembering the sudden burning of her palm and crushing migraine from the safe house, and hoped its temperature change wasn't a herald of things to come.

"I did. And please, call me Mare. You're like part of the family, you know?"

"Not you, too." Casi sighed, trying to hide her amusement.

"Me too, what?" Marielle tried for innocent, but the grin gave her away.

"Luc is only protecting me."

"I'm sure he is, but he wants more."

Did he? Luc kissed her last night and even said he wanted to do it again. Casi shook her head in denial.

"Yeah, he does. He doesn't hold hands with just anyone."

Casi's eyes widened. The little sneak. "Marielle, were you spying on us?"

"Maybe a tiny bit." She pinched her fingers together in example. "I wanted to know how things were going. I watched you guys walk back to the house." Marielle had the same accent as her brother—well, her entire family—liquid and rolling, but mischievous.

"What am I supposed to do with you and your family?" Charmed, Casi wanted to be annoyed but couldn't.

"There's nothing to do but succumb. We outnumber you." Marielle rubbed her hands together and smirked like some terrible movie villain. "And if I know my brother, once he gets over his whole internal struggle of professionalism versus personal needs—and mark me, he will—you won't stand a chance."

She shook her head. If last night was any indication, Luc had already lost the battle and decided to be selfish. Casi needed to figure out what to do with that. She couldn't think about it now. A change of topics was in order.

"How about your reading?"

Marielle snickered. "I see what you're doing, and I'll let you get away with it for now. I'm generous like that."

"You have a question in mind?" Casi shuffled the cards.

"I do. Love is in the air…"

"You better leave me and your brother out of this, or I'm taking my deck and walking."

“Nah. Just teasing. I’m worried about my final in Theory of Computation. Who knew going for my computer science degree would be so hard? I’m awesome with computers. Who needs stupid theory?”

“Theory classes suck in all majors, Mare.”

“Right you are, sista!”

Marielle offered a fist, which Casi obligingly bumped and then placed the shuffled deck of Tarot cards in front of the girl.

“I believe you know the drill. Cut the deck into three piles as you think of your questions and then stack them back together in any order you like.”

Marielle did as told, and Casi quickly laid out five cards in a cross pattern and exhaled a relieved sigh. Nothing weird here, straight up normal. In fact, the cards were super clear in their answer to Marielle’s question. Goosebumps raised on her arms. Maybe not so normal after all. The cards never, ever actually answered a question directly for her before. She had always used their definitions and her college degrees to fake her response. This was freaky, like she might have actual psychic powers—

“Is something wrong?”

The question jolted Casi out of her running thoughts. She offered a smile. “Quite the opposite actually.”

She tapped the center card of the cross, the King of Swords. “This represents your situation. The King of Swords tells me you have the intellect to make important decisions.” This earned Casi a smile. Next, she pointed to the second card, the one lying left of center. “This one represents the challenge. The Nine of Cups is literally a challenge or obstacle, so this is your final exam you're freaking out about." She motioned to the third card, sitting right of center. "This card is for guidance. The Six of Wands is someone highly successful, meaning, I believe the card represents you again. In other words, look to yourself."

Marielle smile grew to a grin. "This is looking terrific."

"Absolutely." Casi pointed to the fourth card drawn directly below at the base of the cross. "This is your focus. The World represents successful completion. And the fifth card"—she tapped the top of the cross—"This is your outcome. The Sun. It's the best Tarot card ever. It represents success and accomplishment. I think your final will be a slam dunk."

"Oh, *Dieu merci*! I was so worried."

"Apparently there's no need to, Mare. But you should still study, of course."

Marielle stood with a beaming smile. "Don't worry. I'm still planning on hitting the books. Sorry I can't hang some more, but I have to swap out laundry before someone screams at me for hogging the machines. Thank you so much again. It's such a relief."

"You're welcome. It wasn't a problem at all."

The youngest Avery bounced out of the room as she had arrived, full of energy and happiness with the world. It must be nice to be so carefree. Casi stood and gathered her cards back into one pile. She picked them up and stared at them. One more go. Wasn't the third time the charm? Quickly she shuffled and then cut the deck. She held her breath and pulled three cards.

The Six of Swords. The Hierophant. The Tower.

Casi's legs gave out and she collapsed, landing

back in her chair. Impossible. No way could those three cards, in that exact order, possibly reappear again. The hairs on the back of her neck rose. Something in her had changed since her abduction. She saw ghosts, started having premonitions in her dreams, and now the cards were real? What the hell was happening to her?

Chapter Thirty

"Hey, Lucky, get your mind back in the game and stop ogling your girlfriend."

Luc tore his gaze away from Casi and nodded at Bastien. They continued walking while carrying a heavy folding table. Somehow in their trek across the lawn, Luc had stopped moving. The afternoon had flown into early evening with all the hard work staging for the party. There would be more tasks tomorrow, since most of the setup had to be done Saturday morning. Reaching a pile of stacked long tables, he and Bastien heaved, placing their burden on the top.

As Luc shook out his arms and then flexed his wounded arm, he was pleased. No pain or stiffness. Even his thigh hadn't really bothered him, only the occasional twinge when the stitches pulled. His gaze drew back to Casi once more. He wasn't sure what task she was supposed to accomplish, but for the last half hour, she'd stood unmoving and stared into the swamp. She looked both pensive and upset.

Bastien tapped him on the shoulder. "What's going on in that head of yours, big bro? Other than getting distracted by a *brûlant fille*."

Luc ignored his brother's *sizzling hot girl* comment as his gut twisted with worry. "Something's wrong."

"*Ouais*, she does seem a bit distracted." Bas gave him a slight shove in her direction. "You're worthless like this. Go on now. *Prends soin de ta fille*."

Yes, he would take care of her, he could do nothing less, especially after getting his first real taste of Casi last night. Luc prowled across the lawn. She flowed in his blood. He'd been protective before, but now it twisted him up inside if she wasn't safe, smiling, and happy.

"Casi?"

She jumped at the quiet sound of her name. Casi turned and faced him. "Oh, hey."

"Sorry I startled you."

"No worries, I was just lost in thought."

Lost in thought, most definitely. But something bothered her, and he would find out what.

"Take a walk with me?"

"Sure." She gifted him with a brief smile.

He grabbed hold of her hand and interlaced their fingers. Tugging her away, Luc didn't care who witnessed them holding hands. He had told a white lie last night when he blamed his kiss on the moonlit bayou. Yes, true in the romantic sense, but deep down, if honest with himself, he had feelings for Casi. They ran deeper than they should, but he really didn't care anymore. His family had seen the truth first. He was done fighting with himself, and he would win the woman he wanted, but first he had to find out why she was troubled. She shouldn't be upset and afraid anymore.

"Where are we going?"

Luc gave her hand a brief reassuring squeeze. "You'll see."

She huffed. "It better not be something creepy again. I really don't need you laughing at me."

"Now, *cher*, I wasn't laughing at—"

"You were."

"Okay, maybe a little." He squeezed her hand again. "I promise it's nothing spooky," he reassured her, and with his free hand he crossed his heart.

"Fine."

They rounded the side of the house, and he spotted the path he wanted. He needed privacy, and he knew just the place to find it. The mix of cypress and willow trees closed in on them, making the gravel path almost too narrow for two people to walk abreast. Okay by him, because he now had an excuse to pull Casi closer. Her shoulder brushed his upper arm with each stride. The increased physical contact soothed him. He would feel completely better after he fixed whatever troubled her.

The gravel path abruptly ended, and Casi gasped next to him as she spotted the screened house in the center of a small clearing. It wasn't large, about twenty-five by thirty feet. The Dutch-gabled roof, sported venting fans on each side—spinning lazily. Instead of solid walls, the open-air house had fine meshed screens between the vertical support beams. He guided Casi to the screen door, opened it, and let her enter before him.

She walked to the center and spun slowly, taking in the decorations. Unlit fairy lights dangled from the natural wood, open-beamed ceiling. An inviting seating area was arranged on the opposite short side from the door. A rainbow mat covered the outdoor deck flooring where two large wicker weaved couches faced each other across a small table. Matching chairs paired on the short side of the table. On the long sides of the small house, built-in benches ran the length of both sides with waterproof cushions on top. In short, sheltered by the surrounding trees, the secluded cabin hidden in the clearing made for a quiet retreat. A place for escape.

"This is wonderful, Luc. Thanks for showing me."

"You're welcome, but it gets better. Hang on a sec."

He walked to the side bench nearest one couch and lifted the seat, exposing a hidden storage area. Quickly he pulled out several soft cushions and pillows and set them up on the couch, before returning and closing the bench's lid. He arrived at Casi's side, took her hand once again, and pulled her toward the now comfortable couch.

"Sit." He tugged her down beside him. "We shouldn't be bothered here. My grandpapa built this for his wife so she could have a place of peace and quiet away from the loud Avery household." Luc angled his body to face Casi better. "Now spill. What's wrong?"

"Nothing, really." She chewed on her bottom lip, a sure sign the complete opposite, in fact, was true. He'd learned she nibbled when uncertain or uncomfortable.

"Darlin', you should know me better by now. You can't fool me. I know something is up, so you might as well share."

She studied her clasped hands in her lap, before exhaling loudly. "Fine." She met his gaze directly. "You're really annoying at times."

He shrugged. Skilled at reading people, Luc wasn't sorry this time his talent played against Casi. He didn't care as long as he could figure out a way to help her. She still wasn't talking, so he lifted an eyebrow and waited her out.

"Okay, okay. I don't know what to say..."

It looked like he'd have to drag it out of her. "How about starting with what happened after lunch? You were all smiles and laughter, and then when you came to help in the yard, you stood staring at the swamp like a baby gator waiting to get eaten by its poppa."

"How do you even notice these things? Alligators eat their young? Seriously?"

"I notice everything about you, Casi. After last night, you must know I'm attracted to you. I care about you, and I don't like it when you're not happy. And yes, gators do, so stop trying to change the topic, and please tell me what's going on inside your pretty head."

"It's silly..."

He held in a frustrated sigh. "I don't care. Spit it out, *cher*."

"I...I...think something's happened to me. Changed me."

"A lot has happened to you." He chuckled. "Be more specific."

She stood and started pacing in the small sitting area. "No, not like that." She pushed her hair off her face as she made another lap. The words suddenly spilled out of her in a long run-on sentence. "Ever since I was abducted, I've changed, like mentally somehow, and I've seen and spoken with Mason's ghost. Apparently, I have prophetic dreams, and now the Tarot cards are real!" Her pacing became frantic.

He jumped to his feet, intercepting Casi, and stopped her by placing his hands on her shoulders. "Slow down, darlin'."

Her wide, spooked gaze stared at him. "I'm freaked out, okay? Magic isn't supposed to exist! There's no such thing as psychic powers! This can't happen. I don't want any of this!"

He tightened his hold when he felt her trembling. "Science can't explain everything. Just because it hasn't been proven doesn't mean it's not out there. Is it so bad to be gifted?"

"How can you say that? Do you really believe in all the mumbo jumbo? A few days ago, I was just plain old me, and now I'm Annie Wilson from *The Gift*!"

"I'm Cajun, sweetheart. I believe in powers beyond our knowledge. I was born superstitious. You can't grow up in the bayou without being surrounded with the mystical. *Prend-lé aisé*. Take it easy. Come here." He gathered her into his arms, and when she relaxed into his embrace and wrapped her arms around him, his stomach flipped, happy in the realization she trusted him. He could feel her pounding heart as she leaned into him. Rubbing her back, Luc waited for her to calm, and when she sighed, he knew she had at least released some of her anxiety.

"What happened with the reading? Did Marielle get awful news?" His own heart sped up a bit with worry for his little sister.

"No," she mumbled into his chest. "Her reading was all unicorns and rainbows."

He gave her a slight squeeze. "Well, that's good, but I'm assuming something happened to get you all riled up."

"Before she arrived, I wanted to practice because, you know, the cards aren't real." She tried to pull away from him, but Luc kept her close. Casi huffed out a breath. "Fine." She settled back. "I pulled three cards all with the same question of what my near future held.

The cards predicted doom and disaster. I reshuffled and pulled three new cards." He felt her shudder. "They were even worse. Marielle arrived, so I couldn't try again."

"And her reading came out good, right?"

"Yeah, it did. She was worried about a final exam. When she left, I went for a third time's a charm." Casi's trembling returned, so he pressed a kiss to her hair as he ran his hand up and down her spine for comfort. "I pulled another three cards and…it's impossible…but they were the exact same draw in the exact same order as last time."

She pulled away from him and peered up at him, eyes wide. "What's wrong with me? This shouldn't be happening. Why can't everything go back to normal?"

His heart broke for her. He hated seeing her so upset. Maybe he could do something to take her mind off her troubles. After all, tomorrow had arrived, and he did say he'd kiss her again.

"Now, sugar," he drawled as he lifted his hand from her waist and cupped the back of her neck. "There has been some good out of all this."

She snorted. "Really? Because I'm not seeing it."

"I've got at least two for you. Mason Webb, no matter how odd the form, he's still in your life. If you didn't have any psychic ability, he'd be lost to you."

"And the other?" she whispered.

"Depending on how you think, your circumstances brought you to me." He inched closer. "I can't say I'm happy for the reasons, but I do know I'm grateful you're in my life. Amazingly grateful."

She blinked at him, and her tongue darted out, and she licked her lips. He didn't bother to hide his smile. "I believe I told you I'd kiss you today."

"You might have said something..."

He slid his hand at her waist around to the small of her back and pressed her close, so her soft curves were against him. Using the hand on her nape, he tilted her head and swooped in for a kiss. He kept it light as he took his time nibbling at her lips, but soon it wasn't enough. Luc needed more. His tongue came out to taste, teasing her to open, which she did on a breathy sigh. And like last night, Casi wrapped her arms around his neck and let her fingers play in his hair.

She tasted like sweet tea and something unique to herself. She tasted right. Casi was his new addiction. Their tongues dueled, but he won when he gave a hard suck and was rewarded with a moan. He broke the kiss to explore and finally taste her soft skin. Pressing open-mouth kisses along her chin, he reached her neck. He tasted down the long column, stopping to lick at her pulse point before continuing downward. Arriving at the point where her neck met her shoulder, Luc couldn't resist giving a teasing nip to the juncture. A breathy whimper escaped Casi, and she tilted her head back, giving him greater access.

He sucked hard, hoping to leave his mark on her delicious mocha latte skin. She pulled his hair, and Luc chuckled. Lifting his head, he claimed her mouth once more in a deep kiss as he walked her backward. When her legs hit the couch, he pressed her down onto the cushions. With one leg straight, he bent the other and placed his knee between her legs and leaned down, giving her some of his weight. His fingers left her neck to plow into her hair, and the other hand skimmed up her ribs, lightly caressing the side of her breast.

Casi stiffened under him and froze. Startled, he broke the kiss and saw her tightly scrunched eyes and furrowed brow. He immediately straightened, releasing his hold on her hair and removed his hand from her side as he half knelt upright on the couch.

They were both breathing hard when her eyes fluttered open, and she frowned at him.

"You stopped. Why did you stop?"

"Casi, are you all right?"

"Of course." She sat up and reached for him, but he stopped her by gathering her hands into his.

"*Non*. Not, of course."

"I'm fine—"

"You're not." He let his thumb stroke the inside of her wrist. "You flinched and then froze."

She shook her head in denial while her eyes filled with unshed tears. "Please…" Her broken and whispered plea cut into Luc.

His heart ached for her. Sitting fully on the couch, he pulled her beside him and gave her a hug. Casi whimpered, then climbed onto his lap and clung to him. He worried about the intimacy, but relaxed when he decided it had been her choice. With a sigh, he rested his chin on her head. She relaxed and gave him her weight.

"I didn't want you to stop," she mumbled into his neck.

He sighed and rubbed her back. "A part of you did, darlin'." The time for a hard conversation, one she wouldn't like, but necessary for both of them, had arrived. "Have you been intimate since your assault?"

She went rigid and pushed away. He gave her a bit of space but didn't let go. Placing a finger under her chin, he tilted her face so he could meet her gaze. "*Non, cher*. We will talk this out."

"I don't want to."

"I know, but we're going to anyway." With a gentle pressure on her back, he asked her to cuddle, and relief flooded him when she did. He idly stroked the bare skin of her arm from shoulder to elbow. "I know this is difficult, and I'm sorry, but if we want to explore this attraction between us, we need to talk."

She nodded her head before burying her nose into his neck.

"*Bonne fille. Dis-moi la vérité*." He kissed the top of her head. "Tell me the truth. Have you been with a man since you were in jail?"

Casi squirmed on his lap before burrowing herself deeper and wrapped her arms around him. "Yes… Twice." Pain and loss feathered her soft reply.

He wanted to tread carefully. If he hoped for something more with her, they needed to get behind her trauma and at least begin to deal with it somehow. "Was it any good?"

She stilled in his arms and held her breath.

"Casi," he continued to stroke her. "Come now, talk to me."

"No, not really," she grumbled. "The first, I just wanted to get it over with and get on with my life. I figured I'd get it done and be all right. It was horrible, actually."

"And the second?"

He heard her sniffle. *Dammit*. Luc hoped she wasn't crying. He stopped stroking her arm and went back to rubbing her back.

"I would have pulled the plug, but I just wanted to

get better. He…he never noticed how uncomfortable I acted, not like you."

"Aw, darlin', I'm sorry."

"Not your fault." She gave a little hiccup. "I really like you. I thought it'd be all right…"

"And it will be. You have my word. Just not today, *cher*."

"I wish it was."

"I know." He pressed another kiss, lingering this time, to her head as he inhaled the honey and ginger scenting her hair. "Have you gone to therapy?"

This elicited a chuckle. "No. Ironic, right? I didn't think I needed counseling."

"Maybe you need to rethink that. If you were working with a patient in the same situation, wouldn't you recommend help?"

"It wasn't like I was raped. They pulled him off of me in time."

He hugged her tight. So careful with others, but not herself. "Sweetheart, there may have been no penetration, but you most definitely were violated. Not only were you ambushed and beaten to near unconsciousness, they handed you over to a man against your wishes, groped, assaulted, and if not for the last-second rescue, you would have been raped. That is reality. You have a lot of trauma you need to work through."

"I know." Her voice sounded tremulous and filled with hurt. His chest ached again.

"You can face this. You're a strong, courageous woman, it's not a weakness to ask for help."

She curled herself into him. "I know," Casi repeated. "You're right…but not today, okay?

Maybe…can you just hold me?"

"Anything for you, darlin'."

He relaxed into the pillows of the couch and rested his chin on her head as he tightened his arms around her. She felt right in his embrace, like she belonged there. Kind of his new favorite thing to do. Luc would hold her the rest of the day if necessary, anything to comfort her and make her feel safe.

Chapter Thirty-One

Selene strode past the front desk of the police station with barely a nod to the uniform sitting attendance as she made her way directly to the elevator. The cache of being the girlfriend of the deceased assistant district attorney allowed her to walk freely around the precinct. Her recent failures annoyed her, but as the saying goes, *there was more than one way to skin a cat.* She knew from personal experience. If she couldn't use Bastien Avery, then Detective Vincent Tate would do the trick. She'd bet Gabriel's horn Tate knew where Avery and the girl were. It was time to make Tate her bitch.

After feeding last night, Selene decided to have some fun and crashed the Roosevelt Waldorf Astoria's Blue Room, which hosted some swanky charity event. She drank, danced, and ultimately left with two handsome willing men on her arms. After kicking them out, she spent the rest of her night pondering her Avery problem, and then remembered Tate.

A few phone calls later that morning, she located him at his French Quarter precinct. Hopefully, he was at his desk and hadn't dashed off between her discovery and the drive over. Exiting the elevator, she marched down the hall but froze when she heard the detective's deep baritone. Selene stayed out of sight and listened in.

"They finally picked up Brock Winston. He alibied out. The Winston kid couldn't have been in the townhouse with Casi." Tate paused, and when no answering voice replied, she realized he must be on the phone. "Winston could still be the partner of the Cyclops, but I'm just not feeling it. Anyway, things are getting crazy here. Be glad you're gone."

He must be updating Avery, proving her point he knew where the Cajun detective hid.

"Remember Nathan Roberts?" Another pause. "Yeah, that's the dude. They found him dead in his car after eating his weapon. The strange thing? His gun was missing two additional bullets." A pause. "That's what I'm thinking. I dug a bullet out of a tree in the park. I'm hoping to sneak in a ballistics test and find out if he's our shooter. The only thing really bugging me? He had no ties to you or Casi, except being a cop."

Selene grinned. She had her confirmation and inched forward so Tate appeared in her line of sight. He stood in an unlit empty room by a desk listening on his cell.

"I'm running the wallet for prints through an Army buddy of mine because, you know, beware the mole." Tate nodded before continuing. "We had another body dropped, but with a twist. Way more violent and there wasn't any ligature marks or signs of restraints, though weirdly no evidence he put up a fight. It looks like our killer is ramping up. Maybe he got sloppy this time. We can only hope. We're still waiting on DNA to see if there was any evidence this time around."

Good luck with that. Selene wasn't human, there would be no evidence the humans would understand. And as for fingerprints? Who cared? She could easily erase all thought and evidence with her puppets if the prints were traced back to her. None of today's technology mattered when you could control other people's minds. It sure sucked to be human.

"How's Casi? You should be able to reassure her the Cyclops is still here in town." Tate nodded. "Yeah, man. Keep her safe and look after yourself. No sign of infection?"

Someone was hurt? Hopefully, it was Avery and not the girl. Perhaps Roberts had done her a favor? A weakened detective would only help her cause.

"Good. Nothing more on my end. I'll call you later and check in. Say hi to Jolie for me." Tate laughed and smirked. "Not gonna. Too bad, Cajun boy. Talk to ya later." He pulled the phone away from his ear and ended the call.

Selene walked into the room, right up to Tate. "*Pardon me, hot stuff.*" Her magic snapped out, as the detective turned, and wrapped around him as he faced her. "*I need some help, and you're the delicious man to give it to me.*"

Snared, his eyes glazed over and went empty. Perfect. She stepped closer to the large man who towered over her six-feet-in-heels height. Hmm, so masculine, maybe she needed to play with him. Absolutely her type and now she completely possessed him. A niggle of worry scurried across her mind. Cassanne Thomas and Lucas Avery had been hers until they weren't. No. Selene had no room for doubt. Every other human she'd enthralled hadn't slipped her leash, even at a distance, proven by both Nathan Roberts and Commander Eckert. Tate was hers.

Selene trailed a finger down his broad, hard chest.

"*Will you help me?*"

"Of course."

She smiled. "Excellent. *I need you to take me to Lucas Avery and Cassanne Thomas*."

The detective stiffened and sweat broke out across his brow. Stubborn, strong, and handsome—the trifecta. Selene pushed her power and laced her words with iron. "*No, no, you naughty boy. You are mine to command and obey. Detective Vincent Tate, you will take me to Lucas Avery. Now*."

Tate swayed at her command as her magic gut punched him. "Yes, ma'am. Please come with me."

He offered his arm like a gentleman, and who was she to refuse? He guided her out of the precinct and to a huge, shiny, silver SUV. Opening the passenger door, he helped her into the tall car and carefully shut the door once she was safely settled. In no time, he sat behind the wheel and started the throaty engine.

A quiet smile curled up her mouth as Tate drove. Soon, the Thomas chit would be dead, and Gabriel's horn would be hers.

****

Gabriel hefted the large metal keg onto his shoulder and left the storage room, striding down the back hallway toward the exit. With the door propped open, he departed the Loo without missing a step and crossed to the bar's van. He could have carried two kegs at once, probably more if he could figure out how to balance all of them, but a normal human couldn't manage all those kegs at once. So filling the cargo space with fifteen kegs took a little longer than necessary.

He set down the last barrel, as the bar's owner

walked up and grinned at him.

"I know you said you could move this all yourself without breaking a sweat, but I'm impressed. I really didn't think you could."

Gabriel hid his smile. "No worries, I'm glad to help." He glanced at the fifteen kegs in the cargo hold and shook his head. "Isn't this a bit much? I think there's about ten kegs too many."

Chris Jeske laughed outright. "Gabe, you've never attended a Cajun party, have you?"

"Can't say that I have."

"Maybe you should stick around there tomorrow instead of driving back. The Avery's won't mind, and I doubt they'd notice you were even there with the crowd expected. This Saturday is your day off, you should enjoy yourself."

"Perhaps I will."

Jeske slapped him on the shoulder. "Drive safely, you hear? Thanks again for volunteering to load and drive."

"No problem. It's my pleasure." Gabriel shut the two rear van doors and gave a tug to make sure they were securely fastened. "I only hope I don't blind any fellow drivers on the road."

The Loo's van was garishly painted a vivid glowing purple. Emblazoned on both sides of the vehicle were large sparkly gold fleur-de-lis emblems followed by bright white swirling lettering declaring the bar's name. Underneath in dazzling yellow print stated—Home of Wilted Lily Ale. The van's outer decorations were an eyesore.

"Don't make fun of my van," Jeske mocked a growl. "It's eye-catching and pulls in the business."

"If you say so." Gabriel backed away from Chris. "I better hit the road. I don't want to get stuck in traffic."

He caught Jeske's nod before turning and getting behind the wheel. After a suspiciously wheezing start, he pulled out of the parking lot. Getting on the interstate, he settled into a lane and mentally went over his plan. It was time to cheat a little. Taking a page from his brother, Remiel's playbook, Gabriel needed to reveal himself to the holder of his horn so she could be prepared. If Casi froze when faced with the siren, the consequences could be dire.

To disclose his identity might be a chancy maneuver, but Remi had gotten away with using an intermediary. Their Father hadn't punished him or, in fact, Uriel either. Both his brothers had nary a word from Dad. It gave Gabriel hope. Selene needed to be destroyed. For centuries she'd taken away the human right of free will, and her body count put human wars to shame. If he had any doubts about killing her, Selene's own words at the bar convinced him of his righteous decision. The siren would never change her colors, and her essence was evil to the bone. Time to send her to where all malevolent beings ended up. She'd sealed her fate and should have met her destiny centuries ago.

He only hoped Casi would be strong enough to carry through with the burden he placed on her. Casi's life's trials proved she was a survivor, a fighter. Gabriel hoped she had at least one more battle left inside her.

Chapter Thirty-Two

Selene studied her surroundings, gazing out the windshield as Tate drove up a long driveway. The old growth of willow trees blocked her view on the sides, but the front remained clear enough as she spotted a sizeable house. In Europe the house would rate as a small manor. With her superior eyesight, she spotted a couple sitting cozily on a swing hanging from the porch.

"*Stop the car.*"

The detective obediently obliged.

She couldn't hold the confrontation on the front lawn, not knowing how many people were in the house. She could handle around twenty before she would fail to keep her focus. Spread too thin, Selene would lose her own self-awareness, and she'd have to be cognizant to subdue Cassanne Thomas, especially if the girl put up a fight.

Between the lacey fronds of two willows, she spotted what looked like a small clearing. It should do. "*Vincent, my dear, please drive to the house after I exit. Park and walk to your friends. Convince them, without telling them about me, to follow you and take them to the small meadow on your right, behind these trees. Do you understand, poppet?*"

"Yes."

She patted his hard-muscled thigh. "That's my

good boy. *Don't delay and there will be a lovely reward for you.*"

Tate smiled as she exited the car and shut the door. He waited for her to safely step away before driving off. Selene gave the couple on the porch a quick glance. They were so involved with each other, they never noticed the SUV, let alone that it had halted. With Tate properly motivated and in her complete control, it wouldn't take him long to arrange her special meeting. Having such a strong, handsome puppet at her beck and call was lovely. Perhaps she'd keep him. She passed through the trees and settled in to wait for her prey to arrive.

In short order, distant voices reached her preternatural hearing.

"Can't you tell me what's going on?" Avery's Cajun drawl revealed the speaker.

"Not by the house. Too dangerous." Tate's deep voice replied.

"If this is, you know, business, I could have stayed behind." Cassanne's soft statement barely reached Selene's ears.

"No, you need to be there. It's important to both of you."

Silence, except for the tread of three sets of footfalls. They were close now. Selene straightened and gathered her power on the far side of the clearing. Tate led the way and walked directly to her side. Avery paused, keeping Casi beside him when he caught sight of Selene.

"Ms. Walsh?" Avery frowned.

"Yes, Detective. I have important information. Detective Tate thought it would be better and safer if I delivered it in person. Isn't that right?" She smiled at Tate.

"Yes, ma'am."

With a puzzled expression crossing his attractive face, Avery led the girl across the short distance and halted in front of her and Tate.

Silently, Selene sent her magic out, wrapping it around Avery and Thomas now that they were up close and personal. Yet the strangest thing happened. Her power slid off them both as if they had a shield against her enthrallment. Why wouldn't her power work on them?

"Ms. Walsh? The information?" Avery sounded impatient.

She guessed she would have to do this the old-fashioned way. "*Vincent Tate, kill your partner. Now*!" Selene crashed her magic into Tate while simultaneously grabbing Cassanne's arm, pulling the girl away from his side. Before Avery could react, Tate attacked.

The former Delta Force warrior didn't disappoint. Fierce and violent, his assault sent Avery scrambling backward as he blocked the larger man's mixed martial arts punches and kicks. If Avery had been a fraction slower, he would have already been dead. The Thomas girl screamed and lunged toward the battling pair.

"No! Stop!" The girl struggled to escape Selene's hold.

"Leave them be, poppet." The woman froze at her words, a look of horror on her face.

"It can't be…"

Selene's mouth curled up in a smile. Her bruising grip tightened on the girl's upper arm, as she yanked

Cassanne close, pressing the chit's back to her front. "Where is my horn? I can sense it's close. Give it to me."

The girl struggled. "Let me go. He's going to kill Luc!"

"That's the point, poppet." Selene used her free hand to encircle the girl's neck to choke some obedience into her, but she fought back. Thomas slammed her head backward, connecting with Selene's chin at the exact moment a sharp burning pain struck her bare calf. Her leg crumpled as the girl slipped from her grasp and ran.

Catching her balance, Selene found the source of her pain. Avery's mangy cat had its jaw wrapped around her calf with its teeth sunk deep, growling. With an answering growl of her own, Selene transformed her hands into claws and pried the feline off her. She hurled the cat, aiming for a tree. Not waiting to see if her aim held true, she turned her attention back to the clearing.

Tate had brought Avery to the ground and had the perfect grip to snap the Cajun's neck until the girl vaulted onto his back, crashing the two of them to the side, rolling away from the prone Avery. Interfering bitch. Selene needed this wrapped up.

Why was Detective Tate just sitting on the ground with the girl between Avery and him? "*Vincent Tate! Finish this*!"

She strode forward, flinging her magic out when a familiar potent energy flooded the small meadow. Gabriel. *Not now*! She had everything she needed right here, but she couldn't chance hanging around.

With an angry snarl, Selene willed out her wings, which punched through the back of her shirt. In the next split second, she launched herself skyward, gaining altitude quickly, and flew out into the swamp. Time to disappear. She may have lost this round, but she was far from done. One interfering angel and some humans would never get the best of her. Eventually Selene would have everything she wanted. After all, she was the better predator with centuries behind her. Her day would come.

Chapter Thirty-Three

Casi couldn't believe her eyes, as her winged, female stalker became a distant smudge in the sky.

"What the actual fuck?"

She couldn't agree more with Tate's exclamation as he rubbed a hand over his face. He looked totally bewildered, and this happened after completely missing the woman who had sprouted pitch-black wings and flown away. At least he wasn't trying to kill Luc, at the moment.

Avery sat on her other side, eyes wide, jaw dropped as he stared into the cloudy sky. Thank God. If he looked stunned, she hadn't hallucinated the woman with the wings.

"Are you all right, Luc?" Casi scanned him for injuries and surprisingly didn't find any serious ones, only some scrapes and bruising. However, that didn't mean he wasn't hurt where she couldn't see. She glanced at his thigh, relieved to see no blood seeping through his jeans. The gun wound must be well on its way to healing.

On a rough exhale, Luc tore his gaze away from the sky and faced her. "Fine. You?" He reached out a hand and traced a finger gently down her neck. Her neck twinged with the light touch. There must be a bruise or some mark where the woman had grabbed her throat.

"I'm good."

"Well, I'm not." Tate surged to his feet and glared down at her and Luc. "Will someone please tell me how the hell I'm here and not at the precinct?"

"You don't know?" Casi frowned at him. "You don't remember driving here and almost killing Luc?"

"What the fu—"

"He can't remember because Selene enthralled him." The sudden new deep voice interrupting Tate had her scrambling and crab crawling backward into Luc, as a brightly glowing figure entered the clearing.

"Gabriel?" Luc placed a staying hand on her shoulder. "It's okay, Casi. This is Gabriel, from the Fleur-de-lis, the bar where my brother's band plays. Remember the text I got about the delivery?" He squeezed her shoulder. "Though I'm not sure how he knows anything…"

The large, radiant man, built on the scale of Tate, walked right up to them. Was no one going to mention the human-walking light bulb? She pressed herself harder into Luc. Neither of the detectives seemed to notice Gabriel's shiny aura. Casi rubbed her eyes, but he still glowed.

The man stared directly at her, and as if he read her mind, his radiance shrunk and seeped into him. "My apologies." She swallowed hard.

Casi blinked the burning afterimage away, and only a man stood above her, dressed simply in a pair of faded jeans and a logo T-shirt from the bar. His brown hair cut short and messy in a hip style. The guy's face carved in hard angles, giving him a sharp edge, yet softened by his warm brown eyes, which seemed to twinkle down at her. He broke his gaze away and fixed it on Luc. "I know quite a lot. It's why I'm here, actually."

"I thought it was to deliver beer?" Luc stood and offered his hand to Casi, who gratefully took it since she felt weak from the fight and her crashing adrenaline. She tucked herself close to Luc, afraid she might be having a mental break after seeing a flying woman and glowing man.

"That, too." Gabriel smiled. "And you're not crazy." The last statement had been addressed to her.

She hadn't spoken out loud. Was he reading her mind?

"What the hell is going on? I tried to kill you?" Vince stared in shock at his partner, obviously scanning Avery and noticing the minor injuries.

"Yeah, you did," Luc replied. "If Casi hadn't tackled you, I'm pretty sure you were about to snap my neck."

"That's…that's…"

"It's okay, man, you weren't in your right state of mind." Luc gave Tate a crooked smile. "I think I need to spar with you more often. You totally handed me my ass."

"Shit. I don't remember. How can I not remember?" Tate shook his head and displayed a wide-eyed gaze. "The last thing I recall was finishing my brief to you on the phone"—he pointed at Luc—"and now I'm standing here, apparently narrowly escaping killing you. This isn't right."

"What time is it, Vince?" Luc didn't take his eyes off Gabriel.

"A little after twelve…" Tate looked up and took in the sun's angle.

"*Bon ami*, it's closer to two."

"With Friday traffic…Shit." Tate ran a hand over his bald head. He took a deep breath, paused, and studied his partner with a thoughtful expression. "I'm like you. You entered your house, and next thing you know, you're in the park with Casi getting shot…with no memory of how."

"Exactly," Luc acknowledged. "And somehow a bartender knows how our memory lapses occurred and how Selene Walsh, a woman I've known for years as a ladder-climbing socialite, could sprout wings and fly away."

"Wings?" Tate's jaw dropped.

Poor Vince, way behind the curve, and he appeared more frustrated than any of them. If Casi believed her senses, this Selene Walsh was the Cyclops, the serial killer who first grabbed her and then stalked her. *Come here, poppet*. She would never forget that turn of phrase. Her own personal terror wasn't even human. Walsh couldn't be, she had wings. Casi swayed, but Luc clutched her tighter, keeping her on her feet.

The big bartender studied them with his astute gaze, taking them in. "Perhaps it is best, if you were all seated again before I explain."

"Well, why the hell not, if it gets me answers. Besides, I'm dizzy as shit." Tate plunked himself to the ground and pressed his fingers to the bridge of his nose.

"Might as well. I'm curious." Luc brushed a kiss to her forehead before helping her find a spot on the ground. He kept his arm draped across her back, his hand gripping her far shoulder, as he tucked her against his side. Casi took a deep breath and released it. She agreed with Tate. She wasn't feeling so hot either, which must explain all the clinging to Luc since the fight. Had she just barely managed to save his life?

Gabriel glanced down. “I was only planning on revealing myself to Cassanne,” he held up a hand. “Yes, I know her, but she doesn’t know me. However since the three of you are so tightly entwined in this and have witnessed Selene as other than human, I suppose I don’t have to stick to my original plan.”

“Um, Ms. Walsh isn’t human?” Tate’s brow crinkled in confusion.

“*Coo-yôn*, she sprouted wings and flew away,” Luc stated the obvious.

“Again with the wings. What wings?”

Gabriel knew her? How? She’d never met or seen the ex-glowing bartender. Casi was pretty sure she’d remember him.

Gabriel held up a hand, stopping the detectives and interrupting her swirling thoughts. “Detective Tate, you won’t remember, but I’ll get to the reason why shortly. First, I assure you, Selene Walsh is not human. She is a siren—”

“A mermaid?” Luc jumped in, apparently recognizing his mythology. It surprised Casi. “Shouldn’t she be in the water luring sailors to their deaths?” His accented words carried a sarcastic taint.

“Not a mermaid.” Gabriel pursed his lips. “This will go much faster if everyone would hold their comments and questions until the end.”

There was power behind his words. Casi felt like a chastised little girl, and she hadn’t even spoken, though her thoughts had echoed Luc’s. She must have not been the only one feeling scolded since Luc cringed next to her and Tate’s shoulders hunched. Appeased, the bartender continued.

"What modern media has made of the sirens was, in fact, not reality. No fins for them, just wings, claws, and fangs. However, they do have magic in their voices like the legends of old. They don't have to sing to use it though. Their voices, much like vampires with their gaze, can mesmerize, can enslave humans. Sirens enthrall with words. She owned you, Detective, capturing you at your precinct. While in her power, you had no control of your actions, no memories of your time with her or of her." Gabriel paused and met Luc's gaze. "It happened to you as well."

"But why aren't we controlled now? Is it because she's gone? There's a distance thing?"

"No, Lucas. It's a Casi thing. It's a *my* thing."

"You're a bartender..."

Gabriel smiled, taking several backward steps, creating a distance from them. "In my current guise, yes. But that is not who or what I am."

Chapter Thirty-Four

He glowed again, shining brighter and brighter, and with the reactions of the squinting detectives sitting beside her, she wasn't the only one who witnessed his aura this time. The light grew blindingly sharp until a flash pulsed outward. Casi cried out, and Luc protectively shoved himself in front of her, using his body as a shield.

Blinking rapidly, trying to clear the tears from her eyes, she gasped as she peered around Luc's shoulder. The bartender had disappeared. In place stood a man, if you could call him that. He stood over seven feet tall, the jeans and T-shirt now replaced with tall boots, black breeches, and a fitted, sleeveless, collared, white shirt. His thighs were massively muscular, and his shoulders were much broader, displaying a huge chest. The reason for this giant build was obvious and gloriously exhibited behind him—wings. Magnificent snowy white feathers overlapping, appearing soft as satin, stretched from his back, filling the width of the clearing.

Casi dragged her eyes away from the wings and dared to stare into his gaze. Brown eyes were now an impossible, unearthly copper. His former short dark brown hair flowed past his shoulders down to his waist, parting for his wings. If she thought his face chiseled before, the angles were now extreme as if a sharp knife cut through hard clay. His white skin held an internal glow, leaking out, giving him an otherworldly appearance, as if the wings, height, and warrior's build weren't enough. Suddenly glad to be sitting, Casi figured she would have fallen had she not been.

Luc's movement drew her gaze as she watched him make the sign of the cross. Her eyes widened. Oh my God! Was he an angel?

"Archangel, actually."

He did read her mind! Gabriel met her gaze and smiled. "You're the...*the* Archangel Gabriel?" Casi's voice sounded timid to her ears.

"I am."

The loud meow drew everyone's attention, including Gabriel's, and broke the tension at the angel's revelation. Trotting from the tree line, Catastrophe approached, tail flagged with the tip crooked at a jaunty angle. When she reached the Archangel, she twined herself between his legs, loudly purring and rubbing against him.

"Yes, you were ferocious. A true warrior." Gabriel chuckled, and between laughs, the awe-inspiring angel morphed back into the bartender. No fancy light show this time. One moment a massive winged being and then poof, back into a man. She guessed the earlier show was for dramatic effect. "We need to talk."

He sat, and Cat crawled into his lap, curling up, making herself at home. Still purring like an outboard motor, Gabriel petted her. "I revealed myself because I figured your next questions would be how I knew what I told you to be true. This seemed the most expedient way. Please don't share what you've learned with anyone beside yourselves, I'm in enough trouble as it is."

"Uh, sure? It's not like anyone would believe us," Casi admitted. Both Avery and Tate nodded in agreement.

"Good, I'll be as succinct as possible. Questions at the end, please." Gabriel met each of their gazes before continuing. "Selene Walsh is your serial killer. The innate psychic or magical abilities linked her victims. She is harvesting the glands to help her maintain a human appearance. The torture is just a bonus for her."

Psychic abilities? Casi didn't have any, well, she hadn't at least until the siren had captured her. Her disbelief in the paranormal seemed silly now since the whole Archangel thing. Shivering, Casi shifted from behind Luc's protective body and eased herself under his arm to snuggle against him. She wasn't going to think too much about the need for cuddling. He didn't protest or comment except to tuck her closer.

Gabriel grinned and once again answered her thoughts. "Yes, you have psychic powers, but they were untapped. It wasn't until you held my horn that your abilities were triggered."

"Horn? As in the actual Gabriel's horn?" Awe filtered Luc's voice.

"Yes." Gabriel gestured to her. "She wears it now."

Startled, Casi pulled the chain from inside her shirt, revealing the horn-shaped charm dangling from the necklace. "This? I can't see this tumbling Jericho's walls down…"

Gabriel's laughter boomed out, carrying a joyful ring. "Not presently. May I?" He held out his hand.

Casi shrugged. She opened the chain and pulled the horn off, then dropped the tiny charm into his palm.

His fingers wrapped around the horn as he fisted it. "Behold"—his hand opened—"a cherished treasure of Heaven."

The three-inch curved bugle morphed before their eyes, growing in size until it achieved about two feet in length. The odd color—a greenish, brownish-gray combination—became more pronounced in its larger shape. The polished gleam highlighted the colorful striations. It appeared like a solid piece of beautiful marble. Looking closely, Casi spotted the eyehook in the curved u-shape. The ring was the only thing unchanged about the horn, so tiny in comparison now, she wasn't sure how it remained attached.

"It is the first Shofar horn in existence, but unlike its modern successors made from ram or sheep horns, this is a bone from a kraken."

"Enough!" Tate threw his arms in the air with a grimace on his face. "Kraken? Sirens? Earlier you mentioned vampires…I feel like I'm in a video game. These…*things* are real?"

"My Father's world is delightfully diverse. You live and work in New Orleans, what do you think? It is a hub of supernatural confluence."

"Vince," Luc interjected. "You saw him transform not only himself but the horn with your own eyes. It's a little late to be a doubting Thomas, since you're here."

Tension built in the air as the detectives stared each other down, pitting their wills against each other.

Tate grunted, breaking first. "Fine. But I still reserve the right to call bullshit."

Luc reached an arm across her to present a fist to Tate, who tapped it with his own. Men. After everything that had happened, she had no problem believing the Archangel. The horn troubled her though. How could she have carried around a priceless religious artifact and not know it?

"I can't believe I was wearing…" Casi gestured to the horn.

"Be grateful you had it on your person," Gabriel responded. "Between the horn and your powers, you broke the siren's enthrallment of the men beside you. Consider yourselves immune." He nodded at the detectives. "Selene can never take control of any of you again."

"But wait…what about me?" Casi thought back to her own capture. "The siren must have ensnared me when she grabbed me in the alley, because it's the last thing I remember before waking in the basement. I didn't have the horn then, so how come I wasn't in her powers when strapped to that gurney?" Her blood chilled at the memory. She should have died horribly on that table.

Gabriel nodded. "I think her attack on you awakened your psychic abilities in a proactive self-defense. You broke from her magic on your own, and then once you held my horn, your skills came fully online. With my relic, you can break others out of her grasp and keep them permanently safe from entrapment."

Luc sighed. "That's a relief, but what about my family? Does Casi have to touch them all to immunize them?"

"She probably has already without knowing, but it's a simple matter of her having the horn on her person. Casi can give out hugs to make sure your family's protected."

"I'm assuming Selene will still come after Casi, right?"

Gabriel nodded. "She wants Casi and the horn."

"*Merde*! The party! Casi couldn't possibly touch everyone. There're too many people. What if Selene grabs the guests and uses them against us? We can't hurt them to protect ourselves, they're family and friends! We'd be overwhelmed in seconds."

"Calm, Lucas." Gabriel raised his hand, palm out in supplication. "Even Selene has limitations on her powers. She could probably handle a dozen easily, but not much more than that before she loses her own control."

Casi sighed in relief. Good to know they weren't facing some all-powerful uber-villain. But the siren stalked her. How could she protect herself? A shiver went through her, causing a scrutinizing look from Luc. There had to be a way to save herself.

"Yes," Gabriel once again answered her unvoiced question.

"Yes, what?" Luc asked, still staring at her.

"My apologies," Gabriel offered. "I'm being rude. It's time for my final words, then I must go back to being a simple bartender for a while."

Luc faced the Archangel with a slight tilt to his head. Casi could see the wheels turning in his mind. He was probably thinking ten steps ahead of her addled, shocked brain. She wasn't wrong.

"Why does she want your horn? And why don't you take care of Selene? You're an Archangel. I'm sure it would be simple for you."

"You'd be correct, Detective Avery. However, there are laws, as I'm sure you can appreciate."

"You can't interfere, right?" Tate jumped into the conversation.

"Correct, Vincent. My hands are mostly tied. I have searched centuries for a way to rid this world of her evil. Recently, by my brothers' actions, I conceived a plan and put it into play."

Oh, hell. He wanted to use her to kill the siren. Casi supposed it would be better than being killed, but how could she possibly take on a supernatural creature? Besides, she'd never killed or hurt a person in her entire life, even during her darkest days. She wasn't sure she could. Fear flooded her veins. Casi looked away from her tightly clasped hands in her lap, meeting Gabriel's gaze. His expression serious yet thoughtful, proving once again he was reading her mind. Enough, already.

"I can't. I won't."

Luc, showing his agile mind, knew exactly what she meant and quickly nudged her behind him once more. "Casi will not be your assassin." Relief flooded her. Why had she worried? Luc would protect her, heck, Tate would as well. "So what if Casi's immune to mind control, she doesn't have any training or weapons to take on this monster. I won't allow it."

"Do you think me so unkind, Lucas François Avery?"

"I don't know you. Practicing Catholic or not, you're asking her to do your dirty work, I'm inclined to be distrustful."

"Luc." Casi grabbed his arm. "Archangel. Perhaps you shouldn't aggravate him. Let's hear him out." She might be afraid of taking on a supernatural creature, but she doubted the angel wanted her death. Casi tried to edge out from behind Luc, but he merely grunted and blocked her.

Seriously? She scooted backward, out of his reach, and moved sideways before inching to sit between him and Vince. No more cuddling with the overbearing caveman. Luc shot her a frown but gave her the space she wanted.

Tate spoke into the gaping silence. “I assume there is a way for a human to kill a siren, and I’d offer the sucker bet it has to do with your horn since Selene’s after it. So since I doubt an angel of our Lord would send us to our deaths, and yes, ours, Casi isn’t doing this on her own. In fact, if there’s a way to keep her out of it, I’m all in. How do we take Walsh out?”

Gabriel nodded. “I can give you the tools, but my hands are tied after that. I cannot interfere more than I already have.”

“Again, so how do we kill her?” Tate asked in all his Delta Force seriousness.

0“With this.” Gabriel picked up his horn lying on the ground beside him. “You are correct. This is the sole instrument of her weakness and why she wants it protectively in her custody, since my relic can’t be unmade—destroyed. Sound the horn in her presence, and the odds will be even.”

“So…what? We carry around a freaking ancient horn until Selene shows, and then one of us blows it?” Casi’s nose crinkled. Did the horn do something like explode Walsh or something like Jericho’s walls?

“First, we can be more discreet.” Gabriel glanced down, and the horn shrunk before their eyes, back into the three-inch charm. He handed the tiny-sized horn to her.

She threaded the chain through the artifact’s hook

eye and fastened the necklace around her neck, letting it drop against her chest. "Neat trick you have there, but how are we supposed to do it? Change the size, you know?"

"Simple." He gently took Cat from his lap, who gave a disgruntled meow as he placed her on the ground and stood. "All you have to do, any of you have to do, is simply will it to do so. It's my horn, and I asked it to obey you." He paused. "It shouldn't matter, but I gave the power to Selene as well. She will be able to size shift it as well. It was necessary so it could remain hidden while she had the relic in her possession." Gabriel turned and walked away.

"Hey, wait!" Luc jumped to his feet. Right before he grabbed the Archangel's arm, Gabriel stopped and faced him. Luc skidded to a halt and dropped his hand. The angel lifted a single eyebrow in query. "You didn't tell us how to kill her."

"I didn't. I'm sure you'll find a way. With your immunity and the horn, you'll figure something out. I have high hopes."

Gabriel left, passing through the willow trees, and headed to a brightly painted van parked on the driveway. She and Tate both got to their feet. They walked to Luc.

"Was he serious?" Casi stared dumbfounded at the pretend bartender who drove the van to the house. "Are we on our own?"

"Apparently so." Luc grabbed her hand, entwining their fingers. "And there's no doubt we'll do as he asks. I want you safe. She'll just keep coming for you."

"We need a planning session for our mission." Tate's dark gaze locked on Luc's.

“That we do.” Luc tugged on her hand to get her walking. Vince fell in step as they headed back to the house.

How were they going to kill the siren? Those words alone boggled her. She shot quick glances at Tate and Avery walking on either side of her. Hopefully, a former Delta Force warrior, a kick-ass detective, and one scared psychic could be a new dream team and not the start of a bad joke or making headlines as the siren’s next victims.

Chapter Thirty-Five

Luc sighed as he shut the door, enclosing Vince and Casi with him inside his father's office. It had taken the rest of the day and into the evening to get some private time. Gabriel drove off, leaving behind all their unanswered questions after they helped to unload the kegs. Party prep filled up the remaining afternoon. When evening arrived, his family wouldn't let them skip dinner or miss visiting time afterward. Especially since they loved Vince and had been happily surprised by his unannounced arrival. Luc finally had to resort to official police business and asked to borrow the office to get away from his interfering family.

"I know where Poppa hides the good stuff. I'm pouring us all a round." Luc sat in the large well-worn leather chair behind the old heavy maple executive desk. Opening the deep bottom drawer, he reached in and pulled out a bottle of top shelf scotch. "Someone grab the glasses off the credenza."

He wasn't surprised when his partner went to the cabinet holding several liquid-filled decanters and empty tumblers. Casi appeared not to be a big drinker. He motioned for her to take one of two chairs in front of the desk. She crossed the room with no argument and sat herself down in the overstuffed, wide, high-back chair. Tate followed shortly, placing the crystal tumblers on the desk before taking the remaining matching chair.

Luc pulled the cork from the bottle and poured generous amounts in all three glasses. Tate grabbed a glass as Luc re-stoppered the bottle. He nudged a glass toward Casi. “You too. It’s been a hell of an afternoon, and I doubt this discussion will make the rest of our night enjoyable.”

Reluctantly, but obliging, Casi leaned forward and grabbed a cut crystal glass. She sniffed its contents before taking a tiny sip. Luc slugged back a generous swallow. His life had been turned on its head. He believed in many things science couldn’t prove, he was Cajun after all. He had no problem with Casi being psychic and definitely had no problem believing in angels with his Catholic religion. But supernatural monsters? Sirens…krakens…vampires…oh my? He supposed in for a penny, in for a pound. He needed to believe in order to keep Casi safe and prevent any more victims from dying. He drank some more.

Vince broke the silence. “It’s surprising the one thing freaking me out the most isn’t Heavenly beings or mythical supernatural monsters turned real, but the fact I almost killed you.” Tate took a gulp from his glass. “I don’t know what I’d do if I had.” He paused as they eyed each other. Luc knew, as well as Vince, the Special Forces trained soldier would have succeeded. Tate faced Casi and raised his glass. “Thanks for stopping me, sweetheart. I couldn’t have lived with myself if had I killed him.”

Casi raised her glass in acknowledgement, and they both drank. Truth be told, Luc knew he was dead when Tate pinned him to the ground. With his wind knocked out, he couldn’t respond quickly enough before

Vincent's hands were on Luc's jaw and the back of his head. He couldn't have done anything to prevent Tate from snapping his neck. It had happened too quickly. Sweat broke out on his skin at the memory. *Damn.* He had been lucky holding Vince off as long as he had.

Luc smiled at Casi before switching his gaze to his partner. "It was an awesome tackle. I'm not sure how she managed to take you down." He compared their sizes and shook his head. "She's on my rugby team next time we play. I want to see her tackle you again."

Tate lifted an eyebrow. "I'm forewarned of her mightiness. I'll pass to your brother and let her pummel him."

"Um, you boys are forgetting the fact I don't know how to play rugby…"

Luc smiled. "You'll learn. It's fun, and we play mixed-gender teams. You'll fall in love with the game."

"That means she's sticking around?" Tate asked.

"I surely hope so, if I get my way." They exchanged one of their silent communications. Tate had the *it's like that* look, which Luc returned with a *you better believe it, she's mine.*

Casi shook her head. "I hate to break it to you all, but unless we figure out a way to kill the siren, there might not be a later."

"Killjoy. Great way to ruin the relaxing mood, Thomas." Vince mockingly frowned back at her. "But she does have a valid point. It's getting late, we should probably work out a battle plan for killing the bitch."

"I wonder what Gabriel meant by the horn evening the odds?" Luc hated not having all the information in his hands. "What's it supposed to do?"

"Who knows?" Vince countered. "Since I have to

believe he is, in fact, the Archangel Gabriel, I'm gonna have to trust his word the horn will help. So even the odds? Maybe it makes her more human than supernatural monster?"

Casi nodded. "That makes sense. So she can't use her voice on us since we're immune, and after sounding the horn, maybe she can't sprout wings."

"Claws and fangs," Luc muttered. "Gabriel said she had wings, claws, and fangs. Maybe supernatural strength?"

"Do you think the horn takes all of it away?" Casi looked hopeful.

"It's best to plan for the worst-case scenario," Vince mused. "Let's prep for no enthrallment and no wings, but expect claws, fangs, and super strength." He blew out a harsh breath. "I'm living in a graphic novel."

"Can we just shoot her?" Luc liked the idea of taking her out from afar. Close contact opened up too many chances of danger.

"Worst case." His partner pointed out again. "We'll have guns and try them, but let's assume it might only slow her down and not kill her, so we'll have to get dangerously close."

"Here's another thought," Casi interjected. "How long does the horn's effect last? If it's merely seconds, would she heal her bullet wounds?"

Luc smiled. "Super healing. Excellent point. We need a backup weapon and method."

"Decapitation." Vince's grin was slightly evil. Luc knew that expression. That smile was usually directed at Commander Eckert, especially when his partner got one over on the asshole. "I'd like to see her heal from that. Nothing can live without a head. There are plenty of machetes around here because your family uses them when you go deep into the bayou. I remember you keep 'em sharp."

"We do." Luc returned the smile. "So we have our weapons down. First guns. My rifle for gators is here. It'll give us bigger caliber to keep her down permanently or slow her down longer."

"I like your way of thinking, partner." Vince raised his glass in a toast, which Luc duplicated.

A comfortable silence filled the room as each of them drank. Luc loved his poppa's office—from the scarred desk, which had seen generations of Avery's behind it, to the book-filled shelves lending a comforting musty smell to the room. He remembered reading in a chair near one of the windows as his poppa worked on the books for his newly opened restaurant.

Jules Avery hadn't wanted to delegate for his shiny new business. A smile tugged at Luc's mouth. His momma had words with the stubborn chef, and the accounts were soon passed over to a real bookkeeper, giving his poppa more time with his family. The family had plenty of money with the mineral land rights, but his poppa wanted to succeed on his own. Much like their poppa, Jolie opened her tea shop all on her own, and of course, Luc made his own money. But as all Avery's knew, the family had everyone's back if the worst should happen.

And Luc would protect them all. This so-called siren wouldn't hurt his family. His gaze drifted to Casi curled up in her chair, her legs tucked under her, staring into her mostly filled glass. As if she felt him staring, she lifted her gaze to his. She didn't know it, but he was keeping her. Not wanting her scared and running, he brought out his poppa's smile, the charming one.

Casi's head tilted as if trying to read his mind. Hopefully telepathy wasn't one of her newly acquired psychic skills. Right now though, he'd put aside their possible future and focus on her safety by killing Selene. He had no qualms about it, he'd revel in the blood staining his hands.

They had the weapons, now they needed a plan. "So how do we find her? Do we try to hunt her?"

"It's a possibility. However"—Tate wore his Delta Force face—"we wouldn't be able to control the ground. I'd rather have the advantage of knowing the terrain."

"Use me." Casi dropped her feet to the floor and sat up straighter. "She wants me and the horn."

"You're not bait—"

"How about the screened cabin?" Casi spoke right over Luc. "I could hang out there, and you guys could hide in the tree line. Or maybe, you know, we could find some place farther away from the house that would work better."

"No."

"The plan has some merit, partner," Vince added. "Picking the location and using Casi allows us to control the situation."

"No way. She's not going anywhere near that creature." Luc glared at Vincent. Casi would never be on the frontline. He thought Tate had his back. In the clearing, Vince had wanted to keep Casi out of it. Traitor. She'd been in danger enough. He couldn't lose her. Tate and him having her six might keep her safe, but the *might* freaked him out. It wasn't nearly good enough.

"Luc, let me do this."

He stood, the chair rolling forcibly back as he pressed his palms to the desktop and glared at them. "I won't allow it."

Casi shot to her feet. "Allow it? You don't get a say. If I want to put myself out there as bait, I will."

"No."

"Okay, everyone, let's all calm down," Tate offered, still sitting. "We can come up with a Plan B."

Casi glowered back at him. "We don't need a Plan B. Plan A is fine. Keep it simple. It's a thing."

Luc's blood boiled. He struggled for calm. He had a flash temper and letting it loose was never a good idea. But damn, Casi needed to stop putting herself in danger. She absolutely would not be involved in taking out a supernatural creature. Luc knew one way to ensure she didn't sneak around his back. He held out a hand.

"Give me the horn."

Her eyes widened, then her lips pursed into a thin line as her brow furrowed. "No." It surprised him she hadn't shouted at him, but her refusal, a soft-spoken denial, appeared composed. Her hand reached up and pressed the horn hanging inside her shirt to her chest.

Luc had enough. He stalked around the desk and stopped in front of her, close, encroaching in her personal space to loom over her. Through gritted teeth, he tried to soften his voice. "Give me the horn…please."

She shook her head and tried to take a step back, but the chair blocked her. "No, Luc, I won't. Gabriel gave me the horn, not you, not Vince, but me. Stop acting like an overbearing asshole."

Asshole? She hadn't seen him at his worst, but she was about to. "You will *not* be a part of this. Give me the fucking horn, Casi." He got into her face, crowding even closer. She stared up at him and shook her head. "Don't make me take it from you." Her eyes grew round, and she bit her lower lip.

Tate finally unfolded himself from his chair, took a step, and gripped Luc's shoulder. "Man, back off. Let's talk this out."

He shrugged out from under his partner's grip but did take a step back and tried to calm down. But with his pounding head and his blood boiling with frustration, cooling off was beyond his grasp. He stared at Vince. "What the hell? You don't want her involved in this anymore than I do. Why don't you have my back?"

"Stop being a dickhead and I might."

He stared at him. "I'm not being a dick. I'm trying to protect her."

"Thank you." Casi spoke up. "I do want your protection and Tate's too. You'll keep me safe. I know you will." She glanced between them. "It's a good plan—a baited trap with a battle ground of our choosing. Nothing bad will happen to me. You won't let it—I trust you."

Dammit. She had to say those three words. He knew what those words meant. Her fear of the police ran deep and rightly so. The pulse pounding in his head found a faster, sharper beat. It meant everything to him that Luc had gained her trust.

"Thank you. I know how hard it is to trust us. So please *trust* me. Putting you in danger is stupid—"

"Stupid! I'm not an idiot. I know the danger.

You're the one being a dim-witted, stubborn misogynist." Her voice rose in volume with her own anger.

Luc stared at her in shock. "Of all the…" He shoved a hand through his hair. "Let us handle Selene. We're trained for it, and you're not."

"Trained? You've fought supernatural monsters before?" Her glare softened as she gazed at him. "No one is safe all the time, Luc."

He took a few more steps back, distancing himself from her. Why was she being so naïve? He'd seen her fear, her terror. Why couldn't she let them handle this? "You're in way over your head."

She shook her head again and looked sad. "I'm keeping the horn. I will be part of this, Luc. I *need* to be a part of this."

His head throbbed harder, and his temper rose again. In the clearing, she had said differently. Of course, *now* she changed her mind and wanted all in. "You're wrong. You need to stay out of this. You're a civilian, and you're going to get us killed by distraction alone." His jaw locked, and he glanced at his silent partner. "I need some fucking air."

It may be childish, but he couldn't stay in the room a second longer. He didn't want to say something he couldn't take back. Luc strode out the office and headed for the front door. Once outside, he picked up his pace, trying to get as far away as possible. His temper flared red-hot. Luc needed to run off his anger.

He was all in. From the moment he'd caught her in his arms at the station, Luc had been lost. *Est'tombé en botte*. He fell to ruin. And if he had to tie her up and lock her in a room, he'd do so. He wouldn't lose the woman he loved.

Chapter Thirty-Six

Luc waited at the base of the wide staircase, sending up a silent prayer Casi hadn't use the back set of stairs instead. He'd kept his distance from her all morning. Now midafternoon, the party had already started, but there been no sign of Casi. He searched, and when he hadn't found her, guilt set in. So now he laid in wait, hoping to apologize for his behavior last night.

In answer to his prayer, she appeared at the top of the staircase. Casi froze when she spotted him below, leaning on the curled end of the banister. He added another prayer. *Please don't run, darlin'*. She stood there frowning down at him. Willing her to stay, he used the moment of her indecision to take her in. God, she was gorgeous.

She wore another borrowed dress, and this one, hands down, was his favorite so far. The fire-engine red color made her latte skin glow. Thin, tiny straps held the dress up, revealing her bare shoulders, the neckline plunged, more than the clothes she'd been wearing, to tantalizingly reveal the top globes of her breasts with Gabriel's horn resting just above, dangling from a silver chain. Her upswept hair showed off her long neck while a few escaped tendrils framed her beautiful face. The fiery fabric cupped her breasts and clung down to her waist before gently flaring out to end an inch or two above her knees. The flirty, pleated bottom would swirl out if she spun and twirled. He'd make sure it did when he danced with her, the added bonus he would glimpse more of her thighs.

He let his gaze trail downward, hoping for sexy, matching red stilettos. Luc had to hide his grin at the practical flat, tan sandals. Spiky heels on the lawn would have been unworkable. Lifting his eyes, he locked gazes with her rich brown-eyed stare. The anger glaring in their depths wasn't a surprise. He hoped she'd take her rage and stride on down. Confront him instead of turning her back and bailing. *Come on, sweetheart. Give me a chance*.

As if Casi read his mind, she took the first step down, until she stopped a few levels above him, giving her a slight height advantage. Still frowning, she folded her arms across her stomach, while her lips pressed into a thin line as if fighting to keep her words from exploding out. The silent treatment turned back on him. He deserved what he got.

"Can we talk, Casi?"

Her eyes widened before narrowing in a glare. "Now you want to talk? Not last night, or this morning, or even earlier this afternoon?"

"Yes. Please?" He held out his hand. "I'd like to explain." She didn't move, only stared at his outstretched hand. He swallowed hard. God, he hoped he hadn't messed it all up, hoped he hadn't lost her trust. Luc would grovel if necessary. "Please?"

"Fine."

Instead of brushing by him as he expected, she took his hand. A bit of hope exploded inside him as he led her to the sitting room. When she tried to drop his hand, no doubt in an effort to sit in a chair alone, he tightened his grip and tugged her down beside him on the couch. He needed her close to him, especially with what he was about to share.

"You look absolutely beautiful, by the way."

She snorted and pulled her hand away. "Compliments will not lift you out of the hole you dug yourself into."

"I suppose not, but I wanted to tell you. It's the truth." He needed to show all his cards, get everything out front. Hopefully, it would be a winning hand. "First, above all else, I'm sorry. I *was* an asshole last night. When my temper blows, it explodes, so I didn't handle the situation well, but there is a reason for my poor behavior. Will you hear me out?"

She tilted her head. "You know I'm pissed at you, right?"

"*Ouais, cher*. I know."

"Your disappearing act today did not make you any more appealing." He nodded. "So you want to talk now? Why should I listen? Everything seems to happen on your terms and only yours."

Casi stood and he leaped to his feet, grabbing her wrist. "I love you," he blurted out, and she froze. Maybe not the best declaration of love ever stated, but the most expedient to keep her from leaving. His finger swept gently over the soft skin of her inner wrist. "I love you."

She shook her head in denial. Raising his other hand, he pressed it against her cheek, stopping the side-to-side motion of denial as he continued to pet her wrist, stroking over her pulse. "I do."

"You-you," she stuttered but didn't pull away. "You can't. It's impossible. You hardly know me."

"Ah, darlin', I do. I might not know everything about you, but I know enough."

"It's only been, what? A week, maybe a week and a half? I've lost all track of time. It's all a mess in my head, but I know it's too soon, too fast."

"Come, sit with me." He dropped his hand from her face. Using the gentle encircling hold on her wrist, he pulled her down once again alongside him on the couch. Luc gazed straight into her confused eyes. "Let me tell you about the Avery men and love. The first I know of is my great grandfather. He fell for his wife when he saw her through a café window. He went in, introduced himself, and asked her out on a date. They were married shortly after. Next came my grandpapa, he met my grandmamma at a *fais do do*. He saw her dancing with another man, and it hit him hard. Struck dumb with love, and then a rage of jealousy swept through him."

"What did he do?" Casi leaned in, closing the distance between them.

"What any jealous man would do. He marched right on over, tapped the other fellow out, and swept her up in his arms and danced the night away with her." Luc smiled. No matter how many times he had heard the story, it never got old. "Still extremely in love today as they were in the beginning."

She returned the smile. "I know. I've seen them. And no matter how much I didn't want to see you today, I couldn't keep myself away from Rene and Faith's celebration. Even if it meant running into you."

He nodded. "Rightly so. Their love and life together is beautiful."

"So did your dad fall fast for your mom, too?"

"He did indeed. One night, Poppa was leaving a bar when he spotted a woman in the parking lot trying to break into her car. He went over to help, thinking she locked her keys inside. When she jumped into the driver's seat and began hot-wiring it, let's say it raised some suspicion. When asked, my momma replied this was her boyfriend's car, well, ex-boyfriend's as of that night. She'd finally caught him red-handed, cheating on her. Her plan was to leave his car in front of the police station, 'cause the cheating ex had several outstanding tickets." Luc grinned. "Poppa told her to scoot over, got in, and started the car for her. He fell head over heels right then and there."

"So the Avery men have this total love-at-first-sight thing, but what about their partners?"

"Ah yes. The women took a bit of convincing and wooing. But they all got their *filles* in the end. And I might add, the women have been exceedingly happy."

"You really believe this?" She wore a slight frown.

The men in his family, when they fell, they went down hard and fast, with no looking back. He had heard the stories of Avery men through the years and the love at first sight, but Luc hadn't really believed the tales until Casi.

"No, not until it happened to me. I thought they were cute family stories."

"So when you knocked me off my feet in the interrogation room, it was actually you who fell?" Her frown had disappeared, but not her skepticism.

He took her hand, interlacing their fingers, and gave a squeeze. "I tried to ignore the feeling. I didn't recognize it for what it was. Plus the war within myself about remaining solely professional hadn't helped."

"Funny, Marielle said something similar. That once you got over yourself, you'd recognize your feelings for me." Casi's frown returned. "Luc, you—"

He quickly held up his free hand, stopping her. "I know. Don't worry, there's no pressure to return the emotion." His grin broke out. "That's where all the convincing and wooing comes in."

He would win his woman. Get her to fall hard for him as he had for her. But first, he needed to keep her safe. His smile fled. "About last night… I am sorry. It's just… I know I went all caveman on you, and it was wrong, but when it comes to you, I'm all protective, possessive, and primitive. The decidedly uncool three P's."

She squeezed his hand. "You *do* make me feel safe, so the caveman act is kind of comforting sometimes, but Luc, you have to understand I don't like feeling out of control. This siren has taken so much from me—my best friend, my security, and the sense of being in charge of my own life."

"I know, *cher*." He brushed a shiny tendril of her hair behind her ear.

"So last night…I wanted to take back my life, be in control, and you stomped all over my determination. Being bait to trap her is something I *can* do. But," her bottom lip went between her teeth. He had the urge to draw it out with his own but knew now wasn't the time. They still had things to work out. Her next words proved he was right. "Do you really think I'd get you and Vince killed?" Her brow furrowed as her brown eyes filled with worry.

He held in his sigh. Stroking his hand down her bare arm, he searched for the words he needed to say, but didn't want to hurt her. "Truth?" Casi nodded. "There is a possibility. If this were a normal situation, we'd use a female undercover who looks like you. Someone trained who could take care of herself if the shit hit the fan. But this is nowhere near normal." Luc gave a slight morbid chuckle. "Look," his sigh escaped him this time. "We'll figure out how to deal with Selene." He stood, bringing Casi up with him. Luc placed a quick kiss to her lips before tapping her nose with his finger. "Selene won't show tonight, there's too many people for her to deal with. So let's forget about her and have some fun. It's time to join the celebration. You have no idea what you're missing."

Casi finally smiled at him and a grateful peace settled inside him. "Lead on, my hot Cajun."

"I'm liking the *my*." He started walking while holding on to her hand. "You think I'm hot, darlin'?"

She snorted. "I'm not confirming or denying. You have enough ego as it is."

"But it's your ego now."

Luc gave her his charming grin as she laughed, and he escorted her to the backyard. *Vrai*. Truth. He would make Casi his, because he was already hers.

Chapter Thirty-Seven

Noise washed over them as Luc led Casi down the porch steps and into the backyard. There were easily a hundred people partying, helping his grandparents celebrate their love. Family and guests ate and drank everywhere. Long tables were decked out with kegs, piles of crawfish, platters of oysters, fried catfish, vats of jambalaya, and he spotted one of his favorites—crab cakes with lime sauce. *Yum*. His stomach growled. He hadn't eaten anything since last night, because arguing with Casi and Vince had left him with no appetite.

The makeshift dance area filled with couples swinging away to the upbeat zydeco song from Bastien's band. Hopefully his brother wouldn't be calling him to the stage anytime soon. They had a special surprise for their grandparents, but Luc really wanted to eat something and have a beer.

He spotted Tate standing with a drink near one table. "There's Vince." He gave a chin lift in his partner's direction. "Let's go get some food and drink."

Casi smiled and let him guide her through the crowd. It took determination since several relatives who hadn't seen him in a while kept trying to stop him and visit. All with grins and knowing looks at him with Casi. However, he wouldn't be thwarted. Starving, he wouldn't feed the family's gossip vine before feeding his own stomach. They could think whatever they wanted.

"Hey," Vince greeted. "It's good to see things have sorted themselves out." He smiled at their joined hands.

"Maybe," Casi hedged, while the traitor Vince chuckled.

"I'm working on it," Luc replied before grabbing a grilled Cajun shrimp skewer and dipped the fish into a bowl of spicy crab dip. Two for the price of one. His stomach was pleased. He snatched a jerk chicken wing next.

His partner raised an eyebrow at his food inhalation. "Hungry? You need a beer?"

"*Ouais*, that would be awesome." Luc deliberately ignored his partner's sarcasm. "Bring one for Casi, too." Vince walked to the next table shaking his head and started filling cups from the keg. "Here, darlin', try this."

Luc held out a crawfish slider. It consisted of shredded crawfish on some baby spinach, topped with jalapeno slices and chipotle mayonnaise, all sitting on a square of thin-sliced cornbread.

Casi took a bite. "Hmmm, this is fantastic."

Vince arrived juggling three cups, so Luc helped his partner out by carefully taking two and handing one to Casi. Luc took a healthy swallow. The Wilted Lily Ale went down smoothly. When he realized Neutral Ground had stopped playing, he bolted a few more shrimp skewers drenched in the crab dip. His reprieve had ended. Sure enough, Bastien took to the microphone with no musicians backing him up.

"Lucky? You out there, man? It's time to get your ass on stage." His brother searched the crowd for him as several of the partiers laughed.

"I guess that's my cue." Luc slugged back the rest of his beer and placed his empty cup on the table. He looked at Casi. "I won't be long." Then he shot a glance at his partner. "Stay with her?"

"Of course."

Reassured, Luc made his way through the crowd, and hopped onto the stage, and stood next to his little brother.

"You ready?"

Luc nodded. "Good to go."

"Right then. Listen up, y'all. We have something special for the celebrating lovebirds. Grandmamma? Grandpapa? Where you at?" Bastien shielded his eyes with his hand trying to find our grandparents.

"Over here, Batty," Rene Avery called out.

Luc spotted his grandparents sitting together underneath the shade of a tree.

"Al' right." Bas rubbed his hands together. "I've written you a song. It's called, *The Road Taken*, the story of your love." Luc and his brother both smiled when their grandmamma clasped her hands to her heart and grinned. "I dragged Luc up here to sing it with me." Bastien looked over his shoulder. "Count us down, Phil."

Phil clicked his sticks four times before smashing down on his tom drum while banging on the bass to set the perfect beat to the new Neutral Ground rock ballad. The band crashed in on the pickup to the next bar. The new song, a wild cross between a Jon Bon Jovi song and zydeco, as only his brother could mix and make work. One more measure and it was time to sing. It opened with the chorus.

So many roads.

So many ways.
Right. Left.
Retreat. Advance.
All my choices led to you.
The only road taken.
The only right answer.
My heart, my soul, and only love.

Luc's gaze found Casi's. She had quickly become his heart, soul, and most definitely his only love. The song may be for his grandparents, but it spoke to him, the voice of the future he wanted and would cherish if he could be so lucky. Bastien took the first verse solo, and Luc would sing the second.

Two lives separate.
Loneliness. Incomplete.
A solo journey,
A dark so deep,
Until Fate intervened,
And opened my heart, skin deep.

Luc sang as Bastien dropped out.

We collided unexpectedly.
Two stars crashing,
Brilliantly blinding,
The darkness disappears.
Two hearts combining,
Never alone, forever binding.

Still not taking his eyes off Casi, he agreed with the verse he sang. Casi and he had collided unexpectedly, quite literally. She lighted his loneliness, brightening his darkness. He smiled as he harmonized with Bas as they sang the chorus again.

This time they swapped when they got to the next verses. He sang first and felt the words soul deep. They spoke to his ideal. He wanted a wife who was also his best friend, someone to make him complete.

The years float by,
We grow entwined,
Two halves now whole.
Best friends. Lovers.
No end in sight.
My life complete with unending joy.

Our love expands.
Sons, daughters, and generations.
A universe of love,
Orbiting our fused hearts.
The journey worth taking,
Our story still unfolding.

The chorus came again before they dove into the bridge together. Singing to Casi, he hoped she'd read his mind and his intentions, yet not get scared.

Time might chase us,
We won't lose the race.
Stronger together, always entwined.
No beginnings, no endings, with love everlasting.

Yeah, time would be his friend. He'd use it to win her, and like his grandpapa, Luc wouldn't lose because they would be stronger together. Casi and he had already proven they made a pretty great team. Now, if only she would believe it too.

So many roads.
So many ways.
Right. Left.
Retreat. Advance.
All my choices led to you.
The only road taken.

The only right answer.

My heart, my soul, and only love.

As the last harmonized notes rang out, the crowd exploded with applause, hoots, and hollers. It would seem Bastien had another hit on his hands, at least with his family and friends. Luc finally stopped watching Casi long enough to take in his pleased grandparents who were grinning and clapping. After witnessing their happiness, he scanned over the crowd before being drawn back to his woman. Casi wasn't smiling or clapping, but at least she wasn't frowning. *Oops*. He hoped singing to her didn't make the hole he had dug any deeper.

Bastien slapped his shoulder, breaking Luc's study of Casi. "You ready for another song, or should I hand you a trumpet?"

"Sorry, Bas. No can do." His gaze drifted to Casi again. "I think I'm going to eat, drink, and dance with my woman."

"Huh, you finally gave in."

"*Elle réchauffes mon sang comme personne d'autre*."

Bastien chuckled. "I bet she heat's your blood. *Bonne chance*, Lucky. Though I doubt you'll need it." With another smack to Luc's shoulder, his brother sent him on his way. "Get lost and give her a kiss for me."

Luc smiled as he jumped off the stage. "Not on your life. Her kisses are all mine. Find your own."

He made his way through the crowd, heading back to Casi and Vince, hoping there might be opportunities to steal some kisses. Luc was in the mood to party.

Chapter Thirty-Eight

Casi couldn't catch her breath as Luc spun her away from him. She twirled and the bottom of her dress blossomed out before she hit the end of their extended arms and then he tugged her back in. The night revolved in bright lights and loud noise as she danced with Luc. Since Luc had apologized, the rest of the day transformed into a dream, all starting with that damn song. He was supposed to sing it to his grandparents, but no, he literally only had eyes for her. Shivers chased through her body in remembrance.

His singing had been so intimate, so personal, even surrounded by a crowd. He had stunned her and made butterflies—the good kind—flutter inside her stomach. It didn't hurt that Luc's singing voice held a sexy rock and roll growl. Surprising, since his speaking voice, so lyrically smooth, was in complete contrast. When he immediately left the stage, jumping off after performing only the one song, and made a direct beeline back to her, her heart started pounding. Her pulse hadn't slowed down since.

Attentive Luc was devastating. He plied her with amazing food, made sure she had something to drink while always somehow touching her—brushing against her, a hand on her waist, hip, or draped around her shoulder. One time he had lightly run a finger down her neck, and she swore her womb clenched.

He'd hold her hand or have his warm touch against the base of her spine as he guided her through the crowds, introducing her to extended family and friends. His obvious proprietary handling should have pissed her off, especially with all the knowing glances from his friends and family. Instead, it had made her feel wanted and special. Go figure. She guessed she must have forgiven him for his behavior from last night. Luc told her he loved her, and it still staggered her. And then he took her dancing, which they've been doing for what felt like hours yet seconds as well. Time had no meaning while they danced.

He spiraled her in, landing her with her back plastered against his front, leaving no space as they swayed. Running his hands down her sides, he settled his grip on her hips—tugging her closer if possible. Luc definitely enjoyed himself. His obvious arousal was pressed firmly against her backside. Instead of panic, only excitement and need filled her veins. Before she could really enjoy the sensations, he spun her again and had both her hands entwined with his as they now faced each other.

She laughed. Luc was an amazing dancer. Casi wasn't so bad herself and enjoyed dancing, but with Luc leading, her game rose to a whole new level. She'd never had so much fun on a dance floor before. Looking up, she caught his gaze and nearly tripped. He grinned, and his eyes…the hazel mostly green, burned with sinful thoughts. Luc held her enthralled. He must have read her own lustful gaze because his grin morphed into a smirk, and his eyes, still hot, now held a bit of mischievousness glinting through his mercurial-colored stare.

Next thing she knew, instead of dancing on their patch of yard, he threaded them through the surrounding couples. When he had them maneuvered to the far edge of the dance floor, he dropped one of her hands and, with the grip on her other, tugged her from the area to behind the stage. Once out of sight, he broke into a jog. He ran them farther into the darkness.

She hesitated. This didn't seem the smartest idea with a supernatural creature hunting her. Luc noticed and smiled over his shoulder.

"I'm taking you around front. Didn't want to be obvious."

"Luc." She laughed, trying to keep up with him. "What—"

His mouth crashed down on her lips, effectively cutting off her words. She rejoiced. Casi had been waiting all night for him to kiss her, especially after all the touching—foreplay on steroids. She opened her mouth, and his tongue plunged in. She tasted beer and Cajun spices, as he probably tasted the same on hers. A moan escaped her, and Luc growled his approval as he stepped them backward without breaking their heated kiss.

Her back pressed against something smooth. She guessed they had only made it halfway around the house, and she didn't care, as long as they kept kissing. Luc held her possessively. One hand dove into her hair, and she felt strands falling from her messy bun. The other on her hip gave a squeeze before trailing downward until he reached the hem of her dress. His palm pressed against her bare thigh as he found his way under. Luc's fingers feathered upward, still staying on the outside of her leg and not trailing inward, but she gasped anyway.

He broke their kiss, and she involuntarily groaned as he pressed his forehead to hers but didn't remove either of his hands.

"You okay, *cher*?" His accent weighed as heavy as his breathing.

"Yes." Luc heard her whispered and panted reply, because next he dropped a quick kiss to her nose, and then he took over her mouth again. This time the kiss wasn't rough and so needy, it drifted more languid and sly, like he had all the time in the world, and he used it to drive her crazy. As if all the touching this afternoon hadn't teased her into a lustful fire.

The fingers under her dress stroked her skin, sensual but not moving to erotic areas. She squirmed, wanted more, needing more. He chuckled. The bastard. With a last swirl of his talented tongue, he left her mouth to kiss her chin, then jaw, before caressing wet open-mouth kisses down her neck. The rasp of his growing five-o'clock shadow was an erotic contrast to his hot mouth making her shiver.

"Luc." She didn't recognize her own voice which sounded low and husky. "Please."

He reached the base of her neck and sucked hard as the hand on her thigh climbed higher and clutched her lace-clad butt cheek. Releasing her tight hold on his shoulders, her arms twined around his neck so her fingers could play with his soft hair. She hitched her leg around his hip, aided by his hold on her ass, and pressed her aching center against the hard length of his erection.

A groan tore from both their throats. Her fear never rose, only an intense arousal.

The hand in her hair dropped to a primitive hold to her nape. “You are so sexy. You’ve been killing me in that red dress all day. *Bon sang*, you drive me crazy.”

He thrust into her, hitting the perfect spot, spiking a tremor and soaking her already damp panties. Luc was the sexy one. His mouth crashed on hers, and their tongues dueled as their lower bodies continued an erotic rhythm, driving her higher and hotter.

Casi had never felt this way. Ever. Not earlier in her life when things were simpler and fresh and certainly not since her assault. Luc had been right, there was a connection between them. She hadn’t seen it through her bigotry, blinded like Luc through his profession. Her life tainted by her distrust after the attack. Both shock and need flooded her.

Could it be? Her heart pounded even faster. She wanted to deny her feelings, but with Luc being brave and stating his love while expecting nothing in return, she hadn’t inspected her own emotions. Casi trusted him. More than that, she knew she was safe with him, cared for him. Loved him? *Holy shit*!

This time she broke the kiss and pressed both her hands to his face, holding him so she could meet his gaze.

“What?” Luc’s voice was hoarse, his breathing unsteady.

“I…” The words she wanted couldn’t pass her lips. So she would offer what she could in this moment. “I want you. Take me upstairs. I need you inside me…closer. I want to be closer to you. Have to.”

Luc gave her a new smile, one tender and sweet. “You sure, darlin’?”

She knew he’d stop. Even now, with her leg

wrapped around his hip and his erection tantalizingly pressed against her core, their blood running hot and need coursing through them both. Casi knew he would only go as far as she could handle. Her safety paramount to him, he'd never hurt her, physically or emotionally.

"Yes. And I'm getting sick of the repetitive questions."

"Too bad, sugar. I'll always be checking in with you," he drawled.

"Hmmpfh." She puffed out. "Hey, Luc." He raised an eyebrow. "Take me to bed or lose me forever."

He laughed. "Show me the way home, honey."

Proving he knew his *Top Gun* references, she laughed in return. Casi dropped her leg and grabbed his hand. She towed him behind her. Looking over her shoulder, she gave Luc a smile and saw a metal shed he had backed her against. Missing his warmth and being draped around his body, she hurried to the front of the house, keeping to his plan of sneakiness.

Casi ran them up the porch, through the front door, and up the wide staircase before Luc's inner caveman took over. He swept her off her feet and into his arms. She squealed in surprise. He stole a burning kiss before jogging down the hallway. Luc entered his bedroom and used his foot to slam the door behind them.

He set her gently on her feet. She read the question held in his gaze, but before he could put it into words, she placed a finger against his lips.

"Don't. I want this. I want you."

He kissed her finger and smiled. Casi took advantage of his compliance and tugged his T-shirt from his black jeans. When she got it free, she yanked it upward, and Luc obligingly took over, pulling it over his head. With her hands now unoccupied, they went directly to his bare chest, pressing against his warm, firm muscles and light dusting of dark blond hair. Luc toed off his shoes as she let her hands wander, her fingers tracing the ridges of his abs.

His hands, in the meantime, weren't idle. He deftly snatched the clip holding what remained of her bun out of her hair and tossed it aimlessly behind him. Her hair fell, reaching the middle of her back. He appeared pleased as he petted the entire length from the top of her head down to its ends.

Luc gave a playful tug on a lock. "Shoes."

Not wanting to remove her hands from him, she too, toed off her flat sandals while simultaneously popping the button on his jeans. Casi carefully slid down his zipper, not wanting to injure the straining bulge hidden behind the metal teeth. Multitasking at its finest. Grabbing the waistband of his jeans, she pushed them past his hips, revealing today's boxer briefs—black. She missed his cherry red ones. It would have matched her borrowed dress. When Luc had kindly stepped on the legs of his pants, his feet pulling them the rest of the way off, Casi went for his underwear. Her hands were halted when he gently shackled her wrists. He raised her hands, placing her palms against his chest.

"Not so fast, darlin'. Let's leave them on for now." She frowned and he chuckled. "I've been dying to unwrap you from this sexy red dress all day."

His hand landed on her waist and feathered downward until reaching the hem. Having touched her all day, he already knew there were no zippers or buttons to deal with. His hand fisted the soft material and leisurely pulled upward.

Thank God the only underwear she had packed from her apartment were her fancy ones—praise be to dirty laundry—she had no qualms over the revelation. Luc's head tilted down, breaking their gazes, and locked on her bare skin peeking into view, his attention completely captivated. When the peach lace of her bikinis with the matching satin bow appeared, he swallowed hard.

"Arms up," he rumbled and with obvious impatience quickly tore the dress up and over her head. The dress went the way of her hair clip as he tossed it behind him. She lowered her arms to her side and studied Luc as he took in the rest of her uncovered skin. His gaze locked on her breasts covered in a matching peach lace demi bra. Her tight nipples poked through the shear lace. Casi didn't shy from her obvious arousal on display. How could she? Especially since a hot, sexy Cajun stared at her with an equal mix of awe and lust.

Luc reached out and fingered the tiny satin bow nestled between her breasts. "You're killing me, darlin'. So gorgeous." He met her gaze and smiled. "Come here." His hand gripped the back of her neck and pulled her close. She willingly went to him and tilted her face upward as he brought his down. Needy yet testing, he kissed her. Questioning if she was still all in. She showed him by sucking hard on his tongue while getting a handful of his toned ass and squeezed. He groaned and broke the kiss.

"It's that way, is it, sugar?"

Casi smiled as his hands seized her waist and lifted her in the air. She shrieked when her body hit the mattress and bounced. Luc leaned a knee on the mattress and clutched her ankles, pulling. Next thing she knew, she was flat on her back as he crawled up the bed, stopping when over her. He braced a forearm next to her shoulder, using it to hold his weight off her. Reaching with his other arm, his hand palmed her face, holding her head in place as he leaned in and kissed her, lazy and sexy. Luc had as many kisses as he had smiles in his arsenal, and she looked forward to learning all about them.

She hooked her leg over his hip and rubbed her aching center against him. Luc groaned, his hand left her face to caress downward and land on her lace-covered breast. His lower body pressed into her as his hand squeezed and his thumb brushed her tight nipple.

With his weight pushing her into the mattress and the hold on her breast, a harsh memory sparked across her brain. Her body flinched, solely reactive and unwanted. The coursing blood in her veins took a turn and pulsed with fear. Luc broke their kiss and flipped them.

She straddled him, heart racing as his hands gripped her upper arms. He stayed in a half crunch, making close eye contact. “Better?”

“Yes.” She nodded, ignoring all her body’s signals to the contrary, trying her best to will it all away.

He laid down, giving her another tender smile as he dropped his hands to her thighs. “You’re in control, darlin’.”

Too late. Flashbacks flooded her brain—terror, pain, rough hands, heavy weight, and hot breath. *No, no, no, no*. Her blood turned to ice, and her muscles locked. Overwhelmed, her personal nightmare crushed her. Casi heard her name, Luc calling her, but it seemed so incredibly far away.

Chapter Thirty-Nine

"Casi!"

Luc launched upright and gripped her shoulders, giving her a sharp shake. The jolt did nothing. Her eyes were wide, unblinking, and blank.

"Casi! Darlin', come back to me."

The skin beneath his hands turned icy cold. She barely breathed. *Shit.* Luc slid out from under her and gathered her in his arms. Moving them to the edge of the bed, he snagged the comforter. He covered Casi and then wrapped his arms around her again, offering his warmth as well as the blanket. She still wasn't responding. What was he supposed to do?

On a huge gasp, Casi came alive, blinking as fast pants of air escaped her. She would hyperventilate at this rate. Luc gripped her chin, turning her to face him.

"Easy, Casi. Slow down. Come on, breathe with me." Her gaze focused on him. "Deep breath in." He inhaled and held it, relieved when she followed suit. "Exhale. Now another deep breath." He watched as Casi continued to slow her breathing on her own. Her chest stopped heaving, and color returned, darkening her skin back to a healthier mocha color. Luc's panic subsided.

His hold on her loosened, but he realized his mistake too late when Casi jumped from his lap, comforter and all. She ran across the room, landing in front of his tall dresser. Her hands gripped the edge, and he saw her fingers turned pale with her tight hold. She bowed her head. His heart broke for her.

"Casi."

"Don't," the lone word came out harsh and gravelly.

He'd give her a moment, but only a short one. Luc wouldn't allow her to shut him out. When his mental count reached sixty, he stood. A minute. She'd had her time. Padding across the wooden floor, he came up directly behind her. Carefully, he raised his hand and placed it over one of hers. He pried her bloodless fingers from his dresser.

Casi whirled on him, slapped both her palms to his chest, and shoved. "Go. Leave me."

Her push hadn't moved him because he locked his legs. He shook his head twice but stepped back a few steps so he wasn't crowding her, not wanting to make her feel trapped. He wouldn't leave her, couldn't leave her. She glared at him when he stayed in front of her, unmoving.

"Fine. I'll go." She spun on her bare feet and managed one stride before running into the outstretched arm he'd flung out to block her. Casi wobbled to a halt, but instead of pushing past, which he would have allowed if she really wanted to leave, she remained standing quietly and bowed her head once more.

"Why?" Her voice broke on the single word, but she swallowed hard, lips pressing into a thin line. "How can you stand me? Why aren't you running for the hills, or throwing me out? I can't stand myself. I'm disgusted. Just be done with me and let me go."

"That would be a hard pass, *cher*. I'll never be

done with you. I love you, Casi."

She whirled, lifting her head, and stared. He could see everything, her every emotion written across her face, in her eyes. Anger. Shame. And yet the most important and most heart wrenching—fear.

"How can you love me? I'm a mess. This is the second time I've wigged out on you. The panic attack at your house and now, losing myself during sex? How many freak outs will it take to earn your revulsion? How many times teasing you and leaving you with blue balls and frustration before you hate me? It will happen. We need to stop…whatever." She waved her hand around in a futile gesture. "Whatever this thing is between us now."

He took one step closer, crowding into her personal space. "*Non, cher*. Never. You could break down a billion times, and I'd never be disgusted. Sexual frustration? I'd be happy to only kiss you for years if it meant you were in my life."

Her eyes glistened, but no tears fell. "It's too hard."

Slowly, he reached and pressed his palm to her cheek. He sighed when she leaned into his touch. "Easy is overrated, darlin'. I promise you right here and now, I will fight for you. Fight for us. Even when you can't."

"Luc." His name whispered across her lips. Closing the last step, he wrapped her in his arms, pressing her tight against him.

He held her until the stiffness left her body, and she relaxed into him. Pressing a kiss on top of her head, he moved his hand to the small of her back. "Let's lie down, *mon coeur*." She allowed him to guide her back to the bed. Halting, he pulled back the light blue blanket and sheet, exposing the mattress. Luc tugged the comforter off Casi and tossed it to the end of the bed. "Go on, climb in."

Silently, Casi obeyed, and Luc was a second behind her. He leaned against the pillows and headboard and then wrapped an arm around her shoulders, guiding her to his side, tucking her against him. She rested her head on his shoulder. With his free hand, he grasped the sheet, leaving the blanket behind, and covered them to their waists. That job done, he slid his arm across her stomach, his hand landing lightly on her hip where his fingers stroked the soft lace of her panties.

"*Parle moi, bébé*. Talk to me. What's going on inside your beautiful mind?"

She sighed and turned, angling closer, her nose pressed into his neck, and her arm snaked around his waist in a soft hold. "I'm tired." The soft exhale of her breath warmed his skin. "I want to be me again. No more nightmares, no more panic attacks, no fear."

Deep down, he knew Casi understood what she had to do to achieve this. She was smart, but in denial. He needed her to say the words. With his hand still stroking her hip, he took a breath and hoped to guide her there. "You know how to make that happen, darlin'."

"Therapy." The word a slight whisper of disgust, but the next came out as a plea. "I knew I needed to from the beginning, but I know what it entails." She shuddered in his hold. "I don't think I have the strength to go there, to open the box and let it all out. I can't relive it again."

"Casi, you are one of the strongest women I know, next to my momma, sisters, and grandmama. You're in fabulous company." He gave her shoulder a brief squeeze. "The box holding your assault is cracked open. I'm betting it was never sealed. All your emotions and trauma have been leaking out, poisoning you every day whether you've realized it or not. Don't you think it's time to throw open the lid and purge it all out once and for all? Keeping it stuffed inside, you'll never heal. I know you know this."

Her hold around his stomach tightened as her fingers clenched. "You're right." Her hand released its hold on his waist and moved to press against his chest, her fingers idly threading through his chest hairs.

"If you want," he hesitated, wanting to tread carefully. "I could go with you."

"Like couple's therapy?"

"Sure. I think it would help me figure out how to help you, us." He buried his nose into her hair, loving the honey-ginger scent. "It scared me, Casi," he mumbled into the dark tresses. "I didn't know what to do when you blanked out. You were barely breathing. I hated being helpless." His confession sent a chill through him. If he wanted her continued trust, he needed to be vulnerable with her, too.

"I'm sorry."

"*Non, bébé*. Don't apologize. Not your fault." He placed a quick kiss to her head. "I'm trying to let you know why I think counseling together will help not just you, but me as well. I want us to work, and I'm willing to put in the effort, no matter how hard or how long, so we can succeed." He held his breath and sent up a silent prayer. "So what do you think? Want to go to therapy together?"

Casi rested against his side. Her hand stopped

petting him, and he waited as she stilled. It had to be her choice, her decision. Just with any alcoholic or drug addict, the person needed to want to be healed for themselves. Holding his breath, he clung to hope.

"Okay."

On a sharp exhale, he smiled. "*C'est bon.* I can't wait to get started." Luc pushed Casi slightly away from him and grinned down. "In fact, you earned a reward."

"A reward?"

"Yes. My version of positive reinforcement." His grin grew. "Do you trust me?"

She nodded. "You know I do. I wouldn't be here practically naked if I didn't."

"I'm going to make you feel good, darlin'." He leaned in and dropped a kiss to her nose. "My mouth," his lips brushed against hers, "and my hands," he palmed her stomach and spread his fingers wide to cover more of her satiny skin, "will be instruments of your reward." He nibbled on her full lower lip before tracing over with his tongue in a silent request. She answered.

Casi parted her lips, and his tongue slid in, stroking slowly into her mouth. He took his time before breaking the kiss and leaned his forehead against hers. "I'll stop anytime you want, or I'll stop if I think it's too much. Okay?"

"Yes," came her breathy response.

He captured her mouth for another long kiss before coming up for air. "*Doce comme du miel.* Sweet like honey." He moved to her neck and alternated open-mouth kisses and hard sucks down the long column until he reached the juncture where her neck met her collarbone. Luc nudged the necklace holding the horn aside with his nose before nipping her skin. Casi's entire body shivered. He eased the sting of his bite with a caress of his tongue. Looking up, he captured her gaze, checking in, and saw only warmth and desire in her brown eyes. "*Je t'aime*. I love you."

Casi gifted him with a sweet smile which he decided to steal with his mouth, kissing her hard. Heat flooded him, and his heartbeat kicked up when she gave a sexy moan. *Yes*. He wanted more of that. Luc wasn't kidding when he told her he would settle for only kissing her. Tasting her, capturing her groans and little mewling sounds made him grow hard as his blood flew south. He shifted his hip so his erection wouldn't press against her. Casi's pleasure was his only design. He didn't want to trigger any panic, only help her find some release. But damn, being so aroused while only kissing, he wondered what would happen when he finally touched her. The rate things were heating up, he wouldn't be surprised if he'd orgasm with her.

When Casi squirmed, he broke the kiss and took a moment to stare at his hand against her stomach, taking in the contrast. His tanned hand looked lighter against her darker smooth skin. Skin so soft, it made his fingers feel too rough with his calluses. She squirmed again, and his splayed hand caressed downward. He fingered the satin peach bow centered in the band of her sexy underwear. Luc really wished his mouth could replace his hand. He wanted to pull down her panties with his teeth and then place kisses along her legs until he reached her hot core. He wanted to taste and feast, knowing if he adored her mouth, he would love the more intimate flavor of her sex.

Later. He knew the day would come when he could indulge. He could be patient. Instead, he took her lips and, licking his way in, kissed her deep. His fingers danced down over the soft lace of her underwear until his hand cupped her between her legs and pressed in. Casi's mouth tore from his when her head fell back as a groan passed her swollen lips. Luc bit back his own groan as she ground against his hand, and he felt the hot wetness soaking her panties. So damn sexy. Thank God he wasn't wearing restrictive jeans, hard and erect, his penis peaked from the waistband of his boxers.

He used his thumb to nudge her underwear aside and finally stroke a finger between the folds hiding her fiery center. Casi cried out again, and her hands flew to his head where her fingers clutched at his hair. Luc pressed kisses to her chin and back down her neck, once again wishing his mouth and not his fingers teased her below.

"Please." Casi's breathless plea needed to be answered.

Luc slid a finger into her. She moaned and tugged his hair, sending another jolt of pleasure through his veins, and his cock throbbed in response. With her so wet, he easily slid a second finger in and pumped both in a leisurely rhythm. Casi rocked her hips, meeting his strokes. He stopped sucking on her neck when she gave another sharp pull on his hair.

Luc smiled. "That's right, *bébé*, take what you want."

He curled his fingers and searched for the hidden special spot inside her. He found his mark. Casi shouted his name as she arched, and her hands fell, one gripping his shoulder and the other on his bicep. Her fingernails dug in, no doubt leaving her own impressions behind. A satisfied smirk curled up his mouth as she rode his fingers faster and harder. Her breaths were short, hard exhales. Casi had to be close. She trembled against him. He brought his thumb into action, finding the tight bundle of nerves and smoothed circles over her nub.

"Luc. Yes. Please."

With his free hand, he lightly gripped her chin, tilted her face so he could watch her. He wanted to see her come.

"Do it." He ordered her. "Let go. Give it to me." Luc's thumb pressed hard on her tiny bundle of nerves sending her over the edge.

She was magnificent. Arching, her eyes flew open before squeezing shut as her mouth opened, crying out her release. *Perfect.* His fingers continued to stroke her as he tried to wring every last drop of pleasure from her contracting core. When she came down, he gentled and finally withdrew.

Casi collapsed against him in a sigh of contentment. Her head landed on his shoulder once more, her harsh exhales warming his chest. He raised his fingers, wanting so badly to taste, but wiped them on the sheet before discreetly adjusting himself, getting his erection situated inside his boxers. Taking a deep breath, he held Casi with a hand to her hip and one to her shoulder, urging her to cuddle closer. He pressed a kiss to her forehead and sighed in satisfaction before dropping his head against the bed's headboard.

He fondly studied her as she returned back to herself, her breathing slowed to normal. Her eyes fluttered open and locked on the bulge still tenting in his boxers. Her hand on his chest drifted downward, but he caught her wrist. He brought her hand up and placed her palm flat, back to its original position.

"Luc—"

"*Non, cher*. Not tonight."

"But…"

He patted her hand before moving his to grip her hip once more. "Baby steps, darlin'. I'm good."

"I want to make you feel good too. You definitely deserve a reward." Her lips turned into an adorable pout.

"We've got time." He chuckled. "All the time in the world."

Casi stilled and then drew her bottom lip between her teeth and chewed. Her obvious tell returned as she mulled something over. With the arm across her back, Luc reached around and used his fingers to tug her lip from her teeth. She frowned.

"But what if we don't have all the time in the world?" Casi tilted her face so she could meet his gaze. "The siren is out there. What if one of us dies?"

His hand left her hip so he could tuck her hair behind her ear. He wanted to see her face clearly.

"I promise we won't die," he made a vow to her.

"You can't know that."

Luc pressed a finger against her lips. "I do know. It's three against one, supernatural being or not. Plus, we have an Archangel on our side. How can we possibly lose?"

Her brown eyes softened as his finger dropped from her lush lips. He used his hand to press her head back down against his shoulder.

"Now, sugar, cuddle close and get some sleep. Leave your worries and let tomorrow come."

Casi sighed and closed her eyes. Luc watched her sated body quickly drag her under once she allowed herself to relax. He wouldn’t let her die. No one, not even a mythical creature brought to life, would take her from him. *Mine*. Just as he was hers. Nothing would break them apart.

Chapter Forty

Casi sat curled on the porch swing, legs tucked underneath her as she sipped some sweet tea. Alone at last. A hard-fought victory on her part. Waking up in Luc's arms had been incredible, but after they had separated to shower and dress, doubts flooded her. Her life was moving too fast. Did she truly love him? Luc clearly thought he loved her. Impossible. They'd only known each other for such a brief time and under high stress. For the love of God, she hated cops. Relief washed over her, so glad she hadn't spoken the three little words back to him.

And yet…

Lucas Avery was amazing—compassionate, sharply intelligent, and so understanding. Gorgeous. From his thick, silky dark blond hair, to his catalog of smiles, add in his expressive mercurial hazel eyes, and his hard, lithe body, it equaled the whole package. The man liked to cuddle! The more she got to know him, the more practically perfect he became. But would it last? He claimed he wanted to work together through the mess that was her life. Yet it all seemed unbelievable in the light of day.

Hence the *me* time. After eating breakfast and helping with the dishes, she'd told the affectionate Luc to bugger off. Casi needed the distance—time alone to think without him looking at her, touching her, and God forbid, kissing her. She couldn't think when he kissed her.

Taking another sip of tea, Casi's mind raced. Luc was too good to be true, and it worried her deep down, because he represented everything she'd always wanted. But every time her life became pretty perfect, the shit would hit the fan. She loved her career in California and had really made a difference in the lives of her kids. Until the unthinkable happened, two of them murdered under her watch, the arrest, and her assault. She had been so broken afterward and never imagined getting her life back on track, but she had. Returning to New Orleans, meeting Mason, opening her shop—everything lined up. Casi felt happy, and then *bam*, her life fell apart once again.

Dammit! If she jumped all in with Luc, would he destroy her? Or would he be everything she wanted? Needed? The man offered to go to therapy with her. Unreal. Maybe time had come to pull her head out of the sand and face the music? After all, she truly wanted to be happy. There had been too many bleak days she tried valiantly to ignore. If she grabbed life with both hands and accepted what Luc offered, the time to work on becoming the best possible version of herself had arrived. Casi wanted to be an equal partner in their relationship, not the weak link bringing everything down. She needed to reclaim her life.

Feeling better now that she'd decided to quit doubting and trust, Casi finished her tea. She stood, empty glass in hand, with a smile. She'd find Luc, kiss him silly, and let him know she loved him. No more hiding. No more second thoughts. She would go all in.

The howling screech came out of nowhere, freezing Casi on the porch halfway to the front door. The horrible sound repeated. She spun, facing the direction of the painful cry. Staring into the dense copse of bald cypress and tupelo gum trees. The Spanish moss draped on the branches added a creepy aura to the woods. Casi held her breath, waiting for the sound to repeat. It did. The small hairs on her arms and the back of her neck rose. The shriek sounded feline.

Catastrophe.

There were predators in the swamp. Cat sounded in trouble. She dropped her glass, and her feet were moving before the next cry sounded. Catastrophe was supposed to stay inside the house, but she constantly escaped. No matter how hard the family tried to keep her indoors, the feline managed to sneak out. Right before she kicked her speed up to a jog, Casi threw a glance over her shoulder. She'd promised both Vince and Luc she wouldn't leave the house alone for any reason, but this was Catastrophe. She didn't have time to waste. Luc would be devastated if something happened to his pet.

She ran across the lawn, and then reaching the trees, she navigated between tree trunks, gaining on the painful shrieks.

Her foot caught under an exposed root, tripping Casi. Flinging an arm out, her hand slapped bark, and she caught her balance. She used her momentum to push away and continued across the uneven terrain.

Casi had to be in time. Though the screeches were terrible, at least she knew Cat was still alive. Maybe trapped or caught in something so she wasn't about to be eaten. She willed her feet to run faster. Rounding a tree, she skidded to a halt. Catastrophe's cries were close, so loud Casi felt she should see the distressed feline. She searched the ground and even looked up into the trees but couldn't find the cat. Frustrated, Casi slowly walked until the cry came again.

Darting forward, she stared in confusion. No one was there, feline or otherwise. The uncanny howl repeated, and Casi's gaze shot downward. *What the hell*? Propped against the bottom trunk of a gum tree laid a cell phone and a small speaker. The cat screech howled again, causing her to jump. She crouched and turned off the speaker. Searching, she saw no one. *Shit*! A trap! Casi sprung to her feet, turned, and ran into someone. Or rather, *something*.

"Where are you running off to, poppet?" The siren stood before her, clawed, fanged, and her black wings tightly furled against her back.

Casi screamed.

Selene lunged. One clawed hand grabbed Casi's arm in a bruising grip, keeping her in place, but that wasn't going to stop her from fighting. She screamed again while throwing a punch. Her fist connected to the siren's jaw. The creature's head snapped left and then slowly turned to face her once again, laughing and showing her long fangs. The siren hadn't even rocked on her feet with the blow, and now Casi's fist felt broken.

Stunned by the pain in her hand and still held by the monster, Casi reached for the horn concealed under her shirt, but she wasn't quick enough. Selene's other hand rose supernaturally fast, a syringed gripped between her sharp claws. The needle stabbed into Casi's neck. Cold liquid with a burning bite stung beneath her skin as the siren depressed the plunger.

"This should bring some peace and quiet. Be a good girl, poppet, and don't fight it." Selene caressed a single claw down Casi's cheek.

Casi's mouth opened with another scream, but nothing escaped. Her vision tunneled. She couldn't believe this was happening again. She sent a silent prayer as her muscles loosened. The arms of the monster hugging her halted her collapse. *Please. Please let her shouts have been heard.* There might be a good chance since she heard the recording, but she had been on the porch and not inside the house. *Help me, Luc*. Her world went black, and there were no more prayers.

Chapter Forty-One

Luc jogged down the main stairs, skipping steps as he increased his speed. He hadn't seen Casi in a couple of hours and had gone searching for her. Enough already. She had plenty of time alone with her thoughts. He'd just come from Casi's room, but it had been empty. At the front door, he flung it open and stepped through. His eyes focused on the empty porch swing where she had been much earlier. *Don't panic. Stay calm.* Maybe her avoidance was payback for his disappearing act yesterday. No reason to lose his stuff. And then he noticed the shattered tea glass lying on the wooden floorboards between the swing and the front door. His stomach flipped.

Casi had given him and Vince her word. She wouldn't leave the porch or the house alone. No going to the secluded getaway house, no taking a stroll or hike. Her promise, which he had sullenly accepted, had given her the privacy she so desired. He knew she doubted their relationship. Though the last thing he wanted to do was leave her alone with her fears, Luc gave her some space. His sisters had taught him well. Sometimes the better part of valor lay in retreating.

"Dammit!"

He should have listened to his intuition and stayed by her side. His instincts, usually correct, screamed at him. Where the hell was she? Maybe in the kitchen?

Perhaps she left to grab something to clean up the broken glass.

Luc entered the house and went left. Almost running into his partner, he skidded to a halt. “Is Casi in the kitchen?”

“Slow down.” He gripped Luc’s shoulder. “What’s lit your ass on fire?”

“I can’t find her.” Luc’s heart raced. “Something’s wrong.”

“She’s not in the kitchen. Call her phone. She’s supposed to always have it on her.”

Merde! Luc needed to calm the fuck down and get his head on straight. He whipped out his cell, unlocked it, and tapped her name in his favorites. When it started ringing, he put the call on speaker. On the fifth ring, her voicemail picked up.

“*Hi, you’ve reached Casi Thomas. Leave your message, and I’ll get back to you.*”

“Call me, better yet, get your ass to the kitchen.” Luc ended the call and met his partner’s gaze.

Vince’s brow furrowed, and he frowned. “She promised. Casi has to be around her somewhere.”

Luc shook his head. “Something drew her off the porch because I refuse to believe she was snatched directly from the porch and neither of us knew.” He stared down at the phone in his hand, mind chasing in circles. His cool brain under fire, gone.

“We could get a warrant and ping her phone. We should be able to track her.”

“*Mère de Dieu*! I’m an idiot!” Luc tapped his phone and launched a GPS tracking app. He glanced at his partner before inputting the chip’s number. “I slipped a GPS chip inside her phone’s case.”

"Good call," Vince praised. "Way faster and sneaky. I approve." He slipped to Luc's side, staring down at the screen. "Where is she? Hopefully someplace stupid like asleep in the backyard."

Come on, come on, come on. He willed the app to go faster. Finally, the map pinged with the state of Louisiana showing. Luc held his breath as the map zoomed in tighter, each refresh getting closer and closer. The app zeroed in on Bayou Lafourche and then settled on a stationary blinking red light, pinpointing Casi's location. It wasn't the house.

"Where is that?" Vince pointed at the screen, pulling Luc from his daze.

He fiddled with the program until their location, noted by a solid blue dot, appeared on the same map as Casi's blinking red light. "She's in the swamp. About five, six miles out."

"That's not good."

It really wasn't. "And with a possible two-hour lead." Luc met Vince's stare and swallowed hard. The siren had to have Casi. He squeezed his eyes shut, trying to shove down the hopelessness flooding his system.

Vincent steadied him with a firm grip to his shoulder. "Hang in there, brother. We need to weapon up and go Oscar-Mike."

On the move, Luc translated automatically. Right. He took a deep breath and nodded, before leading the way out the front door and around to the side of the house. Reaching the exact shed he had pushed Casi against only last night. Where they had hotly kissed. He stopped in front of the door and used the keypad, inputting the unlock code. After the snick, he opened the door and strode in.

Yesterday morning, when he'd been avoiding Casi, Luc had taken the time to gather supplies and weapons, storing all in one place. Three machetes, his rifle loaded with 30-06 ammo, a .22 Magnum, laid alongside a green backpack containing a first aid kit, water, rope, and two tactical KA-BAR knives.

"I have trained you well, my young apprentice," Vince teased, no doubt trying to lighten the mood as they armed themselves. Machetes went into sheaths tied to their thighs, while Vincent slipped the Magnum, with safety on, under his waistband at the small of his back.

Luc pulled out a small electronic device from the backpack's side pocket before tossing the bag to Tate. He powered up the device and inputted Casi's GSP chip identifier. "No real cell service in the swamp. Hit or miss." He held the screen for Vince to see the blinking green dot. "It's a satellite tracker, kind of like a Sat phone. Can't make calls, but it will find the chip I hid."

Vince gave a thumbs up. "Truck or boat?"

"Boat." Luc grabbed his rifle and marched out of the shed with Tate on his heels. He upped the walk to a jog, which turned into a run as they crossed the backyard lawn, heading for the dock. It wasn't easily seen from the house because the dock was located on a larger body of water than the tributary found at the end of the groomed part of the Avery's property.

Reaching the gravel path carved through a cluster of trees, the boat came into view as they ran. Soon their feet pounded down on the warped boards of the dock. Luc's nerves steadied as he jumped into the Blue Bayou Mallard. "Cast off."

Vince nodded and grabbed the mooring line as Luc

reached for the fast Gator Tail outboard motor. Before his partner even jumped in, Luc turned the key, and the engine revved to life. He handed the GPS device to Vince so he could guide as Luc piloted. The loud motor got them moving forward, and he picked up the pace after a few feet from the dock.

"You know this area better than me. If you can open her up, get the rpm's going. We aren't turning for a mile or so. It's time for balls to the wall," Tate shouted over the engine.

Luc didn't think twice and gunned the outboard. He grew up playing within this swamp. The bayou didn't hold many secrets for him. They'd get to Casi and kill the siren bitch. Nothing would stop them.

With Vince navigating and Luc's knowledge, they could take a few shortcuts. Maybe not wise with some of the vegetation floating on the water they had to cut through, but the engine showed its power and mastery of the swamp, never seizing or stalling.

"Slow down," Vince yelled. "We're close."

Finally. Luc manipulated the controls so they coasted. Scanning the narrow waterway, he searched the solid ground on either side, praying he'd see Casi. He fought back his worry, needing his detective side and not the personal worried side. She was counting on him.

Vince gestured to an area a few yards ahead, where the GPS chip should be. Luc hunted for the nearest place they could tie off safely and spotted a fallen tupelo tree. It would be good enough to use and would double as a dock. He pulled up alongside, and Vince wrapped the mooring line around a sturdy branch. His partner's hand signaled forward, taking point as he glanced at the GPS screen before pulling the Magnum from his waistband. Luc snatched his rifle and followed silently behind. His eyes swept the tree and the surrounding grounds for cottonmouth snakes. They like to curl in fallen trees and hang out in the brush by the water's edge. Getting snake bit was the last thing they needed. But at least they had a first aid kit in the backpack his partner was currently wearing.

Luc stepped off the trunk and trailed a few feet behind Vince so neither would be in the way of each other. Tate held up a closed fist, and Luc halted. Squatting, his partner shifted through some molding plant debris.

"Damn."

Hearing Vince swear had Luc's feet moving. Reaching Tate's side, he stared at Casi's phone lying in the muck. His heart sank. How the hell would they find her now? He couldn't lose her when he'd only just found her.

"I love her," Luc choked out.

Vince stood after slipping Casi's phone into a back pocket. He nodded. "We'll find her."

"How? The tracking chip was our ace." He closed his eyes, fighting for calm. "She could be dead already. We're hours behind, and the clock keeps ticking."

"You can't think like that, Lucas. It's not helping."

Luc snapped his eyes open and shoved his hand through his hair. "I know, dammit. But…the freak has wings! How the hell are we going to find them?" He flung out an arm. "The bayou is huge. They could be anywhere."

"Again, not helpful. Think, man. You are a hell of a detective with uncanny intuition." Tate glared at him.

"We know Selene likes to play with her victims, torture them, draw it out. She'll need a place, a building. What does your gut tell you?"

Torture. Luc's panic exploded. His heart rate galloped, and he had to swallow back the bile rising in his throat. Vince noticed.

"Come on, Avery. You grew up here. Played here. This freaking swamp was your private playground. Where, nearby, could Selene have taken Casi?"

Luc shoved his horror down, even though the monster could be hurting his woman right this minute, the freaky bitch. His anger finally surfaced. Vince was right. Luc owned this bayou. He knew it deep in his blood. "There're three possible sites."

"Good man, what are they."

"An abandoned cabin, a hunter's hide, and a crawfish shack." Luc grimaced. "They're all in different directions."

"Pick one, what's your inner voice telling you?"

"If I get it wrong…"

"Then we go to the next one. Casi is tough, she'll hold out. She knows we're coming for her."

Luc nodded. "Right. Let's go hunting."

Vince slapped Luc's back. "Now you're talking. Lead the way. We will save Casi."

Purpose flooded his veins. They wouldn't be too late. Luc spun and ran for the boat with Vince hot on his heels.

Chapter Forty-Two

Casi's eyes fluttered open. Lifting her head, she discovered her new living nightmare and wished she hadn't woken. Once again, she was tied but this time to a chair instead of a table. Her arms were bound tightly behind her back. Tugging, Casi found the rope had been threaded through the slats of the metal backrest and then wrapped tightly around her joined wrists. At least her legs were still free.

As for the siren, she appeared human. Leaning against a wooden wall with daylight peeking between the warped planks, Gabriel's horn dangled from the silver chain she held in her hand.

"Well, my poppet. You took longer to wake than I expected. You're spoiling my fun." Selene wore a creepy smile. She twirled the necklace once before clutching it in her fist. "What? You have nothing to say? Tsk, tsk."

Casi tried to ignore the siren and instead studied her surroundings. They were in some kind of shed. Bare bones and rickety, it didn't have windows, only a missing door with the view beyond pure swamp. A rusted tin ceiling offered little cover, and the haphazard wooden floor as damaged as the walls, let in as much swamp smell as it kept out the elements. A high long table abutted one side of the square hut. On it laid a tipped-over metal bucket and a cylindrical steel cage.

The entire room held a fishy smell.

"It's lovely to have the horn again," Selene purred as she hooked the necklace around her neck. "You, however, have been nothing but trouble." She took several steps forward closing the distance and halted a few feet from Casi. "But now, everything is back the way it should be. I have the horn," she patted the charm lying on her chest. "And I have you." Selene tilted her head to the side and studied Casi. "Why doesn't my voice work on you?"

"Because I'm special." She frantically worked the ropes trying to free her hands, keeping the motions small so the psycho siren wouldn't notice. Maybe if she could keep the monster talking, it would buy her time to get free.

Selene threw her head back and laughed. "Special? No, you aren't. You're worse than human. You have gifts elevating you, but you choose to ignore them. In fact, you probably wish you didn't have abilities, so you could be just one more cow among the herd."

"I'd rather be an ordinary person than a freaky monster who gets off on torture and murder. So go fuck yourself." The rough twine of the rope dug into her wrists. Liquid dripped onto her hands, and she realized it must be blood. Ignoring the pain, she worked harder. Maybe the blood would help her slip free of her bonds.

****

Luc cut the engine and coasted the last stretch, fearing the loud motor would give them away, having no idea if sirens had supernatural hearing or not. "Get ready to jump," he warned Vince. "We need to pull the boat up to secure it."

When they were near to what counted as the shore,

Vince didn't hesitate and jumped, with Luc right behind. They landed thigh deep in the murky green water, but it didn't deter either of them. Slogging forward, they tugged the boat higher out of the water and quickly secured it to several fronds of a bonfouca.

Luc pulled his machete and took point. They had a ten-minute hike ahead of them. The location was definitely accessible via water but getting there by boat would have taken longer, since they would have to navigate around land clumps in order to reach the correct tributary. Luc had decided to go as the crow flew—crossing land instead of going the long way around. Swinging the sharp ax, he hacked a path through the swamp while monitoring the ground. Luc wanted solid earth beneath his feet and no hidden predators lying in wait.

Vince was a silent partner behind him, keeping pace. Had Luc chosen correctly? They were actually heading to the farthest of the three spots. If he picked incorrectly, they had wasted precious time they couldn't afford. He clung to the fact Casi was strong, a fighter. She had survived so much, including her first encounter with the siren. She would make it through. Maybe even rescue herself once again.

The thought of Casi saving herself brought a genuine smile to Luc's face for the first time in hours, but quickly it fell into a frown. He wished for a quicker pace but couldn't chance upping their speed. In the bayou, solid ground could be deceptive, hiding treacherous terrain. Veiled bogs and marshy areas acted like quicksand and were ugly ways to die. If they got stuck, it wouldn't help Casi.

Luc halted after rounding a tree and motioned

Vince to pull up alongside him. There in the distance stood the building he banked all his luck on. The structure on stilts rose from the water's edge, keeping the shed from flooding during storms. A long two-part ramp connected at a right angle led from the muddy ground to the open door. It looked abandoned. He strained his ears and heard nothing except the usual bayou sounds of frogs, birds, bugs, and the constant background noise of water, both drips and plops from the slow-moving swamp. He heard no voices or movements.

"Do you hear anything?" Luc whispered.

His partner shook his head. "We still need to check it out." His dark brown gaze remained serious. "Chin up. I trust your gut. You're rarely wrong, it's uncanny."

Luc nodded. He clung to his nickname. *Lucky*. Holding tight to that thought, he crept forward and hoped for the best.

****

"If you think you're so much better than us, why am I, a mere human, immune to your supervillain power? You're pathetic and obviously losing your touch."

Casi's latest comment set the siren off. Selene launched into a rant, just as Casi had hoped. She raged on about how people were no better than sheep and went on from there. The tirade continued nonstop. It gave Casi more time and kept her from torture by a monster. She froze, eyes widening as Mason materialized behind the fuming Selene.

Transparent, Casi could see straight through him, yet she still could perceive him. She made out his black hair, bright blue eyes, the handsome, charming face she loved and cherished, yet his body was harder to discern, only a hint of a torso, arms, and legs—wispy and faint. Her heart clenched. Was he fading?

"Sweetie," his whispered voice echoed inside her head. Casi shot a glance at the lunatic siren, judging if she had heard him also, but Selene didn't react. "Sweetie, you need to hurry." Mason's lips hadn't moved, yet she still heard him. "Get out of those ropes now. You've run out of time."

Shit! She had stopped trying to escape while staring at her lost friend. Casi redoubled her efforts while more blood streaked downward, coating her palms and the back of her hands.

Selene fell silent and glanced over her shoulder as if she sensed Mason's presence but turned back when nothing was there. "Enough. It's time for a bit of play, poppet." The siren transformed before Casi's eyes. Fangs lengthened in Selene's open-mouth smile, and her raised hands morphed as fingers became sharp claws, however her wings didn't make an appearance—probably because of the size of the room.

Adrenaline pumped, filling Casi's veins as terror flooded her. The siren slowly prowled toward her. Frantic, she struggled harder, and one hand slipped free of the binding. She shook her other hand loose and then burst from the chair, launching herself at Selene. Casi's bloody hand grasped the horn, and she yanked. The delicate chain easily broke. The necklace clasped in one fist, she shoved Selene hard with the other. Surprised by the unexpected attack, the siren fell a few steps to the side, giving Casi the moment she needed. Darting past, she ran for the doorway, until brought up hard by a hold on her ponytail. She was yanked backward.

"Casi!"

Eyes wide, she was shocked by Luc's arrival in the exposed threshold with Tate right behind him. Everything happened at once. Selene pulled Casi tight against her front as claws speared into Casi's stomach. Pain lanced through her like she'd never felt before. Casi screamed.

"No!" Both men shouted in denial.

Casi threw the necklace with the last of her strength.

Chapter Forty-Three

The siren ripped her bloody claws from Casi's abdomen, and Casi fell as Luc caught the necklace. There was so much blood.

"Down!" Vince shouted, and as Luc dropped to his knees, his partner fired his gun, unloading ammunition into the siren. Selene's body reacted to the impacts, jarring with each bullet, and stumbled backward but didn't fall.

The horn! Luc stared at the tiny charm in his hand and hoped Gabriel had their backs. With both his mind and heart he willed the horn to grow. In a blink, the artifact's size transformed into an instrument that could be played.

"No!" Selene charged, leaping over Casi's prone body.

Luc raised the horn to his mouth and blew. The purest, deepest note sounded forth. It rang true and filled the small shack, hitting Selene mid-lunge. The siren transformed. Fangs and claws disappeared as well as her strength. The bullet wounds bled as she stumbled and almost fell. The fumble gave Vince the opportunity to attack.

Tate darted past Luc, who crouched on the floor. Swinging the razor-sharp machete, the blade connected with Selene's neck. With the power behind Tate's blow, the honed edge severed her head from her body and sent it flying. It landed on the table, rolled, and halted when it hit against the crawfish cage. The siren's eyes stared blankly at the rusty tin roof as the body of the monster crashed to the floor.

Not really thinking, Luc shrank the horn and shoved the relic into a pocket while running to Casi's unmoving body. *Please God, don't let it be too late.* She had to be alive. He dropped to his knees and placed two fingers against her neck. He searched for Casi's pulse. Panic bubbled within Luc. He sensed only the pounding of his own heart. He leaned toward her mouth. *There*! He felt her exhale, and with the proof of life, he could now feel her pulse beneath his fingers.

Luc straightened and pressed both hands on Casi's stomach, applying pressure as he shot his gaze to his partner.

"I'm on it." Vince yanked the backpack from his shoulders and dropped to Casi's other side. He pulled out the first aid kit. Vince, with a pair of scissors, gestured Luc out of the way, before cutting Casi's shirt open, exposing five deep puncture wounds.

Luc rubbed his bloody hands on his jeans before grabbing his phone. Unlocking the screen, his stomach sank. "No signal. Damn." He needed to call in a medivac and get her to the hospital.

"No worries. I've got this. She will not die on my watch." Vince had already swabbed clean Casi's abdomen. "I'll need your help stabilizing her in order to get her back to the boat."

"Anything."

Luc followed his partner's orders as they worked together, disinfecting and then sealing the wounds with super glue before swaddling her in a pressure bandage.

No fresh blood leaked through the dressing, a good sign, helping Luc's concern settle.

"What are we going to do with the body…and head?" Vince asked while cleaning Casi's shredded wrists.

"Easy, we'll let the bayou take care of her." Luc stood and crossed to the table. He grabbed the siren's head by her short red hair and strode to the open doorway. Halting at the edge of the ramp perched over the water, Luc raised the head so he could gaze into her blank, dead gaze.

"You got what you deserved. Too fast for me, though. All those lives you took…I hope you're in hell and karma is real."

Luc threw Selene's head and watched it arch over the water to splash down in the middle of the slow-moving river. It bobbed once before quietly sinking. He turned and entered the shack finding Vince lifting the headless body in a fireman's carry, hefting it over his shoulder. He followed Luc's earlier action, and with a corresponding splash, the body hit the water.

The gators would feed well tonight.

Vince returned and shouldered the backpack with all its items restored. His partner glanced around. "What about all the blood?" Between the siren and Casi, it was obvious something horrific had happened here.

"Like I said, the bayou will take care of what remains." Luc gestured to the mismatched walls, the uneven floor, and the missing door. "Next good rain and it'll wash this place clean. Besides, this shed is pretty isolated. Few people come here, and they're Cajun. Most will think a gator might have been slaughtered inside. It'll be fine."

"Good." His gun already disappeared to the small of his back, Vince grabbed Luc's rifle. His partner read his mind. Tate knew Luc would want to be the one to carry Casi.

Luc scooped her up with one arm under her knees and the other across her back. He settled her against his chest with her head resting on his shoulder. Vince nodded and left the building. Luc pressed a quick kiss to Casi's forehead.

"Hang in there, darlin'. I've got you. You're going to be just fine." He followed Vince out the door. Holding his precious cargo, he carefully walked down the ramp and headed in the boat's direction.

He glanced at Casi, relieved to have her in his arms once more and thanking God, he and Vince had arrived in time. Luc wanted to be there for her forever, whether to slay her dragons, support her healing, or just stand by her side. She was the woman he would always love.

Chapter Forty-Four

New Orleans, July

Two months had flown by, and in that time, Casi's life had changed for the better. Completely healed from her wounds, she happily sipped her beer while sitting on a barstool inside the Fleur-de-lis next to Luc. Glancing at the man sitting beside her, she felt so grateful to the stubborn, handsome guy in her life. Deep into her therapy sessions, alone and with Luc, she finally got her life on track. *Crazy*. Why hadn't she taken this step on her own a long time ago? Surviving her latest trial by fire had cleansed her, and like a phoenix rising from the ashes, her life felt brand new. Everything was awesome, and Casi refused to let fear—of betrayal, trust, or the horrors of *what if*—rule the way she'd live her life. She loved Luc, and he returned her love tenfold. And if the worse came to be, she had no doubt whatever happened, they'd handle it together and come out even stronger on the other side.

On the professional arena, she still had her psychic shop, but instead of faking it, she was now the real deal. Casi smiled. Who would have ever believed? She also took the steps to get herself certified in the state of Louisiana, putting her degrees back into proper action. Being a social worker or practicing as a therapist, she wasn't sure which she'd choose, but at least she'd finally have some choices.

Casi nudged Luc in the ribs when she saw Gabriel toss a towel over his shoulder and walk toward them from behind the bar. He stopped in front of them and smiled. The Archangel had decided to hang for a while.

"You need refills?" Gabriel smiled.

"*Non*," Luc answered. "We're good."

"So," Casi drew the angel's attention. "I've been meaning to give you something." She withdrew the charm-size horn from her pocket. "I don't think I should be its keeper." She gave the artifact to Gabriel, who tucked it out of sight.

"Thank you, Casi, and you too, Lucas. You saved many lives and perhaps soothed some souls with Selene's death."

Luc nodded. "It was a group effort."

"Speaking of a group." Gabriel gestured for Luc to turn around.

Swiveling on his barstool, Luc spotted Bastien approaching with a trumpet in hand. Casi caught Gabriel's gaze, and they exchanged knowing looks.

"Come on, Lucky. It's time to earn your pay." Bastien handed the trumpet to Luc, who automatically took the brass instrument.

"Pay? Since when have you ever given me money?" Luc stood.

"You don't earn money. You get paid in joy and happiness." Bas slapped him on the shoulder.

"Of course I do." Luc grunted when his younger brother grabbed his arm and dragged him across the Loo to the stage.

Casi watched as the brothers jumped onto the platform, and Luc took his place on the crowded stage. All eleven members of Neutral Ground performed tonight—twelve with Luc. The excitement in the audience was contagious, the mood bright and alive with enthusiasm. Bastien slipped his electric guitar strap over his head and settled the instrument low on his hips before stepping up to the microphone. With a nod to his drummer, the beat clicked out, and the band started jamming away. Casi had come to really enjoy their weird blend of zydeco and rock. The sound original and all their own.

"Hey there, pretty lady." Vince greeted her as he took Luc's empty seat and signaled Gabriel for a beer.

"Hey there, yourself. I thought you were out searching for your headquarters?" She gave Tate half her attention while still listening to the band.

"I took a break. I've got a bead on two places. Either of them should work." Vince drank some beer and swiveled on the barstool so he had a better view of the band.

"That's awesome." Casi's feet tapped along to the fast beat, kind of wishing she danced with Luc on the crowded floor.

When Casi, Luc, and Vince had returned to New Orleans, more things had changed than her entering therapy. After the seeming disappearance of the Cyclops and the apparently unsolved serial killer case, Commander Eckert finally had his ammunition to make Luc and Vince's life a true living hell. Unfair, of course, because the detectives had actually not only solved the case but took out the murderer as well. But obviously they couldn't tell the truth.

Miserable, Luc finally confessed to Vince. Life was too short, things could change in a split second, so why waste it doing something he no longer enjoyed?

He was finished working for the NOPD, and then Luc shared his new dream. He wanted to open a security firm and protect people. Be his own boss with no more red tape and jumping through hoops, Luc could finally, truly help people in danger. No more Eckerts. Luc handed in his resignation to his captain, who tried to talk him out of quitting. The captain hadn't wanted to lose his best detective, but Luc smiled and said his goodbyes.

Tate had jumped ship with Luc, and now they were the proud new co-owners of *Archangel Security, Inc.* Vince had even recruited some of his former military pals as employees. They currently searched for a building with office space to call their own.

The song ended, and the Loo erupted in cheers and applauses. Casi smiled as Luc put down his trumpet and stepped to the microphone next to Bastien. She gave an internal sigh and mooned like a love-struck schoolgirl. Luc singing made her swoon.

"Hey, all," Luc greeted the crowd before shading his eyes with one hand. He peered across the barroom before locking gazes with hers. "There's a special someone I'd like you to meet. Casi, sweetheart, come up here."

What? No way. She didn't have a talented bone in her body unless you counted her newfound psychic abilities.

Tate stood and snagged her hand, hauling her off her stool. "Not a chance, Vince. I'm not going on stage."

"Oh yes you are, beautiful. It's why I'm here."

"Tate, no."

"It'll be fine. Stop worrying."

The crowd parted for the six-foot-five black man who continued to drag her closer to the band. She hated being the center of attention.

"Here you go, Lucas." Before Vince's words processed, his hands were on her waist, and he lifted her, dropping her on the stage. Luc caught her hand, twining their fingers together before she could escape. Vince smiled at them from the dance floor. *Traitor*!

Luc leaned and whispered in her ear. "Don't be mad, *cher*." He pressed a kiss to her cheek, before taking a step back without letting go of her hand.

She drew her gaze away from the large and watchful audience and finally focused on Luc. Noticing for the first time the sweat glistening on his brow and the slight worried expression on his face, Casi realized her confident man appeared nervous. The answer came when Luc dropped to one knee before her. She gasped, and her free hand flew to cover her mouth. All thoughts of the crowd flew from her head. She had eyes only for Luc.

"*Je t'aime. Tu es mon coeur*." He raised their joined hands, and he gave her hand a gentle kiss to her knuckles.

A slight giggle escaped her. "You do realize I don't understand what you're saying, right?"

Luc's charming smile flashed. "I love you. You are my heart." He swallowed hard. "I told you the story of Avery men and their women. Casi, darlin', you completely blindsided me, and I have never been more happy. I need you in my life, for it has no meaning without you." Luc's liquid accent curled around her with his heartfelt words of love. "Cassanne Roseline Thomas, will you marry me?" With his free hand, he reached blindly into his front pocket and pulled out a ring.

Casi's swallowed hard. Her eyes filled, but no tears fell. There might have been a time in her life when she would have bolted in terror, but not today. Luc proved by his actions she could trust him. Not only that, but she could trust him with her heart, with her soul. He made it easy to love him.

"Say yes!" Someone shouted from the audience, getting a laugh.

"Darlin'?" He gazed at her with all the love beaming in his eyes, naked for all to see. "You gonna leave me here on one knee?"

Casi shook her head and tugged his hand, getting him to stand. She smiled. "Yes, Lucas François Avery. Most definitely, yes, I will marry you."

The crowd cheered and clapped. "*Dieu merci*. You had me worried there for a moment, sugar." Luc took her left hand and slid on the ring. "It's Faith's. My grandmamma wanted you to have it, especially since her husband replaced it with a much larger caret for their anniversary."

Casi studied the engagement ring adorning her finger. So beautiful in its simplicity. The rose gold band twisted with a petite vine of pavé diamonds leading to a heart-shaped three-quarter carat diamond. Character shown through its beauty. "I love it. Did she really want me to have it?"

"You can ask her yourself, *cher*." He gestured through the lights to the back of the room. Casi gasped when she saw the entire Avery clan in attendance. Only Catastrophe was missing. The feline queen happily slept on Luc's bed where they left her before coming to the bar.

"Oh my God!" Casi turned to Luc. "You've been sneaky."

Luc grinned and pulled her in for a kiss. The audience cheered again, and Bastien pulled his brother away. "My turn." Bas kissed both her cheeks. "Welcome to the family, darlin'." She hugged him in return before he stepped away and returned to the microphone.

"Okay, you love birds, off the stage," Bastien ordered. "Go dance with your *fille*, Lucky."

Luc put action to his brother's words and helped her off the stage and onto the dance floor below.

"Al' right, y'all. Let's get this party started!" Bas shouted into the mic. "*Laissez les bon temps rouler*!"

Neutral Ground struck a familiar beat as their newest hit, *The Road Taken*, blasted from the stage. Luc grasped her hand and twirled her away before reeling her back in. Their bodies pressed tight, with no room between them. Casi laughed, her heart filled with joy and love for the man who danced with her. She couldn't wait to find out what the future had in store for them.

Laissez les bon temps rouler. Yes. Let the good times roll.

Chapter Forty-Five

St. Brendan's Church, near Durness, Scotland, Late July

Gabriel waited for Father Campbell to leave through the church's side door, leading to the attached graveyard, before materializing inside St. Brendan's. His gaze took in the beloved small Scottish church. So much history between this Church and the Archangels. He strolled up the nave and stopped at the crossing. He bowed his head to the crucifix hung behind the altar before turning. In a few long strides, Gabriel entered the shrine to the Archangels. The chapel held seven statues standing in a half circle. St. Michael, with his sword stood, in the center. On his right was Raphael, the healer, and on the left was his own statue depicted as the messenger. The remaining Archangels, Uriel, Raguel, Sariel, and Remiel formed the rest of the half circle.

Gabriel approached his own statue. He paused, studying his portrayal and that of his brothers and sister. As with all the statues, they were dressed for combat, with gauntlets, armor, and cloaks. Each had a weapon—either brandished or sheathed to their bodies. Those not holding their weapons held objects of their representations, such as Remiel with his weighted scales. Gabriel's own sword hung at his side as he held his horn upraised in his right hand. He chuckled. The horn wasn't right. Too thin and long before belling out. Not a curve in sight.

Kneeling before his statue, he opened his fisted hand. On his palm laid his horn, only a mere three inches. That would never do. The relic's tiny size would be lost in its cradle. With a slight push of his will, the horn morphed into its rightful size. Now two feet long, the curved bugle gleamed. The Shofar of kraken bone gleamed a blend of green, brown, and gray combined in shiny ribbons. It was time to return his horn to St. Brendan's careful protection.

He pressed his hand against a decorative section of the base's molding. A hidden panel opened to reveal a hollowed chamber inside the statue's foundation. Placing his horn into the indented impression on the crushed blue velvet, the kraken Shofar fit perfectly. Gabriel gazed at his creation one last time before he closed the secret compartment and stood with a sense of satisfaction.

He studied the depictions of his brothers and sister. He, Uriel, and Remiel had set their problems right, leaving his four siblings to take up their own gauntlet. He willed his wings to appear as he prepared to go home. Gabriel wondered which one of his kin would be the next to break a few of Father's rules and get into a bit of trouble.

For a sneak peek, if you missed *Walking Through Fire,* the first book in the standalone Fire Chronicles Series.

Chapter One
Northern Scotland, Near Durness
July 1809

The first tingle of fear raced up Simon MacKay's spine as he found himself alone in the pitch dark—kneeling on rough, wet granite. Waves thundered and crashed around him in the gloom. He must be in one of the sea caves on his estate. A blast of salty, cold air struck him, clearing his muddled, throbbing head to frightening awareness. He staggered clumsily to his feet, pain shooting through his arms and shoulders. He couldn't move his hands.

"Nay!" His shout echoed in the darkness. He was bound to the cave's wall. He struggled, arms stretched tautly behind him, his muscles strained against the ropes tying his wrists. Ignoring the bite of the coarse fibers and the pain of his tortured joints, panic set in. He had to get free. He had to get out. His family was in danger.

A wave slammed in close, spraying water onto his face. Sweat mingled with salt water as he thrashed. The metal mooring ring trapping him clanked against the limestone rock, as his heart raced with equal parts dread and exertion. Clasped hands turned sticky with blood from the rough bindings biting into his flesh. Simon ignored this too.

Ice water drenched him as the next wave crashed against the wall. The chilled soaking froze him in place.

The tide was coming in, and the cave was rapidly filling. He hung his head, and water dripped from his long hair to streak down his face, mimicking the tears he couldn't shed. His body started to shake as shock and disbelief speared his mind. If he didn't free himself, he'd drown, and his family would be left unprotected.

"I canna die like this. I won't!"

He lifted his head and peered into the shadows. Another wave hit him waist high before he felt the dragging pull of the ocean's retreat. He could now hear lapping water.

I will die here, his traitorous thoughts declared, and for what?

A choked laugh escaped Simon, and he shook his head. "Never!" He strained once more against his bonds, but they held fast. Whoever tied the knots had done it well.

How had he gotten here? His last recollection before waking in the cave was leaving the manor and walking to the stable. He entered, but then it all blurred together. His throbbing head held the missing clue. He'd been struck. There had been no warning, no telltale movement.

The next wave hit him chest high, slamming him against the wall, crushing his arms behind him. This time however, as the wave retreated, frigid water remained clawing at his ankles.

Simon prayed the high-water mark wasn't above his head. With no light, he couldn't tell. In his soul though, he knew. He was meant to die, and at the rate the tide continued to rush in, his fate would soon be sealed.

"Damn you to hell, you bloody devil!" His cry was

lost in the booming darkness. He should have known better, should have anticipated. There had been threats. He ignored them all. More fool he. Now he would pay the ultimate price.

He shook with rage as the icy water swirled about his waist. Numb to his physical discomfort, his inner turmoil was dagger sharp. Who had done this to him?

The thoughts of his tormentor fled from his mind when an incoming wave crashed above his head, submerging him. He instinctively held his breath until the arctic wash drained away to chest level. He braced and waited in the darkness for the wave set to finish. He knew the sea's rhythm. It was in his family's blood.

Three. Four. Five. The last wave pulled him from the wall, stretching his arms painfully behind him. He floated back, and his feet found ground. The sea now reached his neck.

Regrets flooded him. Who would care for his family? He would be leaving behind a little sister and a sick mother. Sadly, the sea had already claimed his father, and now she would have the son. Were the men in his family cursed? Simon would disappear, and the MacKay name would die with him. Would the sick bastard who killed him now go after little Jean or his ma? Who would stop him?

A sob escaped his throat, and he ruthlessly bit his lip. He would not die a sniveling coward.

The water lapped his chin and reached higher to caress his mouth.

The bastard would pay. Though he knew not who his murderer be, Simon saved his last thoughts to curse his enemy.

The water closed over his head, submerging him

into a liquid world. He held his breath, willing the water to retreat, but the sea would not be cheated.

His lungs burned, tears squeezed from his closed eyes and mingled unseen in his watery prison. He bit his lips, drawing blood in his effort not to breathe, but his body betrayed him.

Purely reflexive, his mouth gasped open, sucking in air for his oxygen-starved lungs. All they received was the cold water of the North Atlantic.

On the second inhalation, his body started to convulse when the ocean filled his lungs.

On the third, Simon MacKay drowned.

GLOSSARY OF FOREIGN PHRASES AND WORDS

Belle-mere: (Cajun) Mother-In-Law.

Bon ami: (Cajun) Good friend.

Bonne chance: (Cajun) Good luck.

Bonne fille: (Cajun) Good girl.

Bon sang: (Cajun) Damn it.

Brûlant: (Cajun) Sizzling hot.

C'est bon: (Cajun) That's good.

Ça vaut la peine: (Cajun) It's worth the trouble.

C'est le bordel: (Cajun) What a bloody mess. What the hell.

C'est si mauvais? A quel point?: (Cajun) How bad is it?

Cher: (Cajun) Dear. Sweetheart.

Coo-yôn: (Cajun) Idiot.

Dieu merci: (Cajun) Thank God.

Dis-moi la vérité: (Cajun) Tell me the truth.

Doce comme du miel: (Cajun) Sweet like honey.

Elle réchauffes mon sang comme personne d'autre: (Cajun) She heats my blood like no other.

Est'tombé en botte: (Cajun) He fell to ruin.

Fais-do-do: (Cajun) A dance party.

Fais de beaux rêves: (Cajun) Sweet dreams. Good dreams.

Fifolet: (Cajun) Swamp spirits.

Fille: (Cajun) Girl.

Famille: (Cajun) Family.

Fils de putain: (Cajun) Son of a bitch.

Granmè: (Haitian) Grandmother.

Je t'aime: (Cajun) I love you.

Laissez les bon temps rouler: (Cajun) Let the good

times roll.

Mea culpa: (Latin) Through my fault. My bad. My fault.

Mère de Dieu: (Cajun) Mother of God.

Merde: (Cajun) Shit.

Mon coeur: (Cajun) My heart.

Mon chéri: (Cajun) My sweet.

Moi aussi je t'aime: (Cajun) I love you, too.

Non: (Cajun) No.

Ouais: (Cajun) Yeah. Yes.

Parle moi, bébé: (Cajun) Talk to me, baby.

Prend-lé aisé: (Cajun) Take it easy.

Prends soin de toi: (Cajun) Take care of yourself.

Prends soin de ta fille: (Cajun) Take care of your girl.

Que peut-on faire: (Cajun) What can you do?

Qu'est-ce qu'il y a: (Cajun) What's the matter?

Que vais-je faire de toi: (Cajun) What should I do with you?

Quoi ça dit: (Cajun) What's happening?

Sans doute: (Cajun) Without a doubt.

Santé: (Cajun) Health.

Tue es en sécurité: (Cajun) You are safe.

Tu es mon coeur: (Cajun) You are my heart.

Vide ton sac. Tu te sentiras mieux: (Cajun) Spit it out, you'll feel better.

Viens immédiatement: (Cajun) Come Now.

Vrai: (Cajun) True.

A word about the author...

First published in Marion Zimmer Bradley's "Sword & Sorceress" anthology, C J was bitten by the writer's bug and hasn't stopped since. Her award-winning first novel, "Walking Through Fire," a Scottish ghost romance, is published by The Wild Rose Press. She is currently working on the fourth book in The Fire Chronicles, as well as a new Urban Fantasy starring a kick-ass Time Enforcer.

When her pen isn't scribing, you can find her busily cutting and tracking music for film and television. With close to twenty years of music editing experience, her credits range from "Northern Exposure" and "The Muppets Christmas Carol" to "The Kill Point" and "The Middle."

In her downtime, you'll find her curled up with a cup of tea, her cats, and a great book in Tarzana, California.
https://www.cjbahr.com

Thank you for purchasing
this publication of The Wild Rose Press, Inc.

For questions or more information
contact us at
info@thewildrosepress.com.

The Wild Rose Press, Inc.
www.thewildrosepress.com

www.ingramcontent.com/pod-product-compliance
Lightning Source LLC
Chambersburg PA
CBHW051131030726
47504CB00004B/808